EDENVILLE

EDENVILLE

A NOVEL

SAM REBELEIN

WILLIAM MORROW
An Imprint of HarperCollins*Publishers*

EDENVILLE. Copyright © 2023 by Samuel Robert Rebelein. All rights reserved. Printed in the United States of America. No part of this book may be used or reproduced in any manner whatsoever without written permission except in the case of brief quotations embodied in critical articles and reviews. For information, address HarperCollins Publishers, 195 Broadway, New York, NY 10007.

HarperCollins books may be purchased for educational, business, or sales promotional use. For information, please email the Special Markets Department at SPsales@harpercollins.com.

FIRST EDITION

Designed by Leah Carlson-Stanisic
Art by Ivan Kovbasniuk and MariLila/Shutterstock, Inc.
Map by Leah Carlson-Stanisic using art by Antipathique, Adobe Stock Images

Library of Congress Cataloging-in-Publication Data

Names: Rebelein, Sam, author.
Title: Edenville : a novel / Sam Rebelein.
Description: First edition. | New York : William Morrow an imprint of
  HarperCollins Publishers, [2023] | Summary: "Sam Rebelein's debut
  Edenville is an unsettling, immersive, and wildly entertaining read for
  fans of Paul Tremblay and Stephen Graham Jones"— Provided by publisher.
Identifiers: LCCN 2022054306 | ISBN 9780063252240 (hardcover) | ISBN
  9780063252264 (ebook)
Subjects: LCGFT: Horror fiction. | Novels.
Classification: LCC PS3618.E3355 E33 2023 | DDC 813/.6—dc23/
  eng/20230410
LC record available at https://lccn.loc.gov/2022054306

ISBN 978-0-06-325224-0

23 24 25 26 27 LBC 5 4 3 2 1

For all the amazing English teachers I've ever had:

Dan Jones, Sue Parise (a true angel), Ms. Roussin, Mr. Thell, Tracy, Kevin Lang, Kristine Jackson, Darcy Soi, Dan-the-Man Pitt!, Eric Buergers, Paul Russell, Jean Kane, Mark Amodio (who taught me to be tethered), David Means, Don Foster, David Tolley, Tyrone Simpson, Wendy Graham, Michael, Sherri!!, John (who embraced Renfield in its earliest form), and of course, a real hero: Darrah freakin Cloud.

Thank you all for helping me get here.
None of you were monsters.

Affirmations help achieve a sense of safety and hope:
I am a channel for God's creativity, and my work comes to good

JULIA CAMERON, *The Artist's Way*

You can't trust anybody in a goddam school.

HOLDEN CAULFIELD, in J. D. Salinger's *The Catcher in the Rye*

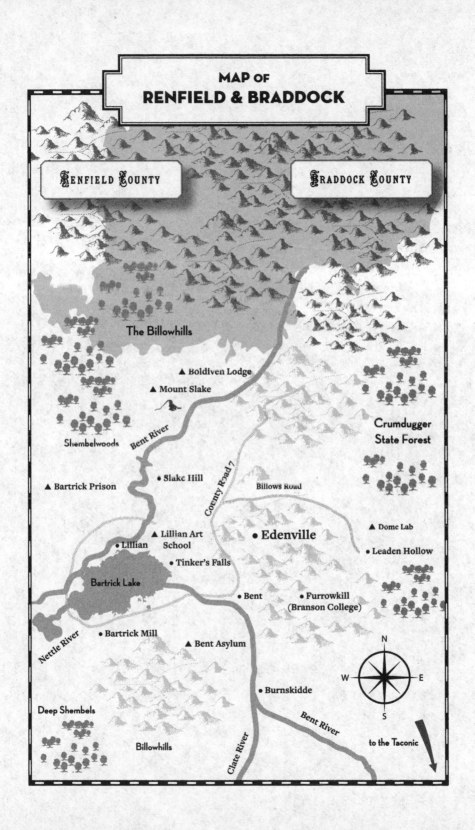

OVERTURE

THE GUMMERFOLK

He dreamt of an attic. Of course, it wasn't a dream, per se. But Cam didn't know that at the time.

The attic had a sharp-peaked roof, as if Cam were inside a perfectly triangular wooden prism. The point at the center of the ceiling ran from the stairs at one wall all the way to the small square window in the other. He wondered what the outside of the house looked like, if the roof was so sharp you could cut yourself along its edge.

The wood of the attic was unfinished, unsanded, splinterous, and rough. Nail ends jutted out all over. The room itself looked like a torture device. In its center was a faded pink sofa with wooden legs carved into human feet. The rest of the attic was bare.

Cam sat on the sofa's middle cushion. He couldn't move. Couldn't blink. Across from him, about a foot off the floor, something was etched into the sloped wood of the wall. He managed to squint, and saw it was a man. Or . . . man*like*. Minimalist, in thick, cakey yellow chalk. Two lines for legs, one down-swooping curve for each arm. And a ragged mass of spiked hair for the head. Someone had taken the chalk and scribbled it in an angry circle several times, digging in until the chalk cracked and caked in odd patterns. In the middle of this hair were two thick, slanted lines. Deep. Gouged hard into the wood.

The eyes hurt to look at. Like gazing into the sun.

Cam struggled to open his mouth, to speak, and as he did, the figure on the wall opened with him. The yellow chalk lines blurred. Beads of red popped like sweat from pores. Dark crimson fluid began to drain from the figure's hair and eyes, to run across the floor in spidery tendrils, throbbing as they stretched in all directions. Fingers poked out between the boards of the attic wall. Dozens of black-clawed, gray-fleshed hands wrapped around the wood from the other side. Yellow eyes and puckered mouths, pressing up against the wall from within. Fingers yanking at the wood, trying to pull it apart, to pop loose all the boards upon which this figure was drawn.

The gummerfolk were coming through.

"Don't," Cam managed to say, the word molasses-ing out of him. "Dooon't."

But his voice was drowned by another. Someone he couldn't see. Some booming, hell-thunder tone that read to him—the poem.

He'd remember it for the rest of his life, word for fuckin word:

> *The Shattered Man,*
> *with wild hair.*
> *You better run,*
> *avoid His stare.*
> *If you see Him,*
> *you are through.*
> *Cuz chances are?*
> *He already*
> *has seen*
> *you.*

On the final word, a board wrenched free with a *snap*. Fingers pulled it back into the darkness of the wall. And the gummerfolk began to slide into the attic.

If they had ever been human, they definitely weren't now. Now they looked like someone had dug the bones out of regular people, held their skins to a flame, and watched them melt. Their shoulders oozed halfway down their sides. Arms bent out of their abdomens. Legs dribbled directly down from their ribs. Their heads rolled, sloshing against their chests. Their faces drooped and their waxy lips opened, closed, like fish on hooks, choking on air. Their clothes were all askew, simple T-shirts and denim jeans, on sidewise and janky. Their hair was tufts of brown wire plugged into the warm clay of their scalps. The gummerfolk, an abandoned project forgotten in the cellar of the universe, squeezed their way out of this bleeding hole, one at a time, and spread like multiplying cells, expanding through the attic. Wobbling and sloshing. Some poorly made cross between a man, a leech, and one of those slippery snake tube-toys you find at, like, Rainforest Cafe.

God gave up while making these.

"Doon't," said Cam, more strained this time, like shouting through mud.

So many of them pouring through the hole. Warbling and swaggering around the attic. Aimless—until their eyes landed on Cam.

The first oodled its way around the side of the sofa. Its arms dangled at its sides, one twisted to the front, the other wrenched behind its back. It opened its mouth and ran its bugged eyes (one falling far down its cheek) over the entire course of Cam's body. He could feel the eyes like snakes upon his limbs, slithering up and down. Tasting him. The gummerthing made slobbery, licky noises. Wavering side to side.

Then fell on him.

It smacked its mouth against the side of Cam's neck, the fleshy bit with lots of strings inside. And it began to chew. To gum, really, because it had no teeth. It gnawed at him, very slowly. And as it did, Cam realized its lips weren't waxy, weak things at all. They had muscle behind them. They were *strong*. It'd take a while, yes, but this thing was going to gum him to death, no doubt about it. In a matter of maybe two or three agonizingly slow, gradually more painful hours, Cam was going to die at the hands of a toothless leech.

Another fell upon his ankle, splatting prostrate onto the floor. It moaned with pleasure, and its eyes rolled in opposite directions as it sucked at the side of Cam's foot, just over the big knob of bone.

Another fell on Cam's arm. Its mouth began to work at the flesh inside his elbow. Gums clenching, squeezing, releasing. He could feel tongues rolling over him. Warm, wet slobbering. Their jaws were strong, *so* strong. But he couldn't move. Couldn't fend them off.

Another gummerthing tripped over the one on the floor and fell into Cam's lap. It made an audible, cartoonish *amph!* as it chomped down on Cam's inner thigh. Another leapt over the back of the sofa, nuzzled

Cam's shirt off his belly, and latched on to his navel. He felt the gums working at his gut. Squeezing, releasing. Squeezing, sucking, releasing. Nudging around the organs inside.

Another fell on his bare toes.

Another swallowed his entire hand, knuckles *grrrinding* between its gums as its mouth *squeeeezed* . . .

At last, one of them waddled around behind him. He heard it crack open its mouth in a big, wet yawn. Drool dripped into his hair.

"Doon't," Cam moaned.

But the thing didn't listen. Of course it didn't. Why would it?

A great whoosh of air as it swooped down and took the crown of Cam's head inside its jaw. It squeezed its gums around his skull and sucked. Some of Cam's hair ripped loose, vacuumed away down its widening throat.

"Doon't." It slid its mouth lower. A snake shoving prey into itself. "Dooon't."

It worked its mouth down, lips wriggling over Cam's eyes. He felt them squish back into his skull, the gums pressing, pressing. Everything went dark.

"Doooon't."

The mouth descended over his nostrils, practically breaking Cam's nose up into his brain, grinding into the nape of his neck and his ears. All the while, more mouths fell on him, all over his body.

"Dooooon't!" he cried as he sucked in air between his teeth. He took a big breath, and the thing swept its lip into his mouth, shoved his tongue back into his throat. It dug its own tongue into him, tasting him gag. It pulsed lower, mouth moving down over Cam's chin, so that the suffocating, warm, wet flesh of its throat covered his entire face. He could taste its bile as it tasted him. Things in its jaw cracked as it widened, and prepared to take his shoulders.

Finally, the scream yawned from Cam's chest in one big "DOOON'T!"

He was awake.

He lurched up in bed. The R train rumbled through Brooklyn's underground, rattling the windows from far below. Lampposts poured a soft orange glow across the ceiling. Quinn snored gently at his side.

He was awake. And he was alive.

"Jesus," he murmured. He took a shaky breath, rubbed at his eyes. Pain lashed through his skull. He grit his teeth, swore at the dim bedroom. He blinked hard, several times. He wasn't crying. Something *else* was in his eyes. Something gluey? He held up his hand, pulled his fingers apart. Fluid separated between his knuckles in thick boogery strands. It was cold. Glacier-cold.

The fuck?

He blinked again, and the poem blared in his mind.

He scrabbled for his phone on the nightstand and typed it all out, though the screen was blurred, his fingers sticky, his eyes throbbing horribly.

He felt like if he didn't write it down, he'd die.

> *The Shattered Man,*
> *with wild hair.*
> *You better run,*
> *avoid His stare.*
> *If you see Him,*
> *you are through.*
> *Cuz chances are?*
> *He already*
> *has seen*
> *you.*

"Ew, why would you have jizz in your eyes?" Quinn asked, brushing her teeth in the open doorway between their bedroom and the bathroom.

Cam, still in bed, stared at the ceiling with bloodshot eyes. "Well, it's not snot. It's . . . rubbery. And sort of white."

"You save any of it?"

"God, no."

Quinn grunted around her toothbrush.

"My hypothesis," said Cam, in his *I have an MFA, therefore am smart* tone that Quinn used to love and now didn't at all, "is that it was a *wet* dream in addition to being a nightmare. That happens, right? You get so spooked you . . . cream the bed? Somehow, I've spooked myself into ejaculating directly *up* the length of my body, into my eyes." He cracked his knuckles, pleased with himself. "My aim must be pretty good."

"Ha. It's not." Quinn spat toothpaste into the sink. "Besides, your briefs aren't wet. Are they?"

"Hm. True. They *are* dry." Cam picked at his beard, thinking, as Quinn smeared on deodorant.

"Maybe something dripped down from the third floor," he said. "A leak or something?"

Quinn glanced at the ceiling. "Looks fine to me. You google it?"

"It'll just tell me I have eye cancer or something."

"And you don't think you have eye cancer."

"Well, I *hope* not."

"Then you know the alternative." Quinn cocked her head, let that dangle for a moment, like he was supposed to fill in the blank.

Cam held up his hands. "I . . . *do* have eye cancer?"

"Ahh. See, this is a perfect example of the rule."

"What rule?"

"*Our* rule. If anything creepy happens in the apartment . . ."

Cam groaned and rolled his eyes, which stung. He squeezed them shut. "Of course. We call the super."

Quinn had a Q-tip buried in her ear now. She nodded. "Because Diego *said* the building might be haunted. So if anything happens we can't explain, we don't be bullshit about it. Don't say it's the *wind* or some shit. Don't say it's an old building that *leaks*. It's a fuckin ghost. If the question is, *Is it a ghost?* then it's a goddamn ghost. We've both seen too many scary movies to be that kind of stupid."

This was true. Ordering Indian food from the place down the block and watching bad horror movies *was* a favorite pastime of theirs. Cam claimed it was inspiration for his writing. But he'd left his laptop open the other day, and Quinn had snooped a little (how can you not?), and she'd discovered he hadn't written anything new in months. He *had* been playing a lot of *Skyrim*, though. So that's what he'd been doing while she was on the roof smoking cigarettes by herself, watching the traffic on the bridges to Manhattan, glittering in the murky night.

"So how are you applying the Diego Rule in this scenario?" Cam asked. "Did a ghost jerk off into my eyes?"

She sat on the edge of the bed, began to lace up her boots. "Who knows. Maybe you're possessed. Maybe you came out of your *own* eyes. A braingasm!" She gasped, clutched his thigh. "New band name, I call it. Braingasm." She went back to her boots. "Ya know, semen burns your eyes. Could be why they hurt."

"Quinn, it's not *brain* semen. How does that make more sense than—"

"It's because your cornea's made of the same cellular material eggs are made of? So the sperm just *dig* in there, thinking it's—"

Cam buried his face in his hands. "Quinn, oh my god."

She clapped her thighs, launched herself to her feet. "Look, I'm just sayin. If it smells creepy, it *is* creepy."

"Well, just because the dude who sold us the apartment said it's haunted doesn't mean it is."

A pang of betrayal needled up Quinn's chest. "Cam, I'm ashamed of you, I really am. You're mister big horror guy, and now you're gonna say some dumb bull like, 'Oh, the dude told us the apartment was haunted but I don't *believe* him'?"

"But we've had no flickering lights, no . . . strange whispers . . ."

"Baby, *you're* a strange whisper." She leaned over, kissed his forehead. Really dug her lips into him to blot her lipstick on his skin. When she released him, he had a bright red *Fight Club*–style mouth just over his third eye. He looked cute, all blear-eyed and snug in bed.

"I gotta go help Kenz with inventory," she said. "I love you, have a good day, don't get ghosted."

And she was gone.

Cam washed his eyes in the sink for the third time that morning. But the water made the sting worse. He felt like he'd coated his eyes in some acidic plastic shell. When he rubbed at them, they seemed to shift around inside his skull.

He sat at the little desk in their bedroom, opened his laptop. He eyed the *Skyrim* icon. Last time he'd played, the game claimed he'd logged over a thousand hours. That . . . didn't seem very healthy.

So he cracked his knuckles. Opened a fresh Word doc. Picked at his beard. Stared at the blinking cursor. Rubbed his eyes.

And began to write.

The words came easily, for once. He found himself writing about the house under the attic from his dream. The man who lived there, one Frank LaMorte, had annihilated his family with a box cutter. All four of his children, peeled like bananas. When he was done, he took great dripping handfuls of them and painted a stick figure on the attic wall. An act so cruel and bizarre, it changed those wooden boards forever, warping them into a doorway to a nightmare realm. When the boards were pulled apart, the house painted over and thrown back onto the market, that blood-figure man was scattered into pieces, the doorway from His realm to ours—broken once more. *He* became angry. He became the Shattered Man.

This was the best work Cam had ever done.

But as he wrote, the burn behind his eyes grew worse. He could barely see the screen, his vision was so bad. Fat drops of cold phlegm curdled out of his eyes and spattered onto the backs of his hands as he wrote, and wrote, and wrote. He followed the story as it twisted in new directions, moving of its own accord. He'd always heard stories do that, but he'd never seen it firsthand. It was strange. Something was curling out of him, stinging his eyes as it needled its way out of its nest in his brain.

Weeks of this.

Quinn asked if he wanted to see a doctor. No, a doctor might cure it, and curing it might dry up the words. Cam adamantly refused, blinking and bloodshot.

Four months later, he had himself a novel. And as suddenly as it'd begun, the burning in his eyes? Gone, without a trace.

See? No doctor necessary.

Cam had exactly three publishing credits to his name before *The Shattered Man*. Three stories in semi-pro magazines that he should've been proud of but wasn't. But he felt, finally, that *Shattered Man* was something important. At last, he'd written something that mattered. An entire novel! He just *knew* it was going to change his life.

Ohh yes. It would change his life indeed.

That was three years ago. Back when Cam and Quinn had first gotten their together-apartment, in Park Slope. Quinn liked the place because it got morning sun, and their windows opened onto the building's courtyard, full of actual trees. She loved that she could fall asleep to the sound of wind in leaves, instead of the trucks and drunks along 4th Ave. She could walk along the entire roof, too, all around the building. She could see the Statue of Liberty, the far-off shimmer of the Chrysler Building . . . Cam spent his evenings bolted to his desk, so Quinn got used to coming up on the roof by herself, with a cigarette and her father's lighter, the Zippo with Marilyn Monroe etched in its side in Warhol colors. She'd put her Spotify on shuffle, stick in her earbuds, and watch the red and white lights tinkling in the polluted dark of the city.

Quinn was comfortable being alone.

Cam didn't mind the sound of traffic at night. But he wasn't born and raised upstate like Quinn. His parents worked at NYU. He didn't know the music of peeper-frogs, trains howling at night through the woods. He'd gone north for his MFA at Branson College, in the mostly-nothing town of Furrowkill. There, he met Quinn (a junior and a theater major at the time). She'd clung to him because he talked about himself like he was important. Quinn felt like river debris at best, bobbing along through life without any direction except *down*. After they both graduated, he asked if she wanted to follow him back to the city.

"Cam, my hometown has only five thousand people," she'd told him. "We *used* to have a bowling alley, and we *used* to have a Blockbuster. I'm from Leaden *Hollow*." Grimacing like the name tasted how it sounded. "So yeah. I would *love* to move to Brooklyn with you. I could get involved in theater! Be in weird plays in black boxes downtown." Which she never really ended up doing (the "weird plays" she auditioned for always seemed to require more nude monologuing and rolling around in milk than she was comfortable with), but it'd been a nice dream to cling to when she'd said goodbye to Leaden Hollow.

Quinn was done with Leaden Hollow anyway. Everywhere she went, she felt like she was kicking up a slow-growing layer of water and sediment. Like the place was gradually flooding itself with memory, as most small towns do. Cam was just an easy buoy to cling to as she floated away from home. She hated herself for those moments alone on the Brooklyn roof, when she yearned to go back.

Such a dirty fuckin trick hometowns play. You can't wait to leave. Then they keep whispering your name on the wind.

They'd been dating for two years already when Cam had the attic nightmare. Quinn was so relieved. Cam had spent their first year in the city getting high and playing *Witcher 3*, sitting around saying "Roach!" in that white-haired dude's gravelly voice. Picking at his beard on the couch, leaving coarse little hairs all over the floor. He'd smoke an entire joint, ramble at Quinn about how he could be the next Stephen King, then turn on the PlayStation. Again.

But the nightmare seemed to give him a new sense of purpose. *Then* he managed to sell the book to a small indie press—some bunch of nerds operating out of a refurbished cider mill in Vermont. Quinn had been stoked. Cam was invited to readings; he did interviews. It wasn't a *big* splash, but it made him happy.

Except Happy Cam was somehow even more smug and irritating than Unhappy Cam. Happy Cam berated Quinn for her taste in food, her music. He was now officially better than her, a successful novelist. And it stung. Especially when she pulled back from theater altogether, and became just another Brooklyn bartender with an abandoned dream.

When the indie press tanked, dragging *Shattered Man* down with it, Unhappy Cam reemerged, and Quinn remembered she didn't like *him* very much either. He was bitter and cynical. Had zero ideas for future books. He slumped around the city for his tutoring job that he hated, grumbling about the SATs and ungrateful high schoolers. Schlepping brick-size test-prep books from apartment to apartment, having all these one-on-one sessions with sixteen-year-olds who couldn't give a fuck, then coming home and demanding Quinn rub his shoulders as he rolled a joint.

Rinse and repeat.

She watched him sink into an irrevocable bitterness. This thing he'd believed would change his life hadn't changed anything at all. He was just as unimportant as he'd always been. He hadn't even written a word since that last cold tear dried up on his keyboard.

Quinn felt she could relate. Turns out, she *didn't* want to grind through audition after audition. Kicking herself, for example, for missing an open call just because someone threw themselves onto the tracks of the F train up ahead. Sitting there sweating in the piss-stink of the subway car, clutching her old headshot, picturing the corpse-cleaners a mile up the track. Fuckin horrible. And she finally had to admit to herself that theater had never been that fun anyway, even in college, without Celeste. Celeste was the one who'd gotten her into acting in the first place. Back in the day.

So then . . . what *did* Quinn wanna do?

Good question.

Over time, Unhappy Cam became somehow . . . comforting. At least rubbing his shoulders gave her something to do. Lines to recite.

"It's okay, baby," Quinn told him, time and again as she dug into his muscles, staring over his head at *Witcher 3*. "You'll write something *huge* one day. I know you will. I know it . . ."

Hoping desperately that this was true.

SHATTERED MAN, WITH WILD HAIR

When Caleb Wentley discovers a small stick figure drawn in chalk on his attic wall, he doesn't think much about it. It's just a yellow set of lines with a weird mess of hair and two diagonal slits for eyes. Creepy, but the previous tenants had kids, didn't they? Kids draw on walls.

But when something starts to whisper to him through the chalk—digging its fingers between the wooden slats of the wall and pressing its mouth against the wood from the other side—Caleb knows something is wrong.

His investigation into the history of the house leads him to a cult-like organization called the Committee for the Reconstruction of the Shattered Man. The Committee tells Caleb that the figure in his attic is only a scale drawing of a much larger design. Thirty years ago, the Shattered Man, a god-like giant from another plane, was summoned in blood, across an entire wall of what is now Caleb's attic. The boards He was splashed across have been scattered around the country (macabre keepsakes for true crime fans), but the Committee is almost done recollecting them. They just need Caleb's help finding one last piece. Once that's in place, and the Shattered Man is whole again, He will open a doorway to a world far more monstrous than our own . . .

In Campbell P. Marion's debut horror novel, *The Shattered Man*, Caleb must race against time to stop the Committee from opening this door, before the creatures on the other side pry their way through. It isn't long before Caleb learns the Committee's ultimate plan for him, and the most important lesson about the Shattered Man: Once He's whole, only fresh death can unlock His favor.

Jacket copy from the back cover of *The Shattered Man*

CHAPTER ONE

THE C.M. BOX

The lounge dedicated to the faculty of the Creative Writing department is not very large. But then again, neither is the Creative Writing department. Madeline Narrows was one of only ten professors.

She sat on the green leather couch facing the mantel in the lounge, her bare feet propped up on the coffee table before her. Madeline liked to be barefoot. It helped her feel the breath of the Earth, she thought.

She closed the book she'd been reading. Its spine crinkled gently in the silence of the lounge. She ran her hands over its surface. *The Shattered Man* bled across its cover in bold, chalky yellow letters. The stick figure with its spiky hair and eerie eyes stared up at her, made her shiver.

Madeline didn't know this writer, this Campbell P. Marion. According to his bio on the book's back cover, this was his first book. He was a young white man with a thick beard and round glasses. He had an MFA from Branson College, about an hour's drive from where Madeline now sat. He wasn't smiling in his black-and-white photo, which was credited to a Quinn Rose Carver-Dobson. What a nice name. It sounded like a law firm. Madeline wondered what their relationship was.

When she ran her fingers over the image of Campbell's face, she felt that he was kind, but that he often chose not to be. She felt that he could be selfish and small, but that he was well-loved by at least one person who believed in him (Quinn?). She felt that he could say mean things very easily, and that his ideas could be dangerous.

Madeline took her fingers away from him. They felt oily and tingly as she rubbed them together, the way they always did when Madeline felt things about people.

She'd enjoyed *The Shattered Man* tremendously. She'd read it in one sitting, in fact. But of course, she'd been riveted because the book had partially been about *her*.

See, every other week for the past three months, the department's student employee (the sophomore boy with the gauges and blue hair) delivered a box to the department's office. This box contained an embarrassingly large assortment of work. Books, magazines, printouts of online publications, newspapers, literary journals . . . All of it dumped into a waterlogged HelloFresh box and delivered from the campus library (where the blue-haired boy spent countless hours poring over archives, digital and physical) to the Creative Writing department in Slitter Hall. The boy didn't know what it was all for, and thankfully, he never asked. Madeline didn't know how they'd explain it to him. Where would she even begin?

At the Alumni House dinner in February (almost three months ago now), Madeline's boyfriend, the handsome and award-winning writer Benny McCall, had gathered all ten Writing professors in a side room of the Alumni House. He poured himself a drink, told them to make themselves comfortable. And he told them a story that only three of the ten people in the room had believed. *These* three took turns reading the boxes every month. Digging through everything they could find by authors who all shared the same initials. The other seven professors didn't speak to them much anymore.

Madeline hadn't been as surprised by Benny's story as the others had been. They'd been dating for three years before he arrived at the college this semester. The concept of having a *boyfriend* at forty-five, with one divorce under her belt already, still made Madeline giddy. But he'd felt . . . different this last year. She'd felt him in his sleep. *Wormy* was the word that came to mind, though she didn't know why. He'd just been acting so strange since he won that fancy literary award last spring. Since he met that woman Catherine Mason. He'd been so . . . aloof.

So actually, she'd been relieved when he gathered them all in that room in the Alumni House, and told them what he knew. *See?* she'd thought. *I knew it. He* isn't *himself.* It'd given her hope that things might get better. And when he asked this sub-department (those three people who'd believed) to begin organizing and sifting through the boxes—

when he asked them to build those machines in the basement—Madeline had readily agreed.

It's difficult to cut things off, especially when your boyfriend is such a fine kisser, and such a wonderful writer.

But reading through the boxes was a laborious, horrible task, with very few exceptions. Because Madeline knew that if she found anything worthwhile, she'd have to report it. And if she did *that*, it . . . essentially meant death to whomever she'd just read.

Which was why she was sitting here with *The Shattered Man* in silence, not moving. She wasn't sure Campbell P. Marion deserved to die.

She laid the book in her lap, front cover up so she didn't have to feel Campbell's eyes on her, staring out from his author photo on the back. She looked up at the wide portrait adorning the wall above the mantel. She picked at her cuticles.

"Damn you," she told the portrait.

The portrait did not respond.

Matthew Slitter, subject of this portrait, was college president from 1971 until '79. He was widely considered an ineffectual, limp-handshake, hippie kind of man. Absent-minded and unfocused. He had tanned, leathery skin, absolutely no hair except the thin crown of wispy long white around the base of his skull. He wore round, wireframe bottle-lenses and blinked constantly, his eyes often red during college functions. His manner of speaking was distracted and whispery. He even carried around a froofy wooden cane like some mock Wonka. And he had this *un*clean smell about him, like sex or musk or weed.

In other words, he seemed pretty much constantly stoned.

But in 1973, Slitter observed something gravely important: a large number of English Literature & Linguistics students were submitting creative projects for their senior theses. When he inquired around the department as to why this was, Slitter learned that many of these students had just come home from Vietnam. Many more had lost friends, brothers, fathers . . .

Slitter drafted a college-wide memo, dated November 1973: "The human heart is too finicky and fragile to contain horror for long. It has too many chambers, too many holes. Material *will* leak out eventually, one way or another. You must express and exorcise, for without an outlet, a tributary, your heart will simply pour out inside yourself, until you're full to bursting. You can die that way. Slowly, over the course of decades.

"So, hell. Let the people write."

Slitter split the English department in two. The Creative Writers remained in Boldiven Hall, which Slitter renamed after himself (why not?). And all the Literature & Linguistics folks moved into new offices in Von Eichmann, the building kitty-corner to now–Slitter Hall. That didn't particularly please the History professors, who'd had Von Eichmann to themselves, but Slitter built a new wing off Von's east end, and the History department grumbled itself into a contented silence.

Slitter Hall was now home to four Writing professors, as well as the entirety of the Philosophy department, upstairs. The building's old auditorium was remodeled, and Slitter instituted biweekly coffeehouse evenings there, where students and teachers alike could come to read their work. For students, it was an opportunity to share the writing they'd kept sacred throughout high school, many of them reading in public for the first time, hoping to maybe get a pat on the back from a beloved professor. For the faculty, it was, honestly, a chance to steal ideas for their own writing. It wasn't like *all* of these kids were going to publish their shit anyway, right?

Soon, students in other departments began to participate in the coffeehouse as well, both as audience members and as writers, sharing poems, stories, songs. It didn't hurt that Slitter insisted there be a spread of coffee and treats each week, all organized by his wife, Belinda. Thanks to Belinda, there was always a glut of chocolate chip cookies, brownies, and oatmeal raisin balls that even the most steadfast oatmeal-haters agreed were quite good.

So it was that the Slitter Coffeehouse Reading Series became a well-appreciated tradition at Edenville College. It showed up on college pamphlets. Slitter Auditorium became a major stop on the college tour. By 1985, the Creative Writing faculty had more than doubled. It became a popular inside joke: "Your kid's a writer? My condolences. Well, send em off to Edenville."

But despite this well-appreciated addition to campus life, Slitter's inevitable forced retirement began in late 1978, when he used the phrase "far out" in another college-wide memo. Alumni worried he might try to turn the college into a commune. It didn't help that he also wasted a fair amount of the college's endowment on "whimsical" projects (and that's cited from a letter to Slitter *strongly* suggesting that "retirement would probably suit you sig*nifi*cantly better than academic life . . . Don't you think?" The last few words of which were heavily underlined.). Matthew Slitter had no defense to this, and quite honestly, he was ready to go himself. If the board had no taste for his "whimsical" endeavors—such as ensuring there were more sunflowers on campus (an act that had also admittedly carried to Edenville a slew of aphids, beetles, midges, and moths), or instating Turtle Tuesday once a semester, in celebration of the snapping turtles in the campus lake—then Slitter simply "didn't want to play anymore," as *he* wrote in *his* letter back to the board.

It was, suffice it to say, a seamless and amicable transition.

In 1990, Matthew Slitter famously vanished, at eighty years old. There were rumors he'd been killed, his body fertilizer for the vast seas of sunflowers now covering the entire western academic lawn (West Campus for short, West Camp for shorter). Slitter's flowers surround the borders of the campus as well, blocking it from view from the road. According to some, Matthew and Belinda (who vanished alongside her husband) are buried somewhere under campus, wrapped up in all those flower roots. And even in this strange new grave-life, motionless in the dirt, roots growing from his eyes, Slitter holds his wooden cane tight to his chest . . .

The point is, it was Matthew Slitter's fault there was a Creative Writing department at all. Which meant, through a long series of accidents and coincidences and just plain bad luck, it was *his* fault that Professor Madeline Narrows was sitting here today, in Slitter Lounge, holding a stranger's life in her hands.

"Damn you," she told his portrait. The old president stood with his chest puffed high, in a field of sunflowers with his ever-faithful eagle-headed cane. Storm clouds brewed above him, lightning frozen midflicker on his glasses. Yellow petals swirled about his feet. He looked very grand and autumnal.

Madeline looked down at *The Shattered Man* again and sighed. Maybe she could pretend she never saw it. Drop it in the donation slot at the Edenville Public Library downtown. Or even better, rip its spine in half and stick it in the shredder. Maybe Benny would never know.

No. He'd know.

She glanced out the door behind her, into the hall. The couch had its back to most of the lounge, including the bookshelves, the big wooden conference table with its green banker's lamps, the bar cart, and the door.

Nothing moved.

But even if he wasn't watching her right now, he'd *know*. And he'd be pissed.

Madeline slipped into her Birkenstocks, rose from the couch, and tucked the book under her arm. She walked out of the lounge, past the window to the administrative assistant's desk. Angie was in her late sixties. She had thick white hair compared to Madeline's mousy brown, and her skin was a rich near-onyx compared to Madeline's clouded blue-vein quartz. Twelve penguin bobbleheads nodded uniformly on her desk. She pointed at the book under Madeline's arm. "Find anything good?"

"Hope so," said Madeline brightly.

"Ohh exciting. He told me y'all are close to finishing."

"Yep," said Madeline, a little less brightly. "We are indeed . . ."

As she walked down the windowless length of Slitter Hall, Madeline passed rooms full of students, all in their last week of classes before finals. Slitter is academically and literally a stuffy building, especially in this last week of April, so the doors to these rooms were open, letting in some slightly fresher air from the hall. She glanced in one room to see Syd teaching her class on short fiction. She paced the room like a caged cat as she croaked on about "Gardner's idea of the fictive dream, which *will* be on the final."

Madeline lifted her hand in greeting. Syd nodded coolly at her. Once, perfunctory. The way Syd always nodded. Then she pointed at the chalkboard with the one arm that ended abruptly above her wrist. "So let's start with this paragraph here."

Madeline passed another room where Chett, hunched and nasally, was asking "literally anyone" to give him their opinion on Woolf's use of free indirect discourse.

"Is Mr. Ramsay thinking this," he droned, "or the authorial narrator? See, that's the beauty of Deleuzian narratology." Clicking his pen. "We get to really *dig* into these questions . . ."

Chett wasn't in the sub-department. He wasn't a believer.

At the end of the hall, Madeline turned toward the stairs. She took them down from the first floor to the basement. Then one flight further, to a door she had to unlock with a special key. As she did, the sounds of muffled machinery rolled over her. Music, too. Tom Jones, wailing on and on about his Delilah, that cheating backstabber who'd laughed when he confronted her. A grinding, crunching song that made Madeline wince.

But Wes *loved* Tom Jones. The music meant he was here.

Good.

She adjusted her grip on the book as she walked down the dim, flickering hall of the under-basement. Hot down here. Metal hot. She could taste gear grease on her tongue. As she walked deeper, it grew hotter. "Delilah" grew louder. Jones cried *why* over and over, drawing Madeline helplessly toward the pounding of the machines.

When she came to the great vault door, she rang the buzzer. A pause, and the door began to crank and grind. She listened to its bolts and bars churn themselves out of the wall. The door screamed open in a hellish, rusted whine—and there stood Professor Wes Flannery, in an apron spattered with blood.

"What?" he said. Behind him, the room groaned with engines. They cranked and banged, and Wes had to shout over their steamy clangor, over the music he had playing on his Bluetooth speaker resting on the metal sink bolted to the wall.

"It's the middle of the day," he said. "There's students around." Benny and Wes had laboriously soundproofed the under-basement, but . . . Murphy's Law and all.

"I think I have someone!" Madeline shouted. She held out the book.

He took it in one big leather-gloved hand. He turned it over, glanced at both covers.

Wes was a pirate captain of a man. Broad and burly, six and a half feet tall. Hairy arms, deeply tanned and thick. The book looked much smaller in his hands than in Madeline's. He towered over her with his electric-white hair, his old barfight scars. The apron, covered in stains. He was her oldest friend in the department. She was not afraid of him. And when he worked down here, his sweaty musk was not altogether unpleasant.

He handed the book back to her. "What's in it?"

"The giant. The tapestry. Us, sort of." She held it to her chest. "Can I come in?"

He stood aside.

Calling it a "room" would be generous. It was a massive concrete block, barren except for the metal slab in the center, the sink, and the massive twin turbines along the back wall, rotating endlessly. Madeline kept her eyes on the floor, avoided looking at the turbines. It was Wes's job to take care of them. He'd traded *that* for having to take a turn reading the box. Madeline wondered if he still thought it was worth it. She hadn't worked up the courage to touch him, to see what he felt like these days.

"The shelves are full," he told her, turning down the volume on Jones. "That girl was the last. We'd have to recycle."

"We're still getting boxes, though."

"Then take it up with your boyfriend, Benny. We're outta room. Tell him not to be greedy."

Madeline sputtered. "I . . . I'm not telling him *that*."

Wes hawked a glob of phlegm onto the floor, by a metal drain. "So what do you want me to do?"

"Well, I haven't . . . *found* anyone before," said Madeline. "And I'm . . ."

"You're having doubts."

She paused. "Maybe."

"So what, you want me to help you hide this?" Nodding at the book. "From *McCall*?"

"No." She felt a lurch of fear.

"Then what do you *want* me to do?" Wes asked gently.

"I don't know," she snapped. She glanced at the large, clanking machine. "I just . . . It just really struck me that . . . We're *hurting* people, Wes. That doesn't bother you? At all?"

He was about to answer when a large cough caught him by surprise. It cracked his body in half. He racked up several wet coughs in a row, then spat again onto the floor.

"Ya know," he sniffed, "maybe one day it will? But this is borrowed time, Madeline. If there's even a chance . . ."

"I get it," she said, not looking at him. Looking instead at the thing he'd just coughed up. It was blue, and reeked of juniper. She swallowed a small lump of bile. "I just don't want to . . . hurt anyone anymore. I feel . . . stuck, Wes."

He sighed. "Here." Held his hand out for the book. Examined it again. Then: "Okay, here's an idea. Maybe we can just . . . bring him in. Keep an eye on him."

Madeline brightened. "He has an MFA. We could hire him!"

Wes nodded, reading Campbell's bio. "Yeah, he's got some credits . . . Why not ask him to be the next writer in residence? Next semester."

"What about that other woman? The, the . . . playwright lady."

Wes shrugged. "Fuck her. A sudden shift in schedule. She can come in the spring."

"What if he doesn't accept our invitation?"

Wes scoffed, handed her back the book. "He'll accept. Because we can offer him what *all* young writers want."

"Strippers and coke?"

He laughed. "Right. No, we can offer the poor asshole a chance at being *important*. What writer doesn't want that?"

Madeline nodded, thinking. "Okay. Sure. Yeah, I'll ask Ben tonight. Thank you."

"Just don't tell him it was my idea." Wes turned from her, ripped off his gloves, began to wash his hands at the sink.

Madeline watched the shelves of the turbines revolve. She wiped sweat from her forehead. It was hot in here, so hot. And the only relief? A barely noticeable breeze from the large dented metal fan whooshing slow overhead.

"Where's the girl?" she asked.

Wes flicked water off his hands, jerked his chin at the lefthand turbine. He led Madeline to it, and waited until one shelf in particular rotated around the bottom of the machine. He pressed a button. The engine jerked to a halt. Steam hissed. The shelf hung at chest height.

The girl had short red hair. She wore a beige bra, a diaper, and nothing more.

Madeline ran her finger up her arm. The girl twitched. Madeline tasted her pain. The bottomless, rusted dark. And she took it. Not all, just . . . a little. Let it soak up through her fingers. Felt it settle into her tissue, her bones.

"There," she whispered. "It's alright. Shhh . . ."

As the hurt crawled into her body, sucking at her marrow, Madeline grew a little thinner, thinner, until Wes said, "That's enough." He slammed the button, the engine whirred back to life, and the girl's shelf swung up away from Madeline's grasp.

"You'll kill yourself doing that," said Wes. He coughed. "You know that."

"Has she dreamt of any wood yet?" Madeline asked.

"My guess is no. But you'll have to ask Benny. *He* drinks the stuff." Nodding at the tanks behind the machine. "He'd know."

Madeline didn't want to ask Benny. She hugged *The Shattered Man* tight to her chest.

Far overhead, the large metal fan . . . whooshed . . .

A vulture, circling its dying prey.

CHAPTER TWO

THE RED YARD

The Red Yard was an old bar. It *smelled* like old bar. Stale beer, ancient sweat, rancid lemons. The booth benches were plywood, the tables some kind of soggy sticky oak, pockmarked with decades of carved names and initials and dicks. The kind of place that might catch you alone, whisper drunk into your ear, a totally sloshed wallpaper arm sloughing off the wall and slinging across your shoulders, *Hey man, lemme tellya somethin . . .*

The Red Yard had seen some fucked-up shit.

It'd first been built as a home for one Simon Routhier, meatpacker and friend of the Rockefellers. A thank-you for something history seems to have neglected to record. The beer garden behind the Red Yard was once an actual garden, filled with flowers, koi, butterflies . . . About a hundred years ago, Simon Routhier had been found *in* that garden, butchered beyond belief. Steaming globs of him spread across the entire space, dangling off the trees, oozing into the fishpond. Like he'd sneezed and suddenly exploded, leaving behind a big red yard.

Simon's fresh twenty-year-old wife, Florence, was arrested at a speakeasy in Manhattan. They asked her *why*, of course. Was he having an affair? Did he smack her around? *Why* did she kill successful meatpacker Simon Routhier, her husband of only seven months?

Florence laughed. According to the *Times*, she laughed all the way to the chair.

Whenever Quinn worked in the Red Yard (most weekday nights), she found herself scanning the small crowds, all the awkward Hinge dates, for telltale signs of something otherworldly and cool. Translucent skin, old pucker scars on the neck . . . It just *felt* like the kind of bar vampires might meet in. When she handed people their beer, she always grazed their fingertips with her own. So far, every hand Quinn had touched here had been disappointingly warm. But she held out hope for evidence of something . . . something *new*.

Doesn't everyone.

Cam had once pointed out, annoyingly, that real-life vampires ("Well, *if* they exist") might not follow the same rules as their mythic counterparts. Besides, Quinn was fairly vampiric herself. The pale skin, the bright, hypnotic eyes. And her hands *were* often quite cold, all skeletal and reddish.

Celeste used to call them witch's hands. From any other mouth, that would sound like an insult. But Celeste had a way of making it sound spooky and powerful. *I can just* see *those fingers cackling over a boiling pot of green*, Quinn remembered her saying, in that smoky voice of hers. And *You just have such pretty hands*, her voice even smokier than usual. Tangling her fingers in Quinn's, that night after homecoming. That awkward night when they were almost more than friends. The night they never got the chance to talk about, before . . .

Well. She didn't need to think about that.

Florence Routhier's picture hung on the wall by the little stage in the corner of the Red Yard, across from the bar, and directly over the dark hall leading back to the bathrooms. The picture had been taken three weeks before Florence burst her husband. She glared out of it with dead sepia eyes, a pinched black-lipstick mouth.

This picture was one of the main reasons Quinn liked working at Red Yard. Florence watched over all. The bar's guardian angel was a legit murderer. Which meant, if anyone tried to fuck with Quinn or the bar or anything at all, Florence could be trusted to intervene. Quinn could feel her lurking in the floorboards. Somewhere under that old bar smell, there still lingered a hint of meat upon the air.

Quinn found it comforting. She lifted a glass to Flo, saluted her, and drank a sip of cider.

She stood behind the bar, earbud jammed in one ear: Iron & Wine's cover of "Such Great Heights." Real sad-girl shit she couldn't play over the speakers because it'd bum everyone out. She had both hands in the kangaroo pouch of her hoodie, fidgeting with her dad's old Marilyn lighter. She'd found that the more solid she made herself, the less likely she was to be hit on. Black boots, loose torn jeans, her old autumn-hued Leaden Hollow High hoodie (go Crows). It was yellow, orange, and brown, the colors of fall leaves. A crow soared across the front. It always made Quinn think of the old fight song: *Go Leaden Hollow Crows! We'll peck you dead, everybody knows!* She wore her sharp bangs low over her eyes, so they twitched whenever she blinked. She'd seen someone do that in a movie once when she was eight, and it'd stuck, the way movie-things will when you are eight.

It was mind-boggling how many men acted like they were somehow the first to ever hit on her, to tell her she had pretty eyes.

"Wow thank you," she'd started saying. "I have literally never been complimented before."

Then again, she *did* have nice eyes, if she said so herself. Gray and ringed, like an old tree. Cam called them oaken eyes—betrayers of an old soul. She liked that. It was better than a lot of what she got at the bar, and she clung to it, deep in her heart. Just as she clung to the hoodie, which had once been Celeste's. Celeste was a size fourteen, and the folds of fabric hung loose about Quinn's body. Like a blanket she could walk around in.

She watched as the Red Yard filled slowly with patrons, the rickety tables in the middle of the floor beginning to creak with bodies, all filing in for the Red Yard Reading Series, which started in about ten minutes. Quinn eyed them all with distaste. She tried to see if she could explode any of them with her mind, like Florence Routhier had maybe once done. She squinted at them. They refused to explode.

Bummer.

The Series hosted three fantasy/sci-fi/horror authors, who read twenty minutes apiece, every other week. It'd begun long before Quinn started working at the bar, and if she'd known about it when she'd started, she probably wouldn't have accepted the job. Because of course, it wasn't long before Cam pulled the ole, "Any chance you could ask if *I* could read?" And of course, the woman running the series had loved him so much

(Cam could really turn on the schmooze when he wanted to) that he was now a regular. But Cam never read anything *new* because he never *wrote* anything new, so every few months, Quinn had to listen to him read the same stupid pages from *Shattered Man* again. At this point, she could almost recite the story word for word: Frankie LaMorte hears a man's voice behind the wall of his attic. He boxcuts his family to bits on its behalf, then paints a sketch of the Man on the wall in their blood. These slats of bloodstained wood are now cursed! They *mutate* you whenever you touch them, they're sooo evil. If you have just *one* piece of the Shattered Man in your possession, you're always wondering if your actions are yours—or His. And if you put Him all back together again, look out! Monsters will claw through the wood from another world.

Whatever. She didn't need to hear all that spoooky nonsense again. She liked the book, but not *that* much. Not that she would ever say that.

She eyed Cam across the bar. The two other authors reading that night sat at one booth, but Cam sat, unsocial, in the corner. He picked at his beard, muttering to himself over a beer, reading through his pages for that evening. So nervous and tight-wound.

She watched him.

He did not explode.

Nothing in Quinn's life exploded when she asked it to.

She'd put five years into this relationship now. Most of her twenties. Her youth! She couldn't just cold-turkey it. She couldn't cold-turkey *any*thing. How many packs of menthols had she crushed up halfway through, thrown into the trash, and stood over like a grizzled assassin above the grave of a nemesis? *That'll be the very last cigarette I ever smoke,* she'd vow solemnly every time. And then she'd buy a new pack, just a few months later, do it all again. If she broke up with Cam, who's to say she wouldn't just . . . buy another pack? So to speak.

And Crows forbid she give her mom the satisfaction of knowing she was right. Yes, Quinn had hopelessly entangled herself with "yet another artist boy adult man," as her mother had called him last Christmas, after about half a bottle of Barefoot rosé. Quinn had done the same thing with that music major her freshman year at Branson. And the same thing *twice* during her senior year of high school. She'd fall for the hairy, tired-looking artist type. She'd push to make the relationship function. And the guy wouldn't even care. Scraps of validation, few and far between.

"You're jjust gonna keep doin the saame asshole," her mother slurred. "Ssmoking the ssame shit. Dead girl walkin! Usin a *dead* man's lighter. Shoulda left it in his coffin like he *asked*."

That'd sent a cold shiver down Quinn's spine. To be fair, Dad *had* asked to be buried with his lighter. It'd been *his* dad's, and he had no son. But Quinn plucked it out of his casket at the funeral, at nine years old. It was her talisman now, like the Leaden Hollow High hoodie (go Crows). Which was ironic, because when she was *in* high school, she had no school spirit at all. Only when she left for college did she acquire a strange hump of pride, and the hoodie became a staple of her wardrobe. Her memorial to Celeste.

She hadn't thought her mother knew about the lighter. But Mother knew everything. That's why they didn't talk much anymore.

Quinn downed the rest of her cider, and nodded at the other girl behind the bar. "Hey, Kenz?"

Kenz glanced up.

"You mind if I . . . ?" She waggled her lighter and pack of Camels.

Kenz shook her head.

"Thanks, man."

Kenz nodded.

Kenz didn't talk much.

The door to the Red Yard opened onto an alley. In summer, it was filled with long picnic tables, screaming families, wasps. Tonight, in the still-bitter ides of early May (does May have ides?), the alley was empty and dim. Wind ripped. Strings of bistro lights swung overhead.

Quinn had to cup her hand tight around the end of her cigarette to keep the wind off. She had to flick the lighter a bunch of times to get the spark to catch.

"Come on, Marilyn," Quinn muttered. She shook the lighter. Tried again. The spark caught, but the wind blew it out. "Look, I know you're pissed JFK had ya killed, but come on." She tried again. Nothin. "Fuck you . . ."

"Well."

The voice made Quinn jump. She almost sucked the whole cigarette down her throat in a surprised gasp.

A woman stood in the shadows just beyond the swinging strings of lights. They tilted in the wind, illuminating her face so Quinn caught glinting hazel eyes—then darkness. The lights swung again. Quinn saw long, dark hair with pulses of white—then shadows.

The woman's voice was a low croak-growl. Rasping and odd. "I was going to ask you for a light, but I might be out of luck."

Quinn gave an awkward laugh. "Oh, just . . . give her a minute."

"What, you talk in the third person?"

"I mean Marilyn." Quinn held up the lighter so the woman could see. "Give her a minute, she'll light your fire. That's what my dad used to say. And then he'd wink and my mom would always punch him. 'William Thomas Carver. Language!'" Quinn spoke around the cigarette, frantically flicking at Marilyn. "She always called him by his full name when she was mad. But the joke was on her, because he *liked* his . . . full . . . Mm." She got a light, sucked hard. Clapped the Zippo shut, and blew out a grateful stream of smoke. "There, see? I always think it helps if I talk about him, too. I know that sounds nuts, but." She shrugged.

"All the truest truths sound mad at first," said the woman, in that gravelly bass tone.

"For sure . . ." Quinn eyed the woman's shadow.

She held out the lighter. "Here. Good luck."

"Oh, would you mind?" The woman held up a hand. And as the lights swung again, Quinn could see there wasn't a hand there at all. Just a rounded knob, covered in a network of overlapping, finely darkened leather straps, all cinched in place with three silver buckles along the woman's wrist. Quinn had the impression that she had multiple sets of wrappings for different occasions. It looked very sophisticated.

"Sure," said Quinn.

The woman slid a cigarette between her lips. Quinn held the lighter to it. The flame caught, no problem, and the woman took half the cigarette into her lungs in a single drag.

Quinn was impressed.

The woman was about half a foot shorter than Quinn, and when Marilyn lit her flickering from beneath, Quinn saw that she was middle-aged, had Korean features. She saw, too, that the cigarette she was smoking was striped blue and white.

"Where'd you get that?" Quinn asked, clapping Marilyn shut.

"It's a Noxboro. They're a local brand where I'm from."

"And where's that?"

The woman took another long drag. She blew out smoke, and said this name like it was magic: "Edenville."

Quinn cocked her head. "And where's *that*?"

"Upstate. About three hours from here."

"I'm from Leaden Hollow," said Quinn, not quite knowing how to add to this conversation.

"Go Crows," the woman said.

Quinn blinked. Then had to look down, remind herself she was wearing the hoodie. "Oh. Right. Go Crows."

"Decent town, I've heard."

"Dull," said Quinn.

There's really not much to do in Leaden Hollow, so the Children's Shakespeare Troupe attracted a large number of kids, including one Celeste Barton, who dragged Quinn with her to audition when they were ten. Despite herself, Quinn's taste for theater blossomed at a very young age in the old barn outside town, every summer. She could still feel the sticky mosquito-heat of wearing a floofy blouse and pantaloons in the smack-middle of August. Humid and crickety.

She felt lonely all of a sudden. The memory of getting dressed for *As You Like It* with Celeste . . .

"Who lights your cigarettes for you up there?" Quinn asked, hands back in her hoodie pocket. "In Edenville, I mean."

"I have a contraption," said the woman. "Sits on the corner of my desk."

"And what brings you down to Brooklyn?"

"Well, the reading." Like this should be obvious.

The woman took a final drag, ground her butt out under her heel, "Well, that's my time," and went past Quinn to the door. "You were great, thank you. Coming in?"

Quinn had barely smoked half her Camel. "I'll . . . meet you in there. Hey, your first round's on me."

The woman smiled, nodded. Then disappeared inside.

First round's on me? Why had she offered that? And why had she almost handed over Dad's lighter so easily? To a stranger?

She gripped Marilyn tight in her pocket, grateful to still have her.

This was the most intriguing person she'd met in a long time. But if Quinn had learned one thing during her twenty-six years of being alive, it was that intriguing people could be very, very dangerous.

CHAPTER THREE

SYDNEY KIM

"Alright everyone. Hello, hello." The woman who ran the readings (Quinn refused to remember her name) adjusted the mic on its stand. She grinned at the audience as she fussed with her tall, wobbly stool, then read off her phone. "Welcome . . . to the seventh year of the Red Yard Reading Series."

Scattered applause. A single "Woo!"

"Here at the Red Yard," she read on, "we celebrate dark tales of all kinds. From bloody fantasy to the most *twisted* horror. We enjoy lighter stories, too, but . . . not as much."

Scattered laughs. An "Amen!"

"We want to start by thanking our *dread*ful host, Florence Routhier. Florence, thank you for letting us be here tonight. We hope you enjoy our tales."

"Thank you, Flo." Everyone lifted their drinks to her picture. She scowled.

Quinn darted her eyes toward Cam. He adjusted his glasses with a pinkie, picked at his beard. So fidgety. She figured he didn't like being in the presence of a ghost who killed men. And in general, she knew he hated readings unless *he* was reading. A direct quote: "You have to sit there and *look* like you're listening the whole time, and you have to remember a *specific* thing they said so you can compliment them after. That's the fuckin thing at readings—everybody loves everybody, even when they're a horrible storyteller. Bullshit." Grumbling as he tamped a fresh bowl of indica with the butt of his lighter.

"Is that how you felt about watching me in plays?" she'd asked.

He'd looked at her and said quickly, in a deer-in-headlights voice, "No. Not . . . always . . ."

Quinn leaned back against the wall, sipping cider. Eyes shaded behind her bangs, hands buried deep in her hoodie (go Crows). She scanned the crowd. The woman with the strapped stump stood in the corner. She seemed to be staring pointedly at Cam. Should Quinn be jealous?

"First up!" The mic warble-screeched feedback. "We have Campbell P. Marion. Campbell is an MFA graduate of Branson College. His short fiction has been featured in several magazines, and his first novel, *The Shattered Man*, is available from Cider Press . . . Press. Cider Press Press." The woman frowned at her phone. She did this every time.

Quinn had always thought it was a horrible name. Maybe that's why they went belly-up.

The woman gestured to Cam. "Give a warm welcome to Campbell P. Marion."

Kenz paused what she was doing to clap as Cam took the stage. Quinn flicked a fingernail against her cider glass.

But that woman in the corner didn't even slap a thigh or anything. Just stood there, the metal buckles along her wrist glittering in the dim lights of the Yard.

She kept her eyes glued to Cam as he cracked open his old copy of *Shattered Man*, smiled awkwardly, and began to read. He read about Caleb's investigation into the LaMorte massacre, how Caleb met up with the Committee, and the Committee's inevitable betrayal. How they tacked Caleb to the reconstructed Man and watched him die, just so His door would open again at last.

As Cam read, Quinn watched the woman narrow her eyes. Her wrapped wrist twitched . . .

"Cuz chances are? He already has seen YOU."

Cam looked up from his book. Maybe half the bar was listening. Someone in the back laughed. Someone else shushed them.

"Thanks," he grumbled, as he literally tripped off the stage to mild applause.

He had barely stepped past the hall to the bathrooms when a woman swept into his path. She had a gristly Wild West voice. Grating and sandy. When she stuck out her hand for him to shake, he looked down and saw it was her left. Cam had the sudden impression that he was meeting a legend.

"Marvelous reading," she said.

"Oh, thank you." He smiled, shaking her hand with *his* left. He glanced over her shoulder at Quinn. She held up his post-reading beer. Cocked an eyebrow at him.

"I'm a writer myself," the woman said, still shaking his hand. She ran her thumb over his knuckles. "Sydney Kim. Syd is fine. I'd wager you haven't heard of my work."

"Ya know, I haven't? But . . . I'd be surprised if you'd heard of mine, so." He tried to retrieve his hand and failed.

"Actually," she said, "I have. And I have a bit of a . . . strange question for you. Would you mind if I . . . *touched* you?"

"Aha. Well. I sort of feel like you *are* touching me." He tried again for his hand. She tightened her grip, grinding his knuckles together. He winced.

"Not with this hand," she said. "With my other."

Cam glanced at the wrapped stump. "Um."

She jerked her head at the darkened hall. "Just for a minute. Writer to writer. Don't make it weird." Which was an odd thing to say for someone who had literally just made it weird. But no one had ever asked to *touch* Cam before. He'd signed books, signed a leg once . . .

"Okay," he said. "Why not." Because he also had the impression she wasn't asking. As far as she was concerned, he'd already agreed. She was just being polite, and she didn't have to be.

He could see all this reflected in her eyes, as they dug into his.

She smiled. "That's wonderful. Just wonderful. The *right* decision."

As Syd led him away, Cam shrugged over at Quinn. She threw up her hands, *The fuck?* just before he slid out of view.

The back hall was sticky, flickering. Thick, cloying mélange of condoms and ammonia. A *Galaga* machine rotting in the corner.

Syd cleared her throat. "I know this is a bit spookier than it needs to be. My *own* invitation to the sub-department," she scoffed, "the *Committee*, you called it—was much more formal. But we're a bit short on time, so . . . apologies."

Cam's ears perked up. *Short on time?* That smelled like stakes to him. Like the catalyst of an adventure. *We need your help. We're almost out of time* . . . And he was suddenly very aware that that's exactly where he was: the beginning of a story. And the feeling that burst inside his chest wasn't fear, but excitement.

There is nothing we all want more than to be inside an exciting story.

"My parents," said Syd, "emigrated from Korea when I was four. My older brother had just been decapitated by a bus and they needed a change. I don't remember Gangjin at all." She popped open one of the three silver buckles along her wrist. She unwound the first leather strap as she spoke. "But I do remember our first home in America. A one-bedroom apartment in Bent."

"In where?"

"Bent," she said again. She held out the strap. "Hold this, please?"

He did. It was sweaty and warm. Smelled like damp skin.

Syd popped open the second buckle. "I slept on a cot by the wall separating us from the family next door. The wall was on my right side." She swiveled loose the second strap and handed it to him. The skin beneath was wrinkled and red. "The family next door sounded . . . happy. I didn't know much English yet, but I heard them laughing and singing, playing board games." *Pop*, the third and final buckle. "I lay on my cot at night, my parents screaming at each other in Korean on one side, that family laughing on the other. I used to put my hand to the wall, so I could be close to them. This went on for years." She unspooled the final strap, twisting it around her fingers. "When I was nine, and I knew enough English to ask our super about that family—who they were, what they were like . . . You know what he said?"

"Nobody's lived there for years?"

She smiled, eyes glinting. "That's usually how these things go, isn't it? Well, turns out the wall was made of old stained barnwood. Their kitchen table was, too. And the family I'd heard? They'd bashed their skulls against the table-corners one by one, over a decade before I ever lived there. When the smell got bad, the super called Bent PD to break down the door. They found a maggot-ridden mash of minds, splattered across the table in wriggling heaps. But the family was still seated around that table. Playing Yahtzee. Laughing. Empty skulls filled with flies. Rolling dice into the gore. The super closed the door, nailed it shut, and *left them there*. He said he was sorry I'd heard them, too. We lived in that apartment for another three years. And that family . . . kept . . . laughing. Here." She handed Cam the final strap.

He stood stupidly with three leather strips in his hand. "You're fucking with me."

"That was my first memoir," said Syd. "*The Other Family*. That table diseased them. And the wall did *this* to me."

She held up her exposed stump. At its peak lay a very small hand. Half the size of a newborn's. Pruned and pink. It was closed in a fist, flat against Syd's skin. But when she freed it to the open air, it began to unfurl. It stretched and flexed its little fingers. Cam could hear the joints pop, like they hadn't exercised in a long time.

Syd blossomed this hand in his direction. "May I?"

"Um," he said. "No?"

"It's alright," she said, in that growling voice. "It won't hurt."

She reached for him.

He stepped back. "Look, I . . . I don't know what you're—"

"But that's the thing, Cam. You *do* know."

She planted her hand on his forehead. Squinted at him as she dug her little fingers into his skin. She was right, it didn't hurt. It felt . . . good, actually. Made his whole head hum. Made his shoulders drop.

"Oh yess," she purred. "Madeline was right. You *knooow*."

"I . . . do?" he said with his eyes closed.

"Yesss. You can *see* beyond the door."

Cam's blood ran cold. His knees gave and he was afraid he might fall—then Syd retrieved her hand, and the feeling was gone. She took the straps from him, curled her little fingers back onto her wrist, and said, "This is terrific. I haven't wasted a trip after all. Cam, do you—"

"Everything cool?" Quinn appeared at Cam's side.

He blinked at her, numb.

Sydney Kim smiled.

"I'll take that drink now," she said, as she tightened the buckles about her wrist.

Quinn clapped an old-fashioned onto the bar. Syd held it up to Cam, sitting on the barstool next to her. "To Flo. I hear that's the proper toast here."

"To Flo," Cam murmured. They clinked glasses and drank. His skull still buzzed, and his beer tasted funny.

Quinn bobbed on her heels, watching the two of them from behind the bar.

"So," said Syd, "do you teach as well as write?"

"Uh, tutor," said Cam. "Test prep for high schoolers."

"I bet that's thankless work."

Cam laughed unevenly. "Yeah, it's . . . not my favorite."

"You ever think about teaching at the college level?"

"Sure."

"Mm." Syd sipped her drink. Her small hand rested in her lap. Cam could feel warmth emanating from it, curling across his thigh.

"Well, I'll cut to brass tacks," said Syd. She sat straighter. "I work for a college upstate. I'm the chair, actually, for the Creative Writing department. We have a *very* reputable program, not to brag. But we find ourselves experiencing a . . . last-minute change of plans. Regarding our writer in residence for the fall."

"Don't schools usually have that kind of thing planned, like, a year in advance?" Quinn asked.

"Usually," said Syd. "We had a playwright coming in, but she had to cancel. My colleague Madeline came across your book and we were all very taken."

"Wow," said Cam. He smiled into his beer. "Thank you. That's . . . very cool to hear."

Syd nodded. "So we were wondering. It wouldn't be a full-time position, but we need someone to attend a few of the freshman writing work-shops, work with them a bit one-on-one . . . We'd provide housing in one of the faculty apartments, and all of the frosh would read your book . . ."

Cam tuned out. *This* was a call to adventure indeed. No more dealing with insane parents? No more schlepping around giant tomes of practice SATs? He'd have an office, he could start wearing tweed . . . And he *knew* something, apparently. Knew something he didn't even know he knew.

How ominous, how *cool*, was that?

"Does that sound alright?" Syd asked. "That can be off putting to some."

"Sorry, what's alright?" He looked up. "What am I put off by?"

Syd chuckled. "I know, it's a big offer."

"Yeah, I . . . I'm just . . . absorbing . . ." He trailed off then, because across from him, Quinn was staring wide-eyed at the floor. Standing very still, hands deep in the pouch of her hoodie.

He frowned. "So wait, what's off-putting?"

"The college," said Syd. "It's . . . Edenville College. Up in Renfield County."

Quinn stiffened even more.

Cam glanced between them, then laughed awkwardly. "I'm sorry, am I supposed to know that name?"

"Well, you went to Branson, right? That's practically next door. Fur-rowkill is only an hour's drive from Edenville."

Quinn looked up. "I know Renfield. I hadn't heard of Edenville, but I've . . . heard about Renfield for sure."

"Is it, like, not a nice place?" Cam asked.

"It's haunted," said Quinn, eyeing Syd. "There are stories. *Bad* stories."

"Well, how come nobody ever told *me* stories about Renfield County?" Cam whined. "I love a good haunting."

"They're not *nice* stories," said Quinn, her jaw working. Something strange happening to her that Cam couldn't quite read.

"It's *supposedly* one of the most haunted places in America," said Syd. "You know that one road in New Jersey where people always see phan-tom trucks and ghosts and whatnot?"

"Sure," said Cam, feeling defensive. "Of course I do."

"It's like that, but . . . the entire county. But Edenville is nice. Especially on campus."

"I see." Cam picked at his beard.

Quinn's head swam. Her scalp itched. Some part of her brain seemed to flit around her skull, tickling the insides of her nostrils and her ears.

She coughed. "I'm gonna run to the bathroom. You keep talking. Kenz?" She nodded to Kenz, who nodded back. Then she slipped away from the bar and walked wheezing toward the bathroom. She felt pregnant or something. Dizzy.

In front of the bathroom mirror (door safely locked, fluorescent over the toilet safely humming), Quinn looked at herself and identified the feeling. It wasn't illness at all. It was sudden, powerful premonition: *Something is coming. For me. For Cam.*

For us.

It reels you in. Those old words came back to her. *Renfield County just . . . reels you in . . .*

It'd found her. It'd sent Sydney Kim as its envoy. It'd already begun to *reel you in . . .*

Quinn put a hand to her chest. She gulped at the old-bar air of the Red Yard bathroom, where Flo could not see her. Could not protect her from what was coming.

When Quinn came back to the bar, Cam and Syd were deep in conversation about what his teaching duties would be, what the town of Edenville was like.

"We even have a Pancake Planet," said Syd. "*Excellent* salads. Ironically."

"Okay," sighed Quinn. "Anyone want another round? Because I absolutely do." She poured herself a shot of vodka, saluted Flo, and downed it. "Whew. Go Crows."

"No, I should get going," said Syd. "I'm heading all the way back up tonight. But . . ." She dug into her purse and produced a business card.

She handed it to Cam. Green and vibrant and plastered with sunflowers. They wrapped around her name, peering up from the cardstock. Round black eyes with yellow lashes. In bold green font:

SYDNEY KIM
ASSOCIATE PROFESSOR OF MEMOIR & ESSAY
ACTING CHAIR, DEPT. OF CREATIVE WRITING
EDENVILLE COLLEGE

"Because this is all so last minute, we'd love your decision within the week," she said, standing and sliding another of those Noxboro cigarettes into her mouth. It bobbed as she spoke. "Just shoot me an email. Of course, if you're having trouble deciding, you're welcome to come up and visit the campus, see the faculty apartments. And remember, it's not a long-term gig, if that makes a difference. Just a semester. With the possibility, of *course*, but."

"We'll talk it over," said Quinn quickly. She offered Syd a tight smile. "Thank you."

Cam was too busy staring at the card. Then Syd's hand was in front of him. "Campbell."

He shook it, slightly dazed. "Syd."

She nodded at him, then at Quinn. "I look forward to hearing from you."

And she was gone. Leaving a blanket of dense, frightened silence in her wake.

"So what spooked you?" Cam asked.

Quinn poured another shot. She savored it, so she had a moment to think of something to say.

She'd never told him about Celeste. Not even a little bit. Had never even mentioned in passing her one experience with Renfield County. How could she start now?

All she could think to say was, "Bad vibes. That's all."

"Yeah," he said, unconvincingly. "Same." He examined the card.

The sunflowers gazed back.

CHAPTER FOUR

REELS YOU IN

Renfield County.

Quinn turned the name over and over in her mouth as she and Cam walked home from the Yard. Just a few blocks, but it felt very long and cold that night, in the ides of early May.

Renfield County.

If *Leaden Hollow* had a strange metallic tang, then *Renfield* was the feeling you get when you eat an entire bag of chips late at night, when that shit greases up your lips, slices into the roof of your mouth, gets stuck inside your molars and it *burns* there. That was the way those words felt upon Quinn's tongue. *Renfield County* cut around her mouth like salted shards of glass.

It was a favorite local saying for a while (it's out of fashion now), that there's about as much chance of something happening as there are roads out of Renfield. Which is to say, there isn't much chance at all, because there *aren't* any roads out of Renfield.

As in:

You think the Whalers (the high school football team for the town of Bent—go Whalers) *have a chance to make it to state this year?*

With that new jerk-off coach? Ha! There's about as much chance of that *happening as there are roads outta Renfield.*

Renfield County lies in a small valley, nestled within a crescent-shaped offshoot of the Catskills called the Billowhills. The Billows, as locals call them, are covered in thick, misty pine. The Shembelwoods, after one Arthur K. Shembel.

The county began as a scattering of Dutch and German settlements, housing the lumbermen and trappers who worked the Shembels, and the miners who dug great gouts from the swaths of limestone and granite dotting the roiling curve of the Billows.

The Billows Road cuts straight through those gravestone-colored hills. Huge jags of rock press against the sides of the road, close to the shoulder. Miles of wire mesh hold it all back from crumbling onto cars. You'll see, if and when *you* drive down this road, that the only thing keeping the Billows Road from collapsing are the rocks that allow it to exist. If the Billows ever turned and decided they'd had enough of roads, they could easily sneeze and trap Renfield inside itself—forever.

Edenville lies on the southeastern edge of the Renfield valley, but there are five main towns overall. Well, Tinker's Falls isn't so much a *town* as it is a hamlet of trailer parks and diners, broken-window auto shops and mud, all carved into pockets linked by narrow forest roads. Bartrick Mill squats along the southern bank of Bartrick Lake, in the center of the county. Even though no one swims in the lake, the Mill is something of a suburban, touristy town, thanks to the rainbowy waterfall coming off the lake into the Nettle River. Renfielders *love* to propose to each other under that waterfall.

A county road runs through the Mill, but winds back out of the valley without touching any other town, almost like it knew it made a mistake coming there at all, then oops'ed its way back west.

Bent, far east along the Bent River, was once a fishing town. But nobody fishes out of the river anymore. Bent's once-pretty downtown is now faded and smoggy, the apartment buildings along the river all smudged black from the fire of '53.

Then there's the upper-class haven of Lillian, where people smell like horses and eat kale.

Edenville is the county's obligatory small college town. Rustic clock tower and all.

Around these bubbles of human life, the Shembelwoods are eager to reclaim anything they can. Braddock County, just east of the Billows, is the only civilization around Renfield for many miles. Far northeast in Braddock is Leaden Hollow, Quinn's hometown.

Because there are so few roads out of Renfield (two, if you've been counting), there aren't many opportunities for outsiders to hear the county's stories. Which is a shame, because there are *so* many. Ask a Renfielder about their spookiest encounter—when the sun has vanished behind the trees, the peeper-frogs in full swing, the Halloween wind ripping, or the snow smothering everything around, glowing alien-bright beneath the moon—and they'll raise an eyebrow, pour a nice tall drink, and spin you a good old-fashioned campfire yarn. Or two. Or nine.

*Every*one in Renfield has a story.

Quinn, who lived safely outside Renfield's Billowhills rim, knew very few of these stories. She knew only that Renfield County killed her oldest friend.

Cruising was a major pastime in Leaden Hollow, especially after the bowling alley closed. And sooner or later, everyone got the itch to check out Renfield. So many whispers among the adults. So many murmurs that it was "bad land." That the people there would "shove you in a van and eat you with a rusted spoon, just as soon as look at ya." According to Quinn's mother, at least.

For Quinn, the itch came about a week after the homecoming dance her senior year of high school. It was October, the breeze carried dead leaf and overripe pumpkin, and she wanted to do something fun. Moreover, she wanted to break the awkward tension she'd been feeling with Celeste. After the dance, they'd hotboxed her car and Celeste had said that really nice thing about Quinn's hands, and they'd leaned *so* close to each other, and . . . and . . .

Quinn figured a little adventure might be the jumpstart they needed to clear the air about that night. Not that she knew exactly what she wanted to say, but she felt like she needed to say *some*thing. She and Celeste had been friends for almost a decade, and now it was all awkward and weird. Why not take a drive?

Celeste, of course, was very down. That's one thing Quinn loved about her. She was always down.

In a way, it was Quinn's fault Celeste was gone. It'd been her idea, after all. That fact had crossed Quinn's mind once or twice over the years. "Once or twice" meaning many, *many* times.

Quinn's mom had even said as much, when they were putting up those useless MISSING posters all over the Hollow's meager downtown and as far out as Mortonkill, closer to the county line.

Out of nowhere, her mom goes, "Shouldna been drivin up the Billows Road at night." Stapling a poster to a telephone pole to emphasize her point, *shunk*. "That's how it gets ya. Gives you a taste, and you think, 'Man. I wonder what *else* is out there.' Just like those ridiculous *Saw* movies you like." Stapling angrily with each word. More staples than any poster needs. "*I've* driven up the Billows Road. Your father, too, rest his soul. But that's how it reels you in. The *glimpse*. That's why there aren't any roads *out* of that place, except the two. Because there's too much shit to hold inside. It's not a valley, Quinn Rose. It's a god." *Shunk*. "Damned." *Shunk*. "Cage." *Shunk*.

So Quinn asks, "What was your story?"

And her mother gives her this hard, flickering glare. She looks away, staples up another poster. Celeste's tan face, framed by that golden hair that always smelled like peach. Mom says, "They told me not to tell."

"Who did?"

Still not looking at Quinn: "The laughter in the bushes." And before Quinn can say anything else, her mother stabs a finger in her face. "Quinn Rose Carver-Dobson, if I ever catch you daring death like that again, I'll make you *wish* Renfield took you, too. Hear?"

Oh. Quinn heard.

For over a decade, Quinn let that be enough for her: *It's bad there. It reels you in and won't let go.* She held that idea close, as the sun began to bleach Celeste's face on all those posters. As the rain curled them into themselves and the wind blew them off their rusting staples, scattering them into the gutters around the Hollow. She held it close as the school psychiatrist interviewed her for some mandatory district thing. As she tossed a flower for Celeste at the RENFIELD COUNTY sign. And as she peered down the other side of the Billows Road, down the peak between counties, and saw countless other flowers in varying states of decay.

She'd never told Cam *any* of that.

* * *

Quinn sat on the edge of their couch, unlacing her boots. It gave her something to do so she didn't have to look at him as he flicked the edge of Syd's card. "*Really* nice. What is that, emerald green?"

"Hey, Cam?" She curled her socked feet under her, protectively, on the couch.

"I'm just sayin. Patrick Bateman would be stoked."

"Cam, listen." She locked him in place with her old, oak eyes. Her bangs jerked as she blinked. She patted the couch. "I want to talk about this."

He stood there, looking at her. He slid his glasses up his nose with a pinkie and sighed. "So . . . we're the meat, huh?"

Quinn lifted her shoulders. "She was bad vibes. You know she was. Here." She patted the couch again. "Sit."

Cam had always called this part of the film "Meet the Meat." Because this is when you learn who the victims in the film will be. In most horror films, it doesn't matter who they are or what they want. Who they're sleeping with. All those teens in that cabin will be butchered by dawn. That group of hikers lost in the woods? Ribbons of flesh in the end, gutted by a creature far more interesting than their petty disagreements and traumatic pasts. The film doesn't care about the meat, and neither did Cam. He often zoned out during the first third of the horror films they watched. He didn't care to learn about the characters. They were nothing more than meat.

We're all rotting ribbons in the end.

But in this story—*his* story—Cam didn't want to think of himself that way. Someone had told him he was important. And the thought that that might be a lie? That Syd was just using him for some nefarious Blumhouse purpose? No.

He sat in the chair across from the couch. "Look, the place can't be *that* spooky."

"I heard about it all the time growing up," said Quinn calmly, hands clasped in her lap. "There's all *kinds* of stories. People go missing there."

"But people live there," said Cam.

"Yeah, but people also seem to die there."

"You mean, like . . . excessively?"

"Yes. Like legit, people go missing there *all* the time."

He scoffed. "What, and people don't go missing in Brooklyn? We're, like, ten blocks from the stab capital of the world."

"I know, baby. But humor me." She scooted toward him. "Like, let's just say we're watching this movie. Okay? And this . . . mysterious woman offers the main dude a job. And she comes all the way down here to offer it *on the spot*. That's movie bullshit, isn't it? Having an in-person conversation when it could've been a phone call?"

Cam gave her that half-smile that said his feelings were hurt. "Come on, man . . ."

"But that's how it goes! You don't read the signs and then you're screwed. You're all like, 'Free cabin? Sounds great,' and next thing you know, you're . . . being eaten by spider people."

"Renfield County has spider people?"

"Cam, there are literally stories about . . . fucking *monsters*. You . . ." She felt a sob clench in her throat. She had to blink to keep tears from boiling into her eyes. She thought about feeding him some examples. Like the guy who sat behind her in pre-calc who said he'd driven up the Billows Road and seen an honest-to-Crows werewolf. Or her cousin Adam who had a picture on his phone of a bunch of men in suits running through the trees at night.

But no. Cam would laugh in her face.

"Look," she told him. "I don't mean to be a dick, but *I* think this job might be a trap. Like a . . . horror movie trap. And *you* know it. But you're being bullshit about it because you're stoked it might be real. Sorry."

"Okay. Aha." Cam put up his hands. "I don't mean to pull this card, but . . ."

"But what if we've been watching too much TV?"

"Yeah, just because she's a *spoooky* stranger doesn't mean she's gonna fuckin . . . skin us. There's always the chance it's legit."

"Really?" And before she could stop herself, the words popped out of Quinn's mouth with venom: "Really, there's a chance they love you *so* much they just make an offer on the spot like that? Does that even happen? Aren't positions like this filled an entire *year* in advance, but they just have this sudden oops of an opening? For *you*?"

Sure enough, Cam looked at the floor, tucked his shoulders in. He closed himself to her. In a very small voice, he asked, "Is that so unbelievable? That they'd want me?"

Quinn sighed and knelt on the floor in front of him. She took his hands. "Babe. She came all the way down here. That's, like, *hours* on the train. She came in person so it was a better *scene*. I know that sounds fucking stupid, but isn't this what you've, like, *trained* for? This is Horror 101: Be alert. They didn't even *interview* you."

He slid his hands out of hers. Stared at the card in his lap. "I know. We shouldn't go. It's just nice to pretend it's not a scam."

Quinn took a breath. She'd really stung him deep.

Truth be told, she actually did (sort of) want to go. It wasn't just Celeste stopping her. There was, so to speak, a clear point in the road that she had never passed. Not with Cam. Not with anybody. And if he went and left her behind, that'd be it. This would be over. He'd have a fine time playing professor and she'd be a crazy superstitious bitch, and *he'd* be the one who got to call her that. Forever. She didn't want it to end that way. So what if, instead, they went up to Renfield and had some crazy-ass adventure, and it *bonded* them? Or convinced her to finally move on from him? What if this was what she'd been looking for? The point in the road that would topple their relationship one way . . . or the other?

Point Celeste.

"Well . . . it *would* be an adventure," she relented.

"And it's short-term," said Cam, perking up. "First sign of trouble, we hightail it back here. But if we like it, we can . . . We can save up for a second car so you can drive yourself around, maybe find a cool bar to tend? Get into some community theater?"

There *was* a sizable dent in Quinn's soul that wanted to dive deeply, *deeply* into community theater and never resurface. She could put on plays in barns again, take her cast out for drinks in the middle of nowhere. She could talk to ghosts again, too, the kind that lived nicely in very old theaters, where the air was *filled* with spirits, so packed tight and so interested in what you were doing that you breathed them in a little when you were alone, and they wriggled around inside your heart, saying, *Very fine adaptation of* Lear *you've got here. I remember when I played Lear, in 1879 . . .*

Quinn loved that feeling.

And who knows? whispered a hidden, hopeful corner of her heart, so quietly she almost didn't hear it. *Maybe we could find Celeste . . .*

"Alright, ya know what?" she said. "Fuck it. We can check it out. As long as you promise me," she held out a pinkie, "that at the first sign of trouble, I get to cash in. I say we both get one veto. If anything happens that either one of us doesn't like, if we get too spooked, we can cash in at *any* time and come back down here lickety-split. Cool?"

"Should we have a safe word?" Cam asked.

"We absolutely should."

"How about . . . bananas?"

"Mm, but what if I really want bananas, then how can I say the code word?"

"Quinn, I've literally *never* seen you eat a banana."

"So?"

Cam rolled his eyes. "Okay, what do *you* suggest?"

She considered this. It could be a name. A very specific name. Celeste had her second-favorite name ever, after her own. Quinn Rose Carver-Dobson was *great*. But Celeste Ichabod Barton had that ring to it. Had a pumpkin spice flavor Quinn loved.

"Ichabod," she said. "Either one of us says Ichabod, we fuck off back to Brooklyn."

Cam grinned. "Deal. I'll call Syd tomorrow and tell her we want to visit."

They pinkie-swore.

Three days later, on May 10, 2019, they drove Cam's old sedan up to Edenville.

CHAPTER FIVE

1896 NETHERWILD LANE

Thunk. Quinn was flicking at the window of the car. *Thunk*. Slamming the first knuckle of her middle finger against the glass, flipping off the landscape as it slid by. *Thunk*.

"Could ya not?" Cam wrung the steering wheel, made the leather squeal under his palms. "You're makin me wince."

Quinn gave the window a final *thunk*, then tucked her hands into her hoodie pouch (go Crows). The car's old wipers whined across the windshield, beating back the big buckshot blasts of rain that kept slapping against the car as they drove north.

"Nervous?" Cam asked.

Quinn rolled her head toward him. "What do you think?"

He scoffed. "Ya know, you should be asking *me* if I'm nervous. It's supposedly *my* job."

Quinn rolled her head away again. "So are you nervous?"

"Not yet."

"Well, there ya go." *Thunk*.

"Quinn."

She tucked her hands back in her lap. Watched a cow pick its way across a field of mud. A lone horse under a tree. A shuttered laundromat. A swampy patch of gnarled birch.

They'd spent an hour on the Taconic, finally exiting into Braddock County about ten minutes back. Cam thought Quinn might perk up when they started seeing signs for familiar territory. She'd been so quiet and lip-chewy the first two hours of the drive. So he'd pointed at a sign,

LEADEN HOLLOW 8 MI., and nudged her. That's when she started flicking at the window. Not the response he'd been hoping for.

The roads became particularly bendy and dense, so he could never quite tell what was coming. More than once, the GPS on Cam's phone, tucked into the cupholder, would tell him to take a road heading, say, west, but the road would curve around east for so long, he'd be sure he was heading in the wrong direction. Until suddenly, out of nowhere, they'd hit the junction they were supposed to turn on. Cam hated it. *This* was why they built cities on grids, to say *fuck you* to nature-roads that bent and swerved at will.

He pointed to hills in the distance, foggy shadows through the rain. "So those are the Billows?"

"Yep." Quinn nodded. "And the Shembelwoods." She pointed to the thick wall of dark green. "Renfield used to be a big lumber hub, but mostly it was this one company. They're still around, actually." She sang what Cam assumed was a radio jingle or something: "Mither Lumber and Co." *Thunk,* she flicked the window. "Big hardware store chain. They've got a location in the Hollow and another in Furrowkill, right by Branson. Actually, I heard the Mithers moved there last year. To Furrowkill, I mean."

"Where were they before?"

"Lillian. They're one of Renfield's oldest families. Huge deal when they moved out of the county. I think there were rumors they tortured animals or something." She couldn't remember how she'd heard this. How this particular legend had slipped past the bars of what her mother called *the cage*. Maybe it'd followed the Mithers to Furrowkill, and spread. "I remember people started throwing rocks through their windows. I don't remember why."

"Weird."

"Well, that's what I mean," Quinn sighed. "*Lots* of weird shit around here . . ." She watched a burnt garage go by. *Thunk.*

They turned west onto the Billows Road, and began to go up. Up, up. The trees began to close in. Fat splats of rain fell from thick branches drooping over the road, their fingers brushing against the top of the car.

Quinn tucked her feet up under her on the seat. She wondered if the trees were reporting back somewhere. If their roots were, like, signaling the All-Tree, somewhere deep underground. She wondered if the county itself had clocked their arrival.

It absolutely had.

The car bumped over potholes. Up, up. Bump, bump. Until at last they came to the crest of the hill—and there it was. The wide green sign: WELCOME TO HISTORIC RENFIELD COUNTY. And in red spray paint beneath: *we missed you.*

Cam stopped, gazing down at the landscape below. Miscolored squares of pasture land, red silos, the winding calligraphic lines of roads, and the gray snake of the Bent River, all nestled into the dark blanket of the Shembelwoods, stretching far out in all directions. There were cozy stains of towns ground into the earth, like colonies of bugs under logs. Like a quaint little jigsaw.

"Doesn't seem too evil from up here," said Cam. He glanced at Quinn. She was staring at the county sign. Her jaw muscles worked.

Cam rolled his eyes. *Theater people are so fuckin dramatic.*

He drove them forward. And with that, they'd officially passed Point Celeste. The farthest Quinn had ever gone. The point in the road at which they'd stopped that night, nearly a decade ago. The point where Celeste had slammed her foot on the brake, and turned to Quinn with dark, bleeding eyes.

Down they drove, and down. Impossibly far down. The drive *up* hadn't been this long, or this steep.

When they passed through the limestone maw of the hills, the woods nudged against the car from either side.

They passed a row of abandoned homes. Doors that were black holes and windows eye-patched with plywood, stubborn jags of glass still stuck inside the frames. They passed a massive burnt barn with a collapsed roof. It took them almost a full thirty seconds to drive by it, it was so large. Then the old foundation of a gas station, no more than a dirty lot, metal bending out of the cement, and a sign that read $1.79 but nothing more.

"So . . . Edenville *exists*, right?" Cam asked.

"Ahh, the old 'Offer him a fake job, then lure him into the woods to harvest his blood' gag. Seen it a million times." Quinn stared out her window at a long knee-high wall running alongside the car. Neatly stacked granite slabs all packed together with a cake of old pine needles, mud, and leaves. She had the feeling that if she knocked one of those slabs loose, her skin would turn to granite, too, or something. Just beyond the wall, the woods ran thick and deep.

"Check it out," said Cam, nodding through the windshield.

The road was widening.

At last, they swept out from under the canopy of dripping branches, and emerged into what looked like the main intersection of the town. There was a small wooden sign. A light-green, flaky-painted thing with a picture of the street (but with horses and carriages) and two brief yellow lines of text:

Edenville
Est. 1788

"Civilization," said Cam.

"If that's the word you wanna use," said Quinn.

The buildings were squat, pastel, and brick. There was an antique shop, a deli, a pizza joint, a fancy furniture store, a used bookstore, a gas station—all nestled against walls of trees, as if "civilization" was fighting constantly to keep the woods at bay. As if mankind had etched very small and precarious pockets of warmth into all that cold bark and fog.

Quinn spotted a blue sign by the gas station, with an arrow pointing down a side street named Rackell, and two words: EDENVILLE COLLEGE.

"Are you turning?" she asked, just as Cam put on his blinker. He cocked an eyebrow at her in a way that said *Obviously*. So she nodded and let her gaze wander back outside the car. She pointed at an ice cream shop, housed in an old-style colonial, with a (probably very cozy) apartment upstairs. "Ice cream."

"Get your hair cut," said Cam, pointing at another old house with a large picture window. Inside, the tiles and fluorescents of a barber shop.

"Well, we *have* to go to Pancake Planet," said Quinn, as they passed a fifties-style diner with a pink neon PP over its door.

"Oh, exclusively," Cam agreed.

Rackell Street grew a tall border of sunflowers along the driver's side of the car. The passenger's side was lined with rustic faculty houses. A particularly large one on a hill was the Richard P. Hardscratt (Class of '78) Alumni/ae House. Somewhere in there was a small parlor that smelled like vacuum cleaner, where the Creative Writing sub-department had formed earlier that year. Where Madeline's boyfriend, Benny McCall, had gathered them all and said, *So. Most of you won't believe what I'm about to say. That's fine. Just humor me for an hour and perhaps I'll change your minds . . .*

But Cam and Quinn didn't know about that yet.

The wipers squealed across the windshield. Cam had the impression that this was the weather to which this town was born. What it loved best. He imagined this place in the sun, baked and dry and blinking in the light. Here, in the shady wet, the buildings seemed to open their eyes and gaze out upon the road, like toads burrowed into the damp ground. Soaked, content, and watching.

Then he saw it.

The entrance loomed out of the rain, rising like a waking stone beast. It was massive and gothic and gray, spindling towers sticking out across its spine, its entire side dotted with slim arrow-hole windows through which Cam could almost see the campus library. And in large kingly letters over the entryway: EDENVILLE COLLEGE, EST. 1879.

"Well, damn," said Quinn. "Eat your heart out, Branson." Branson College has a much smaller entrance.

Cam breathed deep. A lesser mind, he supposed, would be frightened. Would see the jaw of this gate and assume ill energy, ill omens. Cam had no such misconception. This was a scholarly, inviting place. Already, even before passing the small security booth inside the gate, he felt like he was home. He could smell the fresh-cut grass of the quad, the chalk dust lingering in the old buildings. He could almost *taste* it as he waved politely to the security guard.

But then his chest tightened, because of course, Quinn was right. There was the strong possibility this was a trick. Life doesn't work this easily.

But *seeing* the place . . .

Well. Just nice to pretend, is all.

Heading down Main Drive, they passed the quad on their left, surrounded by brick dorms and the looming Haywood Tower at its head, where most freshmen live. On their right was the long glass hall of some science building, roof slathered in solar panels.

Main Drive ended at the brick behemoth of a college center, ivy creeping picturesque up its clock tower. Signs pointed to East Camp and West.

"Syd said West Camp is all the academic buildings," said Cam as he cranked the wheel. "East is apparently the dorms, rec center, dining hall, student theater spaces . . ."

"Sure," said Quinn. She gazed out at the storm-besotted quad. Void of student life.

"Oh, wow," said Cam. Quinn turned to see what he was wowing, and found the entire west end of campus absolutely drenched in sunflowers. They bowed over the sidewalks, curled up the walls of the buildings. And she couldn't be sure, but she thought she saw the flowers turn as they passed, bending into the road and following the car with their yellow-lidded eyes. No, scratch that—she was positive they turned.

They came upon one brick building in particular at the edge of the West Camp lawn. Three big stone steps led up to its entrance. An imposing wooden fence ran along the edge of a parking lot there.

Cam parked and paused, hand still on the wheel. He turned to Quinn. "Ready?"

She nodded. "First sign of trouble and we Ichabod home. Right?"

"Scout's honor."

"You've never been a scout."

"Were *you*?"

"Hell yeah. Sold the most Thin Mints in Leaden Hollow two years in a row, babyyy."

"So, what? You get *two* Big Nerd badges for that?" And he launched himself out of the car. Quinn followed a moment later, feeling stung.

They charged through the rain across the lot, up the three stone steps. Cam shoved through the door, held it open for Quinn. It boomed shut behind them, the sound echoing through the open door of the vestibule, down the length of the wooden hall. It was cool, grave-quiet. They shivered in the sudden air-conditioning, and took a moment to look around. The walls were covered in bulletin boards and plain white paint. There were old posters for classes ("Take ENGL 1301 today!"), student plays ("See *Fefu and Her Friends* this weekend at the Lance Theater!"), movie nights ("See *Pretty in Pink*! 9 PM in Von 209! Free popcorn!"), all tacked layer upon layer over the corkboards. A table jammed against the wall was littered with small mountains of old books, marked *FREE* in black Sharpie on a length of printer paper.

Cam breathed it in. His parents were both professors: history and math, horribly competitive at board games. He didn't talk to them much anymore. Hadn't even told them about the job, in case it *did* turn out to be some kind of trap. But he couldn't help thinking that this smelled like where he belonged. It smelled like yellowing pages, oak, and stone.

"Sorry about the weather." Sydney Kim came around the corner. "But I'm so glad you could make it." The straps and buckles along her wrist had changed color, the straps lighter, the buckles now brass (this confirmed Quinn's suspicion that she had various styles for different occasions). Syd had a large man with her, tall and broad and tan. She gestured to him. "This is Wes Flannery. His specialty is fiction."

Cam immediately liked Wes's vibe. He reminded Cam of the men in action movies who offer sage advice and dual-wield pistols. The man coughed, cleared his throat, and held out his hand. "Hiya. Do you go by Campbell, or?"

"Cam is good." They shook hands. "This is Quinn."

Quinn had once requested he not introduce her as his girlfriend. Something about it sounded too teenagery for her taste, so now she was just Quinn.

She smiled pleasantly. "Helloo."

A very short woman emerged from a side door. "Hello there. You must be Campbell."

"Oh, Cam is fine," said Cam.

"I'm Angie, the administrative assistant. I'm right in here." She pointed. "Syd's the chair, so I'll let *her* show you around. Even though *I've* been here since '76. Just let me know if you need anything."

"Thanks, Angie," said Syd.

Angie smiled at everyone, then went back through her door. Quinn peered in after her. She saw a lobby-like room with wooden chairs, a minifridge, a coffee maker. Angie's desk sat behind a window, and there was some kind of lounge through another doorway. Inside, a wide portrait of a man with a cane loomed over the mantel.

"This," said Syd, "is Slitter Hall. Home of the Creative Writing department. Philosophy is upstairs, but they only have a few majors every year. *Our* classrooms are all down here." She gestured vaguely. "Let me show you your office."

She led them to a small corner room, the door open, key dangling from the lock. It was a cozy, dim space with brown carpet. Empty shelves lined one wall by an empty desk. The opposite wall's shelves were stuffed with books, and a second desk beneath them was littered with papers.

"You'll be bunking with Chett Neeves," said Syd. "It's mostly his freshman classes you'll be working with. He handles short fiction, narratology . . ."

"Kind of a character," said Wes. He cleared his throat again. "Hope you get along with him."

"Wes calls him Sneeze," said Syd. "It's not very nice."

"Well, *he's* not very interesting."

"Cool," said Cam, nodding around at the room. There were two small windows high on the far wall, through which he could see a sliver of sky and the top of a lamppost. He pictured himself sitting there, watching the snow. The lamppost glowing a warm, peaceful orange. "Very cool."

Wes nodded at Quinn. "How was the drive up?"

"Felt long," she said.

"Well, everything *in* Edenville is walking distance, more or less. Depending on how long you wanna walk." Wes coughed into his hand, then wiped his palm hastily on the back of his jeans. Quinn caught a whiff of something sweet. "What do you think, Cam? Like the office?"

He was about to say he loved it, but Quinn cut in on his moment: "Hey, I was just . . . talking about them . . ." Her sentence breaking in the middle, then trailing off.

Cam hadn't noticed it before, but taped to the open door was a piece of paper. A young girl's face plastered across it. She had ashy skin and bright blond hair curling over her shoulders. She stared at the camera with a cold yearning that made his stomach churn. Like she was asking to be seen. *Demanding*, in fact. Then there was the big red word beneath the picture: MISSING. And the name under that: CLARITY MITHER.

"I was *just* talking about Mither Lumber and Co.," said Quinn. She was entranced by the poster. "That's so crazy . . ." Clarity Mither's eyes held hers tight.

"Ah. Yeah." Syd snatched the paper off the door, crumpled it in her hand. "*That* is a bad joke."

"Stupid senior prank," Wes added quickly.

"Clarity has moved on," said Syd. "Transferred to a different school. Someplace up in Vermont. Some other students were sad she was leaving, so they put up these posters."

"Poor taste," said Wes.

"A bad joke," said Syd.

"Ya know," said Wes, "my last day teaching at my old job? I worked at Bent High for a while, and on my last day, I had a few students dress in black. Like it was my fuckin funeral. Hey, we should send her a picture of that." He chuckled and nodded at the crumpled paper in Syd's hand. "She'd get a kick out of it."

"Sure," said Syd. "I'll email it to her."

Cam and Quinn glanced at each other.

"So we're gonna have a bit of an orientation for you next week," said Syd. "You'll get all your information there about the classes and workshops you'll be leading, when all the coffeehouses are . . ."

"Coffeehouses?" Cam echoed.

"Edenville has its own reading series," Syd explained.

"Oh my god," said Quinn. "Just what he needs."

"It's fun," said Wes. "All the students go."

"That's awesome," said Cam, shooting a quick glare at Quinn. A new audience for his work, far from the Red Yard and Florence Routhier's judgmental glare? Yes, please.

"Well," said Wes, clapping his hands. "Let's show you your place.

Key's on here." He reached between Cam and Quinn and plucked the key out of the office door. The key ring jangled as he dropped it in Cam's palm. "We're just goin across the road from campus. We'll go out the North Gate, at the top of West Camp. Wanna follow us?"

"Sure," said Cam. "Thank you, this is . . . I'm very excited. Quinn?"

Quinn was still staring at the door where the poster had been.

Back in the car, Quinn turned to Cam and said, "So that Clarity Mither gal. Probably not in Vermont, right?"

Cam backed them out of the lot. "I'd . . . give it a solid sixty-forty."

"But scale of one to ten, how creepy are the vibes for you so far?"

Cam's mind was elsewhere. As he put the car in drive, he said, "Bout a three."

So Quinn didn't say that *she* was sitting at about a seven. She still didn't like how easy this all was. True, she didn't know anything about the hiring process for colleges. But shouldn't it be more . . , involved? More paperwork before *Here's your key*?

She slumped down in her seat, watching the sunflowers watching her as they passed once more.

They followed Syd's small black car out the side entrance of campus, back onto Rackell Street, toward a brown sign that read NETHERWILDS in peeling font.

"Solid name," said Cam. "Very spooky. Now *that's* a ten outta ten."

Netherwild Lane curved around more trees, and they found themselves facing a ring of town houses running in an almost perfect circle, with a small playground at its center, though "playground" is a generous word. A sandbox, a metal slide, and two swings, one of which was missing a seat. Just two blue-painted rust-chains dangling down.

The doors for the Netherwild town houses all had big brass numbers over them. Syd parked before number 1896. Identical to all the others, except the six had lost its top screw and swung upside down, crying a little, back and forth in the breeze.

At least it'd stopped raining. A dull mist now clung to the ground, sweeping around Quinn's feet as they walked up to the door. Syd and Wes stood expectantly on the stoop, like parents watching Cam open Santa's present.

He unlocked the door.

Inside, 1896 Netherwild Lane was much like the interior of Slitter Hall. It smelled like bricks and old books. There was a small kitchen immediately inside the entryway, a living room beyond. A hall to the right led to a den and a bathroom. There were stairs up to a second floor just past the kitchen. Wes led everyone up, coughing the entire way. There was a small landing with a window looking down over the "playground," a master bedroom, another bathroom, and a set of narrow stairs leading up into shadow.

"Come," said Syd, sliding her stump into the crook of Cam's arm. "I'll show you the writing loft."

"Sweet," said Cam, flashing Quinn a thumb's up as Syd led him away. Quinn watched him walk off with this woman for the second time that week.

"Kitchen's fully stocked," said Wes, leading Quinn back down to the first floor. "I mean, there's no *food*, but all the pots and pans are here. You cook?"

"Uh . . ." For Quinn's birthday last November, Cam had gotten her a HelloFresh subscription, which she'd read as a thinly veiled insult. She'd allowed at least one meal from each box to rot uncooked, until he'd finally canceled it for her. ". . . no."

But she opened some of the cupboards anyway, inspecting the many cracked mugs, stained drinking glasses, plates with dried egg laminated to them. Dented pots and pans, scratched and oddly shaped. Teeth marks?

Wes leaned against the wall and coughed badly.

"You okay?" she asked.

He swallowed what appeared to be a very painful lump. "Oh yeah. I just have a weird lung thing, acts up when it rains." He cleared his throat with an absurdly wet, horrible noise. Then grinned. His teeth were stained some color darker than yellow. "How are *you*?"

* * *

There was no door to the "writing loft." Nothing separating it from the second floor. Just this eerie set of wooden stairs, broken in half so you walked a few steps right, then left. A flaking lacquered banister wound up along the sides.

These stairs were not inviting. Shadows bloomed down them like a net. They were quietly nightmarish now, in the middle of the day, so Cam didn't even want to *think* about them at night, when something could easily crawl down, slip between the columns of the banister, and crawl on all fours into his room, peering up at him from the floor.

"Cozy, isn't it?" Syd growled, already invisible just a few steps up.

"Y . . . eah," said Cam. The steps moaned beneath his shoes, bending with pleasure as he creaked up behind Syd.

"Yep," she said, just as he came around the curve of the stairs and saw the loft for the first time. "*This* . . . is where you're meant to be."

Cam froze. Opened his mouth. No words came. He stepped back.

The triangular roof. The small square window. The pink sofa.

It was the attic from his dream.

"Well, I'm peachy, thank you," said Quinn. She opened a drawer of severely bent silverware. Something slithered among the forks. She slammed it shut, tucked her hands against her chest, and became vastly interested in the floor. "So did you grow up in Renfield?"

"Of course," said Wes. "You hardly find *anyone* who lives here but isn't *from* here. It's actually why I started writing. To get the Renfield *out*."

"That I can respect. You from around Edenville, or?"

"Tinker's Falls. Bit south of here. Locals just call it the Falls." He winked. "Insider's tip."

"I see." Nodding appreciatively. "And do you like it here?" She looked at him now. This was an important question.

A wry smile twitched over his lips. "I don't *not*. I mean . . ." He cleared his throat. "There's an old saying. You can take the man outta Renfield, but you can't take Renfield outta the man. Me, Syd, some of the other faculty . . . We've tried leaving this place. Living elsewhere." He shook his head. "Doesn't take. You can leave home, but home *never* leaves you."

"Meaning what?"

"Meaning you are who you are. I've *tried* other lives. But . . . I'm still me, and *I* am home. So why not be somewhere that understands me? Somewhere that wants me back?"

"Renfield wants you?"

"Oh." Wes laughed. "Renfield wants *every*one."

Quinn couldn't articulate the feeling that cut through her then. Fear at being hungered for? A flattering thrill at being wanted? "Do you think it . . . wants . . . *us*?"

"Well." Wes tsked. "You're here, ain't ya?"

Cam's shoes scraped over the dust along the floorboards. He moved in a slow circle, open-mouthed. "How?" he asked, moving his eyes over every inch of the space. The sharp roof, the wall where the chalk figure had been. *Exactly* as he'd dreamt it, though there was no figure there now. "How did you . . . ? *Why*?"

Syd nodded like she'd been deeply vindicated. "So my colleague Madeline, whom you'll meet, read your book and passed it along to me and the rest of the sub-department. When I read your description of the attic, I knew that you'd seen this room. I stayed here when I first began teaching at E.C. I recognized it."

"Seen? This?" He spread his hands. "I've never *been* here before."

"Your mind has. In a sense."

"Yeah, in a dream."

"Dream." Syd scoffed, stepped closer. "Listen. When Crazy Frank LaMorte paints a figure on his wall in his family's blood, he creates a doorway for an interdimensional being. That doorway is scattered into pieces, and it takes a team of *very* dedicated people many years to reconstruct it. To access that other realm. To do so, they enlist the help of Caleb Wentley, whose psychic abilities, *un*beknownst to him, allow him to locate the pieces of bloodstained wood that bear the Shattered Man's mark. That's the plot of your book, yes?"

"Yes," Cam agreed warily.

"The book you wrote *based* on that 'dream,' yes?"

"Yeees." Even more warily.

She spread her hands. "Then let this be proof that it wasn't a dream at all. Because how else would this place exist?" Syd smiled. She stepped even closer, her gravelly rasp now an inch from his ear. "You have a gift to *see*, Cam. We've *recognized* that gift. It's how we found you. Why we invited you here. You wrote about this place without even knowing it."

He licked his lips, his heart beating very loudly in his ears. "But in *Shattered Man*, this place was . . . bad. Basically a doorway to hell." *Ichabod* tingled on the tip of his tongue.

But Syd was breathing harder now. Faster. And he could not unlock his eyes from hers. "Ohh, but there are *so* many worlds, Cam. Worlds without war, disease, hate. Worlds I would *kill* to witness." Her teeth began to grind. She hissed in his ear. "I'm not just offering you a teaching gig here. I'm offering you something *special*. The most special thing you will ever do. Doesn't that sound nice? Don't you want to see . . . what's out there?"

"Syd?" Wes called from downstairs. "We should get a move on."

She stepped back. Smiled secretly at him. "I think you'll be a great asset to the Edenville community." She winked as she patted him on the shoulder and began to descend the stairs. "I really hope I've convinced you. You're *important* here . . ."

He lurched after her, not wanting to be alone in the attic. Especially because for a moment, as she'd been rasping into his ear, his eyes had begun to sting. As if the attic air had suddenly sucked at them, dried them out.

This was definitely something to tell Quinn. The burning eyes, the attic, the other worlds *beyond the door* . . .

So why didn't he? Why did he get back in the car and start the engine like nothing had happened? Why, when Quinn asked, "What was up there?" did he answer, "Nothin. Just an attic. Don't know why she was so stoked about it."

Why did he have a hard time meeting her eyes, beneath those sharp jerking bangs? Why did he lie to her as he drove them away from the Nethers?

Easy. It was because he wanted to believe. Wanted to believe that he was suddenly The One at the beginning of a very spooky adventure. He *was* Caleb Wentley. And he didn't want Quinn to Ichabod them home before he'd had a chance to answer the call.

Some of *you* probably would have done the same stupid thing. Because it's such a shame to cut a story short before it's even begun. Even when that story might break you.

Thunk.

Cam jumped.

Quinn had her hand at the window. She grinned. "Spook ya?"

"Pfft. You wish."

She flicked the window again, *thunk*. "What's up with your eye?"

"Tired of driving." He blinked hard.

"Want me to?"

"No, I'm good." Not looking at her.

Quinn eyed him for a moment, then looked back out her window at the gloomscape of Renfield County. She watched the gnarl of the Shembelwoods fill the window as they crept back up the hill, then back down into the world.

Thunk. She thought of Celeste. *Thunk*. She thought of Clarity Mither. *Thunk*. She thought of Wes: *You can't take home out of the man . . .*

In the bottom of her heart, Quinn knew this was a very bad idea, coming here.

Too bad the heart is the organ we ignore the most.

Elsewhere

I'll begin by saying that I am . . . stuck in time. I *have* been stuck in time for as long as I can remember. It's an endless loop, thousands of years long, forward and then back through the ages. In each turn of this cycle, I fall through countless realms, and at their bottom, I always tumble back through time, into the beginning once more. Every time I begin anew, I'm the only one who remembers it has all happened *before*. I have the same conversations over and over. Visit the same worlds again and again. I have seen so many planes I cannot even name them all. The Dream-coast, the Valley of the Ruined, Ettoran . . . Ohio. I've seen them all. Many times.

But the story I want to tell now is only a part of this loop. The way it all begins. My cycle will not renew for many more years to come, but if I am careful and clever enough *now*, perhaps I can alter the coming events enough to break myself from this cycle. To step forward into a new day at last, instead of falling backward into a day I have now seen too many times before.

A worm can dream.

But even though I've been through this many times, there are still parts I can't remember. Pieces I can *never* recall. As far back as my memory can reach, I know that I have only ever wanted one thing: To return to that world that used me. To squeeze the life from it as it did me. And to stop. Fucking. Falling.

It's been . . . a long time since I last awoke in that distant field. Since I was last dragged into that hall by those philosophers in their scarlet robes. Them and their madking, that fucking *High* Lord. Upon waking, I always find myself staring up at a clouded blue sky, blood running down my face. In that first fresh moment of the cycle, I can never remember where I've come from, or what this place is. I don't even remember that this isn't *my* face that's bleeding, but a mask. A skin. I only recall, bleeding and fogged, that this is the beginning. I have fallen back in space and time, and I am lost to the cycle once more.

I should learn to expect it by now, I suppose. Confused and bloodied and wrapped inside a strange skin. I should learn to remember that's how it all begins. But the problem is, so much *time* passes between each new beginning that I find it nearly impossible to keep it all inside my head. It's only later, after it has already begun, that I remember this has all happened to me before.

As I lay there in the field, feeling the dead grass and hard dirt beneath my fingers, I close the eyes of this body and try to think. But my head throbs, and in this moment, the only thing that ever comes back to me is that old chant, from the days I spent stuck in that cage in that other world. Those children who used to dance around me in the mud. Threw clods at me and laughed at me. *Jopp Yennigen's in another skin again. Jopp Yennigen's in another skin again,* they'd sneer. They'd try to break me open. Pop the skin I wore and pluck me out like I was some *thing* to be examined instead of loved. Eventually, their parents ("scientists," they called themselves) locked me in the dark, and forgot about me.

When the rough hands dig beneath my arms, at first, I think, *Good Christ—it's those fucking children.* Back from the dead, though they have not technically been born yet. I scream, fight. I'm back on that world, surrounded by cage bars, mud, and laughter. But then I'm struck by a thought. *Good Christ?* Without thinking, my mind has uttered an expletive that doesn't exist on this world. And as soon as that thought comes, I calm. This is the moment when pieces begin to fold back in. *You have been here before, Yennigen. Remember: they only have Christ on Earth.* You *will be on Earth soon.*

The hands drag me out of the sun, into a dim hall of ivory and jade. The hall is wide. So wide, I can barely see the walls, can see only that they are covered in lengths of faded tapestry, maybe four along each wall. I blink at them, head pounding. They all depict what seems to be a great bird and many stars. Through the bird extends a kind of spine, from the head down through the tail. The spine in each tapestry is composed of a series of galaxies, stacked one atop the other. Suns, constellations, planetary marbles all circling each other, spinning down toward the tail feathers in a weaving, mostly straight line. In the head of the bird, where the mind resides, is something vast and dark. A swirling morass of thread and inky color.

The roof of this hall is triangular and tall, so that its very peak is wreathed in shadow. Animal eyes flicker at me from beams far overhead. Large white pillars line the center of the hall, each bearing a brilliant golden sconce bent into some spiderweb pattern I don't immediately recognize. The metal tines twist and crack like veins, spiraling upward into a series of wax orbs, wicks flickering. The flames shimmer along the stems of their sconces, crackling like electricity. *Oh yes,* I think, watching them pass as I am dragged toward the head of the hall. *These are crafted in the shape of neurons. And the depictions on the tapestries . . . That spine, the mind . . .*

How could I ever fuckin forget?

I'm dragged further from the sun, deeper into the hall. I lift my eyes and see at the end of it a tall and narrow throne, carved of the same ivory that adorns the rest of the space. Shooting through it are pulses of jade, and they *do* pulse. A low rhythmic hum I can almost hear. Upon the throne sits a robed shadow. The robe is a brighter scarlet than those of the men who dragged me from the field (*philosophers,* I remember now they call themselves *philosophers*). It is beyond blood, brilliant enough to be the red of berries, *berries.* It has been so long since I've had berries. Eons, waiting locked in that dark, forsaken cage. Waiting and waiting and at last—the escape, the war in my name, the hope . . . Only to fail once more. To fall back down in this stupid goddamn world. *Again.*

I vow to make it back there, to enslave the sneering children of those "scientists," and make them farm berries just for me.

That'll show em.

The philosopher on the throne grips the arms of his chair. Long pale fingers stretch from the crimson sleeves of his robe and curl around the ivory. The jade veins pulse strong beneath his palms. He wears the hood of his robe low, over his eyes. But I can see the steam curling from them. Can picture the black hollows smoking within his skull.

Those who are shown multitudes—gifted more visions than they can comprehend—begin to rot from the inside out. Their mind begins to boil. The manyworld is too vast to be contained within a single human mind. When one tries, one bubbles and pops.

How could I possibly *forget?* I wonder again. *How could anyone forget . . . all of this?*

"Praise to the Mind," comes the voice of the man on the throne. It booms through the emptiness of the hall. And in echoes from the shadows all around, beyond the pillars and lining the walls, many voices call: "May It guide us."

"*Praise* to the Mind," booms the voice again, so loud his robe seems to shake, the green veins of the throne pulsing harder, brighter beneath his fingers.

"May It bring us answers," comes the echo.

"*We* do not question the intelligence nor the *will* of the Mind," calls the throne.

"It thinks for us all."

The throne lifts his head. I can see now the glowing yellow embers of what were once eyes. Small and charred. Whatever visions this man has seen, they've come powerfully, frequently, over a great period of time. Whatever he's been shown, it was clearly enough to keep him on this throne, in power. But it's brutalized him.

His small burnt eyes flare like flames given air as he booms, "We do not attempt to *answer* the grand riddles of the Mind."

"They are too intricate for us," calls his chorus.

"We do not attempt to *decode* our own fates."

"They are too labyrinthine. Even for you, High Lord."

"We are grateful for *any* knowledge It may stoop to bestow upon us."

A roar from all around: "*Praise* to the Mind!"

"Good fuckin Christ," I murmur. So many things are coming back to me now, as my body slowly regains consciousness. For instance, Earth has the most satisfying swears. Christ was a fiction, of course, like most Earth myths about the cosmos (if they only knew). But when faced with such grandiose horror as this, it's a small comfort to be able to swear deliciously. I taste it like a rich decadence. And I realize my voice is higher pitched than I'd expected. I remember now that I am wreathed in some womanskin. I cannot recall her name. I remember burrowing into her, what it feels like to steer her tall, muscular skin. I can even bring her face to mind, but . . .

No matter. I won't be in her long.

The philosophers who dragged me from the field shove me from behind. I fall onto all fours against the smooth ivory. My head still throbs from the fall. This entire body feels broken, used up. I'm surprised by how weak I feel, but I've probably thought that before. Shit, I'll probably have that thought again.

Then the throne says something I absolutely do *not* remember him saying, nor do I expect I'll remember it *if* I'm ever here again. It catches me so completely off-guard.

He says my name. Not my skin-name. My true name.

I do not like when people know my name.

"Jopp Yennigen," he booms. "Traveler from another vertebra."

Pins and needles canter down my arms. I look up, and he meets my gaze. Steam unspools from his eyes in silver tendrils, whispering upward to the ceiling. The yellow coals within—they burn.

"How the shit do you know that name?" I ask.

He smiles. A wide, smug grin. "*I* am the Philosopher High. It is my station to know."

I laugh. His precious Mind probably told him my name, if I had to guess. But if he wants to be coy about it, fine. "Congrats. But that isn't yours to know. So spit it back out."

One of the philosophers behind me grabs my shoulder. "Do not *order* the High Lord."

"I'll eat that hand if it comes at me again," I say, turning to him.

He draws a crude hatchet from his blue leather belt. "You'll eat iron first."

"Eddick." The High raises a hand. The man behind me steps back, sheathes the hatchet. Glares at me.

The High chuckles. The smug fuck. He has too many teeth. They gleam in the yellow and green dim of the hall. "I was warned of your insolence, Jopp Yennigen. Warned you might not cooperate."

"Oh, I'm not cooperating?" I say. "You *dragged* me here. Forced me to my knees. How would I be cooperating right now?"

"Even so," the High Lord says. "I was *hoping* you might be a willing participant. But I can see now that will not be the case. No matter. In fact . . ." He looks at the ceiling. Something like ecstasy passes over his face. "Ohh. How childish of me to *hope*. How mistaken I was to give in to my heart, when this is so obviously a matter of the Mind. Everything about you has proven true, Jopp Yennigen. Mere minutes you are here, and already, everything I have been shown . . . is coming true."

He laughs. Big, throaty *HA*s. Then he thrusts his hands into the air and bellows, "Praise to the Mind!"

From around me, the echo, booming through the hall: "Praise!"

"It never lies!"

"It knows."

"The dreams It grants are *truth*."

"Better than truth."

"See!" The High Lord stabs a finger at me. He yells so loud the finger quivers as his words shake the hall. "I spoke of this! I said our world would be saved. In my dreams, It showed me a traveler. It said they would come from the stars, *up* through the Spine of the manyworld to save our home, and they are *here*. Philosophers, rejoice! The Mind has granted us a boon at last. Our savior has arrived. Jopp Yennigen . . . is here!"

Drums burst into life. Huge, pounding thunder from all directions. A frenetic chaos of sound, the drummers hidden in the dark. *Doomdoom doomdoom doomdoom doomdoom*. On and on. Deafening.

Yes, I think. *Yes, I remember* so *much now. The fall. This High son of a bitch. And even what is to come . . .*

I gaze at the tapestries upon the wall. There flies the great bird, soaring among the darkvast of the beyondstars. The column of galaxies and constellations curving down its back—the interwoven vertebrae of the manyworld—is what most refer to as the Spine. What lesser Earth-minds call the multiverse. All those shapes and colors and suns and spheres, all stacked like floors of a helix-shaped building, spiraling upward toward the Mind.

Toward God.

The drums grow louder. I look up at the Philosopher High, beaming down at me, lips stretched wide and triumphant. Over the drums, he shouts, "Drag it to the well."

"Yeah, that's right," I yell, ears filled to bursting with the drums, drums, drums. Hands shove their way under my arms, hoisting me off the floor. "Yeah, you fuckers, yuk it up!" I feel my anger rising with the beat, this body's blood beginning to heat. Hatred burns through me, makes me writhe against my skin. *Doomdoom doomdoom doomdoom doomdoom.* I'm screaming down the hall as they drag me away. And the Philosopher High just grins at me as I wail: "Yeah, you called it, asshole! Your *savior* has arrived! Ohh man, are you fuckin saved!" I laugh as they shove me back out toward the sun. I cackle. I howl. I hate this, I hate it, and I *know* that I am helpless to stop it all from happening to me again, for the millionth time.

But this time, I promise myself, harder than I have ever promised before: I will *not* fall.

"Yes!" I cry. "Fuck yeah! I'm here, jackass! Jopp Yennigen—is here—again!"

BLOODYWOOD, BASEMENTS, AND A BALD MAN NAMED BENNY

In the Christian Bible, the Serpent "tricks" Eve into partaking of the Tree of Knowledge. God is angered, because his religion is focused on control. Freedom of knowledge is not for Man, according to God. In reality, the Serpent was attempting to *help* Eve. To guide her toward a better understanding of the intangible universe. In reality, God is the one who tricked Eve. He punished her for wanting to See.

The giant is a different beast. The giant's Mind shares often, is *happy* to share Its thoughts with us, the cells of Its body. Otherwise, It would be lonely, wandering through the darkvast of the beyondstars by Itself. It must turn inward, to us, for company and comfort. We must be able to appreciate that.

Christianity would have you believe that God works in mysterious ways. Well so, too, does the Mind. But the Mind does not treat knowledge like a devil's trick. Even though It may *seem* frightening, because It is so much bigger and smarter than us—the giant's Mind will never trick you. Why would It? It's the one who thought you up.

Cassandra Maywell, *A Historian's Guide to Living Long* (3rd ed., 1993)

CHAPTER SIX

YOUR VERY LAST CIGARETTE AND A TRIP TO PANCAKE PLANET

Quinn was a firm believer in a God who controlled the Shuffle button. There was something *in* there, among all the circuitry and hardware, that decided what song would pop up next. It wasn't something electric, nothing computerized, it wasn't tangible at all. Quinn believed this deeply, even on her most nihilistic, raincloudiest days. You could pull up Spotify or Pandora or your old iPod Shuffle or whatever the hell, hit randomize—and the universe would speak to you. "Come On Eileen" might play, and then you *had* to come on, because something behind the lyrics was sending you a heads-up. "All These Things That I've Done" by the Killers might reach out with its gentle opening notes and say, *Hush now, girl, it's alright.* Or "Everybody Wants to Rule the World" might tumble through your earbuds, and you could *feel* something in there, speaking to you from beyond the stars.

This was the closest thing to a religion Quinn had. It was rare that she knew *exactly* what the songs were saying to her, but she never lost the faith that if you put your shit on Shuffle and let Whoever take the wheel, you'd find yourself in the warm embrace of Something More. Something that would let you know, just for a moment, you were not alone.

In the three months between their visit to Edenville and the beginning of the fall semester, Quinn drifted through her entire life on Shuffle. She stood on the roof at night while Cam buzzed around the apartment, getting more and more excited for his "first adult teaching gig," as he called it. The conversations he had with his parents on the phone drove her nuts. The pride in his voice. She just couldn't shake the feeling that it'd all fall apart. But what was she supposed to say? He *wasn't* special? None of us are? We're *all* just meat?

No. Better to just stick to the roof, letting her phone bounce her from one song to the next.

Her breaks at the Red Yard found her lurking in the alley outside, watching families eat burgers and squirt mustard everywhere. Shuffle God kept serving her a bunch of bummer-tunes as she watched them all. Lots of Civil Wars, Head and the Heart. Fiona Apple, Lana Del Rey. But what was she supposed to *gain* from all this? From being thrown into, like, "New York, I Love You but You're Bringing Me Down," which she hadn't listened to since tenth freakin *grade*? What was the universe trying to communicate by serving up this memory of the backseat in her mom's old car, driving home from some bullshit Christmas party? Christmas after Dad was never enjoyable, and the song still made her throat clench, all this time later. Still reminded her of the way he looked after he slid off that bridge in the rain.

What was the universe trying to tell her?

Even now, as Quinn wandered through downtown Edenville, Shuffle God's logic eluded her.

Fleet Foxes' "White Winter Hymnal" played as she stood on the corner outside the Edenville General Store, squinting at the street and really trying to figure this out. What was the significance of *this* one? It wasn't even winter, it was late August.

She felt like she almost had it when a hefty drop of rain split itself from the edge of the general store roof and landed perfectly on the end of Quinn's last cigarette. Black tar and nicotine splashed against her fingers. There was a puny hiss, and the cigarette died.

"Well, shit," said Quinn. She flicked the dead butt into the gutter. "Fuck you, too."

It was a clouded day, mercifully cool for late summer. Jeans and hoodie weather, which was Quinn's ideal habitat. But the clouds didn't help the fact that she felt like she was having a staring contest with Edenville. Like they were both waiting for the other to make the first move.

She considered this raindrop to be Edenville's first open act of aggression. So far, in the one week she and Cam had been here, nothing significant had happened, and she was starting to feel itchy. Cam spent his days on campus, doing Shuffle-God-knows-what in his office, and his evenings up in the attic, writing (except Quinn never heard the sound of clicking keys, when she'd stood listening at the foot of the attic stairs once or twice). Edenville didn't *have* any "cool bars" to work in, so Quinn spent her days wandering around town, sort of at a loss for things to do. She'd walked through campus a bit, but that felt like Cam's territory. He thought he was so freakin fancy, chattering her around the college center café like he owned the place and hadn't just been there a few days. Plus the sunflowers freaked her out.

She'd found a few trails through the woods behind the Netherwilds. They were pleasant enough, and reminded her of summers with Celeste, picking cottonwood fluffs out of the air. Until she thought she caught one of the bushes along the trail following her. So that was the end of that.

But did she tell Cam this? Nooo. He'd call her paranoid. And maybe she was. She'd even briefly wondered, when she'd given Kenz a spare apartment key (just in case) if Kenz would hide bodies in their apartment while they were gone. That was a pretty paranoid thought to have, right? Right?? Maybe she was freaking out about being here more than she was ready to admit. Even "good ole 1896," as they'd started calling their little town house, felt haunted. Not creepy per se, just . . . invasive. Constantly peering over Quinn's shoulder. Watching her sleep. Very rude.

And speaking of rude . . .

Quinn wiped the black cigarette spatter on the back of her jeans. She dug her pack of Camels from the kangaroo pocket of her hoodie (go Crows) and opened it again. Still empty. Bummer. She'd sort of been hoping a new cigarette would materialize.

She crushed the pack, tossed it in a trashcan on the corner, stuffed her hands back into her hoodie, and looked around. *Now what?* What was "White Winter Hymnal" telling her to do?

The general store was a long, squat building with large stuffed animals filling its picture window. Quinn had walked by it every day for a week, but had not yet talked herself into walking inside. That was because she'd never seen anyone in there except the woman behind the counter, a little old lady with red-white hair and a perpetually pink cardigan. She'd never seen that lady wearing anything other than that same pink cardigan. Or perhaps she had several perfect copies filling her closet, like a cartoon character.

Quinn stared into the store. Packs of cigarettes lined the wall behind the counter.

She didn't particularly like old ladies. The ones in Leaden Hollow tended to leer at her through their car windows as they drove by. They picked at her hair and told her they wanted to bottle her youth, drink it all up. They told her she'd have nice babies. They treated her like an object, which Quinn understood—they'd been treated like objects themselves. But still.

"Fuck it." She took a breath and went inside the store.

The bell over the door *ching*-ed loud enough to make Quinn jump. Ms. Cardigan looked up and smiled. "Mornin."

"Hello," said Quinn, too high-pitched. She realized she hadn't spoken to anyone yet that day. She and Cam had become experts at drifting away from each other over the summer, like slow-moving screensaver icons, bouncing against corners. This morning was no exception. Cam had left for campus without a goodbye.

"Can I help you find anything?" the woman asked.

Quinn scanned the series of short shelves filling the store. It was beautiful in its quaint cliché-ness, with its blue carpet and dim fluorescents, the shelves decked with everything from plungers, boxes of nails, and gardening gloves to coloring books, jawbreakers, and boxes of stretchy rubber dinosaurs. She felt like she was walking into a jigsaw puzzle or an *I SPY* book.

She approached the counter. Up close, she saw that there was only one brand of cigarette on the back wall. The boxes were striped blue and white. A little fox insignia peered out from under the brand name: Noxboros. Sydney Kim's brand.

"What are those like?" she asked.

The woman gave a slow turn and gazed at the wall behind her like she'd never seen it before. She gave another slow turn back to Quinn, made a disgusted face, and shook her head. "Ohh, if you have to ask, you won't like them."

Quinn was vaguely offended. "But . . . they're the only ones you have."

"They're the only ones sold in the entire county. Made local, up in Lillian."

"Well, that sucks."

"You must be new. Did you just start at the college or . . . ?"

"No, my . . ." Quinn hated the word *boyfriend*. Made her feel so . . . not-grown-up. "My *fiancé* is teaching there this semester."

The woman nodded. Quinn felt that she'd fed a dangerous shadow-energy into the world. She shouldn't have called Cam her fiancé out loud.

"What department is he in?" the woman asked.

"English. Er, Creative Writing."

"Ohh. You shouldn't marry writers, though. You always end up in books."

"That's what I've heard." Quinn pointed at the Noxboros. "So why won't I like em?"

"Ohh, you could give the old Noxboro fox a shot." The woman slowly turned again, pulled a pack from the wall with a trembling hand. She smiled as she booped the cigarettes. "$9.79, dear. How long have you been in town?"

"A week."

"Enjoying it so far?"

"I spose."

"Well, my name is Deborah. Let me know if you enjoy those." Pointing at the pack in Quinn's hand. "You have such a young tongue, it might not take well to the . . . local flavor."

"Okay, thank youuu," said Quinn, spooked and already halfway to the door.

Sure enough, when she tamped the pack against her palm and lit up the first striped cigarette, it was horrible. Tasted like dirt. Coated her tongue in a weird, greasy film. She coughed and chucked the butt on the ground, dug it in under her heel. She looked, watery-eyed, through the store window. Deborah was shrugging at her from behind the counter. *Warned you.*

Quinn stuck the pack in her pocket and continued to wander.

She passed a shoe store that looked warm and inviting, lit by several shaded lamps dotted throughout the shelves. She paused outside the window. She had a sudden memory of being in third grade and missing school one day to go to the dentist. It was just a regular checkup, nothing particularly bad or memorable. But her mother had taken her on errands for the rest of the day, and Quinn had been amazed at how many places *existed* while she was in school. Furniture stores and Home Depots. Stop & Shop, the Goodwill, the bank. She hadn't realized, until this very moment, how calm that day had made her. That this random memory of this random afternoon, nearly twenty years ago now, was her definition of contentment.

As she stared inside the shoe store, another kind-looking old lady (a Black woman with a golden nameplate) began humming around the aisles, sliding shoeboxes in and out of shelves. Quinn read her name through the window: Brenda. Brenda caught Quinn's eye and waved. Quinn smiled awkwardly, then fled.

It was funny how this entire place seemed to reflect that day in Quinn's memory. All the stores along Rackell Street seemed so cozy and inviting. And for whatever reason, all the women tending them reminded her vaguely of her grandmother. All of them smiled through the windows so warmly, so kindly, that it almost broke Quinn's heart. She felt too small to deserve it. She wanted to run from them, to dive into a deep lake and never resurface.

But at the same time, she never wanted to leave. She wanted to run into The Silver Cat, the shop selling incense and singing bowls and tarot decks and shit—wanted to run right up to the kind old lady in there with the long silver hair and say, *I'll take it from here. You go on home, Margot,* or whatever her name might be. And there she would stand, behind the counter, until she died.

Perhaps that was the point. Perhaps Renfield *wanted* her to feel that way. Perhaps she shouldn't give in. Or perhaps she *was* being paranoid.

Perhaps, perhaps, perhaps.

She stood under the awning of The Silver Cat, staring through the glass with a longing she couldn't define.

What was she doing here?

"Hello?"

Quinn turned. Standing across the street, in the doorway of the ice cream joint, was (of course) a kind-looking old lady. She had dark-brown skin, round glasses, and a little spoonful of ice cream in her hand. "You seem downtrodden."

Quinn felt a sob bubble up her throat. "Ma'am . . . I *am* downtrodden."

"We have free samples." The woman waved her little spoon. "This one's chocolate-marshmallow."

Well, shit. Quinn loved chocolate *and* marshmallow.

The next thing she knew, she was standing in the shop with its black and white linoleum, its lazy wooden ceiling fans. She ran the chocolate-marshmallow back and forth over her tongue, and before she even knew what was happening, she asked, mouth full, "Can I try the caramel coffee one?"

The lady laughed and got another teensy spoon. "Good, isn't it?"

Quinn nodded.

She tried four more flavors before buying a cup of Birthday Cake. She sat by the bay window and looked out at the clouds. She felt like she wanted to put a gun in her mouth, she was so fuckin content.

Then she noticed the bulletin board by the door. There, among all the flyers for piano lessons and plumbing services and all kinds of shit—was another MISSING poster for Clarity Mither. Young and blond and probably very dead. It struck Quinn that they hadn't chosen a smiling picture of her. Maybe there wasn't one. Maybe Clarity never smiled, and Quinn could respect that.

Celeste never liked to smile for pictures, either.

The air in the shop seemed to sour as Quinn gazed back at Clarity Mither, missing since February. Six months now.

She shuddered. All around her, from every direction, Quinn felt the mother-eyes of many, many women. Watching her eat. Watching her fatten herself up for the kill.

She was being stupid. She'd been wandering around in a daze for a week, daring Renfield to do something to *her*, too. She hadn't done shit to find out anything about *anything* that had happened to Celeste. Hadn't done anything for her relationship either. She was just sitting here, letting Edenville cover her tongue with cream and tobacco.

She and Clarity stared at each other from across time.

Cam walked around campus that first week with the notion thorned in his brain that he was a very special boy. He didn't quite know *how*, but he knew, dammit. The psychic lady told him so.

Syd came to check on him once, to see how he was "settling in" and to invite him to the semester's first coffeehouse, which would be followed by a reception in the lounge in his honor. Other than that brief visit, the department had left him alone in his office "to write," as Syd had said with a wink.

Except he hadn't written anything. He'd had no more dreams. His eyes continued to burn, which was concerning (it'd been years, of course, since they'd done that), but no more cold phlegmy tears squeezed out of him. He wanted badly to ask someone what exactly he was supposed to be doing, what this adventure was *about*, but the opportunity never arose. He was starting to feel that his specialness was pretty precarious, and he'd been avoiding Quinn just in case he had to admit that.

Then he met Sneeze.

While Quinn was eating ice cream across town, a voice wheezed into Cam's office: "You must be Campbell."

He turned in his desk chair, where he'd been (unsuccessfully) pretending to look busy, and discovered a hunched man standing in the doorway. Under his arm, he clutched a thick manila folder stuffed with a foot's width of uneven paper scraps. He had his jaw cocked to the side, and he sneered down at Cam as he tongued the backs of his teeth.

Cam stood, stuck out a hand. "Cam is fine. You must be Chett."

Chett Neeves made a disinterested noise in the back of his throat, then strode by Cam and dropped his folder on his desk. He sighed, sat, and analyzed Cam from a distance. Cam awkwardly lowered his hand.

"I read your book," said Chett. "We *all* did."

"Thank you."

"I didn't care for it."

"Oh."

Chett wore an open tweed vest that he now smoothed over his small paunch. "I detest genre fiction. I'd been looking forward to having another playwright around for a change, but Syd insisted." He swiveled away from Cam in his chair. "Well, as you know, the semester begins tomorrow. You'll be lecturing in three of my sections this week, and then the students will all have a chance to meet with you *twice* to discuss their work one-on-one over the following month."

"Yeah, Syd explained all that to me."

Chett turned, raised his eyebrows. "Oh, so I can't?" Then turned away again, began sifting through his big folder. "My classes tend to read more grounded work than *horror*. We're starting the semester with *Finnegans Wake*."

Cam couldn't stop himself from saying, "Gross."

Chett either ignored this or totally missed it. "Mmhm. Well, you can say whatever you like to the kids. *They* should have read your book over the summer as well."

Cam felt a sharp thrill run through his blood. "And they can ask me questions about it?"

"If they so desire."

Cam nodded. "Cool."

"Indeed," said Chett, flipping through papers, already elsewhere. "Very . . . *cool*."

"Settling in?"

Cam looked up, startled by a new voice for the second time in two minutes. A thin woman in a waifish sundress clung to the doorframe. She gave him a smile so fragile he felt like he could flick it and watch it shatter.

"I think so," he said. He fiddled with the lever of his chair. It *thunk*ed down a full foot. "I've never had my own office before."

"And you don't now," Chett grumbled.

The woman leaned into the room. "Hello, Chett."

"Madeline."

The woman stuck out a hand. "Madeline Narrows, poetry. I'm the one who discovered your book. So really, you have me to thank for bringing you here." As they shook hands, something flickered over her face. "So . . . I'm sorry."

"For what?"

"Bringing you to Edenville," she said. "I'm sure the city is much more exciting."

"No, we've been having a good time here so far. My girlfriend and I are staying in the Nethers."

"Oh, you like it there?"

"She asks," said Chett, "because it's supposedly haunted."

Cam laughed. "My girlfriend says everywhere around here is supposedly haunted."

"She isn't wrong," Chett grumbled.

"Well, I'm just down the hall," said Madeline. "If there's anything you need and Syd's not around, just knock."

"Thank you, I will."

"Also, I have my own printer, so if the department one is acting up—which it always is—feel free to stop by."

"I will definitely take you up on that, I'm sure."

She smiled again, turned halfway toward the door. Then paused, rubbing together the fingers of the hand Cam had shaken. Almost as an afterthought, she said, "Are you . . . coming to the reception tomorrow?"

"It's *for* me, isn't it?"

Another delicate smile. "Sure, but you never know. You could be horribly introverted."

"No, I'm looking forward to it."

"Good." Her face did something he couldn't read. Excitement, worry, then something else. "You'll get to meet Benny."

Cam cocked his head. "Who's that?"

"Our writer in residence last semester. Associate professor now. You'll get along great. Anyway. We'll chat more tomorrow night. Nice meeting you."

She glanced around the office, her smile fizzling into a worried, almost frightened look. Then she was gone.

Cam swiveled in his chair, back and forth for a moment. He spun all the way around and looked out the window behind him, then spun back and looked at the chair against the wall, next to his desk. Mere days from now, a student would be sitting in that chair. A student would be listening to what Cam had to say. A student would be sitting *right* there, watching Cam like he was an adult, like he wasn't less than a decade older than them.

He felt another swell of pride. He was a special special boy indeed.

"The readings are a scam," said Chett. "*I* never go. And if you ask me, the new guy simply isn't human."

"I'm the new guy."

"The *old* new guy." Chett finally looked up. Gave him a cold stare. Clicked his pen, *cuh-click*. "Benny McCall. First Black nominee to win the Bent Literary Citizen Award last spring. Madeline's boyfriend? Got his own office now, down the hall." Chett nodded at it. *Cuh-click*, he clicked his pen. "Moved him*self* in there after he weaseled his way into Syd's good graces last semester. When he told his little tale at the alumni house dinner back in February . . . Well. Syd was *very* impressed. I," *cuh-click*, "was not. I'd steer clear of McCall if I were you. Your last-minute addition to the department is a bit . . . fishy, you ask me." He gave the pen one final *shlick*.

"What, like they're gonna drug me and eat me?" Cam asked.

"Who's to say? I've been in this department for fourteen years, and it's been . . . odd . . . since McCall arrived and that girl disappeared."

Cam blinked. "You mean . . . Clarity Mither?"

"Indeed. Her mother, Greta, put up a big stink, but they never found a body."

"I . . . thought she was in—"

Chett tapped his temple. "You *thought* what they told you."

Cam frowned into his lap. "Huh" was all he could think to say.

"Then again," Chett went on, "students have *always* disappeared around campus. A group of freshmen evaporated about a decade ago." He pointed a pen at the wall that separated them from the parking lot. "Last seen at that old biology building, in the field back there. Apparently, we used to have a biology professor that most of the students *hated*. This was back in the '40s. They called her the Edenville Butcher. Gray clay for skin, steel wool for hair. The works. They say if you were bad—she was the dormitory mother for Kleave Hall, on the north end of the quad—she'd threaten to slice you into pieces. Legend has it she's still in that field house, carrying out experiments with her most devoted students." Chett clicked his pen. "See, mischief isn't *new* here, but it's been . . . somehow worse. Since McCall joined the faculty full time."

"I see," said Cam, wondering who'd sent this man to act as the horror-movie harbinger for him. "Well . . . thanks for the info."

Chett clicked his pen several more times, then turned back to his papers. "Don't say nobody warned you."

"Just the Cobb salad for me," Quinn told the waitress. "Thanks."

"You got it, shug," said the little old lady, swiping Quinn's menu out of her hands. The menus at Pancake Planet were strangely wet, and Quinn was glad to be rid of hers.

Cam sat across from her on an identical orange pleather booth-bench. He gazed sideways out the window at the misty evening street. There was a candy store across the way, and from all the way over here, through two sets of windows, Quinn could see another kind old lady behind *that* counter as well.

"Have you noticed," she asked, "that, like, everyone in town is a nice old lady?"

Cam looked theatrically around the diner, fixed his eyes on a family of five, eating dinner-pancakes (which are just regular pancakes served at six p.m.). He turned pointedly back to Quinn.

"I mean, like, everyone *running* the town," said Quinn. "Our waitress? The women in the shops?"

Cam shrugged. "It's a small town."

"Meaning what?"

He shrugged again, shoulders even higher this time. "I'm just sayin."

"Well, I don't know what you're saying. Thank you." Quinn smiled up at the waitress as she gave them silverware and plastic cups of water. She and Cam sat in awkward silence as the waitress laid down napkins, forks, spoons, knives, and arranged everything with the utmost care.

"So was your day normal?" Quinn asked. "No, uh . . . spooky clues or anything?"

"No spookiness," said Cam. "My officemate hates me. But he doesn't seem to like anybody, so." He shrugged a third time. "Hates the *old* writer in residence in particular."

"Why's that?"

"Don't know. Maybe he's jealous the guy's dating one of the poetry profs. And I guess he charmed his way into the department pretty easily last semester."

Quinn picked up her knife between the tongs of her fork, balancing it gently. "Who was the old one?"

"Some guy named Benny McCall."

"You've met him?"

"He wasn't at the department meeting today." The afternoon's meeting had been an incredibly boring routine thing where they went over best practices and gave Cam a map of the campus. Maybe this McCall thought he was too important to show up.

"Okay," said Quinn, watching her fork waver. "So we've got a missing student. An elusive professor. And the old ladies."

"Uh-huh." Cam looked out the window again. He blinked hard. "Ya know, that doesn't add up to much of a bad time."

"Still." Which came out smaller than she meant it. So small, in fact, it sort of hurt her throat to say, like she was swallowing her own voice. In the last few months, she'd been noticing she did this a lot.

"Look," Cam sighed, adjusting his glasses with a pinkie. "I just want to get the semester underway before we really start picking at why we *shouldn't* be here. You know?"

"Well, come on, man," said Quinn, dropping her silverware. "You can't just . . . play along a little?"

"Quinn, we're at a Pancake Planet and *I* ordered a fried chicken waffle wrap. *You* ordered a salad. What do you mean, I'm not playing along?"

"Why do you say *a* Pancake Planet like there's more than one?"

"They have a location in Bartrick Mill. It says on their menu."

"Well, *locals* just call it the Mill." She snapped her fingers, *Aha*, right in his face. "How's *that* for playing along?"

"Alright, I don't know what you want me to say. You think the old lady Edenvillians are running an insidious operation with the college's Creative Writing department? And they baited me into coming here so they could . . . what? Turn *us* into old ladies? How are you suggesting this is all related?"

"Well, isn't there a saying about how if it *seems* connected, it is? Like Occam's razor or something? The simplest answer is usually the right one. Sherlock says that."

"Sure. Thanks." The waitress put food down in front of them. Cam's waffle wrap was a monster of a dish. He dug into it, in a way that made Quinn wince. Chewing, he said, "So what do you want me to do here?"

"Be . . . interested, for one. Geez." She cut into her salad so she didn't have to look at his smug fucking face anymore. "I thought this was supposed to be a fun thing. This big adventure."

"I am having fun. I'm having a goddamn waffle wrap for dinner. I just don't *also* feel the kind of alarm you want me to feel for some reason."

"Okay. Sorry."

They ate in bitter silence.

"What, are you dropping it?" asked Cam.

"Yeah, we can drop it," said Quinn. "It's fine."

"Okay. Jesus."

They ate in even bitterer silence. Took turns looking out the window. Quinn watched the candy-store lady wipe the counter. She wondered if the woman was happy or haunted or both.

That night, she wondered what it was about that conversation that'd rubbed her the wrong way. Why was Cam pissing her off *so* much? She loved him, didn't she? He was smart, wasn't he? Then why wasn't he playing his part? Why was he sliding into this cliché horror-movie role of the denying husband? It sucked. It fuckin sucked.

It didn't help that he retreated once more to the sooty night-shadows of the attic as soon as they got home. He was only a creaky set of stairs away, but it felt like a mountain.

She sat at the top of the slide in the Netherwilds playground, choking down a Noxboro as the frogs and crickets chirped among the trees.

Alright, she decided. *Enough of this moping around. You gotta* do *something, girl. You gotta dig in, find some shit out. Read some microfiche, like they do in the movies.*

The library. That's what I'd do if this were a movie. I'd go to the library to investigate.

She carried that thought into sleep. Into a dream about Clarity Mither, standing on a hillside without a head.

CHAPTER SEVEN

THE LIBRARY

Cam was putting on a tie in the bathroom when Quinn appeared in the doorway. "Yooo, first day of school!" she said, with effort. "You stoked?"

Cam fucked up the tie-knot. Unraveled it, started over. "Woohoo."

"Nervous?"

"Not particularly." She watched him fuck up the tie again.

"Here." She slid up behind him, slung her arms up under his, and began tying it for him. She rested her chin on his shoulder. Watched her handiwork in the mirror. He smelled like himself. Like that apartment he'd had off-campus at Branson, when they'd first started dating. Oak barrel beard oil, mint candles, fresh paint. She breathed it in. When was the last time they'd touched?

"When's the last time you wore one of these?" she asked.

"I don't even remember. Winter formal?"

"You haven't worn a tie since we were at Branson?"

"Have you *seen* me wear a tie?"

"Guess not." She watched herself work for a moment. "So Edenville has a dress code?"

"I'm trying to make myself look more adult. Where'd you learn this?" He felt like he was watching his mom tie his shoes before the first day of first grade. He almost wanted to shove her away.

"*Merchant of Venice*," said Quinn, pulling the knot tight to his collar. "My senior year. We all wore ties. Remember?"

"Riight." He didn't remember.

Quinn folded down his collar, then held him and smiled at him through the mirror. "You're gonna be fan*tas*tic today, baby."

"I know. Uh, thank you."

"I love you," she offered.

He smiled, turned to her. "I love you." He kissed her. "What are *you* doin today?"

"Thought I'd walk over to the library. Explore some county history."

"But it's a gorgeous day. You don't want to play outside?"

Quinn scrunched up her nose. "And do what?"

He shrugged, pressing past her out of the bathroom. "I don't know. Witchy shit in the woods."

"I'm not going in the *woods*." Appalled that he could even suggest this. She followed him into the bedroom, where he was tying his own shoes on the edge of the bed. "Actually, I was . . . trying to google some shit about Renfield last night, while you were working?"

"Okay."

"Because I know you think I'm superstitious or whatever. Which is an absurd thing to think, by the way. But I . . . couldn't find anything."

He cinched one shoe tight. "Guess I'm not so absurd."

"On the contrary." She held up a finger. "That means it's *more* interesting than I could have hoped. Because the interesting stuff is buried. I thought the library should have some archives or . . . something, so."

"I see." He cinched the other shoe too tight.

She watched him. "Do you think that's weird?"

He sighed. He was always sighing at her. "I don't know, Quinn. If you want to play spooky, be my guest. But I didn't know we were coming here to seek it *out*."

So he did think it was weird. Cool.

She regretted helping him with his tie.

The funny thing about living in a place like upstate New York is that lots of things seem to be housed in old homes and barns. Quinn's dentist back in Leaden Hollow operated out of a refurbished stable, all the appointment rooms old stalls. When she threw out her shoulder building a set for that production of *Pillow Man* at Branson, the chiropractor she'd seen had his office in the living room of an old colonial. This lends the entire land a quaint, homey feeling. A recycled, haunted feeling, too.

The Edenville Public Library was no exception. A large white building with a Queen Anne tower and a widow's walk. As Quinn strode into the little gravel parking lot, she could see through the windows on the second floor to the children's section. Bright pastel walls, painted characters from Wonderland, the Hundred Acre Wood, Beverly Cleary. They were somewhat poorly done. The cartoon bears were lopsided and eye-bulgy, but beautiful in their homemade-ness. There was a bathtub on the balcony, filled with pillows. Easy to imagine hunkering down in there with a book for entire afternoons, entire *days*, during the summer.

"Fuck yeah," Quinn murmured, taking it all in. "Go Crows."

Behind the library was a wall of poplars. Their leaves shimmered in the breeze, glittering in a row of emerald chandeliers. Beyond them, a sunken brook. A barbed-wire fence along its bank, rusted and torn. A bullet-holed sign reading BAD WATER.

But inside, the library was inviting and blissfully, artificially cool. The second floor wrapped around a banister overlooking the center of the main floor. A full circle of second-floor windows poured sunlight onto all corners of the library. The cartoon bears and rabbits and things all gazed down upon Quinn, like saints in a literary church. It was a beautiful space. Old book and mothball and well-loved carpet. The walls were covered in decades' worth of small-town memories. An entire stretch of the entryway was filled with certificates for kids who'd read enough books in a single summer to earn a coupon to that ice-cream joint Quinn had been to the day before. Another wall was slathered in children's drawings, pictures of book signings from local authors (including Sydney Kim), and pictures of posed sports teams like the Edenville Butchers, who apparently played football, and the Bent High Whalers, who apparently played soccer. The sports-team pictures dated back to the eighties, growing more faded, more ghostly, as they aged.

Quinn read through a number of captions beneath pictures, mouth open in an endlessly fascinated slackjaw, overwhelmed by the small town–osity of it all. She found herself suddenly validated, as if her memories of Leaden Hollow *meant* something. Because *she'd* earned a gift card to McCoy's Pizza one summer for reading thirty books. *She'd* played soccer for a season (she'd hated it, but still). That could be her on the wall, grinning on one knee, in her bright blue Whalers jersey.

What was it Wes had said? *Home never leaves you. Why not be somewhere that wants you . . .*

How much did Cam really want her? Who else waited for her in Brooklyn? Kenz?

How badly did *this* place want her?

"Can we help you?"

Quinn jumped. She'd been so taken in by the pictures on the wall that she hadn't heard the two women approach. But there they were, standing a foot away, smiling identically, robotically, at her. The women were almost exactly equal in height. They both wore pastel blouses tucked into mom-jeans. They were both pushing seventy. She couldn't tell which one had spoken.

She named them immediately.

One had several pairs of glasses rattling around on her head, around her neck. Two were stacked on top of each other just above her hairline. All the lenses were smeared and scratched and old. She held another bright red plastic pair in her hand. *She* was Glasses.

The other woman, wider and a bit gruffer, Quinn named Spider. She had only *one* pair of glasses, but from the very edge of their gleaming black frames hung a very small spider. He dangled there, in a shaft of sunlight, wavering a little, to and fro. He had a drunken aspect that suggested he'd attached himself to something he hadn't meant to. Now he was just along for the ride.

Quinn could relate.

"Hi," she said, waving. "I just moved here, I—"

"Ohh!" The women were surprised, elated.

"You *just* moved?" asked Spider.

"You must have family around," said Glasses, looking worried.

"I grew up, uh . . . up in Leaden Hollow," said Quinn.

"Hmm," singsonged the ladies. They wrung their pale, veined hands and gave each other gossipy looks.

"An interesting town," said Glasses.

"Not as interesting as *here*," said Spider.

"Not at all," agreed Glasses.

"But still," said Spider, "the Hollow has its haunts."

"Have you *been* to Edenville before?" asked Glasses.

"It's . . . too far a drive," said Quinn. "The Billows Road is—"

"Ohh, true," said Spider darkly. "The *hills*."

"The *hump*," said Glasses.

"The *wall*," they said together, low and ominous.

"Keeps people out," said Glasses.

"Keeps things *in*," said Spider.

"Yeesss," said Glasses, worrying the red pair of spectacles in her hand. "There are far more uses for *hills* than you know of, Miss . . . ?"

"Quinn."

"Quinn," said the women together.

"Well, welcome to Edenville," said Glasses. "I'm Cindy."

"Marcia," said Spider, her little companion wobbling on his thread. "Have you seen the campus yet?"

"I have," said Quinn.

"And the flowers?" asked Cindy. "Did you like the sunflowers?"

"Ohh, aren't they pretty?" asked Marcia.

"Aren't they *nice*?" asked Cindy.

"Sure," said Quinn. "Well, listen, I'm not gonna bullshit *you* ladies, so . . . I'll just ask it straight-out?"

"Ohh, something important," said Cindy to Marcia.

"Something *good*," smiled Marcia.

"Go on," said Cindy. "Ask. There are as many reasons to hide a question as there are roads out of Renfield."

"Right," said Quinn. "Well . . ."

She took a breath.

She'd never said this out loud before.

But fuck it. If the stories about this county were true, her thing was probably the *least* crazy tale these ladies had ever heard.

She let the breath out.

"Essentially, my . . . *husband*," she upgraded him from fiancé, "was offered a job at the college, and I followed him because I . . . thought it might be some kind of trap. My friend went missing in Renfield when I was in high school. It was a . . . rite of passage at our school to drive up the Billows Road and see what was so scary about the county. No offense."

"None taken," said the ladies together.

"Okay. Well, we . . . saw something," said Quinn. "My friend Celeste and I. Celeste Barton." The ladies blinked at her. "Celeste Ichabod Barton."

"A fine name," said Cindy.

"Never heard it before," said Marcia.

"Bummer. Anyway, I was hoping to come up here to avoid my husband getting wrapped up in anything . . . ya know, bad. We were supposed to be, like, on the lookout together but I'm worried he's maybe not himself. Or he *is* himself and . . ." *And he's just an asshole.* "But then I've been thinking. I could try to find out what happened to her. My friend. And maybe I could stop something similar from taking my husband. So I . . . came to the library. Um." She fidgeted with her dad's lighter in her pocket. "That's it."

The women took a moment to absorb this. They swayed a little on their heels. Eyed each other.

Then tittered madly, throwing their heads back and dabbing at their eyes, it was so funny.

It was weird to watch. Strangely horrible.

Cindy said, "That's so funny, we had *another* young lady come through just last summer, for a *very* similar reason."

"Almost exactly a year ago, in fact," added Marcia.

"In *fact*," agreed Cindy.

Quinn waited a beat, expecting more. The women beamed at her.

"What happened to her?" she prompted.

Cindy shook her head. "Just stopped coming in."

"Up and thin-aired on us," Marcia added.

"Said she was compiling some kind of *his*tory report."

"Looked at all kinds of articles and things."

"We actually made a little box."

"We *did* make a little box!"

"Yes we did."

"Left it right over *there*."

"Figured it would save us time."

"If we ever had another . . ."

"Explorer?"

"Explorer, yes! That's such a good word for it."

"Another seeker."

"Yes, we made a *seeker* box. All that girl's notes and references collected in one place."

"Just in case."

"Anybody was after."

"The same thing *she* was," they said together grandly, like the punchline to an incredible joke.

Quinn didn't get it.

Quinn, in fact, shifted a step away from them. "And . . . what was *she* after?"

"Answers," they said. The women shuffled forward as one, closing the distance between her and them like *that*. They had not stopped smiling.

Quinn had a sudden image of them floating around the library at night, eyes glowing, feet bobbing inches above the floor. She saw them shoulder to shoulder, wearing Tim Burton-colored socks and grinning their Muppet-wide grins, each packed with cartoonish Claymation teeth, all sharp as knives. She heard them hissing as they floated around in the dark, on patrol. Saw them whirling around a corner, their spotlight eyes zeroing in on some kid who'd snuck in after closing. They snarled—and descended. Swooping down like killer birds. Maybe the entire town was patrolled that way. All the little ladies swooping around at night in repetitive, circular patterns.

She had to literally shake her head to clear this image from her mind.

"And where's this box?" Quinn asked, trying hard not to make any sudden moves.

Cindy pointed a bent, arthritic finger across the room, to a shelf behind the circulation desk. There, a big waterlogged box marked HISTORY in black Sharpie. "We left it right over there."

"Well, awesome, I'll just set myself up here." Quinn thumbed at a table behind her, its back to the wall. "If that's alright?"

"Perfectly alright, dear," said Spider.

"*More* than alright," said Glasses.

"In fact!"

"Wouldn't you know?"

They took a breath together, but Quinn interrupted them: "Lemme guess. That's where she sat."

The women sighed like deflating balloons. All the theatrical steam went out of them. Cindy said simply, as a totally normal person, "Truth be told, Quinn, this is a pretty frequent occurrence. Every few months, another young woman comes by to explore the county's history."

"They all have their reasons," said Marcia sadly.

"Their *games*," added Cindy.

"I just moved here, they say."

"I want to know some *history* about the area, they say."

"I want to know what killed my *dad*."

"But it's always a young woman," said Cindy. "We find that men tend not to *dig*."

"They don't cope well with mystery," said Marcia. "Women will shake their heads and say, *No, I do not accept*. But men are more . . . limited in their thinking. They tend to *sink*."

"So *good* for you, not sinking," said Cindy.

"And best of luck!" they trilled in unison.

Before Quinn could respond, they scuttled away down the non-fiction aisle.

To Quinn's immense disappointment, there was no microfiche inside the box.

"Dammit," she told the box.

The box did not apologize.

Quinn shivered when she put her fingertips on its cardboard surface.

It'd felt very heavy on the brief walk from the shelf to the table. And when she popped the lid off, she felt the box inhale, as if to say, *Here I am again.*

She coughed, just to have some noise in the cathedral quiet of the library, then looked around to see if the women would shush her. They were nowhere to be seen.

There was a thick stack of emails at the top of the box, printed out neatly and paper-clipped together. After Quinn was done rooting through the box to see if there was any microfiche (big bummer), she flipped through the emails one by one, and saw that they were all from the same woman, to the same guy, on the same night, according to the Gmail header at the top of each page. This woman kept asking where he was, why he wasn't responding. Her emails became increasingly desperate as the night progressed. Each one detailed a piece of Renfield's history. Some were only a paragraph. Some were pages long.

Another shiver tightened Quinn's spine. She saw herself sending email after email to Cam. Saw herself sinking under the panic of Renfield's influence, just as this woman had done before.

She set the emails aside.

Below them was a layer of old articles and newspaper clippings, faded Xerox copies of out-of-print texts. Quinn rifled through these for a long time. She read about the founding of Bartrick Mill and Bent, the fishing boom the county had enjoyed around the turn of the last century, and its subsequent collapse. She read about the rape of the Shembelwoods at the hands of the Mithers and a few other families who lived in the mansions around Lillian in the late 1800s. But even better, Quinn read about the mysterious disappearances that began to plague the county's lumber camps and pulp mills in the late 1920s. Lumbermen reported strange sightings deep in the Shembels. Men from the limestone quarries and lead mines around Tinker's Falls reported the same. Starting in 1929, the Mither Plant actually had to close on full moons, because the men refused to work. Strange beasts, unexplained deaths. Lights in the sky. Escaped cannibal convicts from Bartrick Prison, living in the ruins of the machine works by the Mill. Cave-ghouls, five-legged rats. The whole goddamn gamut.

Well. *This* was the Renfield County Quinn had expected.

But there was nothing about the thing that had taken Celeste. The thing they'd seen on the road that night. Nothing about the faculty at the college, either. Just a brief mention of Matthew Slitter's disappearance, back in 1990. He'd been beloved among students, according to his obit from the *Lillian Journal*. The obit also mentioned that the campus sunflowers were his doing.

Thanks a lot, she told him, putting his obit aside. His picture, a tiny black-and-white, glared up at her through rounded spectacles. The tufts of white hair on either side of his head looked like mad professor poofs. He looked like an evil Larry David.

Quinn creaked back in her wooden chair. She huffed up her bangs, thinking.

She picked up the stack of emails and shuffled through it more thoughtfully. She watched the timestamps on the emails go back, from two in the morning to half past midnight, to 11:21, back all the way to sunset. She was reading someone lose their mind in reverse.

She stacked them in order, and began reading through them in earnest.

Dear Tom, began the first email, So I've been a really bad sis. I meant to email you *days* ago but I just . . . kept not doing it. That's lame of me, I know, but there it is. Sorry. Well, it's Friday—no school tomorrow—so I figured I'd have a drink and finally finish writing this fuckin thing. Idk why I've been so weird about it. But I had a drink, then I had three drinks, and now I'm sitting on the floor of my bedroom with no lights on, hittin Send. Sorry haha.

Apparently, the woman's mother had just died. In her emails, she described to her brother how sorry she was for pulling away after their mother's death. She wanted desperately to make sense of their mother's passing. Wanted badly to reconnect with her brother, who was AWOL this entire night of emails, as far as Quinn could tell. At the heart of all this, there seemed to be one question on the woman's mind: Was her mother's death something that was always going to happen—or did Renfield *make* it happen?

Rubber-banded together at the bottom of the emails was a set of ancient photographs. When Quinn went to undo the rubber band, it cracked apart, and stuck to her like a dead worm. She had to shake her hand hard to get it off.

The pictures were grainy black-and-white. Polaroids and negative-strips and more. The first photograph was of a family, standing all together in their Sunday best. At the bottom, someone had written in long-faded ink, *Renfields, Thanksgiving 1927*. The family's eyes were white and blank. They weren't smiling. They had their hands on each other's shoulders, like if they lost contact with each other, they'd simply dissolve.

Quinn hadn't known the Renfields were an actual family. They must be very old blood, dating back to whenever the county was founded. Like . . . seventeenth century?

She turned the picture over. A sticky note was plastered to the back: *Left to right: May, Henry, Lawrence, Adelaide, Robert, Baby Girl.* Quinn turned the picture back to see who was who. May looked like she was probably the daughter. Maybe fifteen or . . . twenty, Quinn couldn't tell. Everyone looks so soulless and beaten down in those old photographs. Especially *this* family. Gaping like ghouls from ninety years ago, all glaze-eyed against the flashbulb.

Henry was definitely around ten. And Lawrence must be the dad. He stood with his hand on young Robert's shoulder, his other somewhere behind Adelaide's back, whom Quinn figured was the mom. She had her hand on little Robert's *other* shoulder. The poor kid (maybe about four) sat stiff in a chair with his lips parted, staring dumb at the camera. He held a sleeping baby in his arms.

They stared at her.

Quinn placed this picture aside. The ones beneath it depicted such a vivid story that she almost got up and asked if the ladies had cranked the AC or something, because she was suddenly cold, so cold.

First: a farmhouse. Two stories, rustic. Summer, and the grass was tall. The farmhouse, however, did not look inviting. It looked squat and sad. In faded pen, in the bottom corner: *Renfield Farm, 1926.*

The next picture: *Renfield Barn.* Even less inviting than the house. Dark and deep, and all the stalls were empty. It loomed so high the picture didn't show the top of it.

Then:

Renfield Living Room, doused in pools of black shadow.

Renfield Kitchen, covered in the same inky black. A single ladies' shoe pokes into the bottom of the frame. Somewhere off-camera, a woman's body on its back on the floor.

Renfield Stairs, absolutely drowned in shining dark.

Bathroom, May. Poor teenage May Renfield, slumped on the toilet. A ragged circle of shadow torn through her chest, her stomach.

Adelaide, sprawled across the kitchen floor. The owner of the shoe from the picture before.

Henry, slumped in an armchair. Quinn could see straight through him, to the buckshot holes in the wall.

Baby Girl. Quinn had to squint at this one. She could only see the crib, and the puddle beneath it. But what was *in* the crib? Did she want to see?

The next picture told her exactly what was in the crib. And no—she hadn't wanted to see.

But she held that picture for quite some time, because there were others beneath it. Pictures that were probably worse. She realized that *these* pictures would show her one of three things. One: Lawrence's body splayed across the floor in some other room. The bedroom, maybe, or inside the barn. Maybe outside. He was the only one missing so far, him and Robert. Both of them might have been killed. Or Two: Lawrence's body wasn't *in* these pictures, because he was the one who'd killed every-one else. Or Three: Lawrence's picture was the last. The one where he'd put a gun in his mouth.

Slowly, Quinn slid the picture of the crib to the back of the stack. The next picture wasn't Lawrence. It was the space between the house and the barn, covered in wintry white. A dark trail led from the snow around the back door to the shadow of the barn.

Quinn turned to the next picture. Farther down the trail. Closer to the barn.

Another picture, even closer.

And another.

The last picture in the stack was badly blurred. She squinted at it. She felt like she couldn't get her eyes to focus on it. Should she be looking at it at all? Maybe it was blurred on purpose.

She saw poor little Robert Renfield, lying facedown on the floor of the barn. She saw that his head had been blown away. But what was on the wall? What were those dark lines, those slick curving . . . shapes . . .

Another shiver ripped through her. A deep, endless shiver. One she'd feel all the way to her grave. Because suddenly she *knew.* She knew what was on that fuckin wall. Lawrence Renfield (she was sure now this had been him) had painted it there, in blood. Had dipped his hands into the ragged wound of his own son and smeared that son across the wall. She kicked herself for not recognizing it *immediately*. Lawrence had done it with a shotgun, not a box cutter. But she'd know this story anywhere: Crazy Frank LaMorte murders his entire family, paints a Man on the wall in their blood. The Man who *told* Frank to kill them in the first place. The Man from another world.

If you see Him, you are through, she thought, pulling the sleeves of her hoodie down over her knuckles, to stop her hands from shaking.

Cuz chances are?

He already

has seen

"Finding anything good?"

Quinn almost fell out of her chair. "Jesus!"

Cindy put a finger to her lips. "Hush, Quinn. This *is* a library."

"Sorry, you just scared the hell out of me," said Quinn, forcing a laugh. She put a hand on the box. "Is this the only one you have?"

"Unfortunately. It's all the material our *other* young friend left us with last summer. Poor thing."

"And you don't know what happened to her?"

"Oh . . ." Cindy shook her head, frowning. "We don't really ask that kind of thing around here. The answer is never good. The best explanation I can offer is . . . already in front of you." She gestured to the box on the table. "*All* of our recent history is tied to that family. What Lawrence painted on that wall? Horrible."

Quinn turned the picture of the barn over, so He wouldn't look at her anymore. "What do you mean?"

"We call it the giant," said Cindy, fiddling with two pairs of glasses at once. "That's what Lawrence called it, anyway. In prison. But *this* was the point that young woman was trying to prove. That everything around here, everything we can't explain—which *is* quite a lot—is tied back to this." She tapped her finger against the back of the picture. Quinn felt a jerk inside of her. *Don't touch it.*

"You see," said Cindy, "when Lawrence Renfield killed his family, their blood soaked into the ground of that farm. Ran into the river and the lake. People say that blood was angry. Radioactive, even. So full of pain and horror. Lawrence was a fine father, provided well for Adelaide and the children. History doesn't say *why* he suddenly turned and gunned them all down with his twelve-gauge. But when he did, he let the chaos of his mind infect the entire county through their blood. And when he drew that *thing* on the wall, he made that wood radioactive, too. For sick fun, perhaps, or in hopes of *gaining* some of that madness, people tore that barn down and took pieces for themselves. Now, that wood is scattered . . . everywhere. And every waterway the blood entered, everything it touches—cursed. The entire valley. So the story goes, anyway."

"Yeah, I'm . . . familiar," said Quinn. Her head was spinning. This must be a joke. She could feel the county itself laughing at her. Replace the name "Lawrence Renfield" with "Frank LaMorte," and you had yourself the plot of *The Shattered Man*. A story about a sudden familicide. Bloodstained wood that warped your mind. A nightmare-Man, whispering to Crazy Frank so he could build a doorway in blood. So *He* could come through to our world. And if anyone ever rebuilt that doorway, gathered all that wood together again . . .

But that was fiction. Cam made it up, after he had that . . . dream.

Didn't he?

Quinn licked her lips. "But nobody knows where all the wood is now, right?"

Cindy snorted. "Not by a long shot. I'd say finding it *all* would take a very concerted effort over a very long period of time. The barnwood has a sort of biblical property. Like Jesus's fish and loaves, there seems to be many more pieces of bloodywood than there should be. Everyone's seen *one*, at least. You probably have, too. You just didn't know it."

"I see," said Quinn. She thought of all the wooden things she'd touched since she'd been here. The table at the ice cream shop. This table, here. The banister of the stairs at good ole 1896. The door of Slitter Hall.

"And the running theory," she asked, "is that *all* of Renfield's stories are somehow caused . . . by this?"

"Well." Cindy adjusted the pair of horn-rimmed glasses on her nose. "Legend has it that when Lawrence drew that giant, he was accessing something very, very evil. We *all* believe, Quinn. We *believe* we're all tied in some way . . . to the giant."

"Can I borrow this?" Quinn asked, tapping the photo with a knuckle.

"Of course. May I ask why?"

"I want to share it with my husband. I think he needs to know."

Cindy spread her hands. "Then by all means."

Covering her fingers with her sleeve, Quinn picked up the picture without touching it. She slipped it into her kangaroo pocket, with her Noxboros and Dad's Marilyn Zippo.

"You can just leave all this here," said Cindy, meaning the spread of papers and shit on the table.

"You sure?" Quinn asked, rising from her chair. "I want to keep looking tomorrow, if that's alright."

"Positive, dear. We'll clean it up and it'll be fresh for you in the morning. Oh, it was *so* nice to meet you. And good luck with whatever you're doing. I'd urge you to be careful, but I feel it might be a moot point."

Quinn laughed weakly. Her knees wobbled. "Yeah, it . . . probably is."

On her way out of the library, Quinn spotted a poster she hadn't noticed before. The Edenville Players were putting on something called *No Longer Lawrence*, by a man named Carter Moone. Quinn had never heard of either of these things, Moone or his play.

"Hey, what's this play?" she called out.

Marcia was the one who emerged this time. Her spider still clung to her glasses as she shuffled up and frowned at the poster.

"Ohh," she said. "Moone wrote that in 1955. The only play he ever wrote. He lived as a recluse in Bent until he died. He was blind, poor man. Dug out his own eyes, they say. They put it on every year. A big deal."

That didn't answer Quinn's question. "What's it about?"

Marcia shrugged like this was obvious. "The giant, of course. The Renfield massacre and why it happened."

"Cindy said no one knows why it happened."

Marcia smiled. "Moone knew. He was a *seer*. He knew Lawrence was different somehow, in the months before he killed his family. He was . . . suffice it to say . . . no longer himself. Hence the title. Closing night is actually tonight, you're in luck!" Marcia clapped her hands. "It's *such* a fun time. *Very* well-written."

"I do love a good play," said Quinn, gazing at the flyer. Around the words, filling the perimeter of the page, was a map of the county, stained almost entirely red.

"We *all* love stories around here," said Marcia. "And the theater is just on the other side of town, down Birch Road? Very easy to find. You should abso*lute*ly come."

"Yeah," Quinn nodded. "I will. I . . . absolutely will."

So it all connects to you, she told the picture in her pocket as she stepped unsteadily outside. *Clarity, Cam, Celeste . . . Every story in this place connects somehow . . . to you.*

CHAPTER EIGHT

SUNFLOWERS

"Now, this is a class of sophomores," Chett Neeves explained as he marched down the hall. He moved surprisingly fast for an older hunched guy in a vest. Cam struggled to keep up. "They may know the school slightly better than you, but don't let that intimidate you. You're an adult, dammit."

"Yeah, that's why I put on the tie," said Cam.

Chett wheezed. Cam guessed it was a laugh. "I love it," said Chett. "The *tie*."

As Cam fiddled self-consciously with his tie knot, Chett paused outside an open doorway. A few students ducked through without looking at him or Cam. Cam peered inside. There were maybe ten of them in there, gathered intimidatingly around a big table. Their JanSports and Herschel backpacks and *New Yorker* totes sat wilted on the floor by their Vans-clad feet.

"Now." Chett ran a thumb into his nostril, flicked something off to the side. "What do you want them to call you? *I* insist upon Professor Neeves, but it's up to you."

"Mr. Marion would be fine."

"Good." Chett nodded his approval. "Surnames create a better psychic barrier between them and you."

Cam didn't feel like he deserved much of a "psychic barrier" between himself and these beginners. He'd spent the last two hours sitting at his desk, fiddling with a new short story. He'd sat down feeling great, cracking his knuckles and ready to work. But nothing came. He stared out the window, gathering wool, feeling his eyes throb. He no longer felt the ego boost Syd's little spiel in the attic had given him. He felt like an imposter. An imposter whose eyes continued to burn.

Chett's voice became a Peanuts adult-drone as Cam took off his glasses and rubbed at his eyelids. "Womp womp wompwomp?"

"For sure," said Cam.

"Womp," said Chett. And he led Cam inside.

Cam sat, head throbbing, in the corner of the room, as Chett clicked his pen rapidly and worked quickly through the syllabus ("Any and all late work will receive a zero . . ."). Finally, Chett waved a hand at Cam. "Now. *This* is Campbell P. Marion, as you may have surmised. You should refer to him as Mr. Marion. *Not* Professor Marion, as he is not technically a professor."

Cam felt eyes land on him like a swarm of flies. The room was small, and he felt very close to all these very young people. When he was their age, thirty-year-olds had seemed so wise and grounded. But here *he* was in this stupid tie, twenty-nine, feeling abysmally like a hack.

"Hello," he said awkwardly.

Chett womped on: "Mr. Marion is, of course, our writer in residence this fall. His specialty is horror, as you know if you read *The Shattered Man*, which you *should have*. But even if you're not interested in horror, Mr. Marion can still womp womp womp, womp womp. Womp womp? Womp. So please give your attention to Mr. Marion."

Again, all eyes turned on Cam.

"Uh," he said. "Well . . ."

He began to stumble through *The Shattered Man*'s evolution. The nightmare, the gummerfolk. He didn't mention the eye-goo. But even as he spoke around it, his eyes began to water. He dabbed at them with the cuff of his sleeve. It left an odd yellow smear along the fabric. He frowned at it.

"Can I ask a question?" A student wearing an E.C. sweatshirt (purple and green) raised his hand.

"Sure," said Cam, blinking. "Absolutely."

"Do you really write every day? I know everyone says that's the key, but isn't it hard to—"

"Of course he does," said Chett. "Don't be ridiculous. Anyone else?"

Cam didn't know how to reel the moment back. Didn't know how to say *no*, in fact, he *didn't* write every day. Most days he didn't write at all.

So what the hell was he doing here?

"Passable work, Campbell," said Chett after class in the hall. He gave Cam a light clammy clap on the shoulder. "They seemed to enjoy . . . you."

"Thank you, I had a fun time. And actually, just Cam is—"

"Lunch!" said Chett, ambling toward the parking lot door. "See you at the next one."

"See ya," said Cam, standing suddenly alone in the stuffy Slitter hall-way. He picked at the stain on his sleeve. It'd hardened into a cold yellow patch.

Wes turned the corner from his office, slinging a messenger bag over one broad shoulder. Cam sensed that there was some kind of shift duty at play, that they were taking turns keeping an eye on him. "Hey hey. How'd your first class go?"

"Chett said I was passable."

"Then it was probably a slam dunk. That's high praise comin from Sneeze. You lunch yet?"

"Just about to."

"Let's do it. I'm buyin. Happy first day."

Wes led him outside. Immediately, the radiance of the sunflowers al-most blinded Cam. He even said aloud, "Good lord."

Wes laughed, then coughed. Cleared his throat. "Yeah, takes a little getting used to."

As they walked, Cam could feel the sunflowers turning with them, rustling in the still, warm air of late August.

"So are they . . . alive?" he asked, feeling ridiculous.

"No more than any other flower," said Wes, walking a pace ahead. The flowers were packed so tight along the sidewalks that Cam worried Wes would turn a corner and be gone, leaving him lost in the middle of a flower-maze.

"Fun fact," said Wes over his shoulder. "Slitter's father was friends with Boldiven Grittwood." He glanced at Cam. No sign of recognition.

"Famous painter, philanthropist, back in the day. Lillian elite. Anyway, Slitter Senior was in Boldiven's last class at the Lillian Art School, before the damn thing burned down in 1920. You can always spot a Lillian painting because there's a splash of yellow somewhere on the canvas. Lots of art schools use similar signatures. In the Hudson Art School, it's a splash of red. Slitter wanted these sunflowers to make the campus his own piece of art."

"Pretty big for a splash of yellow," Cam observed.

"Yeah, and I don't know if Slitter's dad really gave a shit, but." Wes shrugged. "Here they are." He hawked phlegm onto the sidewalk.

They emerged onto Main Drive, and could see students walking around, skateboarding down the street, lounging on the grass in front of the library. Cam felt safer here. He looked back at the sunflowers littering West Camp. One in particular seemed to cock its head at him.

Wes held open the door of the college center. The front entrance was a span of orange tile, running off into halls to administrative offices, the post office. Just inside the door loomed a large brass sunflower with a bronze bee in the center of its eye. Wes swaggered past it, toward the café. Dozens of tables were scattered throughout the sunny atrium. Cam recognized some of Chett's students, who eyed him as he entered, and whispered to each other as he passed.

"Martha, you are a fuckin *sight*," Wes announced, coughing again and clearing a huge blob of phlegm from his throat as he approached the sandwich counter. The woman working there waved him off playfully. "You are the only one who makes my subs correctly," Wes told her, and they engaged in a playful flirt that allowed Cam to wander toward the salad bar. As he worked his way down it, he bumped into another of Chett's students.

"Hello again," Cam offered.

"Hi," said the girl. She was dumping tofu in a plastic container.

"What's your name again?"

She told him, and he immediately forgot it a second time. He took a beat before he said, "Can I ask you something?"

"Uh . . ." She glanced around. "Sure?"

"Am I getting a weird vibe about being the writer in residence? I don't mean to say I'm, like, famous or anything. But I feel like I'm getting . . . looks."

"Oh." The girl frowned. "Well . . . No offense, but it's sort of weird because the guy who was here last semester was just . . . sort of a creep. So I think people are maybe wary? Of you? No offense."

"You mean McCall?"

"Mmhm. I didn't have his class or anything, but I got that vibe just from . . . other girls. And the coffeehouse readings. There was even a rumor he *stole* some freshman girl's story."

"Stole how?"

"Like she brought it into her workshop with him, but then *he* read it at the next coffeehouse."

Cam frowned into the pile of lettuce. "Strange."

"I know. Anyway, I'll see ya." She darted away.

"Ready?" Wes appeared at his side, a giant sandwich tucked under one arm. "Hey, you wanna hear another Edenville superstition?"

"Always." He didn't.

"Don't eat the salad before you head to West Camp. The sunflowers'll know you've got their brothers in your belly."

Cam dropped the salad tongs back into the lettuce. "I'll just do some soup."

Quinn was sitting on the concrete steps of Slitter Hall. Her hands were stuffed deep in the pockets of her Leaden Hollow hoodie (go Crows). She was smoking a Noxboro and grimacing badly. Her leg bobbed fast.

"You look grossed out," said Cam as he approached with his soup.

Quinn chucked her cigarette on the ground and heeled it to death. "God, they're horrible, but I had such an itch. Dude, I have the *craziest* thing to tell you."

"Did you want to have lunch? Because I—"

"No, no. I want to show you something. A *clue.*" Her eyes flashed.

"For what?" Cam asked.

Quinn spread her hands in a grand marquee. "The year is 1927."

"Oh boy. Ya know . . ." He glanced around, but all he could see was sunflowers, no students. "I said I'd hold office hours now."

"Then let's talk in your office. But I'm *telling* you, this is important. You'll give a shit. Even *you* will give a shit."

He *gave* an exasperated sigh. Shifted his soup between his hands. "Alright." And jerked his head at the door. "Let's walk."

Halfway down the hall, Quinn became conscious of the fact that she was following him puppy-dog style as he stomped across the old wooden floor. In some deep part of her, she hated that she was doing this, that she was cartoon-skipping along while this man she was now claiming was her husband wouldn't even look at her. Just kept grumpily marching with his soup to his office as she chattered at him.

"And he took the kid's blood, the little *kid*," she went on, gesturing wildly as he unlocked his door. "And he painted this . . . fuckin . . . *guy* on the wall."

"Some Satan shit?"

"Not even." She followed him into his office. He collapsed into his chair with a sigh. It clunked, fell about half a foot to the floor. Quinn leaned back against his desk as he fiddled with it. "The librarian said she doesn't know *what* it is. Nobody does. Called it the giant."

"Ominous," said Cam, as he fiddled with the chair.

"Yeah, but here." She held out the picture, keeping her sleeve over her fingers so she didn't touch it. "Check. This. Out."

Cam took it in both hands, touching it all over. He frowned. "It's blurry."

"But don't you *see*?"

"See what?"

"*That's* the Renfield giant."

He stared at it. "I don't see anything. Where did you get this?"

"In the library. They have a whole *box* of this shit."

"Hm." He stared at the picture some more. His eyes throbbed.

"Well, isn't it?" she asked.

"Isn't it what?"

Quinn scoffed. "The fucking Shattered Man! Isn't *that* the Shattered

Man? I mean, that whole story I just told you. Don't you . . . Don't you *recognize* it?"

Huh. Actually, he did. It wasn't *that* uncommon, killing your whole family. But that blood-figure on the wall . . . Was *this* what Syd thought he knew? The truth behind his "dream"? If so, he couldn't let Quinn Ichabod them home before he knew more.

He flicked the picture onto his desk. "Well, I don't know *what* I'm looking at, but it gives me a headache." He dug into his eyes with the heels of his hands. "Quinn, I don't . . . I don't know what to do with this."

"My point," she said, "is that it's *yours.* Your story. And there's a play about this guy tonight. We should go. We *have* to go. We could learn something."

"Learn what? What is all this bullsh—"

"Something about what's *happening* here," she said, voice rising. "I mean . . . did you know about this? You're acting all . . . defensive and nonplussed."

"Did I what? Know that this was a true story before I wrote *Shattered Man*? No."

"Exactly. Then how did you . . ." She stopped. "Wait a minute. What do you mean, before?"

"What?" Blinking at her.

"You said *before* you wrote the book. But what about after? I mean, did you know about this *after* you wrote the book but before I told you just now?"

"What?"

"Did you *know* this was a thing?" She pointed at the picture on the desk.

"I didn't know about the stupid . . . Renfield massacre, no."

Quinn stared at him for a full beat. Then narrowed her eyes. "What *did* you know, then?"

"I didn't *know* anything, Quinn. Why do you—"

"No." She shook her head. "No, no. You said that too specifically. You didn't know about the *massacre*, but what *did* you know about?"

Cam lifted his hands, made a noise like he was trying to decide how to lie about this. Finally, he let out a big breath. "I just . . . Okay. I knew there was something going on between me and Renfield. Because of the attic. It's . . . Our attic? That's the same attic from my dream. *Exactly* the same. Quinn, I *dreamt* this place." He couldn't stop a sliver of pride edging into his voice. "I don't know exactly what's in that picture, but I know *I'm* connected to this place . . . somehow. Actually, I'm going to the reading tonight to—"

"You didn't tell me that," she said quietly. "You didn't tell me . . . *any* of that."

"Well, I'm telling you now. I didn't want you to freak out and say Ichabod so soon. But they're asking me to give a reading tonight." He allowed himself to smile.

Quinn jerked her head back. "But I want to go to the play. I *have* to go."

"Well, I've got the reading. And there's a reception after. For me. *I* have to go to that. So."

In the past, Quinn would have broken down. She would have gone to the reading, too. Cam would have expected her to go. But not today. Today, she lifted her chin and said, "Well, bummer, because I'm going to the play."

Cam rolled his eyes, then closed them tight, wincing. "Fine."

"Well, it's not fine with me. You lied to me."

"I didn't *lie*. I knew I was important somehow, but—"

"Oh, you're important."

"Apparently." A warning in his tone.

Quinn blinked. Then twisted her face into the most repulsed, appalled look she had ever mustered in her life. "You *knew*."

A smug smile dragged across his mouth. "Yeah. But I think it's sort of cool. Makes me feel like I'm actually a part of something for once."

"Part of something?" she parroted. She barked a laugh. God, she wanted to punch him. Look how fucking *proud* he was that he knew something she didn't. "You're a part of *this*," she said, gesturing between them, meaning *us*. "Why the fuck didn't you say anything?"

"Well, I didn't—"

"You let me look like a fuckin idiot rambling about the little old lady conspiracy and—"

"I didn't want you to—"

"We could've Ichabod-ed our way out of here from the get. Fucking. Go." She stabbed a finger into his chest with each word, pressing him back into the chair. Then took a deep breath, tried to dial it back a bit.

Their fights were typically like this. Cam sitting very still, listening as Quinn ranted about his latest offense. He was saying everything so calmly, while Quinn felt like she was losing her goddamn mind.

"You *said* you wouldn't be bullshit about this," she said. "You're being bullshit."

"Hey, *you're* freaking out because you read some nonsense in a library."

"I'm freaking out because I read some nonsense in the library that *you* already knew and didn't tell me. Shit you fucking *dreamt* about, three fuckin years ago!"

"I'm not *lying* to you. I'm just not . . . sharing everything before I have it figured out. Like, cut me some slack. I'm—"

"Slack?" Quinn felt the window peering down at her. Felt the sunflowers bending up to glance inside, fascinated by this fight. She felt the world churning around her, but she couldn't help her voice from breaking, she was just so pissed. "Slack for *what*? For being a supreme self-centered prick? For not keeping me informed about the clearly Very Bad Stuff happening here? Caleb *dies* at the end of your *own* book. Do you not remember that? The Committee reels him in, uses him to find the pieces of the Man, then they *slit* his throat so they can open His door. You think you're important because this story you 'thought up' is happening to *you* like some fun little-boy fantasy, but your selective fucking *brain* doesn't remember you're in peril. Peril *you* wrote about!"

"Okay," said Cam. He adjusted his glasses with a pinkie. "How about this. It's my first day of a new job. Hm? A job I *actually* have, by the way. So cut me some *slack* for being stressed about this new job. I'm trying to write something because they keep telling me my writing *means* something. For once. And I got nothin. Nothing! So oh my god, I'm *sorry* I didn't tell you, but it just didn't come up. I'm *sorry* it feels like we're in a book right now, but it's already different, so it's fine. Caleb didn't *have* a girlfriend. If this was actually the book, I'd be here alone, and our house would have a history. 1896 doesn't *have* a history. Nobody was murdered there, nothing is happening. I'm sorry about this one weird coincidence. But fucking drop it."

"You're being the bullshit husband," said Quinn, voice shaking. "You're being the guy who says, 'There's no ghost, babe, go back to sleep. You're being delusional.' And you said you wouldn't be. You promised me we'd be rational people about this, not . . . *caricatures*."

"I never said you're being delusional," Cam said evenly.

"But you're not *listening* to me," she said. "You don't even care."

"Yeah, because you're being a fuckin crazy superstitious bitch!"

They sat in wide-eyed silence. Quinn felt like she'd been shot. She put a hand to her stomach, and almost expected her fingers to come away red.

Cam spared her the humility of having to respond. "Look, I'm sorry." He dug his keys out of his pocket, shoved them at her. "Take the car. Go see the play."

"You want me to drive around at night by my*self*? In Renfield?"

"I don't fuckin know what you want. *I* want to read my work to people who will be impressed by it, and I wanna do what I came here to do. There's no immediate threat here, Quinn. There's a hint of a threat *maybe*, and I'm keeping an eye on it."

"No." She yanked the keys out of his hand. "You're stoked it's keeping an eye on *you*."

He jerked his eyebrows and looked away, a look Quinn (correctly) assumed meant the word *bitch* was flying through his head again.

"I guess I'll see you at home tonight," he said.

"It's not home."

"Whatever. Fine."

"Fine."

They sat there for another moment, before Quinn lurched off the edge of the desk and walked out of the office without a word.

When she emerged outside, she realized she'd drawn blood from her palm, the keys digging into the flesh of her hand. As she stormed to the car, the sunflowers bent away from her, pretending they hadn't been eavesdropping through the wall.

CHAPTER NINE

CAM MEETS MCCALL

Cam's headache continued to blossom throughout the afternoon. For three hours, he sat wincing in the corner of Syd's "Truthfully Blurring the Truth in Memoir" class. He kept picking at the crusted yellow patch on his sleeve, eyes watering, head clanging.

Syd watched him coolly. She kept her braced wrist crossed neat over her other hand (the buckles were rose gold today, the straps white leather), and as Cam answered questions from students, rambled about his work, gave them writing advice he felt vastly underqualified to give ("Adverbs are sorely overrated")—he kept thinking about her little hand, curled up beneath those braces. It made him anxious, knowing it was in there. Didn't it need to breathe?

When class was over, Cam camped out in Slitter Lounge, pretending to write beneath the grand portrait of Matthew Slitter, with his sunflowers and eagle-headed cane. Cam remained there, blinking at a mostly-blank Word Doc, until it was time for the coffeehouse. Then he closed his laptop with a sigh and wondered how he'd ever written a book in the first place.

Writing *is* super hard, to be fair.

When he opened the door to Slitter Auditorium, the only two people there were Madeline and Angie, laughing together as they spread out tables of treats.

"You're early," said Madeline cheerily.

"I know, don't let me bother you. I'll just sit over here and stay out of the way."

"Your eyes okay?" Angie asked.

"Allergies," he mumbled.

Madeline nodded understandingly. "When I started here, the flowers did a number on me, too. You'll get used to it." She put a hand on his wrist. "Do you have anything you can take?"

For a moment, just her asking that made him feel better.

"I'll survive," he smiled.

Madeline's fingers twitched. She took her hand away. "Here. Have an oatmeal raisin ball. They're a coffeehouse staple."

Cam took his ball to a seat in the front row, in the corner. He chewed, watching the women set up. They fiddled forever with plastic wrap, unveiling several moist-looking trays of cookies and brownies and lemon squares. The sound was very loud in the empty room, echoing off all those folded red felt seats. A coffee maker steamed contentedly at the end of one of the tables. Cam kept wincing, his right eye twitching.

Madeline flashed him a grin. "You, uh . . . You get to meet Benny tonight."

"Looking forward to it." Cam smoothed his tie over his stomach, brushing oatmeal-crumbs onto the floor.

"He's a terrific writer," said Madeline.

"She's biased," said Angie.

Madeline gave her arm a playful swat. She leaned into Angie, whispered something, and both women giggled. Cam watched them, sucking oatmeal out of his teeth.

Gradually, the seats began to fill. When the majority had butts in them and half the treat-tables were empty, Angie dimmed the lights. Madeline appeared at the podium. She looked even thinner under the bland spotlight. Her eyes more sunken. Her hands containing more small breakable bones, more poppable veins.

"Good evening, everyone," she beamed, adjusting the mic stand on the podium. It looked very large in her thin fingers. "Welcome . . . to our *first* Slitter Coffeehouse Reading of the semester! We are *very* excited to have this lineup for you tonight. First up, we have Professor Sydney Kim, reading from her new book of essays. Then we have Taylor Sheffield, now a sophomore, welcome *back* . . ."

She read through ten names. Cam sat there picking at his beard until *his* name came out of her mouth. "And last but *cer*tainly not least, our writer in residence this semester: Campbell P. Marion. Whew." She cocked her head, like, *That was a workout*. "Soo many amazing voices here tonight. Let's get the ball rolling with Sy—"

The auditorium door banged open. Light sliced inside. An entire roomful of heads whipped toward it. And with them, Cam saw—for the first time—the silhouette of Benny McCall.

Fluorescence from the hall burned across his umber skin. Where it washed out Madeline's printer-paper features, it made McCall glow. Cam was surprised by how handsome this man was: tall, broad-shouldered, bald, no beard, and cheekbones so sharp they could open bottles. He wore a black suit, a red tie, and shining shoes.

And then he spoke. A jangling, broken sound. Like someone was running his voice through a fan filled with shards of tumbling glass and stone. It fluttered up and down between octaves.

"My apologies," he announced. "I'd like to remind you all that students are *not* allowed to park in the faculty lot." He strode into the room, enunciating his words with each step of his sparkling shoes. "It forces *us* to park farther away, which makes us late. Which makes us *less* inclined to be charitable when we grade. Looking at *you*, Ryan. I recognize your mom's van." He swept razor-eyes over the crowd. A boy in a denim jacket slunk low in his seat.

But then McCall smiled, and all was well. His face was so radiant. "But I'm happy to be here. I just parked on *top* of your car, Ryan. Hope that's alright."

Mild, spooked laughter. Except from Ryan.

McCall passed Cam on his way up the aisle. He nodded, like some wealthy Bond villain. Cam waved in return, like an idiot.

McCall grunted into a seat right behind him. Cam picked at his beard again, willing himself not to turn around.

"Professor McCall, everyone," said Madeline. She smiled up at where he was sitting. "Well," she cleared her throat, "our first reader this evening is Sydney Kim, reading a section from her new book of essays, *Rancid Skin*. Everyone snap for Professor Kim."

To Cam's absolute horror, everyone snapped for Professor Kim.

He felt McCall's eyes digging into the back of his skull as Syd stepped behind the podium. Felt them boring into him for the entire five minutes that Syd read. And he felt them still when the next person (Madeline's student Taylor) got up to read. And the next. And the next.

By the time it was Cam's turn, his head was throbbing loud. He took his place behind the podium as everyone snapped for him, each finger-pop like a firecracker next to his ear. Madeline beamed at him from the side of the stage.

"Hi there," said Cam into the mic. A few muted hellos echoed back from the shadows beyond the lights. He fussed with the mic. "I thought I'd read from my first novel, *The Shattered Man*, which . . . Some of us talked about it today, actually. Um . . ."

McCall was moving in his seat, shifting and wincing around. Cam got the sense this man was rarely comfortable in his body. He kept jostling his elbows up and down, in and out, tangling his ankles around each other, running his tongue over his teeth. He kept doing that, he kept rubbing his tongue over his teeth. Cam could see it bulging out the sides of his cheeks. A thick knob of muscle.

Finally, McCall settled in. He slid down so that the shining top of his head barely peeked above the top of his seat. He cocked his eyebrows at Cam, as if to say, *These fuckin chairs.*

Cam couldn't imagine this man on an airplane.

"Yeokayy," said Cam. "Well. Here goes." He pulled it up on his phone, and began to read. The same section he'd read a hundred times.

McCall folded his hands together before his face, shielding his mouth from the room. His eyes were bright and sharp as Cam read about Caleb, the gummerfolk, the Committee, the regathering of the bloodywood . . . and the opening of the Shattered Man.

For Cam's entire reading, McCall didn't move. He stared at Cam over the tops of his knuckles. An owl, glaring down its beak at a mewling rat it's about to chew up and spit back out.

Cam glanced around the auditorium. He saw Wes, Syd, and Madeline all giving him that same tense look. McCall had a hungry glint in his eye.

Quinn's voice fluttered through his mind. *They slit Caleb's throat at the end. Don't you remember that?*

"And as Caleb tucked the bloodstained wooden board beneath his arm," Cam read, "he had the impression that the Committee was watching him. Like cats about to pounce."

Chett Neeves was the only one in the department who didn't attend the reception in the lounge. Cam met a few of the other faculty members: two playwrights, three prose writers, and some poets who kept frowning into his face with garlic breath. The only light in the room was the cozy green glow of the banker's lamps on the table. From the corner, Wes's little Bluetooth speaker played a mix of Mungo Jerry, Tom Jones, and Harry Nilsson. The table was laden with glasses, booze bottles, and leftover snacks from the reading. Cam found himself enjoying it all, which was a surprise. He usually hated parties.

He asked for a whisky, and Wes poured him a glass of Johnnie Walker. Blue Label.

The department didn't fuck around with its booze.

"I'm surprised you're allowed to have alcohol on campus at all," said Cam.

"Yeah, that's another Slitter policy. Anything good for creativity is good, period. Seniors can even sign up for a key to the lounge's bar-cart. But you have to have, like, a 3.9 GPA or some bullshit. Cheers." Wes clinked his own glass of Blue Label against Cam's.

"Seems like ole Matthew made some pretty big changes when he was here," said Cam.

"Oh yeah. Can't imagine any other department in the *world* would provide its students with liquor. But Slitty believed in the power of good stories."

"So where'd he vanish to? I mean, *that's* a good story. Right?"

Wes shrugged. "Probably murdered, if I had to guess. Some pissed-off trustee. Who knows." He sipped his drink. "Them's the breaks. That's a popular saying around here. 'People go missing all the time. Them's the breaks.' Even Bent's *mayor* went missing, last spring. Just *poof*, gone. She was a pistol. Catherine Mason." He smacked his lips.

"Old flame?" Cam asked.

"Pfft. Yeah, right. I never knew her personally. I'm just saying, it happens all the time around here. Fucking . . . bullshit place," he grumbled. "That's why I want *out*."

"You moving?"

Wes gave him half a smile over the rim of his glass. "In a manner of speaking."

Before Cam could ask what that manner was, a thick hand fell on Wes's shoulder. "Gentlemen!"

Benny McCall.

Madeline hovered a foot behind him as he stuck out a large hand for Cam to shake. That jangling, broken-glass voice again: "Inspired reading, Cameron. I've been *aching* to meet you." Something about the way *aching* rolled out of his mouth made it sound exuberantly sexual.

Cam swallowed. "Uh, it's . . . Campbell, actually. Well, Cam is fine."

"Of course. My mistake. Well. Benny or McCall is fine with me." McCall pumped his hand hard. Then nodded at Wes. "Wesley."

Wes sipped his drink.

"So!" McCall clapped his hands. "What are we drinking? I *love* drinking."

He ran his tongue around the outsides of his teeth, making his entire mouth bulge.

They were actually a nice bunch. The more Cam talked to them, the more he got a sense of their work and their lives. For instance, they all had something in common: they started writing as an outlet, to get over their shitty Renfield childhoods.

Wes had grown up in Babylon, a trailer park just outside Tinker's Falls. His father lost his mining job after The Big Accident, which Cam gathered was shorthand for something any Renfielder would be familiar with. Wes's dad took the sudden unemployment out on Wes, though Wes always had a hunch it wasn't just the alcohol that made him violent—it was something he'd breathed in when the mine collapsed, coughing up dirt from far below the earth, right into Old Man Flannery's lungs. Wes believed this because the only time his father ever left him alone was when he smoked his Noxboros on the porch at sunset. Old wives claimed Noxboros could combat negative Renfield energy for as long as they burned. Perhaps the smoke cleared Old Man Flannery out, for a few minutes at a time. Wes's first collection of stories was *A Cigarette's Worth of Time*, because that's how long the violence would stay out of his home. He always wondered if his father smoked on purpose, though he knew that was wishful thinking. Fathers tend to be too self-involved to understand their impact on their children.

Madeline had been driven to a brief stay at the Bent Asylum for "hysteria and nerves" when she was thirteen. Her mother wanted her to be a ballerina and a model. Madeline had gotten used to eating a very small bean salad for dinner each night. Had gotten used to blind dates with older high school boys from affluent Lillian families, in their blue-and-silver Lillian Academy ties. Had gotten used to the blowjob lessons her mom made her older sister give her, so Madeline could "keep her man by the balls." But she *never* got used to the way her mother would crouch by the side of her bed at night, clawing at her hair and gurgling, *Such a good little girl, make her just the way we want. So good, so pretty, so thin . . .* Over and over until dawn.

When she emerged from the Bent Asylum at fourteen, released back into her mother's care, Madeline discovered that she was able to touch other people and receive their pain. She held her mother for hours as the woman wheezed into her arms. It shrunk Madeline's bones. Made her guts constrict. But it made her mother's breathing easier. Made their home more bearable. She called this her "blood talent." She actually *thanked* Renfield for it.

Madeline ate so much pain over the years, first as a guidance counselor at Bent High School, then as a poetry professor at Edenville. Scooping up the angsty, bitter poems about lost high school loves, stifling home lives—all forms of middling liberal arts oppression. Her first book of poetry: *The Sour Taste of All Your Spiders*.

The only person who didn't seem to have a story was McCall. He didn't talk about himself or his writing. He just stood there, drinking and listening.

At one point, they were all standing by the leather couch. Wes was talking about some book he liked when McCall abruptly sucked air through his teeth and pointed at Cam. "By the way, I just loved *your* book."

"Oh. Thank you."

"I don't know what he said that just reminded me of it so I *had* to say something, but I just thought it was excellent."

"That's . . . really nice, thank you," Cam smiled.

"Mm." McCall ran his tongue around his teeth. He leaned forward, eyes growing wide, and with that strange, glassbreak voice, he recited, "The Shattered Man, with wild hair. You better run, avoid His stare . . ." He shook his glass. The ice rattled. "Haunting. A very good, very . . . *haunting* little poem."

"Thanks," said Cam, for a third time. Smiling proudly.

"And I think it's clever, your . . . descriptions of something bleeding into our world. From . . . somewhere else."

"Well, don't fire me, but I think I accidentally stole the idea. My girlfriend was just telling me earlier about some old Renfield urban legend . . . ?"

"Ahh. Of course." McCall crunched a cube of ice between his teeth. Chewing, he said, "The giant."

"Yes! I mean, it wasn't really on purpose," Cam backtracked. "I mean, I must've . . . read about it somewhere? And forgotten? I don't know."

"So funny how the subconscious works like that," said McCall. "How it . . . incubates information and ideas. Without you even noticing."

"But you didn't *see* that attic anywhere beforehand," said Syd. "You *didn't* know."

"No, that's true," said Cam. His eye twitched.

"You want another?" Wes asked. "Here, I'll take your empty."

He vanished from the semi-circle surrounding Cam. Only then did Cam realize he was surrounded. The rest of the department had gone. Just the five of them now.

"So as far as you know," said McCall, "you made that story up."

Cam laughed nervously. "I . . . thought so, yeah." He glanced at Syd.

"Hm." McCall crunched another ice cube, keeping his eyes on Cam.

"Say more about what you're writing now, Cam," said Madeline. She looped her arm around McCall's back. He ignored her.

Cam looked at Wes, pouring whisky. "Oh, well . . . Nothing really."

"Nothing?" Syd asked.

"Don't you feel inspired?" McCall asked. "Just *being* here?"

"I don't know, I haven't really . . ."

"You haven't written *any* more about the Shattered Man?" Syd asked.

"Uh," said Cam. "No, I . . ."

Wes handed him his drink.

"Here's a question," said Syd. "At the end of your book, the Committee manages to find *all* the scattered pieces of wood that make up the Shattered Man. They rebuild Him, they enter His doorway, and they leave Earth."

"Right," said Cam. "And they basically just end up in Hell. His Hell."

"But there are *other* worlds, too, yes? Better ones?"

"Oh, that wasn't . . . in my dream," said Cam awkwardly. He flicked his eyes around the group. "My dream didn't say."

Wes's speaker had gone quiet. The room was silent.

McCall breathed loud through his nose. "Well. I'm sure you'll figure it out in the sequel. We're all *very* curious."

They nodded enthusiastically, way too close to him.

"Sure," said Cam. "Of course."

"I do *love* stories," said McCall. "Seeing. Transcribing. The mind is truly capable of anything." He raised his glass. "To the mind."

Everyone echoed, "To the mind."

". . . mind," finished Cam, a second late. Several pairs of eyes watched him over the rims of their glasses as they drank.

"You know," said McCall. He ran his tongue around his mouth. Laughed. "The thing about your idea is . . . Well. Someone has already written it."

Cam blinked. "I . . . don't know what you mean."

"Your book," said McCall. "Someone has already written it."

"But I wrote it three years ago. I . . . It was based on a *dream*." He glanced at Syd, hoping for some validation here.

She said nothing.

"Of course," said McCall. "But when you awoke *from* that dream, I'd wager that you were crying. Is that right?"

"How did you—"

"But they weren't . . . normal tears. Were they."

"No."

McCall smiled. "That's because they weren't tears at all, Cameron. In fact, we call it Aether. It's the stuff that binds *our* world to many, many others."

Cam glanced around. "I . . . don't follow."

"You saw that attic," McCall explained, "or a version of it, anyway, when your consciousness was *pushed* through the fabric between realms. And when your mind returned to your body, having seen the gummerfolk and the Man, it was soaked in . . . Well, *some* call it ectoplasm. Dream resin. Spinal fluid. *We* call it Interplanal Aether."

Slowly, Cam shook his head. "I'm sorry. Ya lost me. You *so* lost me."

Syd spoke up. "In your book, you call them the Committee for the Reconstruction of the Shattered Man. We don't call our*selves* that. We call ourselves the sub-department of the Creative Writing team."

"What," said Cam.

"And we don't call that nightmare thing the Shattered Man," said Madeline. "*We* call it . . . the Renfield giant."

"Okay, hold the fuck on." Cam adjusted his glasses with his pinkie. "You're saying I had this dream because my brain . . . flew to another world? And got soaked in . . . space juice? And then continued *leaking* space juice when I wrote it all down."

"Precisely," said McCall.

Cam stared at him. ". . . what."

"Here." McCall drained his drink, addressed Madeline for the first time (she was still barnacled to his side). "Where's that copy of *Shattered Man*?" She went to a box in the corner marked *C.M.* She took his book from the box, and brought it back to the group.

McCall waved Cam over to the couch. Cam plopped down onto the green leather, and McCall sat in the chair facing him. McCall cracked *Shattered Man*'s spine and lay it flat on the table between them.

"Okay." McCall took some pages out of his breast pocket. "*This* was written by a student last semester. She had no prior awareness of your work." He unfolded the papers and smoothed them out over the coffee table, sliding the blade of his palm over the creases. "And *this* was written by a young girl in 1974." He took out another sheaf of papers, significantly dryer and yellower. He unfolded them and splayed them out next to the first stack.

Cam watched, silent. Something weird was happening in his chest. A swimmy feeling that made him simultaneously excited and overwhelmed. Like he was a small-town musician *finally* signing his life to a big-shot manager, but something far down in his gut was telling him, *This man will not be kind to you . . .*

"And *this* one," said McCall, voice cracking, "was written by Carter Moone, a playwright and member of the Lillian elite. Moved in the same social circles as Boldiven Grittwood and Jacob Slitter, Matthew's father. He shared *this* piece at a holiday party in Lillian in 1948."

This set of papers was the driest and yellowest by far. McCall removed them delicately from his breast pocket and placed them on the table with the utmost care. He unfolded them gently, and instead of smoothing them out, just let them lie. He sat back, folded his hands over his stomach. He smiled, gesturing at the short stacks of paper on the table. "Please. Take a look."

Cam looked around the room. All eyes were on him.

"They're identical," he said, not looking at the pages. "That's the point, right?"

McCall lifted a hand. *Indeed.*

"Well, they're not *exactly* alike," said Wes. "Not word for word."

"No," agreed McCall. "There *are* variations in diction and style. Each individual voice shines through. For instance, you have a line of dialogue *here* . . ." McCall sat forward, pointing to a section on *Shattered Man*'s third page. "And if we turn to Moone's piece . . ." He picked up the old, yellowed papers and flipped through to their third page. He held it out. "The same line of dialogue in the same position. Moone's is slightly longer, but his work tends to be a bit wordy overall. However, the text on both pages is shaped largely the same. See?"

He was right. As he held the page next to Cam's, Cam could see exactly what he meant. Some of Moone's paragraphs were longer, some shorter. But both pages began and ended in the same place in the story.

Cam flipped through the other stacks of paper. Their third pages all looked the same, too. As did the fourth page. And the fifth.

He stood. "I don't understand how that's possible. I mean . . . Right? This?" He pointed at the papers. "Is fucking impossible."

McCall gave a short, sharp laugh. "Yes, I suppose that's . . . what I was hoping you'd say."

"Well, then what the fuck." Panic needled into Cam's voice. "This was *my* idea. That's not possible. That's not . . ." *That's not fair* was the thought that crossed his mind.

"Nothing is ever *made* up," said McCall. "Ever. Ideas exist . . . in the Aether. They're simply transmitted. From elsewhere."

Syd chimed in. "Carter Moone believed that when Lawrence killed his family and painted that giant, he did something so insane it ripped a hole in the very fabric of our reality. When the barn was taken apart, that hole was scattered into pieces. But it can be built again."

Cam sputtered. "But what's the point of, of *seeing* this shit if it's already been seen?"

"Because we haven't seen *all* of it yet," said McCall. "What we're trying to accomplish here is using pieces of work *about* the giant in order to rebuild Him. Your gift to see is exactly what we're interested in. You wrote about the giant without ever having set foot in Renfield. You can *see* where pieces of Him have gone. Where people have taken them over the years. *You* can help us rebuild His door."

"But all I've seen of the other side of that door is monsters," said Cam. Remembering the gummerfolk made him shiver. "Why would you want that?"

"We believe there are *better* worlds on the other side of His door," said Madeline. "We just need help getting to them."

Cam's head throbbed. He could barely focus on what they were saying. *Quinn was right. I'm in my own fucking book.*

McCall went on. "The Renfield barnwood is something of a commodity. People have trouble parting with their pieces of it. And you'd be surprised where some of those pieces have ended up. Even . . ." He pointed up at Matthew Slitter. Cam followed his finger, and his eyes fell upon the eagle-headed cane.

"He made himself a cane out of cursed wood?" Cam asked.

"Why not?" said McCall. "He believed it had tremendous power. He still has it with him, wherever he is."

Cam stared at the papers on the table. His eyes stung so bad. "I don't . . . So . . . What do you want from *me*? I can't see *where* the pieces are. I mean, I don't—"

"Right." McCall began to fold up all his papers. "We've pooled our resources here and we have *quite* a few pieces between us. Syd's found most of them. Finding things *is* her blood talent, after all."

Syd saluted him with her small hand.

"Personally," said McCall, tucking papers back in his pockets, "I inherited a number of pieces from Mayor Catherine Mason. She was a . . . good friend. I was sorry to hear she disappeared, but them's the breaks, of course. Before she did, she bequeathed her collection of bloodywood to me." He smiled, pleased with himself.

"What if someone destroys a piece?" Cam asked. "Aren't you screwed then?"

"Oh, it can't be done," said McCall. "Renfield won't *let* you. The barnwood can never be burned or pulped."

"Sorta like *Lord of the Rings*," added Wes. "You try to melt the ring and it . . . puts up a fuss."

"So it *is* possible," said Syd, "to find all this wood and reconstruct the door. That's why we've been gathering information from seers like yourself. To find the remaining pieces."

"Which is why your work is so vital to us," said McCall. "Even if it's not really yours."

Cam shook his head. "This is fucking insane."

"Don't feel bad your book was unoriginal," said Madeline. "All art is mad in its own way."

"I don't think that's helpful," said McCall.

Cam shook his head more. He felt like his brain was sloshing around inside his skull. He closed his eyes. "I . . . thought I was supposed to write something *important* here. Syd *said* that—"

"You do have a chance here," said McCall. "To write something *world*-changing—but no one will ever read it. It'll just be for us."

"But why *not* publish it?"

"Well, there are . . . other initiatives out there who would love to know what *we* know about the door. Most of them are benign. Collectors, kids with too much time on their hands . . . We had a run-in just last month with a true-crime fanatic who had the actual *gun* Renfield used in 1927. If those people knew where we kept the wood, they might attempt to steal it for themselves. And we don't like sharing."

"But . . . But you don't even know where the doorway *leads*," said Cam, his voice rising. "If you're saying that the entire county is cursed *because* of this doorway, why would you *ever*—"

"It's a leap of faith," said McCall. His tone made it clear that this was the end of the discussion. Cam glanced around the group. They watched him, breathing steadily.

"It's a lot to process," said Madeline. "Simply put, Renfield is a depression on the face of this earth. We've all been victims to it, in one way or another. But there *are* better worlds up there somewhere, free from this depression. Worlds we can reach with your help. We just need the last few missing pieces."

Wes coughed loudly. "And we're running a bit short on time."

Cam blinked. He glanced at the door.

"I understand," said McCall. "You don't believe us."

"I . . . don't know how to," said Cam. "I feel . . . I don't know."

"Of course. Well." McCall looked around the group. He spread his hands. "Would you like to meet Him?"

"Meet who?"

McCall laughed. "Your Shattered Man, of course. Come." He rose. "He's just downstairs. In the undercampus."

CHAPTER TEN

THE EDENVILLE PLAYERS PRESENT: *NO LONGER LAWRENCE*

A crooked old lady with a poof of thin yellow hair (through which Quinn could see her pink wrinkled scalp) handed Quinn a program on her way into the theater. The program was about three pages long, printed on white paper and unevenly folded by hand. Quinn loved it. She held it to her nose and breathed.

Shouldn't be breathing that shit in. You're supposed to be solving a mystery here, finding Celeste, helping Cam, not . . . whatever this is. Whatever this odd contented feeling was. This growing sense that she somehow belonged here.

The Edenville Stage-Barn was a massive creaky building with an impressively deep stage. An ocean of orange-cushioned seats filled the house, and high above, in the rafters, ceiling fans churned lazily. It was ten minutes until curtain, and the space was maybe two-thirds full, which Quinn thought was impressive for a Wednesday night. She didn't know how many people lived in Edenville, but it certainly didn't give the impression of containing more than two thousand or so. Nearly two hundred of them were here tonight. Clearly, this play was as well-loved as Marcia had told her it would be.

She flipped through the little program bitterly. She was furious at Cam, but angry at herself as well. Because, of course, there *was* the possibility that . . . he was right. Maybe she'd connected dots that were, like . . .

just dots. Maybe everything was fine. Or maybe the county was already digesting her. Slowly.

In the back of the program, she came across a brief history of the play. In bold Comic Sans: "We all know the story. On August 28, 1927, Lawrence Renfield was kicked in the head by a mule."

She almost laughed out loud. That detail hadn't been in the library box or in *The Shattered Man*.

"In the months that followed," she read on, "Lawrence's wife and children (as well as his friend and neighbor Otto Mason) observed a change in Lawrence. He became distant and agitated. He spoke of bad dreams— nightmares about other worlds, where blood ran from the trees. Adelaide, Lawrence's wife, described the man as 'no longer himself.' Otto told her she was probably overreacting.

"This is the story of what happened to Lawrence, his family, and his friends over the four months that led up to the Renfield massacre in December 1927. This is the story of how the giant came to be."

What if Cam was no longer himself? What if he was being reeled in and hollowed out? What if Syd had done something to him in that attic? What if . . . What if there was a chance he could be saved? And even more enticing—what if there was a chance Celeste could still be saved as well?

Quinn realized exactly why this play had wide appeal. If Celeste was just dead, that was one thing. But if she was something *else*? Like, if Cam was just an asshole, that was unfixable. But if he were being possessed? If he were actually a decent guy warped by Renfield's radioactivity? *Then* there was wiggle room. A crack of hope that Quinn could jam her foot inside, keep the Cam-door from slamming shut forever.

If it wasn't his fault, Quinn wouldn't have to give up on him.

But that was a fool's hope. Because he'd been an asshole long before he'd even *heard* of Renfield. That door had shut long ago. Why was she still rattling the knob?

"Anyone sitting here?"

Quinn jumped, slicing her finger along the edge of the program, "Shhhit. Sorry. No, no, you can take it."

The person who took the seat turned out to be the latest in a long line of little old ladies. She smelled of rancid pineapple and Windex. Her dark red hair was so stiff, Quinn could hear it crunch when she moved her head.

"I know there are plenty of other seats," she said, "and I hope you don't mind. I just like to sit *next* to someone when I'm at the theater. Helps you feel the energy of the play, don't you think?"

"I can appreciate that," said Quinn. She sucked at her finger. "Are you related to anybody involved? Cast, crew?"

"One of the gentlemen was a student of mine. He graduated, oh . . . seven years ago? I think he's playing the neighbor, Otto Mason."

"Where do you teach?"

"Lillian Academy." She held out her hand. "Winnifred Hetch, though everyone calls me Winnie or, of course, Ms. Hetch."

"Quinn," said Quinn. "Quinn Rose Carver-Dobson."

"Oh, a very sharp name," said Winnie. "Lots of hard syllables." She began digging in her purse. Leather and mint wafted out of its maw. "Nice of you to trust me with your full name, by the way. I could be a witch. Could use your name to cast *blood* magic."

"Renfield does seem like a place that'd have witches."

Winnie shook her head, produced a lip balm from her purse. "Noo, the ground is much too poisonous. Real witches would never have it. I've never met a witch, but . . . I can imagine." The way she said that made it sound like she had met plenty of *other* creatures.

"I'm sorry," said Quinn, "I'm not from around here. Am I supposed to know you? I just realized you said your name very grandly."

Winnie smeared her lips. "Oh?" Smacked em. "Where are you from?"

"Leaden Hollow. My husband just got a job at the college." *Why am I lying like this? I didn't even* mention *the city, and he's* not *my goddamn husband.*

Winnie chucked the lip-tube back in her purse. "I've heard Leaden Hollow is dreadful."

"I've heard the same thing about Edenville."

"Depends. Anyway, the Hetches are an ooold Renfield family. Like the Masons or the Mithers or the Grittwoods."

"Okay."

"You've never heard of them either."

Quinn frowned, then, "Oh! Mither! Yes. Clarity Mither was the one who went missing from the college."

Winnie rolled her eyes. "Pfft. She never. She's at some summer intensive somewhere. She calls home every few days."

Quinn blinked. "She . . . she *calls* home."

"Of course. She isn't *missing*. Her mother just *thinks* she is, for some reason. Couldn't stop talking about it over bridge last week, when I finally agreed to play. She talks to Clarity *on* the phone and then claims it's not her, it's someone else."

"Who?"

"Who knows. Not me. I don't have the mind for that kind of thing."

"Geez," Quinn murmured. She glanced around. The seats around them were filling.

"Her mother," said Winnie. "Greta? She's a bit loony, that's all. Got the Renfield under her skin. But them's the breaks." A light shrug.

Quinn leaned in. "So that's real? I mean, that's a real story people tell?"

"About Clarity Mither?"

"No, the *blood*." Quinn glanced around again. Little old ladies, everywhere. "The curse on the county. I thought it was maybe just a . . . weird story. But it's true, isn't it? Renfield blood soaked into the ground, mutated everything. The barnwood, too."

"That's what they say." Winnie frowned. Her eyes flickered between Quinn's, studying her. "But yes, people believe it. *I* believe it."

"But what does it . . . do? The blood."

Winnie threw up her coconut-stink hands, red nails flashing. "Whatever it likes, I imagine. Changes people. Takes them. I bet you ask anyone here, they'd *all* have a story. We've seen ghosts, tree-monsters, things that were *not* cockroaches . . . It's just part of life. The land here is a bit *hungry*, that's all. Ever since December 1927, when old Lawrence Renfield sent his family to heaven." She cocked an eyebrow. "I used to jump rope to that rhyme."

Quinn frowned and sucked at her wounded finger. It was already done bleeding, but it occurred to her that the program was made of paper and the paper was made of wood, and now that wood had tasted her.

She shook the thought away. "Yeah, truth be told, this whole thing makes me think of my . . . partner. He's been kind of different since we got here. And I don't know how to complain about it without making it seem like . . . he can't win with me, you know? But I *know* something is going on with him. I confronted him about it this afternoon and he . . . was just a prick."

Winnie nodded gravely. "I validate your concern. If you have a gut feeling about something, trust it."

"You don't think I'm being . . . oversensitive?"

"Oh no." She leaned in, talked out the corner of her mouth. "You may have noticed that most of the people who live here are, well . . . ." She roved her eyes around conspiratorially. Several Winnie copies sat near them, laughing and gossiping with vacant grins. White poofs of hair filled the space with a nauseating cloud of perfume.

"Was it supposed to be a secret?" said Quinn.

"No. We've all come from other places around the county. I grew up in the Mill, for instance. Things tend to happen *all* over Renfield. But Edenville is the farthest town from the lake, and all the rivers. There's a clear gradient in stories around the valley. They thin out the farther away from Bartrick Lake, and the site of the old Renfield farm, you get. Edenville is, true to its name, a nicer town. So we flock." She threw up her hands. "Sue us."

"So you *all* have experiences?"

"Mmhmm."

Quinn asked her next question all in one breath: "Has anyone seen a woman in a hospital gown dragging a dead deer around?"

It was Winnie's turn to blink at Quinn. "Is that . . . something *you've* seen?"

"A long time ago, yeah."

Winnie drew a breath through her nose. "Well. I don't know anything *about* it, but . . . I believe it. Did it *mean* something to you? This woman in the gown?"

"It meant everything," said Quinn. "She killed my friend."

The lights dimmed. The women began to applaud. Color floated up onto the stage and a frazzly-haired woman came out, beaming through crooked teeth.

"Hello ladies," she said. "Welcome to our special closing-night performance of *No Longer Lawrence,* by Carter Moone, on the ninety-second anniversary of Lawrence's kick in the head." A smattering of applause took her by surprise. "Ah. Yes. Good. Thank you. Um. Please turn off your cellphones and . . . be aware that this play contains some of the *usual* adult content." She rattled off a very long trigger warning. "But before we begin, we have an announcement from one of our own." Her face tightened, deadly serious. "Please give your attention to Greta Marie Mither."

Winnie was impressed. "Oh my." She clapped. Everyone else clapped, so Quinn clapped, too.

The woman who wandered onstage was pale, and had the darkest rings beneath her eyes that Quinn had ever seen in real life. She had tight white curls around her head. Quinn had the sense they'd very recently been blond. The woman swallowed a large lump before she addressed the crowd: "Hello. It's been a very . . . long time since I've spoken to you all. And I apologize for that." She fidgeted. "But I have a request for you now. Many of you know that my daughter Clarity has been missing for several months. And . . . I'm at the end of my rope. If any of you know anything about her disappearance, please, please, *please* let me know? Clarity, if you're out there," she gazed into the dark of the audience, "please come home to me. I miss you. I love you. Your father loves you. Your brother and sister, Charlie and Jess—*they* love you. Please. Come home. I . . ." This part seemed particularly difficult to say. "I've been thinking of coming back to a meeting. If you'll all have me. I've been thinking of . . . unburdening my mind. I just . . . I want to know what happened to my daughter. I want to know. I . . ." She paused, jaw quivering. "That's all. Thank you. I hope to see you next week. Praise to the Mind."

She wandered back offstage. No one clapped this time. Murmurs throughout the room. Whispered echoes: "Praise to the Mind."

Winnie leaned over, breathed butterscotch in Quinn's ear. "Greta was a *won*derful member of the Society. But she moved away before we could initiate her properly. Now she's been sniffing around the last few weeks.

Keeps wandering around campus, putting up Missing posters. Poor thing. Bless her heart."

Quinn's skin felt hot and scratchy. She felt even less sure of herself. Clarity wasn't missing at all? There wasn't any mystery to it except Greta's own madness? Were those truly the breaks? That picture from the library *had* been blurry, after all. Maybe . . .

Quinn slid down in her seat, gripping her program tightly in both hands.

The play began.

When Quinn was in middle school, they all read *A Midsummer Night's Dream*. It ate up a solid month's worth of curriculum. They even watched the movie with Kevin Kline (except they skipped over the really sexy parts, which was a bummer). Then the adults shoved every seventh-grader in Leaden Hollow Middle (go Blue Jays) onto a bus and sent them to the Accabon Theater downtown to see a community production of *Midsummer*. Quinn couldn't remember anything from that production—except the magic flower. Whenever the magic flower came out (a purplish-pink, plastic-lookin thing), the actors would pluck a shining star from the prop. They'd hold a brilliant dot of LED white between their fingers, then drop it in the eye of Demetrius, Lysander, Titania.

Quinn was mesmerized. How did they do that??

It was probably pretty simple. They used to have finger-lights like that in cereal boxes. You could pretend you were ET. Pinch the button, and release.

Easy.

But Quinn would *never* figure out how they did the things they did in *No Longer Lawrence*.

The play opened with a phantasmagorical sequence set to "White Winter Hymnal." That was the first kicker. Shuffle God had *just* played that for her. She was riveted, unable to blink. According to God, she was *exactly* where she needed to be.

Before the song hit, the sequence began with a silent, empty house. Kitchen, stairs leading up, a doorway into the living room. The furniture had been scraped away. Wide blankets of dark stain pooled over the floorboards of the entire set. Wind whistled outside, cold and lonesome.

A man strode onstage, thumbs hooked in his suspenders. He looked around the hollow house, clearly angry.

"That's my student," Winnie over-enunciated in Quinn's ear.

Quinn nodded appreciatively. So that must be Otto Mason, the Renfields' neighbor.

Otto moved in a full circle round the kitchen, growing angrier and angrier.

Then he spat onto the floor. And the "Hymnal" began.

Men burst onto the stage, carrying furniture. They placed it precisely where it belonged: a dining table in the kitchen, an armchair in the living room, a crib up the stairs. Next, the men carried in large frozen sheets of what looked like red Jell-O. They laid the sheets down, fitting the pieces together like a jigsaw. They hammered them down onto the floor with chisels and picks. An hour later, in Act Two, it would become clear to Quinn what this was. When Lawrence gunned down his family, their blood had frozen across the floor. The neighbors had hacked it apart with hammers and buried the sheets of bloody ice in the backyard, behind the barn, where it thawed into a brook in the spring. From a certain perspective, the county curse was the neighbors' fault.

As the "Hymnal" went on, the men returned carrying bodies. They carried a limp woman to the kitchen sink, stood her upright. She had a ragged hole in her stomach. Quinn could see straight through it. They carried on a young boy (*Henry*, Quinn thought), a teenage girl (*May*), and a swaddled baby, so fresh she was still unnamed. They placed these bodies around the set. The men took one last lap round the house, examining their handiwork. Then dispersed. And Lawrence Renfield came onstage. He led little Robert, grim, by the hand. The two smiled thinly, the way dead always smile. Lawrence guided Robert upstairs. As they went, Quinn noticed that the bloodstain along the steps was shimmering under their feet. In fact, the sheets of frozen gore around the entire *house* were beginning to ripple. They were melting. Moving. And before she knew it, they were rising. Running in small rivulets up, up, and swimming through the air. They dove into Adelaide's ragged wound. They filled her up until she was whole again. And there she was, unholed, washing vegetables at the sink. A book flew out from Henry's chest, unpulped itself, and he sat in the armchair in the living room, reading. Buckshot and splinters plucked themselves from May's body, reattached to the door of the second-floor bathroom just as she stepped inside and shut that door behind her.

Lawrence stood on the second-floor landing, watching the blood on the floor sweep itself up, thaw itself out, and swim back into its owners. When everyone was whole again, Lawrence took a deep breath. He took a shotgun from behind a sideboard. And in the concluding moments of the "Hymnal," he went around the house and blew out everyone's blood all over again. *Blam*, Adelaide crumpled over the sink. *Boom*, Henry's book went flying through his stomach, out the other side. Lawrence stomped back upstairs and boomed May out of existence through the bathroom door. Quinn ducked her head, not watching as he smack-smack-*smack*ed the butt of the gun into the crib. Robert made a break for it out the back door, upstage. Lawrence followed. He stuck the end of the barrel against the back of Robert's head, the poor boy crying on his stomach in the snow.

Boom, the head was gone. Where did it go? How did they do that? It was just . . . gone. No lighting trick. No smirking crew member hiding backstage with a rope. Robert's head fucking *exploded*.

Lawrence dragged the headless thing deep upstage, where a scrim began to glow with the image of the barn. The song ended, and Quinn watched in horror as the man dipped his hands into Robert's torn stump of a neck, then splashed him across the wall in absolute silence. It took him five full minutes to paint the giant, and he did it all in total, ear-ringing silence. For a flash of a second, just as he was dipping back in, the actor's face looked like Cam's.

When she saw Him there, in full color, she knew for sure. Cam was wrong. She wasn't imagining anything. She wasn't being paranoid. *That* was the Shattered Man. He didn't quite look like the cover of Cam's book. Didn't look how she'd always imagined Him, when she'd read the book herself. But all the same, Quinn knew for a fucking *fact* that it was Him. His two gently curved arms, two straight legs. And the head. The head was nothing more than a madman mass of hair, screaming around the pair of slit-eyes. The blood of the eyes was rich and dark.

Quinn didn't move a muscle for the rest of the play.

After the "Hymnal," time reversed even further, then moved forward linearly to carry the audience through the last four months of the Renfield clan. Quinn watched a mule kick the shit out of Lawrence. She watched Adelaide express her concerns about him (Lawrence, not the mule) to her friend Edna Mason, who expressed *her* concerns to her husband, Otto, who told her she was probably being hysterical. Eventually, the play ended with a truncated version of the massacre, the neighbors burying blood behind the barn, and the melted blood running down into the Masons' crops the following spring. Their son, Otto Jr., ate a bloodied pod of peas. And three hours later, he hung himself in his room.

As they cut him down in the play's final scene, the detective who'd been working the massacre chomped his cigar. He was an old mustached man with sad eyes. The other characters all called him Walt, though the program referred to him as Detective Harren.

"This," he declared, to no one in particular except the audience, "will only be the beginning of the madness. We'll *all* be mad soon, in our own little ways."

Quinn sensed movement in the corner of her eye. She glanced over. Winnie was mouthing the words along with the actors.

"Oh, come on," said Rook, the Renfield County Sheriff. An overweight man with greasy black hair. "We won't *all* be. I won't. *You* won't."

"No, Rook," said Detective Walt Harren. He slipped his hat back on his head. "I'm already madder than I care to admit."

The Sheriff scoffed. "Really. How can you tell?"

Harren looked down at his hands. The cigar smoked tiredly between his lips.

"Because last night," he said, and Winnie said it along with him, "I tried to eat my own son. I *chewed* on him, Rook. Swallowed three of his fingers before my wife pulled me off him. And I don't even remember it happening."

"Your student was great," said Quinn. "He had me chokin up in that scene when he found his son hanging."

"Oh, truly wonderful," said Winnie. "The *best* production I've seen of that play since the *last* production I saw."

Their shoes crunched on the gravel lot outside. Crickets sang at the edges of the woods, in the field behind the barn.

"Yeah, that was . . . fun," said Quinn. "That's a weird thing to say about a play that ends in multiple brutal murders, but . . ."

"But it *was* a rush," said Winnie. "I just love seeing a good story I know by heart, you know? I find it comforting." She glanced up at the sky. "Speaking of . . . You've heard of the Historical Society, no?"

"No."

"Oh! Well. It's a kind of . . . book club. We meet on Wednesday evenings, every week. Our meeting *this* week was canceled—Anniversary of the Mule and all—but you should come next time. I think you'd get a lot out of it."

"What do you . . . do?"

"Discuss history, of course! We share legends and campfire stories. All kinds of things."

"You just sit in a circle and chat?"

"More or less." Winnie kicked at a rock, sent it tumbling into the shadowed grass beyond the lot. "We'd *love* to have you. Seven o'clock, in the library basement. And it's not a *creepy* basement, it's an event hall. Sometimes there's community dinners down there. Spaghetti lunches. It's nice."

Quinn wasn't reassured. People don't need to make disclaimers about normal basements. "But I don't have any stories to share."

"Talk about your . . . deer woman. Or your husband. The point of the Society is validation, Quinn. We *validate* what every one of us has been through." She turned, walked to her car.

Quinn was just thinking, *Like I'm gonna voluntarily enter a weird basement*, when Winnie called back over her car-roof, "You're not mad. If you feel your husband is slipping, he probably is. It was nice to meet you, Quinn Rose Carver-Dobson."

Quinn was taken aback. "Likewise, Winnifred Hetch."

With that, Winnie climbed into her car and was gone, leaving Quinn alone in the Renfield dark. Surrounded by the stars and crickets and new facts.

Clarity wasn't missing. Cam was probably communicating with some evil mind-warping giant. And no one knew anything yet about the thing that'd taken Celeste. The woman with the deer and the hospital bracelets in her hair.

CHAPTER ELEVEN

A TAPESTRY OF GORE

When McCall said the giant was "just downstairs," that was a bit of an overstatement. Cam realized this as they walked the long dim hall of Slitter's sub-basement, lined with *very* unused offices. Mouse shit scattered across the rot-carpeted floor. Spiderwebs nestled in every corner. Musty piles of books, dying in empty alcoves. A white-brick classroom loomed through an open doorway, filled with broken, ancient wooden desks still in rows, filled with ghosts.

The first locked door, at the end of this hall, was tall and metal, heavily barred. McCall approached it, dug a thing of keys from his pocket, located a bent brass one, and unlocked it. The door screamed open. Humid shadows lurked within. McCall stepped aside and looked at Cam.

"Uh," said Cam. "Please. After you."

"Cameron." McCall smiled. "Come now. *Every* college campus has tunnels underneath. Besides, if we wanted to harm you, we would have done it already. Don't you think?"

Cam glanced into the open doorway. It looked too creepy for its own good.

But he stepped through anyway, putting his back to McCall. McCall stepped inside after him, the other professors followed, and the door slammed shut, sending a sonic boom down the length of the hall. Locking Cam in with a group of people he barely knew.

"As late as the 1990s, I believe, they were sticking faculty down in these offices," said McCall. "Can you imagine?" He waved at wooden doors they passed. Cam had the impression that terrible things were on the other sides of them, cocooned and waiting. The air was so dry and warm he began to sweat.

McCall paused at a second door, rummaging through his ring of keys for a large, dark one that looked more knife than key. Something steam-hissed, something Cam couldn't see. It made him flinch, turn around. The sound was coming from a door behind him. A door featuring a very new-looking lock. Three locks, in fact. And a wheel that looked like it belonged on a bank vault. Machinery ground and banged on the other side of this very locked door. Cam thought, for a moment, he heard someone cry out.

McCall finally found the key he wanted, unlocked the door, and swung it open. Just inside was the mouth of a wide tunnel, lit by a single string of industrial caged bulbs, running away down the tunnel's throat. They dangled from a latticework of roots, looping up and down out of the ceiling in a massive pale tangle.

Waiting patiently, at the lip of the tunnel-mouth, was a golf cart.

"Wanna drive?" McCall asked. "Straight shot."

"You go ahead," said Cam.

Wes and Syd fit themselves onto the seat-bench on the back of the cart, with only a mild lack of grace. McCall and Cam squeezed into the front. Madeline made an attempt to climb, smiling, onto McCall's lap. The cart groaned beneath them.

"The weight, baby," he said. "We don't *all* need to come."

"That's okay," she said, climbing back off. She made a brave face. "Being near Him hurts, anyway. I'll see you later?"

"You bet."

"I love you," she added as McCall drove away, not looking at her. An embarrassed vibe rippled over the cart, but Cam wasn't sure if he should be embarrassed for McCall or Madeline.

"Where are we going?" Cam asked. He was gripping the sweaty leather edge of his seat. Worry prodded at the back of his ribs.

"The old site of the Lillian Art School," said McCall. "It had tunnels, too. Rumor has it Boldiven Grittwood built the undercampus himself, so he could meet his lover in secret. A freshman at E.C."

"Gross," said Syd.

"To each their own," said McCall.

"And the giant's down *here*?" Cam asked.

"Oh yeah."

"Why is it so far away?"

McCall smirked. "Patience."

They drove in silence. Cam was about to ask how far they were going to go (*We must be driving for miles*), when the smell hit him. The charred, gristly smell. The tunnel grew narrower. The earth was blackened. It reeked of smoke.

McCall pulled the cart to a stop before yet another very-locked door, dug into the dirt wall of the tunnel. Everyone got out. Wes coughed.

McCall jangled his keys again, searching. "This is the southern edge of the School's main studio. Or its basement, at least. It was beautiful once. A series of cabins on the edge of Bartrick Lake. Son of a . . . bastard." He couldn't find the key he wanted. "A bit of history for you: When Grittwood first began teaching at the Lillian Art School, at the beginning of the First World War, he found that a number of his students were sketching and painting the same subject. Four or five of them. He feared there might be a . . . plagiaristic conspiracy afoot, so he called them all into his office. The students denied any knowledge of each other. All in different classes, had only met in passing, etc. When Grittwood placed their projects alongside each other, much like I did for you, the students were shocked. Outraged. Depressed. They'd *believed* their work to be original.

"Grittwood came to believe it was some kind of . . . cosmic joke. A vast prank played upon him, and his students, by God. Well, God had a sense of humor, so what? Grittwood thought nothing of it. But do you know what his students were painting?"

He looked up from the keys, smiled at Cam. "Your Shattered Man. Before He even *existed*. They were seers before we even knew there was anything *to* see. They painted pieces of Him. Slabs of bloodywood lying in grassy fields. Cutting boards covered in severed fingers and half-cut vegetables. One painted a coffee table with a bloodstained corner, skin and hair clinging to it, a body facedown in the background."

"'Death Fall,'" said Syd. "That one's my favorite. Like a sick Edward Hopper."

"That was over a decade before Lawrence Renfield painted the giant in that barn," said McCall. "When police asked him if he'd drawn the figure *based* on these paintings, he had no idea what they were talking about. Ironically, if Grittwood had had any foresight him*self*, he could have fashioned much of the giant off those paintings alone. It's a shame most of them were lost when one of his students burned the school to the ground in 1920. The poor young man, one Casper Millett, claimed that if he couldn't have his ideas to himself, *no one* could have them." McCall shrugged. "Typical bullshit . . . human behavior. Holy shit, fucking *Jesus*." He finally located the key he wanted, slid it into the lock. "The School was very close to the Renfield farm, you know. The nexus of the bloodspread. In fact, that's precisely where we are now. Directly *beneath* the Renfield barn."

He unlocked the door, shoved it open, and revealed an apocalypse of a classroom. Desks overturned, moldy and writhing with bugs. The carpet stained, peeled, curling up at its edges. Shadows of smog creeping up the walls. Two high windows, far, far up, let in a foggy light. It looked like the kind of room you see only in survival horror video games. Like a set. And you could *feel* it. You could *feel* that something inside this madness of a room—was breathing.

"Go ahead," said McCall. "It won't bite."

"I . . . sort of feel like it will," said Cam.

McCall laughed. "Oh please." He dipped his head, swooped a hand grandly at the door. "Be brave."

Cam was torn. On the one hand, it's not every day you get bowed to by some Bradbury ringmaster. If the opportunity arises, you'd be sort of foolish *not* to go on that adventure.

But on the other hand, this is how people get hurt. You'd have to be someone who *wants* to get hurt, to step inside that room.

Does enjoying this type of story mean we want to hurt? Is it self-harm, to enjoy reading nightmares?

Cam chews on this for a moment.

Then steps inside the room.

The room is dark, deep, and wide. Smells of mildew, ash, and sulfur. This place feels older than it can take, has had too many layers built over it. Things bubble up when that happens. They grow from the old place and bloom cruelly, moaning, into the new. Cam has this sudden understanding that the sunflowers around campus have been feeding on this place, drinking from its burnt insanity. All those roots spindling up through the tunnel . . .

They build entire cities on top of other cities. Seattle, London, Rome. Entire civilizations, forgotten in the layer-cake of the under-earth. This school is one of those. And as it cries into the dirt, the flowers grow from its voice. Renfield County has been moaning for a long, long time. The shit on the surface now? Is just its latest layer of skin.

All this, and McCall hasn't even turned on the light. Cam hasn't even *seen* the room. He's only smelled it. Felt it cake up his sinuses with a wet, clay-like stink.

"When was this place built?" he asked.

"1823." McCall stood silhouetted in the doorway. "It was originally a ladies' school for the daughters of the Lillian elite. The place was . . . cruel. After a time, the Lillian School for Girls became synonymous with madness, melancholia, witchcraft . . . This is all in the old files, in the college library's bottom floor. The white-glove floor. The girls all bullied each other to bits, then started seeing ghosts in the dormitories. The Class of 1869, nearly forty-eight *percent* of them were sent to the asylum in Bent. An even crueler place, that. Madeline would know."

McCall told this story as if he enjoyed it. A Greek god endlessly amused by the torments people play on each other. He smiled so his teeth showed, and Cam caught a flicker of tongue. It swept to the corner of his mouth, then curled up onto his cheek. Farther up than any human tongue should be able to reach.

"The school shut down in 1871," said McCall. "Three years later, it reopened as the Art School. But you can still *taste* the bitter, pubescent psychosis. Underneath all that char. And what better place to hold our tapestry than this darkest, cruelest of spaces?"

Cam swallowed. "Tapestry?"

McCall shrugged. "For lack of a better word . . . for *this*."

He turned on a pair of brilliant work lights. Cam blinked in the sudden flicker-glow. His eyes adjusted, and his blood turned to ice.

The tapestry was a massive mess of broken hunks. Not just wood, but many jagged chunks of it. Big splintery boards and gnarled old withers, rotten and warped. All of it stapled and nailed and lashed together. When Cam looked more closely, he saw there was actually a pattern to it. The pieces fit together in some kind of puzzle-shape. And he saw that they weren't all ragged, these pieces. Some were polished and nice. Painted over in various colors. Well-sanded and cared-for. There was *such* a variety. Cutting boards, tabletops. A chessboard and the lid of a jewelry box. So many pieces jammed together, Cam didn't even see the figure traced along them until he stepped back, took it all in. And there He was. Outlined in a dark, rich brownish-red. Hair striking out in all directions. Cam recognized Him immediately. That was the horrible, blood-chilling thing. He *recognized* it.

"He's . . . fucking huge," said Cam. The giant stood nearly fifteen feet tall and eight feet wide.

McCall nodded. He gazed admiringly at the mosaic bolted to the wall. "He has . . . grown over the years. Not sure how, but He has . . . multiplied His cells. Extended each part of Himself through legend and myth. Fish and loaves." He breathed deep, and recited, "The Shattered Man, with wild hair. Beware his eyes, beware his stare . . ."

"Jesus," said Cam. "Jesus Christ. You're actually *doing* it. And then you're just gonna . . . walk through?"

McCall gave a light shrug. "Why, what else would I do with it?"

Well, obviously, you couldn't destroy it. It was the most beautiful thing Cam had seen in a long time. Beautiful in a *Beetlejuice* kind of way. He couldn't stop looking at it. He walked up to it, put his hand on it. It thrummed.

"I wouldn't," said McCall. "People have lost their minds touching only a *piece* of this. To touch the entire picture . . . Well, *almost* the entire picture, but still. It could be . . . unhealthy."

Cam backed away, rubbing his fingers together. He could still feel the thrum, as if the wood had splintered into his heartbeat. Fed on him, with every pulse. He felt needles pulse up into his eyes. He squeezed them shut, shook his head. His skull burned. Whispers seemed to stream through his mind, and away again, as he shook the thrum out of his hand.

"What's the significance of this?" he asked, voice low and shaking. "I mean, in *my* book, it was just some thing outta Hell. But you don't want to just walk into a nightmare, so . . . what is He? Really."

McCall lifted his chin, as if he had been waiting for this. He took a breath and said, "I am so fucking happy you asked. Because *this* is the fun part. Carter Moone, Casper Millett, all the others whose papers I showed you tonight—all of their journals bear reference to a creature they call . . . the Leviathan."

Wood creaked in the tapestry. Cam took another step away from it.

"Imagine," said McCall, "our entire universe as *one* vertebra in a vast spine. Other universes stacked atop one another, further up and further down from us. Imagine, then, that this spine resides within the body of an unfathomably large being. In some vertebrae, they refer to It as an enormous snake. An elk. A bird. But Moone saw the Leviathan as *this*." He pointed at the giant. "*This* is what he believed we live inside. Our entire reality, just *one* disc of a cosmic spine. And at the very top of this spine . . . is the giant's Mind. The Mind is what grants visions of the rest of Its celestial body, but *only* to seers like yourself.

"The very center of Its Spine," he continued, "is the axis through which the rest of Its body may be accessed. In *this* world, that happens to be Renfield County. Happens to be the Renfield farm. Which is why *we're* here. And why, when Lawrence killed his family, he was actually acting on the madness of a mind far greater than his own. A mind that reached straight down through the center of Its body, and spoke to him."

"The mind of a . . . space giant," said Cam.

"Indeed," said McCall. "Or a bird."

"Or a dragon," said Wes.

"A . . . dragon," said Cam.

"Could be," said McCall.

"F . . . flying through space?"

"Or swimming," said Syd.

Cam stared at them. "What."

"You see," said McCall, "across the Spine, every world has its own group of devotees to the Mind. Interpreters of the thoughts of the Leviathan. The Committee in your book was one such organization. They *praise* seers, those who are chosen by the Mind to travel Its body. See, in reality, the giant pulls your mind up and down His Spine, soaking it in Aether. This 'spinal fluid' between worlds may burn, but it contains information about the manyworld. Things ordinary people cannot possibly comprehend.

"In the halls of these devotees, they display their tapestries depicting the Leviathan. They call these the Tapestries of the Great Unknown, because no one has ever—*can* never—grasp *all* the complexities of the . . . bear, or whale, or however their particular plane pictures the Leviathan. Some believe Renfield was attempting to appease the Leviathan by depicting It here as he understood It, and offering his family as . . . Well, I don't know *what* the hell he thought. Truth be told, I'm never particularly impressed by Lawrence when we meet."

"When you what?"

"Again," McCall waved him away, "most of the credit for this reconstruction goes to Professor Kim and Catherine Mason. Why Ms. Mason chose *me* to carry on her work, I'm not sure. But I'm honored." He ran his tongue hungrily about his mouth. It roiled, like a snake in its den. "So many of the owners of this wood refused to part with it. In fact, *most* of the people I gathered these from did *not* take kindly to me. It's so funny. These pieces hurt them, and they *know* that, but people cling to them like they're these . . . lifeboats. Pain, you know, is recursive. I think that's why people take comfort in the idea of the Spine. It's a linear existence, clearly organized, rather than one that's caught in the same loop. Renfield is caught in the same loop. Those stuck here cycle through the same patterns their parents went through, the same patterns their children will endure . . . But the Spine isn't like that. In the manyworld, you can always move up. Always a better world up there somewhere. But of course, you can always move further *down*, too. There's always worlds . . . further down.

"Point is, Cameron, He *called* to you. From his Mind to yours. But with this, we can call to *Him*. We can walk the entire length of His Spine. Together." He punched Cam's chest. "You and me. Us." Gesturing at Wes and Syd. "The believers. You're part of something *great* here. A long lineage of people trying to understand . . . this. Trying to find some better world in His embrace, free from the poison of this place. And choosing *not* to be a part of that, simply because we won't publish your work? Would be a mistake. This *is* your great work. You cannot remove yourself from this mythology, Cameron. It *chose* you, for reasons we may never understand. You're special. *You* are going to help me—us—access better worlds, further up."

"But how do you . . . know all this?" Cam asked.

McCall paused, thought, then gave a bitter smile. "Because it is my station to know. So. Are you in?"

Do it, whispered the thrum in the back of Cam's mind. *Do it. Do it. Do it.* The same nightmare voice that'd read him the poem in his dream, over three long years ago.

"Yes," he said, grinning. "Yes, I'll write for you."

"Amazing," said McCall. He held Cam's shoulder, nodded at him. Cam felt a strange rush of pride. They needed him. He was the specialest boy around.

McCall flicked the light switch. The room clicked dark. But Cam could still feel the giant's eyes. The eyes were the darkest part of the tapestry. Lawrence pressed hard there, digging his son into the wood. The eyes saw all. Cutting through Cam's skin, right down to his soul. Despite the shiver running down his back, Cam felt a thrill that he was being seen at all.

McCall closed the door, locking it tight. Wes coughed, clapped Cam's shoulder. "Come on. When we get back to campus, I'll drive ya home."

Wes hacked up a lung as he scraped McDonald's trash off the passenger's seat. The car floor was littered in everything from old Amazon packages to ripped-up cardboard to soggy dollar bills. When Cam was finally able to climb in, his shoes sank into the layer of debris. He was grateful it was night, so he didn't have to see everything that was down there.

"There are ten people in the department," Wes said as he drove. "Benny approached all of us about six months ago, asked for our help constructing the tapestry. Out of the ten he approached, only three of us were crazy enough to agree. Because only three of us are dying."

Wes braked at the stop sign by the campus's North Gate. He hoarked into his hand, reached up, turned on the dome light. Held out his palm. In the soupy glow of the Toyota's smelly yellow light, Cam saw a patch of phlegmy blue spattered across the man's skin. Wes wheezed painfully between his teeth.

"Doctors don't have a fuckin clue what's wrong with me. The only explanation I *have* is that it's some kind of Renfield shit. I even had a specialist in Lillian ask if I grew up near any barnwood. I told him yeah and he threw up his hands, gave me the old 'Them's the breaks.'"

"And you believe that?"

"Why not?"

"Just seems like such a weird catch-all to me."

Wes coughed. "Look. My dad . . . He had a plank of that wood. He'd hold it onto my chest and *push* it down. Rub it into me so I'd get splinters in my chest. In my *nipple*. Cam, I had a splinter in my fuckin left nip when I was nine. Doctors say they don't know what's wrong? Well, that's the first thing that comes to mind. Dad on top of me. I couldn't breathe because . . . Not just because of the board, though it didn't help. No, when he'd get on me, his face was right *here* and he kept breathin gin in my mouth. That's *gin*." He thrust his hand in Cam's face. "Smell it. That's blue fuckin gin I've been coughin up."

Cam obliged. Sure enough, it had a juniper-y lilt to it.

"That doesn't make sense," said Cam.

"Why do salmon start rotting right after they have sex? Why do we have poison fuckin frogs in the Amazon? Nature doesn't have to make *sense*, Cam." He punched out the light and wiped his hand on his jeans.

They drove in silence as the car rolled up the Netherwild hill and purred to a stop in front of good ole 1896. The living room light was on.

"Dad's plank," said Wes, "is on that tapestry now. Where it belongs. I've actually *left* Renfield. Twice. Both times I've ended up coming back. I've been *grateful* to come back. Felt more alone out in the world than I did in here. The people here understand. Ya know, Syd put her hand on me? Told me *exactly* how many days I have before I really need to be finding a cure somewhere on the other side of that tapestry. She did that . . . for all of us. So whatever Benny's selling, I'm buyin. My other option is the fuckin grave." His face darkened. "You don't know how good a deal you're gettin. I vouched for you, Cam, I really did. So . . . Don't fuck this up."

Cam wasn't quite sure how to take that. "Thank . . . you."

"Alright." Wes coughed, puffing out his cheeks. He nodded at the living room light. "Go be with your someone."

Cam drifted into the house.

Quinn sat curled up with a bag of cheese puffs, watching TV.

"Hey," he said.

"Hey." She eyed him. "How was it?"

"Strange. You?"

"Fucking bizarre." She crunched a puff.

Cam loosened his tie knot in the doorway. His eyes twitched. His brain hurt. *Do it.* "Well, I . . . think I'm gonna write for a bit."

"On brand." Quinn crunched another puff and stared at the TV.

He fidgeted for another moment, then left the room without a word.

He found himself standing in the attic, staring at the spot in the wall where he'd dreamt the Man. His temples throbbed. He got his laptop and stood before the couch. He stared at the couch. The spot where he'd been gummed to death.

He took a breath.

He sat. Bounced.

"Huh," he said. He ran his hands over the cushions. "Well, this—"

Something yanked his head back over the edge of the couch. His body arced as if electrocuted. He grasped the cushions in both hands. His fingers dug into the fabric. The pain was immense. He felt the Aether squeezing out of his eyes. Like someone shoving a tube of goo out through his tear ducts. It'd never been like this before. Never been *close* to this. Agony. Skull melting. Cold, freezing cold. His eyes were being pushed out of his head. Grinding, squelching, "Oh God . . ."

And the things he saw. Images flashing through his mind. Brilliant and blinding and fast, flickering rapidly like a broken projector.

When it was over, he caught his breath, wiped the ice-cold ooze from his face. It smoked on the back of his hand. He swept it off in long yellow smears on the couch, wheezing and shivering.

He opened his laptop. And he began to write:

Elsewhere

Deadman's Well

We burst into the blinding daylight. I'm laughing my fuckin head off as the procession follows us out of the hall. Everyone is in scarlet robes. The drummers, wide instruments lashed to their chests with strips of blue-dyed leather. The fire-bearers with their ornate golden torches, carved into the same patterns as those sconces in the hall. And the four throne-bears, carrying the Philosopher High into the sun, one at each corner of his ivory chair. The asshole lets them sweat beneath his weight. His broken eyes steam endlessly.

All of their scarlet-robed chests bear the insignia of the great bird, wings spread wide. Inside Its body swirls Its manyworld Spine, and the Mind.

They're all so *serious*. Makes me laugh even harder. I laugh so much I begin to cough. Big dry hacks, ripping out of me as two of the red-robed idiots drag me into some mud-village. My head flops back and I can see the tall peaked hall behind us, gleaming all perfect white and shimmering ribbons of jade. The hall stands cared-for and clean, but the rest of this village is muck and stink. Dirt streets, animals and children running wild. A man pisses in a narrow alleyway. There's a pub with a wooden sign (the painted outline of a beer-mug), creaking in the wind. The moaning fracas of a brothel, sunk-eyed men and women draped over the second-floor banister, watching me pass. A mutated thing throws itself at the bars of a cage on the side of the street. It has patchy hair and whip-scars all along its purple, wrinkled naked body. It screams at me with broken teeth, gripping the bars of its cage until a fat man whips its back, "Get *down!*"

Women stand on their porches in drab dresses and crimson sashes, watching me go by. All their dirty faces, staring at me. A melody of charring meat and smoking wood fills the air. I choke on it, coughing so hard I gag on something wet. I hack up a spatter of red. The philosopher who almost hatcheted me before (the High Asshole called him Eddick) nearly drops me, flinching away as I drool blood. The woman clutching my other shoulder hisses at him, her voice as mocking and sharp as steel. When I hear it, I remember: she'll be the one who shoves me down the well.

"Steady, Eddy," she says. "Don't drop the alien."

"Apologies, Marran," says Eddick. He hoists me up higher, digging his fingers under my arm. "She's slippery."

"*It*," Marran corrects. "You must remember. It is not its skin. *It* is the thing that curls within."

"Apologies, Marran," he mumbles again.

Eddick is right. I *am* slippery. This body has been fighting me ever since I took it. The old personality that *used* to live in this skin was, I assume (I've never really met her), quite strong. The stronger, bolder ones tend to rot more quickly—their last form of resistance against me. This woman is no exception. She has *not* made her home hospitable to squatters like myself. That's why Eddick and Marran have to keep adjusting their grips. My flesh is quite literally sliding around on my bones.

I will have to procure a new skin very soon. Otherwise, I'll be slithering around on the ground as . . . as myself. A mere pile of worms.

One of my molars is loose, so I suck it up out of its hole, turn my head, and spit it at Eddick. He almost drops me again. "Sh . . . It spat on me!" He gives Marran a wild look. He has my body's blood flecked across his cheek. "Will it jump into me? I . . . I don't want it magicking me, or—"

"Steady, Eddy," Marran hisses. "It won't jump, not today. High Lord says. Now, *calm* your fucking self."

"Jopp Yennigen needs another skin again," I sing at him. "Jopp Yennigen needs another skin again . . ."

"Stop it!" he cries, a gruff mix of hysteria and rage. To Marran, "Should we stop our ears?"

"It can't spell. It doesn't magick. You're *fine*. For Mind's *sake*, get a rotting grip."

I laugh. It's just so hilarious. These fools are all so . . . inconsequential. I could burst from this body anytime I want. Abandon this sinking ship and rip into Eddick. The only thing keeping me from swallowing him is that I've tried it before, and it didn't change a thing.

All the while, the drums beat on behind us. *Doomdoom*, they call. *Doomdoom*. A young man, perhaps a teenage apprentice, runs ahead of the procession ringing a bell. He calls to the crowd beginning to pour into the street: "Make way for Yennigen! Make way for your savior! Make way!"

The townspeople part before him. On either side of me, walls of staring faces, murmuring mouths, frightened eyes. None of them look very saved to me.

"Make way!" cries the apprentice, bell clanging wildly. "Your savior has come at last! Make way!"

"I don't think I'm saving anybody," I chuckle. "It's all inevitable. We've allll been here before. I've killed *you* many times." Eddick ignores me as I wheeze at him, his jaw clenched tight. "But I've learned it's not worth the effort. No, killing you would only . . . delay the . . . inevitable . . ."

I trail off because there it is: the inevitable.

The well.

The deadman's well is a waist-high ring of mossy granite stones in the center of the village. The bucket-rope ends in a noose, and dangling from that noose is a bloated, decaying man. Shirtless, skin a mottled gray. He hangs just high enough that everything below his waist is hidden within the well. The crows have been at him. Chunks are missing from his cheeks. His lips are ragged and I can see his teeth. His nipples have been chewed away, but the marks there look man-made. His stomach has been opened and he hangs in great drooling loops from the swarming wound along his gut. Maggots, beetles, and flies wriggle in and out of the many holes where his skin has sloughed apart.

As soon as I see the well, I smell it, too. I gag, and behind me, the Philosopher High laughs upon his throne. "Do you not *enjoy* the flavor of rot, Yennigen? To me, it smells . . . of home."

Doomdoom.

Eddick and Marran shove me to my knees. The smell is overpowering, and I marvel at their ability to keep straight faces as I breathe in wave after gagging wave of deadman. The torchbearers gather round us in a ring, and the drummers follow suit. *Doomdoom doomdoom doomdoom,* they bang on and on.

The throne-bears carry the High Asshole into the town center. They lower the chair to the ground and step back. Their arms tremble from the effort. They waver on their feet, exhausted.

Clouds have begun to congregate. The half-dozen torches gathered round us are actually pulling their weight now. Fire flickers over everything. The faces of the villagers peering down at me from behind the red wall of the philosophers, the beating drums, the well—all of it lit crackling orange and stormcloud gray as the High thrusts his skeletal hands into the air. I'd hoped we could skip the whole spiel (we do this every time), but he calls out grandly, "It has been three hundred years! Three entire *turns* of the loom of the sun, since our land was first afflicted . . . by the rot."

Doomdoom, the drummers add a dramatic flair to his sermon.

"Our forebears," the High continues, "came across the Ersatz Sea from Oldland in the hopes of discovering a new home. A place where they could be free to contemplate the mysteries of the heavens, far from the oppressive thumb of Oldland's oligarchic rule."

"Yeah, y'all really left oppression in the dust," I mutter, eying the four throne-bears, clearly dehydrated and on the verge of collapse.

"These men and women," he goes on, "were the *first* philosophers. The first to receive dreams of the manyworld. Debaters and alchemists and students . . . of the Mind."

Doomdoom. I wince. My ears are ringing.

The High lowers his gaze and his twin tentacles of socket-steam survey the crowd. "*They* came to this land when it was virginal. Green. Rolling hills and plentiful fields. Woods full of fruit and game. Home to no other man, but blooming with cattle and water, vegetable and bird. It seemed a blessing from the Mind, this place. Those who had followed Its dreams in Oldland thought themselves the receivers of a great gift in exchange for their devotion. The first philosophers lived here in peace for years, as the sun wove its thread many times across the sky. But then . . . my ancestor, Dellia the Old . . . had a dream."

Doomdoom.

Nausea creeps through my gut. I'm aching for this to be over.

"Dellia's dream, it is said, *boiled* her eyes from within. She wept when she awoke. Thick, freezing tears that *burned*. And she knew the Mind had graced her with a new vision. A new . . . nightmare."

Doomdoom. The entire village is rapt. This is their church, after all. How often do Christians tire of hearing the Nativity story?

"In Dellia's day, we knew little of the Mind. We knew only—*believed* only—that It existed. But It told Dellia that It dreamt to us because It was lonely, soaring through the darkvast on Its own. The vast is a cold, isolating place. And It has never encountered another creature like Itself, not in all the eons It has flown through the shadows beyond the stars. For a long time, we understood only that we existed within the womb of a friend, but Its true nature eluded us. Until It *showed* itself to Dellia that night. *She* was the first to see . . . Its Spine."

Doomdoom.

"She witnessed things throughout the manyworld that we cannot even fathom. *She* understood the death-migrations of the coastmen. *She* could decipher the language of the vines. She knew the final resting place of the ageless wandering child. And *she* was the first to be shown . . . the rot."

Doomdoom.

"The Mind told Dellia that *this* well is the very center of our world. *This* is the locus that connects us to all else. The axis of the backbone of the bird."

"Bit of a narcissistic idea, don't you think?" I murmur. Marran shoves me from behind, silencing me.

"The Mind sang to Dellia of Its woes. It had mourned Its isolation for eons . . . until It went mad. And in Dellia's dream, this madness shot down through the entirety of the Spine. It passed through our well, down, all the way to the very bottom of existence. In its wake, depression and disease spread outward from *this* point in every. Single. World. Every vertebra along the Spine grew a nexus of loneliness and despair."

Doomdoom.

"Men were driven mad. Brought their families to the well and sliced their throats into its maw, compelled by voices they could not name. Their blood poisoned our water, tore a hole in the very fabric of our world, opening our home to *filth* from vertebrae further down. The rot turned our crops to grime for miles in every direction. It sickened our children. Turned our cattle and horses and even the vermin beneath our feet into . . . unspeakable things. The village filled with panic. Men took their own lives. Took each other's. They were *eating* their own children, like starving wolves."

Doomdoom.

I have to stop myself from rolling my eyes. *Yeah, yeah. Mutated the animals, killed the crops, turned everybody crazy* . . . Every plane in the manyworld has the same problem. Some celestial poison that infects a specific radius around the center. It differs. In some worlds, it's a giant mold. In others, it's a sadness in the air. Sometimes, it's fuckin . . . bugs. Everyone in the manyworld knows some version of this tale.

"The Mind," he continues, "told Dellia that this madness took root at the very bottom of Its body. For decades, we have sent envoys down the Spine to find this root and pluck it out, but none have ever returned. Until, that is, the Mind told *me* we would have a savior. One who has traveled the Spine before, and will do so again. A savior more capable than our mortal envoys. One who *will* find the root of this rot, at the bottom of the Spine, and destroy it. Jopp Yennigen, *you* will be the one to save our world . . . from chaos."

"Doomdoom," I say, just as the drummers strike another beat. "Yeah, this is great and all, but . . . I think your understanding of this situation is bullshit."

Murmurs among the philosophers. The drummers glance at each other.

The Philosopher High snarls, "This is heresy, Jopp Yennigen."

"No, trust me. I've *been* to the 'bottom of the Spine,' and it's just led me back here." *Over and over again.* "There's no root to pluck out to heal everything. No *fix* for this . . . cosmic depression. I don't even think your bird gives a shit about *you* at all. And actually, I bet your envoys have found another plane they enjoy better than this one. I think they abandoned you. And I think you're a fool to believe I'll do anything different, just because you say I should."

More murmurs. The High's fingers work at his throne, clawing bitterly at the marble. A tense silence settles over all.

Then the High spits laughter. Throws his head back, and howls.

"Jopp Yennigen!" he cackles, my true name echoing throughout the village. "This is *exactly* why you are our savior! Because *you* doubt. That is *exactly* what the Mind told me to seek. A doubter. I am tired, Jopp Yennigen. Weary of living in a world cursed by something that, no matter how many visions I am granted or how hard I philosophize, I *still* do not fully comprehend. You say the heart of the poison in the veins of our world does not exist? Well." He points one long, bony finger at my face. He spits the word, "Fffie on you." Saliva flies from his lips. "Fffie on what you think you know. *I* say there is a root to this rot, and it is below our well. *You* will find the root of this evil and wipe it out. Or I will hunt you down, collar you like a dog, and find it my*self*."

I don't know what I expected him to say. But hell, maybe this time I'll actually do it. Maybe this time, I *will* find the root and cure everything. Maybe all this cancer and horror will get sucked back up the manyworld into the skull of the cosmo-bird or whatever it is. Maybe this time, the High will finally let me be, and I'll be left in peace to rule that world that imprisoned me. I'll have more berries than I can stomach.

But no. I shouldn't hope. Not even for a moment. Hope is a heart-thing, and hearts are dumb. I don't even *have* a heart. I'm alien fucking worms.

The Philosopher High thrusts both hands into the air once more. "Praise to the Mind!"

"Praise!" ring the voices of the village.

"We welcome this boon, O Mind," calls the High.

"We accept your thoughtfulness," everyone calls back.

"And now," the High points at me again, "we'll pour it in."

"Death unlocks the door," chant the townsfolk. "Death unlocks the door."

Marran and Eddick shove me against the well, shove my face right up against the corpse so that his stink fills my lungs. I can't breathe. My head swims. My body is dying, right out from under me. And *still*, the High lectures on: "We have killed many to reopen this gate for our envoys. Offered *thousands* of lives to this deadman's well. We pray that *this* will be the last."

Somewhere within her robe, Marran produces a long, shining knife. I see only the glint of it, out the corner of my eye.

Eddick fidgets. "I . . . I thought it couldn't die. Do we slit its throat?"

"No," says the Philosopher High. "We do not."

"Sorry, Eddy," says Marran, as she grabs his hair and rams the knife into his neck. The blade is so long it pierces all the way through, popping out the other side of his throat. She rips it forward, hacking apart the tubes and cords, nearly severing his head from his body. I feel his blood splash hot onto the back of my head, see it cascade into the mouth of the well, plunging into darkness. The dark laps at it greedily. Eddick collapses against me, gurgling and sputtering, pouring out into the well.

Something, far down inside the ground—begins to burn. Eddick's blood sizzles against it. Cold light creeps up the wellstones. I imagine the many other deadmen these crazy idiots have hung here. Each one rotting through, bones showing, necks eventually snapping, remains tumbling down into the wellmouth, down through the very center of the Spine.

"Good luck, Jopp Yennigen," says the High. "May your journey be fruitful. May you bring us the peace we have so long craved. And may you always be in the thoughts . . . of the Mind."

"Fuck you," I tell him, just before Marran grabs my ankles and tips me over into the well.

Down, down, I fall, laughing all the way. The burning light down below grows brighter. Becomes daylight.

Becomes Earth.

CHAPTER TWELVE

SUNDOWN

The next week was a puttering, "Wednesday again already?" kind of week. Neither Quinn nor Cam would be able to say where it had gone, when the calendar turned itself over into a stifling first week of September.

Cam poured out pages of material. Every night, he sat in that attic. Fat drops of eye-jizz slopped onto his hands as he typed, hunched over the computer on his lap, on that old pink sofa. He typed so fast, at first he didn't even notice the glops of glue globbering out of his eyes, spattering against the backs of his hands, onto the keys. Barely felt it gumming up between his fingers and the laptop, tying him to the keys, to the words, in thick phlegmy ropes as he typed, typed, typed.

Yennigen brought to the well. Yennigen falls to Earth. Yennigen murders their way into a new skin, yet again. Yennigen *always* needs a new skin again.

Cam wrote on, trusting in the importance of these visions, though no pieces of bloodywood revealed themselves.

Yet.

Fluid gummed up his keyboard, made the little fan on his laptop whir loud. His eyes stung like fuck, and there were times he had to stop writing, clutching at the dusty cushions of the sofa, squeezing his eyes shut against the pain. Once, they hurt so bad he thought his eyeballs might melt right out of his skull. His eye-bleeds during the writing of *Shattered Man* were never this bad. Now, the pain almost made him think it wasn't worth it.

Almost.

But the clarity that came *after* this pain was orgasmic. It felt so *good* to slap that laptop shut and know he could rest easy, he'd done important work. Soon, his eyes might swell and burst, sure. But in the meantime, getting the words out was *mwah*, chef's kiss. He'd drop into bed hours after Quinn, skull burning but heart content.

If Quinn was concerned about him, she said nothing. They barely spoke the entire week, drifting silent through the same home. Something had cracked between them, but Cam didn't care. He was a full-on special boy at last. So what if he'd broken his word to her? So what if he'd lied? He was finally, *finally*, working on something that mattered.

On Tuesday, he ran into McCall in the hallway. McCall asked him how his teaching was going, and Cam admitted he was having trouble focusing, he was doing so much of his own work. He'd even zoned out during a workshop with a student (the girl he'd met at the salad bar), because he'd squeezed an entire bottle of eyedrops into himself beforehand, and the burning still hadn't stopped.

"Well, that's an awkward situation for sure," said McCall. "Just let me know if any of them are writing anything . . . useful."

"You got it," said Cam, blinking so hard that McCall was just a blur. "Hey, do you have any interest in a story about . . . alien worms? Is that helpful?"

McCall screwed up his face. "Is *that* what It's showing you? No. Jesus. No, we *only* want the location of the wood, Cameron."

"Of course, but—"

But McCall had already walked away.

Wes stood down the hall, in the doorway of his office. *Don't fuck up*, he mouthed.

Quinn spent her afternoons wandering town, smoking Noxboros. So grimy and bad. The music she was listening to was grimy and bad, too. Shuffle God was having a laugh with her, playing her the sticky-sweet notes of "Sundown" by Gordon Lightfoot. The song purred into her ear as she stood on the corner, watching a little old lady drive by, eyes hidden by dark shades, lips pulled back in a silent sneer.

They were doing this a lot now, the little Edenvillians. They'd leer at her, silent, through windows, from across the street. It felt somehow sexual, like they were so struck by her they couldn't speak. They watched her as Lightfoot sang on about his back door.

She didn't eat any more ice cream.

She brought the photograph of the barn back to the library, and Marcia clutched it to her chest with both hands.

"Did you like the play?" she asked.

"Loved."

"I thought you might." Marcia leered at her.

The entire town was leering at her.

Except for Cam. Cam was straight up avoiding her. Ducking his head and mumbling into the other room every time she said hello. *Fine by me*, she thought.

She returned to the library every morning, poring over the seeker box, digging through fable after fable. A woman in Bent who grew a face from the crook of her elbow in '63. A man who skinned his Great Dane and wore her for a week in '82, crawling round the neighborhood until the cops gunned him down.

The creativity of this place astounded her.

But nothing in the box told her anything about Celeste. She walked the streets for hours, wandered far from the Netherwilds. But nothing spoke to her. At night, she sat on the playground slide and watched the glowing window of their little attic. She hadn't gone up there yet. Didn't want to. She watched and smoked. Smoked and watched.

Things finally changed on Wednesday night.

"Fuck!"

Quinn froze, cheese puff halfway to her mouth. She paused the episode of *Nailed It!* she was watching, and looked at the ceiling of the living room. Cam's voice again: "Fuuuck."

She approached the bottom of the attic steps, scraping orange grit off her fingers with her teeth. "Cam?"

A wriggling, groaning sound.

"Cam!"

"Yeah?" He sounded annoyed, sweaty.

"What's happening?"

"What?"

"Why are you yelling?"

"I'm not."

A pause.

"I'm coming up," she said.

"Don't."

She stomped upstairs to find Cam on the pink sofa, digging into his eyes. He blinked up at her. She thought she caught a thin curl of steam or smoke or something, coming up from his left eye.

"Jesus Joseph," said Quinn. "What's happening up here?"

"I'm writing."

"What, are you typing with your eyeballs?"

"No, I've got more of that . . . shit . . ." He dug at his eyes with his thumbs. "Fuck."

"That's a fucking infection. You *need* to get that checked out."

"I'm fine."

"Cam, your brain is rotting. Again."

"It's not *brain*." He sniffed, indignant. "It's Interplanal Aether."

"Oh, Interplanal Aether was my second guess after brain-juice." Quinn crossed her arms. "What is this?"

"It's like ectoplasm," said Cam, irritated. "It's—"

"I mean, what is this, like why are you leaking fucking ectoplasm?"

"Oh, I'm having visions, baby," he said, wiping a long snotty ribbon off his eye. He grinned at her, crimson eyes blinking, face sweaty, fingertips stained pale-green. "For work."

"*What?*"

"They're using it. So I can help them find the wood."

She narrowed her eyes. "What. Wood."

"*The* wood. For the Shattered Man."

Quinn stuck her chin out. "Like your fucking *book*? They're rebuild-ing the giant *like in your book*, and . . . This is . . ." She ran her hands over her face. "This is what we *just* talked about. I can't believe you. You didn't say anything."

"No, because I knew you'd want to Ichabod your way out of here."

"Well, yeah!" She was shouting now. "That's exactly what I want to do!"

"Well, I didn't want you to cash in yet."

"Cam, you're clearly, like, dying. The giant is *bad*. You shouldn't be involved with anything even *remotely* related to it. Campbell." She took a step toward him. "This is what I said. Renfield does *horrible* shit to people. And here it is, directly related to something horrible going on with *you*."

"What am I supposed to . . . I'm trying to be helpful."

"I don't want you to help *them*," she said. "I *want* you to be safe with *me*."

"What does that even mean?"

Quinn took another step closer to him. "Did you know a guy used to live in the Mill who *ate* his own kid? And just last year, they pulled *thirteen beetles* out of this woman *while* she was alive. They were crawling around under her fuckin skin, they don't even know where they came from! This is a *bad* place, Cam."

"Well, it doesn't seem bad to me."

She sputtered for a moment. "Are you *broken*? Do you not see that you're being taken advantage of? What happened to the guy who *recognized* that—"

"Stop!" He beat a fist into the couch. "Stop, stop, stop it! The *one* thing I've always *ever* wanted was to be part of something important. I *got* published and you know how important it was?" He made a zero with his hand and shoved it in her face. "Fucking not at all! So if I have a chance to *see* something amazing? Then fuck it. I don't need to be published. I don't need you. Fuck off."

Quinn held her chin up. Tears welled in her eyes. "Cam. I think it's time for me to say something."

"Oh, seriously, I'm trying to work." He blinked at his laptop.

"I really need you to hear this."

He picked at his R key.

She took a breath. "Icha—"

Cam lurched forward. He gagged. Sludge belched out of his eyes. He clutched at his temples and screamed, the veins in his neck bulging bad. Quinn could see tendrils of smoke curling out of his eyes as guck curdled out of the ducts of him and ran down his cheeks in snotty-colored chunks. She could *hear* it squishing from his body. He gurgled and gagged and laughed at the ceiling of the attic.

She backed away from him, hand to her mouth in fear, revulsion, panic.

Finally, he gasped. His eyes sprang open. He took several deep, hitching breaths. He lifted his head and his eyes were bloody, swelling from his skull. Trembling, he reached for his laptop. Cold steaming yuck dripped down his face. Breathing through his mouth like he was drugged, Cam swiped it limply onto the floor. He typed.

"Cam," she said, her voice uneven.

"I have to write it down," he murmured.

"Cam, we have to leave. You . . . you have to see a doctor, or . . . something."

He turned those bloodshot eyes on her and screamed, "I don't need a fucking doctor! Just let me write in peace! Get out! Go *back* to the city for all I fucking care! Just leave me alone!"

Quinn stared at him in shock. He was hunched over his laptop, typing furiously.

She drifted down the stairs.

Drifted to the kitchen, where the car keys lay on the counter.

She stared at them. From all the way down here, she still heard Cam's fingers slamming on the keys.

She could. She could drive all the way back to Brooklyn. Fuck this. Fuck him. It was only six forty-five, she could make it down to the Red Yard before they closed and get herself a very tall drink.

But then, an idea.

She *could* go home. Or she could go to the one place where she would be validated. Where a group of women would understand her plight completely.

After all the leering, she'd decided to avoid it. It was probably asking for trouble. And in a basement? No thanks.

But . . . they'd be starting soon. She'd be welcomed with open arms.

Even as she marched out the door, and saw the gathering storm clouds overhead, Quinn knew this was the wrong decision. She knew, as Cam wheezed to himself, type-type-typing in the attic, that she was royally screwing herself over by not taking the car and bouncing.

She wondered what Celeste would say. Would she be supportive? Or would she give Quinn the look that dying addicts give to new ones?

Save yourself, that look said, *before it's too late for you, too.*

But Quinn, marching alone through the Netherwilds, didn't listen.

Cam, his eyes burnt and horrible, suddenly knew *exactly* where the next missing piece of the tapestry was. And it had only cost him this pain. This little pain. He would write this down and it would be worth it, and all it had cost him was a little bit of pain.

CHAPTER THIRTEEN

HISTORICAL SOCIETY

She was so mad, she didn't feel human. A furious nausea brewed in her gut, and followed her overhead in the clouds. The air was humid, threatening to burst into hot rain at any second. A sob bulged in the back of Quinn's throat, tumorous and dizzying, as she marched down Rackell Street to the library.

Something eyed her from the edge of the parking lot. She paused, eyed the thing back. It scampered away.

"That's what I thought!" she yelled after it.

She burst through the library's double doors. Lightning strobed as she darted her eyes around the space. Five silent seconds as she took in the room. Thunder grumbled.

The library was dark and purple-shadowed. Light in orange strips, coming through the windows from the dying sunset outside. The only light *in*side burned from some hall off to her left. An open doorway, brown-carpeted, wood-paneled. A yellow light glowed in the ceiling. A paper sign taped to the wall: HISTORICAL SOCIETY. And an arrow, pointing down.

More thunder as Quinn took a step closer. Then stopped, suddenly afraid. Afraid *because* she was afraid. Because she was watching herself walk willingly toward some obviously Very Bad Thing. It was starting to storm outside, her boyfriend was literally losing his mind, and she couldn't believe how perfect it all was. How balls-to-the-wall Very Halloweeny.

Turn. The fuck. Back.

But she took another step.

Oh, so you want to die?

And another.

Because this is how you die.

And another.

She could see now that the arrow on the sign pointed down a narrow set of shitty, black-stain-carpeted stairs. At their bottom was a set of brown metal doors. Doors meant to be thrown open. So perfect and dented that Quinn wondered if the props department had hinged them there for *her*.

She went down a step. It creaked. She stared at the metal doors. Through their windows, she could see yellow tiled floor.

She crept down another step. And another. And when she finally reached the bottom, she put her hands on the bars, took a breath, and *shoved* the doors open.

The air moved as if she'd popped the lid on some pressure-sealed room. Wind gusted in behind her, over her, and her hair blew all in her face, so she was temporarily blinded, and it took her a moment to register what was going on. When she did, she just said, "Ohp." The sound you make when you walk in on someone in the bathroom. It just . . . took her by surprise.

She was standing in a large, yellow-linoleum room. Some kind of ancient event hall. The ceilings were low and cave-like, all rot-tiled and old. Doors led off into the distances, into darknesses and dim, blinking fluorescences. Shutters along one wall, closed against a kitchen. A light on back there, winking through the corners of the shutters. Quinn imagined after-church dinners served through that window. Potluck lunches and pancakes. Even now, someone clanked around in the pots and pans, hidden behind the shutters.

In the well-lit middle of this space, in this heart of some labyrinthine underground, there sat a circle of brown metal folding chairs. And in these chairs, there sat many, many—little old ladies.

"Ohp," said Quinn.

And all the old ladies—turned to look at her.

They grinned.

"Quinn!" said Winnie. "Oh my god, you *made* it."

"I would've bet fifty dollars she wouldn't," muttered Marcia, on the far side of the circle.

"What made her change her mind?" Cindy muttered back.

"Maybe something *else* made it up for her," said Deborah, the woman from the general store.

Brenda, from the shoe store, leaned forward and waved to Quinn. "Hi there. Helloo!"

"H . . . hello," said Quinn. She wanted to add, *I'll just be backing away now.* Because she had seen enough TV to know that she should absolutely not, not *ever*, under any circumstances—

"Have a seat," said Brenda. She gestured to a short stack of chairs leaning against one of the columns holding up the ceiling.

Quinn didn't move. "I didn't mean to barge in like that," she said.

"Oh, not at all," said Winnie. "We *wanted* you to come."

"So many don't," said Marcia.

"But *we* all did," said Winnie. Pointing a finger round the circle. Her wrist jingled with golden gaudy baubles. Her nails were deep red. "Everyone here came. And that's always the first step. So." She pushed hair delicately out of her face. Like obviously the fact that they were all in this room right now made them all very special and strong. It probably did, Quinn didn't know. And she didn't really *want* to know. Didn't need to know anything more about what was happening here, why they were all gathered underground, leering. Peering at her over their little glasses, from under their stiff wigs. This was a mistake. She didn't know what she'd expected.

But when she took a step back, they all *tensed*. Lifted an inch out of their chairs. She froze again, palms up, *don't shoot*.

"Have a seat, Quinn," said Brenda. "Please. No need to run away." She laughed. "You're *safe* here."

"I see," said Quinn. She moved her eyes around the circle, and found Greta Marie Mither sitting with her arms crossed. She looked even more wrung-out up close. She must've only been in her late forties, but she looked so gaunt and tired that she fit right in with the rest of them. She offered Quinn a limp smile.

"Plenty of chairs," said Cindy. She nodded at them, the chairs. "Go ahead. Pull up a seat."

"Go on," they all murmured and nodded. "We're so happy you made it. Cop a squat, sister. Have a seat. Saved one for *you* . . ."

Quinn shook her head slow. "Thank you . . . very much. But . . . Well . . ." She glanced at Greta. Her resemblance to Clarity was striking. And subsequently, her resemblance to Celeste.

"Okay." Quinn threw up her hands. "Sure. Why not."

Which felt like the stupidest thing she had ever done.

But what was she supposed to do? *Not* have a seat? How far into the rabbit hole would *you* allow yourself to fall, if it was you here, in Renfield County?

She felt squeezed under the weight of their eyes as she grabbed a chair and scraped it across the floor to Winnie, who scooted over a screech of an inch so Quinn could fit. Quinn settled into the ice-cold chair, and she and Winnie smiled at each other, like they were enemies somehow.

Now that Quinn sat among them, their musk wormed its way up her nose, into her brain. A sneeze-inducing mix of several different brands of stuff, all woven together into a thick cloud. Mentholated perfume and vanilla and cigarettes and mothball and cream. It clung to Quinn's tongue. She held to the edges of her chair. Her throat clenched.

"Well," sighed Brenda. She smiled around at everyone. *She* was holding a clipboard. "Let's get started." She leaned in. "Welcome. To the Edenville Chapter of the Renfield County Historian's Society. You all made it *some*where tonight. And that's a feat. But." They all said this part together, to each other: "I'm glad you made it *here*."

"Great," said Brenda. "Does anybody want to read us in today?"

"I will," said Winnie, clearly confident this was a very big thing she was volunteering to do.

"Great." Brenda handed her a laminated sheet.

Winnie cleared her throat, glanced at Quinn, smiled at Greta, and began to read. Quinn tuned out and took stock of her surroundings. She recognized more than half the faces here. All the women who'd been working in town, the librarians, women she'd seen at the play, the frazzle-haired director—and Greta. Greta and everyone else watched Winnie read with stern reverence. Quinn thought she caught a whiff of music—some big choir of women—singing out from the dark. She peered around over her shoulder, looked out into one of the many dim hallways. Some ghost-song echoed out from it, far away and dim, but audible, and even . . . blooming a little. Growing just the tiniest bit more triumphant and Christiany.

Winnie finished reading. "And praise to the Mind."

"Praise to the Mind," said the circle.

That caught her attention. Quinn turned back to the group and leaned over Winnie's shoulder, tried to see what was on the laminated sheet, what weird prayer she'd just missed. But Winnie was already handing it back to Brenda, who clipped it quickly to her clipboard.

"Okay, great." Brenda smiled up at everyone again. "It's the first Wednesday, so we'll be reading from our First Lesson today. Do we have any . . . Oh, shoot, I forgot! We wanted to vote on the date of the library book sale."

Quinn sat silently as they voted on the date of the library book sale.

"Great," said Brenda, writing it down. "The twenty-fourth it is. Okay. So. Who wants to read the First Lesson today? We usually have a tradition that the new girl reads, but tonight we seem to have *two* new girls. Not that you're new, per se," she said to Greta. "But . . . which of you wants to read?"

"You go ahead," said Greta, waving at Quinn and squirming impatiently in her seat. "I'm just here for the ceremony. I don't need the readings."

"Ceremony?" Quinn echoed.

Brenda was shoving a book into her hand. It was small, old, and weathered. Perhaps a bright red once, but not anymore. Worn down and yellow-paged. In greasy gold font, the spine read, *A Historian's Guide to Living Long (Third Edition),* by Cassandra Maywell.

Quinn accepted the volume graciously. "Okay. What, uh . . . page?"

"Thirteen," said Winnie, very close to her ear.

Quinn creaked open the book. It smelled delicious, the way all well-loved books should. Page thirteen was the beginning, apparently, of Chapter One: *What Is the Mind?*

Quinn glanced around, gave everyone a tight smile, cleared her throat, and began to read: "The Mind. This is one of the most important truths a Renfield Historian must embrace. Because at the end of any road down history addiction . . ." She paused, looked around again. They smiled at her uniformly. "Because at the end of any road down history addiction is something waiting to take advantage of you and your story, whatever it may be. There are *many* monsters and spirits who prey upon those who have questions. Which is why—"

"—it's best not to have questions at all," they all said with her.

"Great," said Brenda.

Quinn read on.

It grew into progressively weirder stuff, but thankfully they never said anything in unison with her again. They listened in intense silence as Quinn read three entire pages of gobbledygook about history addiction, which seemed like a condition wherein one becomes addicted to solving mysteries. The trouble with that in Renfield was that mysteries got addicted to *you,* too. "Things will sniff you out and peel you raw in this valley," wrote Cassandra Maywell. "They'll eat you and vanish you and squish you flat." So come to the Society! Kick your addiction to legends and myths! Before *they* get addicted to *you.*

That seemed to be the agenda the book was pushing. Giving over the burden of your questions to a mind far greater than your own. A mind that had answers for everything. *The* Mind.

When she reached the end of the first section, Quinn carefully closed the book. "So I feel I have to ask. What story do you think I'm addicted to?"

"Well, that whole barnwood business," said Cindy.

"You've been *sinking* into that box," said Marcia. "You spend *hours* staring at it."

"I do?" Quinn didn't feel like that was true.

"We didn't even want to give it to you at first," said Marcia.

"But it's our job," Cindy shrugged.

"I'm not addicted to that story," said Quinn. How many hours *had* she spent in the library this week? She didn't feel like it was abnormal.

"It's okay, honey," said Winnie. "We've *all* been there. It sucks you in. Take Greta here for example. No offense, Greta."

"None taken," said Greta, bobbing one foot. "I get it. I'm sucked."

"I'm just trying to help out my . . . boyfriend," said Quinn. "That's all."

"Oh, we were all just trying to help *some*one," said Cindy. "It's never just about *you*. Sometimes it is, but . . ."

"But we *all* have brothers or step-sisters or partners or aunts or . . ." Winnie tried to think of another thing. She waved her hand. It jangled. "Sometimes, people vanish into the muck. And you can't help them, so you have to help your*self*. That's why we're all here. Because we're trying to be *smart*. To follow our Mind instead of our hearts. I sought answers on my own for a long time. A *long* time." She zoned out for a moment, to indicate just how long a time it had been. "But then I realized. I would never be able to find those answers on my own. I needed to *give* myself over to a mind greater than mine. A more intelligent power that already knew, and could *show* me, everything I ever wanted to know. Because It thought everything up in the first place." She cast a loving glance around the circle. "So it doesn't matter *what* makes me afraid. I'm not alone when I have all Its other ideas to keep me company. And sure, the price for knowledge was . . . interesting." She cracked her neck. "But it's been worth it. And I know I don't just speak for myself when I say that, but for all of us."

"Praise to the Mind," said Brenda.

"Praise to the Mind," said everyone else.

Quinn sat very still.

Greta cleared her throat. "My heart has . . . led me astray. I have hoped . . . But hope is a heart thing. I'm being," she appealed to the group, "*smart*. Giving up my heart for the Mind. May It be praised."

"Praise to the Mind," said the group.

"I know my little girl is out there," said Greta, her voice trembling. "I just don't know *where*. But you know who does?" She pointed at the ceiling. "It does. So I'm paying that price," pointing at Winnie. "Praise to the Mind."

"Praise to the Mind!"

"And Greta, I wish you the best of luck in finding her," said Winnie, before turning to Quinn and rolling her eyes.

"Well, great," said Brenda. "So who wants to share first?"

Winnie raised her hand.

"Great," said Brenda. "Winnie, go ahead."

"I'll try to keep it short," said Winnie, adjusting herself in her chair.

"Great," said Brenda.

"I feel *good* tonight," said Winnie.

"Great," said Brenda.

"So my name is Winnie."

"Hi Winnie," said everyone.

"And I am . . . a recovering Historian."

The women nodded understandingly.

"It's been almost eight years since my metamorphosis," she said. "And I've been thinking lately, ya know . . . I'm wondering if I've swung too far in the other direction. You know I'm watching *Call the Midwife* now for the *fourth* time? I just feel comfortable in the stories *I* know. I can't watch anything new, it drives me nuts. I mean, I can't believe I went to that damn play . . . and I knew all the words!" She threw her hands up, shook her head, mouth open in mock shock. "I'm surprised at myself. I really am. It's just funny watching myself be . . . someone new."

The women all nodded at each other again. They knew what she meant.

As Winnie spoke, Quinn glanced around the circle again. All these women had been drawn inexorably toward some piece of the Renfield mythos. Some splinter of light below the darkness, if there was one. And the stories they'd sought—had destroyed their lives. Consumed them, just like that woman who wrote those emails in the seeker box. Just like Quinn was being consumed *right now.*

So why wasn't she running?

Winnie sniffed. "Anyway. Thanks for letting me share."

"Thank you for sharing," said the women.

"Great," said Brenda. "Who's next?"

The next woman told some lengthy, complicated story that became gradually less and less intelligible. Quinn gathered that there was something about an animal in her shed, her son-in-law's credit card debt, something about her "practice in the Mill," and "I just know I could afford to do it if I could work, but with my *ankle* . . ."

She concluded by saying, "It just makes me want to know that there's a reason for it, you know? Like . . . what exactly *is* this thing? But I made a promise when I was thirty-seven that I wouldn't end up like my uncle. Not at all. Not. At. All . . . So I haven't gone in that shed." She gave a loud cry-laugh. "Haven't opened it since that night. If I was in a movie, I would have opened it. But whatever lives in there is just gonna keep livin in there. And here I am. And I'm not food." She dabbed at her eyes. "I am not food . . . Thanks for letting me share."

"Thank you for . . . sharing," mumbled Quinn, half a second after everyone else.

"Great," said Brenda. She grinned. "Do *you* want to share, Quinn?"

"Oh, I . . . really just stumbled in here. I'm sorry, I don't mean to . . ." They were staring at her with openly concerned faces. She breathed them in. "Well. Truth be told, I *have* been . . . looking into this one story a *lot* lately. Two, actually, so . . . You got me there."

The women frowned as one.

Quinn glanced over her shoulder. That faraway choir had stopped singing. As if they listened, too. The halls around her were dark, silent, flickering. She took a breath. "So . . . My *partner* has been seeing the Renfield giant in his dreams. And he thinks he can see the pieces of the giant in his dreams as well, which is . . . But I wonder if I'm overreacting here because I . . .

"Well, when I was in high school, I had this friend. Celeste. And she . . . We were super close. But we had this weird moment at homecoming my senior year. Like, we were *just* friends but then for a second, we . . . weren't. I don't know. We never got a chance to talk about it, because the next weekend, we went for a drive up the Billows Road. We lived in Leaden Hollow, and it was sort of a tradition to go check out the *county*," she said the word spookily, as it deserved. "So Celeste was driving and I was in the passenger's seat. And we come to the peak of the Billows Road, right? The big sign that says, WELCOME TO HISTORIC RENFIELD COUNTY. And you have to drive *down* the hill at that point, so we were looking *down* into the dark.

"And we see this . . . woman. In the road. Striding through our headlights and the mist, and she's in this hospital gown. Flapping open in the back so we can see her ass. And she has about four or five hospital bracelets on each wrist. She has her hair in this ponytail and it's tied with *another* bracelet. And in her hands—just *digging* her fingers into the neck of this thing—is a deer. A big dead buck, with its antlers dragging on the ground, and its neck has been snapped, and there's this thick trail of blood and chunks leading back off the road. Coils of dead deer guts just . . . steaming on the pavement like . . . dead summer worms.

"So this woman stops. Turns. Looks at us through the windshield.

"And it's her. It's Celeste. She's in the car with me but she's *out*side, too, looking in."

Quinn's voice broke. She didn't want to say the next part. The part when the woman wouldn't move, and Quinn kept shoving Celeste's shoulder, saying, "Dude, fucking *drive!*" And finally, Celeste cracked her head to the side. Locked Quinn with eyes that were suddenly pale moons swimming with gray inky tendrils and pumping black veins. She had a small bead of blood rolling out an ear. She grinned.

"Hi Quinn," she said, in a voice that wasn't hers. "You look really pretty tonight." Celeste began to lean toward her, tilting her head. "I just wanna chew on you. Come on. Let me suck up your stomach through your mouth, Quinn. Like a vent at the bottom of the pool. Lemme hollow you. It'll be so nice . . ."

She came within half an inch of Quinn's face. Quinn could feel Cel's breath in her mouth. But it wasn't even Cel's. It was thick and sulfurous. Made her gag.

And thank Crows it did, because that's what broke the spell of having Celeste so close to her again. Quinn ducked under her, dove across her legs, and slammed the gearshift into reverse. She pressed her face into Celeste's lap, jammed her hand onto the accelerator.

She couldn't remember what happened after that. She remembered Celeste screaming at her, clawing at her back. She remembered getting in the shower the next day and feeling the sting all along her spine. She remembered looking in the fogged mirror and seeing the long red fingernail-welts along her skin. But how did she get home? And where was Celeste? Where was Celeste's car?

No one knew.

No one would ever know.

Quinn sniffed. "So I figured if I . . . moved here for a while, I might figure out what happened to her. But now something's happening to my fucking boyfriend and I . . . I don't know what I'm doing here anymore. If he wants to rebuild the giant with those other idiots, I say let him." She stuffed her hands into her hoodie pouch and tucked them between her legs. "That's it, thanks for letting me share, praise to the Mind."

"Thank you for sharing," said the ladies. "Praise to the Mind."

Quinn hung her head and waited for someone to say they knew the beast that had taken Celeste. *Someone* must recognize her. They had to.

Silence.

Marcia coughed.

Quinn looked up. The ladies were glancing at each other.

"What?" she asked.

"Your partner," said Cindy. "What does he write again?"

"Horror," said Quinn. "He wrote about the Renfield giant without knowing it. He had these . . . visions pop out of his eyes. Said he knows where the pieces are."

More glancing around. Some of the women straightened in their seats. The silence was very loud and very thick.

"What?" said Quinn.

"He *knows* where . . . pieces of the bloodywood may be?" asked Winnie.

"Oookay," said Brenda, clearly trying to nip whatever this was in the bud. "Ha. Girls . . ."

"I guess so," said Quinn. "I mean, I don't know *exactly*, but . . ."

"He knew," said Marcia, her voice low. "He *knew* . . ."

"Right under our noses," said Cindy. "For *weeks*."

"Come on now," said Brenda. "We said *when* this happened, we'd be rational. *Everyone* should come willingly."

"Oh, she wouldn't come if she knew," said Deborah, shaking her head. "I can tell. She wouldn't want it."

"It would be good to see him," said Winnie. "For those of us who live in houses. It's . . . been a while."

"And we'll be bringing a *gift*," said Marcia. "A gift he's been expecting."

"She can join me," said Greta. "I'm drinking tomorrow, too."

"Will he go for that?" asked Deborah. "Two in one day?"

"He will," said Cindy.

"He did for *us*," said Marcia.

"He diiid," Cindy purred. "And he *said* she would come. He's been waiting."

The murmur that this was a very good idea (whatever this idea was) went around the group.

"Ladies!" said Brenda sharply. "Some of us haven't . . . *been* . . . in a very long time. There's no need to . . ."

But the others began to lick their lips.

"He'll be so *pleased*," said one of them.

"He'll be *thrilled*," said another.

"He predicted she would come."

"We didn't even *realize* until she said—"

"Girls," warned Brenda. "I think it's important we take a bre—"

"What if she doesn't want to drink?" asked Deborah.

"Once she sees him, she'll understand," said Winnie.

"She can watch *me*," said Greta. "Make her watch him do it to me, and *then* she'll see."

"It'll be nice," said another lady, "just to see him. Even if it's too crowded."

"He already *knows* we're coming," said another.

"He sent this gift for *us*," said another.

"So maybe it's a test!" said Winnie. She leaned into the circle and snarled cruelly. "Maybe we're *supposed* to bring her, whether she wants to or not." Her jaw clicked sideways.

Jaws aren't supposed to do that.

"Maybe," said another woman. Something was happening to her knuckles. They cracked and shifted. "Maybe he'll let her ride the chair."

"No one touches the chair," snapped Marcia.

"It's my turn," said Greta. "Maybe he'll let *me*."

"Besides," said another lady, "we'll be delivering *the gift*."

Things were cracking and popping all around Quinn. The women's bodies were rippling, shifting, snapping. Winnie cracked her head toward Quinn.

"You'll look *so* nice," she said, "when you've been changed."

Quinn bolted out of the chair. They grabbed her from behind, threw her onto the floor. They swarmed her. Pinned her down and sneered into her face. Dripped saliva in her mouth as she screamed, kicked. They cackled. Their bodies began to break.

"Girls!" Brenda hollered. "LADIES!"

They turned and hissed at her. Winnie stood tall. She opened her mouth. Her jaw popped off its hinges. Her teeth cracked apart, rattled away down her throat. Her cheeks split. Green-black bones began to rip from the dripping wound of her face.

Quinn scrambled off the floor. "Stop her!" Someone smacked her, sent her flying against the stack of folding chairs. She cracked her head against the column, tumbled against the chairs, and splashed onto the floor, chairs clattering over her, burying her. She shoved at them limply, dizzy and shaking with fear, until a thick, hairy green stump of bone slammed onto the floor by her face, cracking one of the linoleum tiles in half. Quinn froze. Winnie's voice, distorted and gurgling, "You're not boss, Brenda."

Brenda's bright blue heels came into view, swinging up and away as her body crunched and tore. Eight slick, green-dripping legs unfurled onto the floor. An insect click in her voice: "You are not vanishing this poor girl tonight."

"For Mind's *sake*," Winnie hissed. "This is what he wants. Let. Us. Pass!"

She gave a chittering cicada roar, and charged. She and Brenda crashed to the floor out of sight, hissing and scrabbling against the linoleum. Quinn lay still, afraid to move. All around, women howled as they began to change. She heard their bodies popping, snapping, the wet-sapling twist of tendon and bone.

A great rending, a brilliant wet spray of blood, and something smacked onto the tile by Quinn's face. It spurted dark green ooze from the torn twitching tubes of its inhuman neck.

Quinn screamed. A real throat-shredder.

Then she was up in the air, jerked back and forth and carried away through one of those many doors. A door that led to dim, cobwebbed stairs. Stairs that led down, down, into the dark. A dark that glowed, and when Quinn's eyes adjusted, she saw that she was being carried through a tunnel clogged with spiderweb. Some dirt tunnel burrowed into the earth far, far below Edenville. She was being jostled and dragged and jerked through absolute *miles* of thick, sticky web. Clinging to her face, getting in her mouth. And as she went deeper and deeper into the gagging dark, Quinn could feel some huge, insane presence below her. Beating and thrumming in the ground. Singing open-mouthed in a chorus of many, many throats. Like a massive party. A city.

A hive.

Outside Lillian, March 1974

I'm sure there are other fluids further out. Swirling galaxies of blood, bile, saliva. Entire constellations of bone marrow. But all I've ever seen of this creature, whose wings supposedly span billions of realities—is Its Spine. The only juice of Its body I have ever encountered is this goddamn *goo* between vertebrae. Call it Aether, call it resin, call it whatever you want.

It's shit, is what it is.

And when I tumble down from the world of the philosophers, down through the Spine toward Earth, *boom* from the sky straight at the muddy ground   I emerge absolutely *covered* in it. My body's throat retches as I rise shakily to my hands and knees. I spit a great glob into the mud. Shit dribbles off my chin. My entire body is trembling. The fluid has no scent, no taste, but it is cold. As cold as the darkvast of the space beyond space. The space only the Leviathan knows.

I rise, trembling, to my knees. Sit back on my haunches and breathe, face tilted to the sky. I open my eyes. Dusk. My body shivers and aches, but I always remember enjoying this moment. Peaceful. Earth-birds singing. Quiet, no breeze.

I sigh a huge breath into the evening. The brisk air is almost refreshingly warm compared to where I just was, between worlds. This is the first time I feel like I've been able to breathe since the fall.

I look around. The field is mostly mud, wet and frigid. Trees line its perimeter. A dirt road, a shit-wooden fence. Some kind of farm.

It's a change-season here on Earth. The sky is a hard blue. I can't remember if it's spring or autumn. I wipe my hands on the legs of my pants and rise gently to my feet, careful lest I wobble again and drop.

A voice calls out from behind me: "You're tall."

Startled, I whirl about.

Kneeling in the mud behind me is a young girl. She must be no more than ten years old. She has light skin and long dark hair, braided in one shining coil, falling along her shoulder. She watches me with keen, sharp eyes.

I blink at her. I don't remember her. Why can't I hold all these things in my shitty *head*? Sure, it's been an age or three since I was last here. I should be kinder to myself. But for some reason, I'm particularly rattled by this girl. Frustrated. Scared. I don't want her to know me. Every time I'm known, it gets me in trouble. Just look at what happened with the philosophers. They think I'm looking for that depression-root right now.

Fuck em.

"I'm what?" I say.

"You're tall," she says again. She cocks her head. "You're taller than my dad. And I always thought *he* was tall."

It's true, this womanskin is intimidatingly big. Six feet tall, broad-shouldered and muscular. The body of a warrior. I sometimes regret that I cannot remember her name. She deserves better. But that's life, I suppose.

"I wish *I* was tall," says the girl, scrunching her face.

"You'll be tall someday," I tell her, rubbing the back of my head. "Maybe." Then, suddenly worried, I add, "Did you . . . see me arrive . . . here?"

"From the air? Of course." She rocks on her heels, excited. She doesn't seem frightened by my actively rotting appearance. Not at all. "Yeah, the air started to burn and then you *flew* through. Like you were falling."

"Uh huh." I watch her for a moment. Trying to decide what to do with her.

Then she says something that rattles me even more.

"I waited for you," she says. "I waited a long time."

My head throbs. My body is still dying around me. "How?" is all I can think to say.

She smiles, like she's thrilled even to be speaking to me. Like I'm some kind of celebrity.

"My name's Catie," she says. "Well. Catherine. Catherine Mason. But I think that sounds too formal. When I finish high school, I might have people call me Catherine, because then I'll be an adult? But for now, I like Catie."

She bobs some more.

"I see," I say. "You haven't answered my question. Catie."

"Oh! *How* did I wait for you?"

"Yes."

"Well, right here. In the mud." She frowns. "Is that alright? Should I have waited inside?"

"No." I close my eyes and shake my head. Run both hands through my still-soaked hair, raking out a smear of ice. I flick my fingers at the ground, spattering spinal yak on my feet. "I mean *how* did you *know* I was coming?"

She cocks her head again. Like it's obvious, she says: "Because you always come. You always will. Sometimes, you just don't remember me."

I stare at her.

"Where is this?" I ask.

She perks up. "You're in Renfield County, New York. Just outside the town of Lillian, population thirteen hundred. We're in the Falls school district, but my dad says we *technically* live in Lillian. And because the schools are better in Lillian, he pushed for me to . . ."

As she continues, the bad throb in my head gets worse. Almost as loud and terrible as the drums of the philosophers. *Doomdoom. Doomdoom. Doomdoom.* It's so loud I . . . I can't do anything but stare at her.

"This . . ." I say. "This is Renfield."

"Mmhmm." She nods cheerily. "We're right by the old art school. See?" She points through the trees at a blackened building. A lake shimmers beyond. "And over there is the old Renfield farm." She points through the trees on the other side of the field, at a sunken shell of a house. "I'm not supposed to go in *either* of those places."

I sigh. "Of course. Don't know where I *thought* I'd be."

Catie giggles. "But you always ask that. About where you are."

"Do I?"

She nods again. Waits. Then frowns like I've missed my cue.

"So you arrive," she says, more slowly. "First, I say *my* name. Catie Mason. Catherine." She rolls her eyes at *Catherine*. "And then you say yours."

I don't know how else to respond, so I just say my name. My real one.

"I'm Jopp. Jopp Yennigen." And to my intense surprise, she says my name *with* me, just as *I'm* saying it. She has this look in her eye like she's reciting the lyrics to a favorite song.

It's maddening.

Doomdoom.

"No one knows that name," I say.

"Well, I do."

Then why don't I remember her?

Doomdoom.

She leans forward, lets her hands sink into the mud. Hardly a whisper: "I had dreams about you, Jopp. Visions. I thought maybe it was just in my head, but . . ." She leans even farther forward. "I could *tell* it was real. Because every time I dreamt of you, I cried. It *hurt*. It scared me. But that's how I knew you were real."

"I . . . see." I'm about to fall apart. This body is fading around me, throbbing into nothing. If it dies all the way, I'll slide out of her pores and fall to the mud in pieces. *Doomdoom.* My eye twitches. *Doomdoom.* I need someone new.

"What happened to the barn?" I ask. My eyelids flutter. "There should be a . . . barn here. A door."

"It fell," she says. "And people took it apart."

I manage to frown. *Doomdoom.* "But what happened to the . . . figure?"

"Oh, He's everywhere now. Always watching. Remaking the whole valley the way *He* wants it to be. My dad says the giant has His eyes on the entire county."

Doomdoom. "How long ago? How . . . scattered is He?"

She scrunches her face as she does the math. "About . . . fifty years? It's 1974 now. My grandpa was one of the ones who cleaned up the blood in the first place." She lifts her head proudly. "His name was Otto Mason. He's famous. He's in that play that Mr. Moone wrote!"

"I see." I can barely keep my eyes open *doomdoom.*

"There was *soo* much blood," she says *doomdoom.* "That's what he told me. Some people blame him for everything that's happened, cuz he buried the blood in the first place, but how was *he* supposed to know?"

"Right." *Doomdoom*.

"Anyway, I wrote a *bunch* of stories about you. My teacher said they weren't very realistic, but I was just writing what I saw in my dreams."

Doomdoom. My head rolls on its neck.

"And now," she says, "I'd like . . . I mean, I *know* what you are. Not exactly, but I know what you . . . do? I guess? And I won't mind if—"

I burst into her. Explode out from this dead womanskin, letting it deflate behind me in a puff of air. It *poofs* like a used bag. The eye sockets yank apart, go hollow. The mouth *ooohh*-s back in an empty toothless moan. I push away from that dead mess and burst into the face of this little girl. Wriggle into her mouth, past her tongue, down her throat. Shove into the corners of her eyes, up her nose, and then whoever Catie Mason was, she's gone now. I popped her right out of her skull, wrapped my tails tight about the joystick of her brainstem, and began to use her shell for myself.

Sorry.

Typically, there's a moment at the end when skins fight back. Just before I pop their souls from their brains and burrow myself in there instead, they thrash. Wriggle and squirm and panic as I yank them out like a cork from a bottle. They do this without exception.

Except Catie Mason. She doesn't fight at all. In fact—she welcomes me. She blooms for me with pure, virginal energy, and when I slither inside her mind, she simply wilts away with a sigh. She really *was* waiting for me. Even at ten years old, she already wanted to die. She drifts around in my muscles and tissue, grateful to no longer be in control of her life anymore. Her consciousness is done sliding through the Spine. Her consciousness is done doing pretty much anything.

I shake my new hands and head, trying to whip the wisps of Mason off me, the way a dog whips water off its fur. But I can never quite shake a small, lingering hum. A feeling, in these bones, that Catie is thrilled to be in the hands of something sublime. Not to brag.

I lick my new lips. Squint at the field in the dull sunlight. I turn. There's a farmhouse behind me. Lights on inside. An old green pickup truck squats in the gravel driveway. Other houses farther back, nestled into the snarls of leafless trees.

I rise from the mud, brush off my knobbly little knees. I examine my little skirt. Pinch it, give it a twirl. I like it. Catie had good taste. I work to keep it clean as I bury my old skin along the tree line.

I skip to the house, pleased to be out of that dead skin, away from the grasp of the philosophers, and free from that fucking *tomb* in that old world. I feel good. Content. I remember now that the next chapter of my cycle is calm. All I have to do is let Catie's body grow up. Suffering through four years at Lillian High will be the worst torture I'll have to endure, but that's a fair trade for decades free on Earth, where there are berries. Berries! It'll be fun here. *So* fun.

I skip up to the back door of the house and yank it open. I peer into the modest kitchen. Stuff boils on the stove. Something meaty's in the oven.

It's nice to smell food again.

I run my hand along the wall. It's covered in an old wallpaper, pastel yellows and pinks. Stripes and flowers. The floor has a red runner rug and I kneel, dig my fingers into it. It's rich and scratchy. Smells like musty snow.

Someone in another room clears their throat. I jump, turn about. The door to a den is open just a crack. A middle-aged man in suspenders sits behind a desk, surrounded by cigarette smoke, reading a paper through small round glasses.

I breathe deep. I'm too young to smoke cigarettes now, but I can't *wait* for them. When I turn eighteen, I'll buy my first pack of Noxboros. They'll taste horrible, but they will be mine.

I stomp up the stairs into a short hall with a window at its head. In one room, a young man hunches over his desk, and I wonder if this entire family is just men at desks. He looks absorbed in homework, the little lamp at his side burning supportively. I'll have to figure out his name somehow. Richard? Rick? Reggie? Something with an R. I don't remember.

I do manage to figure out, without drawing too much attention, where the bathroom is, the master bedroom, and then my room. I creak my door open and peer inside. It's dark. The only light is the window over the short bed. A sad little prison-cell shaft of sun. The ceiling is sloped. I have a desk, too, and a little vanity. I sit before the mirror, examine myself, turning my face this way and that. I'm pretty. If I remember right, I'll grow up to break a lot of hearts. It'll be annoying and my back will start to hurt, and then I'll be scared all the time because of how swollen my chest is getting, everyone keeps *leering* at it. I'll bleed into my underwear in gym class. Christ, if I recall correctly, middle school will be an even worse roller coaster than high school.

Roller coasters! I forgot. I get to visit the Braddock County Fair one summer soon. I'll get to ride all the rides. It'll be a trip with my soccer camp, all the kids together in a big school bus. I'll sit in the very back with Kurt Motherwell, and even though I'll still be a young girl, I'll show him things I remember from being a woman. He'll be excited and impressed at first, but then he'll be self-conscious and he'll cry. He'll call me a slut. That's okay, I'll call him worse things in high school. By the time we graduate, he'll be in a padded room in Bent Asylum.

I giggle, remembering all these Earth-things. I'm remembering how much *fun* I get to have here.

Then I pause.

I turn.

I stare at the desk, hiding in the shadows far from the window.

I pounce on it, rip open a drawer. Pencils, crayons. Slam *that* one shut, yank open another. Notebooks! I snatch one up, flip through. School notes. A *lot* of school notes. Christ, what kind of nerd takes *this* many notes? There's about half a dozen notebooks in this drawer and they're just fucking *notes*.

I slam that drawer shut, too, and yank open a third.

A black, leatherbound volume, bound shut with a strap of hide. I pick it up gently, unwind the leather strip, and crack it open. On the first page, Catie has written *Dreams & Tales*.

I sit on the edge of the bed and begin poring over the book. The first entry is from September 1972, and she's updated it regularly all the way until now, which is apparently March 1974. She's had countless dreams, nearly the entire book's worth, and most of them are about me. Some of the dreams play out like sleep paralysis. Catie lies rigid on her bed while strange creatures accost her. She calls them gummerfolk—an adorably childish moniker. They poke and prod at her, go through her things. In one terrifying encounter, they rifle through the drawers of her vanity and eat all of her makeup, all the jewelry she'd saved up to buy. She lies there, unable to do anything but watch them have at it, mouths bent back, wide and dark, gums gnashing at lipsticks and earrings and plastic pearls.

As Catie got older, her dreams began to play out like story ideas. She even had visions while she was awake. The book gradually turns from a dream diary into a book of tales. She has so many visions and daydreams, I cannot count them all.

She dreams about the philosophers.

She dreams about Matthew Slitter.

She dreams about *me* entombed in the dark. Dreams of the day I was discovered, the new body I took and how I used it to commandeer that airship, flying it to the hole in the air of that war-torn world, hoping for escape—but falling back down at the beginning once more.

She dreams of the Renfield giant. Dreams of the envoys of the philosophers, searching uselessly for that rot-root at the bottom of the Spine. Eaten by Yckwolves or tangled in vines, lost in the forests of the Dreamcoast. Fucking fools.

"These nightmares are just Its silly little thoughts," Catie writes. "The same way I doodle when I'm bored in class. There's no reason to be afraid of them, because *I'm* just a thought, too. Everything is just a thought in the Mind of God. So really, I'm lucky to get these glimpses of Its other imaginings. All of It is beautiful."

She even has a full drawing of the Leviathan, which she depicts as a giant whale. Alongside it, another entry: "I saw the Mind last night. I flew all the way up Its Spine, and It sang to me: *I don't want to feel lonely anymore. Swimming alone is such a bore.* Wow! Even God feels lonely. I felt bad because I feel lonely sometimes, too. I feel—"

Someone calls from downstairs: "Catherine!" Mother, I presume. "Richie! Dinner!"

Richie. Of course. I remember Richie. I *hate* Richie.

I close the book, shove it back in the drawer, and skip out of the room down the hall. Richie, about three years older than me, is coming out of his room. He's tall, lanky, and easily shovable, so I shove him as I skip by to the stairs. He bounces back against the wall, "Hey! You little jerk." He chases me down the stairs. I squeal with joy and launch myself into a chair at the dining table, looking around eagerly. Steaming piles of green beans, a big thing of dinner rolls, mashed potatoes . . . Here comes Mother, carrying a plate of sliced chicken. She's young, still beautiful. Her hair is in tight, dark curls around her head. She jerks that head at me. "Catie, grab the gravy, will you?"

"Catie grab the gravy," I say automatically. I taste it on my tongue. "Catie grab the gravy." I repeat it all the way into the kitchen, grabbing the gravy dish, and back. I'm happy to do what Mother says. I'm elated to even hear her voice. I'll cry at her funeral thirty years from now. Richie will give the eulogy.

Richie is tearing into a roll at the table. "You coulda broken the back of my head, idiot."

"Hey," says Mother, taking her seat. "No idiots, and *no* breaking heads." She points a finger at me.

I grin. This is fun, this is already *so* much fun. I kick my legs under the table.

Soon, Father is at the table, too. We're saying grace, which I don't remember the words to. Then I'm sent to my room to do homework, which I also don't know how to do (who *gives* a fuck about algebra). Then Father calls to me: it's time for *Star Trek* on the television.

I sit on the floor, my back against the couch, surrounded by my family, watching fake stories about space, and I am very, very happy to be alive.

During a commercial, I look back at Mother, sewing in her chair. "Can I have some berries?"

"What . . . kind of berries?" she asks, appalled. Father peers at me over his newspaper from his chair.

"Any berries," I say.

"Catherine, you hate berries," says Father.

"No I don't." My body bristles.

"I've never seen you eat one," says Mother.

I pout. "I want Earth berries."

"The hell are Earth berries?" says Richie.

"Catherine, please," says Mother, annoyed.

"It's *Catie*," I snap.

They all blink at me, shocked.

I glare. "My *name* is Catie and I *want* some fucking berries."

ESCAPE FROM THE UNDERCAMPUS

Tonight the Mind sang to me of the Philosopher High. Really just big whooping whale noises, but I understood. It said that when a seer receives enough visions, their mind gets soaked in the knowledge of too many vertebrae-worlds to name, and their eyes just explode. This seer declares themself the Philosopher High. And because their consciousness kept flying up and down the Spine all the time, it eventually just fused with all the other High-brains, on all other planes. So the High becomes *the same person* across the entire Spine, a single consciousness *assimilated* (our vocab word this week) across countless bodies. Not one person, but a *bunch* of people all slammed together in a straight line.

Anytime one High-body dies, the Mind anoints another, and grants *them* visions until *their* eyes explode and *their* brain fuses with everyone else's, too.

Philosophers call this the *synchronicity*. The Mind even told me how to spell that!

Because of the *synchronicity*, the Philosopher High sees all and knows all. They have many names, all at once, across every plane. Old Deadjack, Slit Garrity, Dellion the Fourth (that's the one who throws Jopp Yennigen into the well). All kinds of names.

I hope one day I get to be a Philosopher High. It's exhausting being alone inside my mind.

Entry dated April 29, 1973; Catherine Mason, *Dreams & Tales*

CHAPTER FOURTEEN

AUNTIE ETHEL'S ETERNITY TRUNK

The latest mischief was Uncle William's stories. He used to sell them to the *Lillian Journal,* made five dollars off each one they printed in the Sunday edition. William had a stockpile of stories he was still working over, and he packed them with his clothes in the big steamer trunk when he headed out to see Cousin Ida in Ohio for Easter. But when he got off the train, opened the trunk in Ida's spare room—the pages were blank. Every single word he'd typed over the last *year* had simply vanished. The pages were all accounted for, but they were all the fresh snow-white of empty pulp.

William was horrified. He blamed his wife, Gladys, he blamed Cousin Ida. He blamed the strangers on the train. But *why* would someone steal his stories? And why replace them with blank paper?

William's daughter Ethel, who was only twelve at the time, was the one who suggested the trunk had eaten his words. The trunk had eaten things before.

Five years earlier, great-grandpa George had traveled with the trunk to a wedding in Massachusetts. When George opened the trunk in his hotel room, three of his shoes were gone. Well. Nobody in their right mind would take just three left shoes.

The family had never been able to explain it.

Two years after *that,* Eliza had taken the trunk to the beach. She packed her most valuable jewelry and her nicest dresses, because she was trying to impress a young man from Branson College. When she arrived at the beach house, however, the trunk was completely empty—except for three left shoes.

So when Ethel pointed out there was an explanation for this behavior, the family listened. It wasn't exactly a *rational* explanation, but one that made sense nonetheless: The lid of the trunk was fashioned from Renfield wood. A strip of the giant's leg, or perhaps an arm, was stained across its surface. A thick ripple of reddish-brown, cutting diagonally across the lid.

The family began to wonder. Who . . . bought this trunk? *How* had it come into the family? What—

"The fuck is this, what am I reading?" McCall turned the pages over, read the title again. "What the fuck is an eternity trunk?"

Cam sat hunched in the chair across from McCall's desk. His eyes were crimson, pupils almost nonexistent. He dabbed at the corner of his left eye, rubbed his fingers together.

"That's what they end up calling the trunk," he said. "I don't know if they ever refer to it specifically in this draft, but . . ."

McCall's office was vastly different from Cam's. Where Cam's office felt like an unused rec room, McCall's was reminiscent of a mausoleum. Wide, well-lit. Deep purple carpet, a grandfather clock ticking loud. Two hardbacked wooden chairs with maroon leather cushions (bolted in with big brass bulbs), facing the big oak fuck of a desk. One of the legs on one of the chairs used to be made of Renfield wood. It's in the undercampus now, on the tapestry, and the chair wobbles bad. The desk even has one of those timeless green blotters, floating gracefully on the oak.

This corner room has a nice view of West Camp, the two student theaters, Von Eichmann Hall, and the flowers. The parking lot shimmers in the heat.

The lush carpet here smells like something primordial, something you only notice after you have been in the room for a very long time. At night, the chain on the banker's lamp on the corner of the desk swings ever so slightly, and if you listen very close, there are whispers in the hum of the fluorescent lights overhead.

"And why," said McCall, "am I reading about this old-time family's steamer trunk?"

"Well, the lid. It's a piece of the tapestry," said Cam.

"I understand, but . . ." McCall tsk-ed and flipped through the pages. He ran his tongue around his mouth. "But what is all this bullshit . . . character development?"

"It's the story," said Cam. He tried to peer over the desk. "What part are you at?"

McCall held the sheaf of papers to his chest. "Look, I don't *need* to know who Auntie Ethel *was*. Or William or Gladys. This was all in your vision?"

"I saw the trunk get passed around, yeah." Cam rubbed at his eye again. "I added the names and the bit with Ethel's birthday party this morning."

He'd had a lot of time to write because Quinn hadn't come home to bother him. He'd spent the entire night leaking onto his laptop. Hadn't even noticed she was gone until he'd seen the text around one a.m.: *You're a pusillanimous ASS! Mom came to pick me up. Staying in Leaden Hollow tonight . . . Don't call . . . Still mad at you . . .*

"Whatever," he told the phone. He didn't even bother texting back. Figured she'd send him a novel of a text later, explaining what an asshole he was. Fair trade for fourteen hours of uninterrupted work.

McCall let out a deeply irritated breath. He flipped through several pages to the end of the story, skimmed several lines. Finally, he cleared his throat and chucked the papers onto his desk blotter. "Thing is, Cameron." He rose and began to walk around the room, so that Cam's back was to him. "I think you've mistaken me. I didn't *need* an entire piece about the wood. You didn't need to write an entire thirty-page story called . . . 'Auntie Ethel's Eternity Trunk.'" Ohh, the sneer in his voice as he said that title.

Cam turned in his chair. "But I . . . spent all night on it. I *saw* it."

"And I'm thrilled. But as I said the other night, I don't particularly need your *writing*. I just need the idea."

Cam was hurt. "You said my work mattered."

"Your *visions* matter. Your dreams. I don't care about one family's struggle to maintain positivity while their furniture keeps eating their belongings."

"Well, I think it's a good story," Cam grumbled.

"And it's a shame that no one will ever read it." McCall ran his tongue around his teeth. "But you're part of something *bigger* now, Cameron. Better than just . . . writing stories." He leaned back against his desk, hands in his pockets. "Where is the trunk now?"

"That's at the very end," said Cam. McCall frowned, took up the pages again. "See? There's a coda."

"Oh my god, a *coda.*" McCall flipped to the end, read quickly. He raised his eyebrows. "Well!" He turned the page toward Cam so Cam could see his annoyance at the fact that, "You wrote thirty fucking pages and all I needed was this one paragraph. Why?"

Cam's voice came out small and stung. "I thought it was . . . good. I thought you cared."

"I do," McCall muttered as he read the coda. "Just not in the way you . . ." He blinked. Read over the ending again. Stood straighter. "Are you sure about this? The name? Or is this just more bullshit? Because most of this is useless bullshit." He flipped through the pages. "Bullshit, bullshit."

"Well, one *bullshit* would have sufficed. But yes. I'm sure. That's the whole point." Cam wiped Aether off on his jeans.

"Huh. I'll be fucked," said McCall. "Right under our noses this entire time . . ."

He tossed the pages at Cam, who held them delicately in his lap. McCall picked up the phone on his desk, dialed. "Angie? Reserve the van for tomorrow. We're going on a raid."

"Ohh," Angie's voice on the other end. "I *love* a raid."

McCall hung up on her.

"What raid?" Cam asked. "Raid what?"

"Wood raid, of course. You're invited. Everyone is! Should be fun. Fine work, Cameron." Then he plucked Cam's story from his hands and chucked it in the trash.

"Whooaa," said Cam. "What the fuck."

"I got what I wanted off it." McCall shrugged. "What else do you want me to do with it?"

"Well . . . do you think it's good?"

McCall laughed, then gave him a pitying look. "Please." He went to the corner, where he opened a cabinet in the wall, revealing several expensive bottles of booze. He started to pour himself a drink.

"So that's it?" Cam asked.

"That's it. We'll go check it out tomorrow. Syd's miniature friend," he wriggled his fingers, "will be able to tell if the lid's the real deal or not."

"But you didn't like my story."

McCall made a face. "I didn't even *read* your stupid story."

A beat.

"Why are you being such an asshole about this?" Cam asked.

McCall turned to him, fresh glass of whisky in hand. "Best save that tone," he said. He took a loud, slurping sip.

"But you're a writer, too. Don't you . . . care? About the *work*?"

McCall gave him a very level look. He licked whisky off his lips. *That tongue.* "I never said I was a writer."

"Then . . . what are you?" Cam asked.

McCall grinned. "Someone interested in getting the hell out of Earth."

"And going where? Where do you think the door leads?"

"Oh, I *know* where it leads."

"So . . . where?"

"Elsewhere. I'll be honest, I'm not *quite* sure there are better worlds out there. But there are certainly . . . different ones." McCall slugged the rest of his drink. "Well. Thanks for stopping by."

As the door to McCall's office (which Cam now remembered he'd moved him*self* into, which seemed about right) slammed shut behind him, Cam officially began to suspect that Quinn was right: he might be in over his head. The thought that she could be correct made him angry, and he simmered in that anger for the rest of the day, stoutly refusing to text her back, or to see if she'd texted him again.

Of course, if he'd been a better boyfriend, he might have noticed that *first* text didn't even sound like Quinn at all.

CHAPTER FIFTEEN

SHARDSOAP & LADY-HUSKS

The cell was about six feet by seven. Its walls were cement, the floor very hard-packed dirt. There was stuff buried in it. Weird jags and bumps of things. Quinn wriggled a chunk of something loose. It turned out to be an old Elgin watch. The same kind her grandma used to wear. She wondered how long it'd been stuck there, if she could dig through the floor to escape. But even that small amount of digging for the watch had bent one of her fingernails dangerously, had sprent a thin line of blood across the face of the Elgin. So Quinn spent the rest of the night fetaled in the corner, nursing her hand and hugging her knees, wondering what in the absolute bull-fuck she was gonna do now. It even crossed her mind that this was her fault.

The women had carried her all the way down here, cackling, and had quite literally chucked her into the cell. She hit the floor hard, and a sick green fluorescent ho-hummed itself to life overhead. The door to the cell was a big wooden bolted thing. Medieval-looking. When they locked her in, she'd slammed her shoulder over and over against that door until she heard something in herself pop.

"Fuck!" she told the door.

"Quinn."

For a second, she'd thought the door had spoken back. She gaped at it, holding her shoulder. Then Cindy's face peered through the small window in the top of the door, blinking through thick orange-lensed bifocals.

"Cindy, where's Brenda?" Brenda seemed like someone she could reason with.

"Ohh, I'm sorry," said Cindy. "Brenda was . . . disemboweled. They've been trying to vote her out for a while anyway. She was *such* a control freak with those bookfairs." She glanced off to the side. Stone clattered somewhere outside the cell. "I . . . shouldn't be talking to you. I'll try to find you some blankets."

"Cindy, wait! Cindy!"

Cindy was gone.

That's when Quinn had dug into her pocket for her phone. One of the ladies had taken it. They'd left her Marilyn lighter (thank Crows) but no phone.

There was a toilet in one corner, industrial steel. A sink, just as blocky and metallic as the toilet. A cot on a metal wheeling frame, along the wall opposite the sink. When Quinn sat on it, cockroaches swarmed out of its seams, so she left it alone. A small wooden shelf dangling precariously over the pillow held two faded leather volumes: *Legends of the Lumbermen: Myths from the Shembelwoods in the Twentieth Century* and *A Historian's Guide to Living Long*. She'd have to crawl over the shit-cot to reach those books, so it seemed wiser to let them remain a mystery.

The sink had a soap dish. A thick bar of clouded glycerin soap, something floating within. Quinn couldn't identify what it was. But it reminded her of the bars of soap her dad used to buy when she was little. The ones with small animals floating inside, or sharks or dinosaurs. Quinn used to measure time in those bars of soap. She felt herself whittling away at Time itself when she scrubbed them down after school, at night before bed, in the pre-dawn gray before climbing onto the school bus. She loved the feel of the sharp little plastic thing inside, the edges of it scraping into her fingers as she began to reveal it. She'd line up the figurines on the shelf over the sink in the bathroom. By the time Dad died, she had a dozen of them. After the funeral, she threw them all away.

After Cindy left, Quinn had rocked herself for quite a while under the single buzzing fluorescent. From her position on the floor, she could see the one high window of the cell (just a hole with three black iron bars), and a ceiling of rock outside. When she'd finally cried as much as she figured she was going to, she got to her feet and looked out. No way could she get out through the bars in the window. When she peered outside, on her tippy-toes, there was nothing but more cave. A tunnel stretching away into purpley-black. She fell back on her heels, wiped rust flakes off her palms, and turned. Blinked. And laughed. She fell to her knees. She screamed, "What the fuck!" several times.

There, in the corner of the ceiling just above where she'd lain for hours, was the husk. How she hadn't seen it before, she didn't know. But she certainly saw it now.

It looked like a cross between a broken cocoon and the hollow shell of a cicada. Like a human being had crawled up there and flipped over into some Spider-Man pose, hands and legs gripping the walls and ceiling behind them as they gazed down upon the cell. Then they'd split down the middle and wriggled themselves out of their skin, leaving behind everything, even their teeth and eyes. The fingers curled up, empty and dried. The mouth was cleft in two and the teeth leered jaggedly on either side. The transparent eyes were bloodshot and glazed, pointing in wildly different directions. Green and black tendrils of wet moss stretched out from the husk, across the walls and ceiling. A waterfall of dried brown blood cascaded down along the corner. Something had shoved out of this, dropped to the floor, and walked away.

How had she lain under this for *hours* without noticing it?

When she was done laughing and pulling at her hair, Quinn began to gag. She rushed to the toilet and gagged up stringy lines of spit for a long while. She couldn't remember the last time she'd eaten. She didn't know what time it was.

She went to the sink to wash her hands. Thankfully, the tap worked and even more thankfully, the water looked like actual water. It had a sulfurous stink to it, but beggars and choosers and all that. Quinn rubbed the soap between her hands. Pain sliced into her palms. She dropped the bar, looked down at her shaking hands. Ribbons of flesh had been stripped away. Blood oozed thick and dark from a series of cuts, deep in her skin. She washed her hands under the water, clearing away the blood. She counted five stinging lacerations in total.

"Fuck!" she shouted again. She picked up the soap delicately, by a corner, and held it to the light. She could see now the strips of color inside. The rainbowy fracas of several lines crisscrossing around inside the glycerin.

"The hell . . ."

Her eyes swept over to the window, and she caught sight of four sets of glowing eyes, under four mothbally wigs. As soon as she saw them, they tittered and ducked away out of sight. Quinn threw the soap at them as best she could, which wasn't very good at all. It landed limply a foot away from her.

"Fuck you!" she screamed. The ladies outside the cell giggled away into the dark.

In their place, a gentle voice furled through the bars: "I'm sorry about them. This is why I hesitated to come back."

Quinn thrust herself at the window. Greta Marie Mither stood below, giving her a very worried look. She was wearing a scarlet robe, with a blue and gold sash cinched about her waist. The hood fell back behind her head.

"Greta," Quinn whispered. "You have to help me out of here."

"Oh, that's not possible," said Greta. "I'm sorry. They're too thrilled to have you. *You* should be thrilled."

Quinn pressed her mouth to the bars. "I am not fucking thrilled. *Please*. This is a mistake."

Greta shook her head. "I'm sorry. That's just not the way it's done. I've already spoken to him." She laughed. "Of course, he already *knew* you were coming." She shook her head, impressed.

"I don't know who the fuck you're talking about," said Quinn. "You have to *help* me."

Greta frowned. "We *are* helping you. You're going to transform into something new. Something more intelligent. And—"

"I am fucking intelligent!"

"*And*," said Greta, "you're helping *them*. You'll help them find the door."

"What? I'm not helping anybody find that stupid wood."

"But you don't know how important it is. Quinn, they *don't* want to hurt you."

Quinn shoved her bloody hands through the bars. "They literally *just* hurt me."

"Ohh, they didn't mean that. That was just a practical joke! They play it on everyone. They did it to *me* a while ago, back when I was first down here. See?" She held up her hands. They were vastly scarred. "They call it shardsoap. It has something to do with not rubbing away at something until it hurts you. Some Society nonsense. It's a . . . a rite of passage." She chuckled.

"Rite of . . ." Quinn gripped the bars, digging the metal into her wounds. "Greta, I don't want to *pass* anywhere. I want to pass the fuck *out* of this cell. I . . . Look." She stuck her face farther out through the bars, stretching her skin. She knew she looked insane, but she was trying to impress herself upon this woman as much as possible. "I lost someone, too. She was young and blond and she . . . Not that it matters she was blond. I'm just saying your daughter *reminds* me of her. I can *sympathize*, Greta. I understand your loss. But . . . Whatever these women are offering you, it's not worth it. Trust me. You have to help me out of here."

Greta drew back. "They wouldn't like that."

"Yes!" Quinn hissed. She shoved her face into the bar-gap so hard her eyes watered. "I know!"

"Listen, it's just a simple little ceremon—"

"So I can end up like that?" She pointed behind her at the leering husk upon the wall. "*That's* your little ceremony?"

"Greta!" Someone called. "Get away from her window!"

"Sorry," said Greta. She pulled back, lifted her red hood over her eyes. "I can't release you. You'll see. This will all be mutually beneficial, I promise. You have to *let* them help. I almost didn't let them help *me*, but now . . . Now it's all I want." She was fading back into the shadows of the cave.

Quinn shook the bars. Her palms stung like crazy. "Greta! Please! Please help me!"

Greta was gone. Quinn stared after her with such tearful despair that she barely heard the cell-door open. Barely felt the hands on her until there were a *dozen* hands on her, yanking her off the window and dragging her into the tunnel.

Quinn screamed and kicked and bit into the soft arm of one of the women dragging her. She hissed at Quinn and turned a boiling shade of green, odd colors pulsing through her veins. Quinn drew back.

"Are you excited?"

Quinn swiveled her head around. Deborah had appeared at her side. She leered at Quinn. She, too, was in a crimson robe.

"No," said Quinn.

"Oh, you should be. Not everyone is lucky enough to meet *him* so soon after joining the Society."

"I'm not a member."

Deborah waved her hand. "It's just a little ceremony. You'll be fine."

"I'm already not fine!"

They brought Quinn to a wide-open cavern, swarming with old women. They all wore bright red robes. They milled about, sipping from Styrofoam cups, playing cards at folding tables, chatting over dominos. Their perfume stink was abysmal, but at least they weren't whatever they'd morphed into in that basement. The only decoration in the space was what seemed to be a massive woven tapestry of the Renfield giant. It spanned maybe thirty feet tall and twenty feet wide, covering one entire wall of the cavern with brown thread. The thread-eyes of the giant burned over all. He wove a planet Earth between His fingers. And down His back ran a shimmering spine of planets, galaxies, and stars.

They positioned her on a stone dais, no more than a flat-level bit of rock slightly higher than the rest of the floor. From here, Quinn could look out over the sea of bristly white Q-tip poofs of hair. She could see the many black mouths of tunnels in all directions, and the sea of crimson robes. The women held her in place. Greta appeared next to her, offering a small smile and a wave.

Someone was putting something on her. She shoved it away, fought like hell, until she heard Cindy saying, "Hey, hey, you're alright."

She turned. Cindy was holding a green-black sarape. She beamed. "See? A blanket."

Quinn pulled it about herself. Mumbled, "Thanks."

"Of course. Just try not to get blood on it."

Quinn slapped it spitefully with both hands, smeared them all the way down.

And then, from a darkened tunnel at the far corner of the space, came the laughter. Deep, booming. The cackling of a mad king, a demented bar-

barian. A belly-laughing, bloated-emperor guffaw. It boomed throughout the cavern. "Ahh ha ha ha. AHH haha, AHH HAHAHAHA HAAA HA HA HA AHHH!"

The women began to laugh with it. They dropped their rummy cards and their coffee cups and they stood at attention and they laughed. They cracked their jaws wide, threw their heads back, eyes bugging out. They belted laughter at the ceiling, at each other, at Quinn. They laughed right in her face, clutching at her arms with those nobbly old hands. Cindy gripped the edges of the sarape and cackled right into Quinn's mouth. The entire cave filled with the booming, insane laughter of these women, and whatever voice lay beyond.

Light bloomed into the chamber. Foggy and pale. As it lit the ceiling, the laughter grew louder. Closer. Quinn saw a gigantic shadow shoot through the center of the light. The head of some hobbling thing, weaving its way down the tunnel as it laughed and laughed and laughed.

At last, it arrived. Light splashed across its face, across the cracked teeth in its jaw, its grayish-purple skin. It cackled and hooted and spat. It clunked across the stone floor on giant, spidery metal legs. Four of them, six feet tall, one at each corner of its wide, brass throne. The legs were hobnobbed, homemade. Tubes and car-parts and strange strips of metal all soldered together. One of the thing's little hands (nails long, jagged, and brown) clutched what looked to Quinn like a joystick.

It took her several seconds of watching, heart hammering, to recognize that this *thing* was actually a man. A bent little man in a chair with four legs. Some kind of mobile throne he was operating with a fucking *joystick*. He laughed as he maneuvered himself closer and closer to Quinn. The women parted before him, giving his large, pounding metallic legs a wide berth. They continued to laugh with him as he came within a few feet of Quinn. Then he ground to a halt, steam hissing from the joints of his throne. He grinned down at her. Gears clunked.

His was a cold, croaking old-man voice: "Well, well. Ms. Quinn Rose Carver-Dobson."

His legs clanged and steamed and were still. Silence rippled out. All around, the women grinned up at him. "You smell as I expected." He ran a black tongue over his teeth.

His skin was wrinkled and hairless, and Quinn could not account for its purplish hue. Nor could she explain why he had no eyes. Where his eyes should have been, thick plastic tubes ringed with brass were clamped to his sockets. They stretched out from the sides of his head, back around to the rear of the chair. He turned, laughing around the entire cavern, and Quinn saw the glass tanks strapped to the back of his chair, a thick yellow liquid sloshing around inside. Air-pumps whirred above the tanks. The man grit his teeth, squeezed, and thick yellow sludge slurped out of the sockets clamped to his head, through the tubes, down into the tanks. Smoke curled up from the seam where tube met man. It fogged the mouth of the tube and whispered up toward the ceiling of the cave, as he turned back around to face her.

She managed only to say, "Who are you?"

"Questions!" the man roared. He laughed. The cave laughed with him.

He yanked his joystick back, and the front legs of his chair let out a whining grind. They reared up off the floor, kicked at the air like horse's hooves. They slammed back down onto the rock so hard it cracked. "To-night! We celebrate the elevation of two women. One, known to us and very dear. Temporarily lost, but returned to us now. Greta Marie Mither."

Roaring cheers and clapping hands. Greta gave everyone a shy but queenly wave.

"And the other," continued the eyeless man, "new to us, but no less dear. A seeker, just like you. Like *all* of us." He announced her name like she was about to wrestle. "Quinn. Rose. Carver. Dobson!"

Cheers. Hoots. Hisses. Applause.

"Oh, I don't . . . want . . . that," said Quinn. "I don't . . . I'm not here for any . . . ceremony or . . ." She tried to back away. Cindy held her shoulder blades, held her in place. She even pushed them a little, in opposite directions. Quinn's spine creaked and she winced, fell forward, cried out.

"Of course you do," said the man. He grinned. His teeth were horrible. Yellow and shattered. "I have seen what you want. I *know* what will satiate you, my dear Quinn Rose Carver-Dobson."

"Stop saying my name. It isn't fair if I don't know yours."

"Ha! This is true!" he roared. "She does not know my name! And yet, tomorrow! We will celebrate as she and Greta Marie Mither drink of me."

"I won't drink shit," said Quinn. "Especially not from *you*."

"Quinn, don't be rude," said Cindy.

"No!" She jabbed a finger at the shriveled man. "Talk about rude? Who. Are. You. What the *fuck* is all this?"

"My dear," said the man. He smiled again. A wide leer under those eyeless sockets, those twin glass tubes. He raised his eyebrows. Bushy white worms, squirming over the glass. "Do you not recognize me?"

Quinn squinted at him for a moment.

And the realization shook her to a core she did not know she had.

She shook her head. "You're . . . That's not . . . How . . . ?"

"How!" He laughed, and around him, the women tittered darkly. "That is exactly what we are here to cure, Quinn Rose Carver-Dobson. Your *questions*. Because it *is* true. Believe it.

"I," pressing his joystick forward, rising grandly to his chair's full height, "am Matthew Thomas Slitter. And *I* am your Philosopher High."

CHAPTER SIXTEEN

WOOD RAID

The department van was once used to shuttle the Senior Writing Seminar students on ski trips, far up the Billowhills to the Boldiven Lodge. Every February they did this, until the E.C. board of trustees found out these trips were notorious for fostering student-teacher liaisons. The Lodge apparently had a vast number of hot tubs. Practically one in every room.

"But it was *what's*-her-name," Angie narrated cheerfully as she bumped along behind the wheel, "who really got the board pissed. That poetry professor, always wavin around her Lambda Award? Hooked up with what's-*her*-face, that redheaded junior? She was a trustee's daughter? Whew." Angie shook her head. "That *really* pissed off the trustees. And Ken—back when he was college president—he put the kibosh on the trips after that."

"Angela," said McCall shakily from the back of the van. "Would you mind focusing on the road?"

"Hell, I've been driving for fifty years, I *know* roads," she called back. She lifted herself in her seat to peer over the wheel, a feat she barely accomplished.

Cam was in the front with her, clinging to the oh-shit handle. McCall and Madeline were in the middle row, and Wes and Syd filled up the back bench. There was another bench behind them, where McCall had told Cam they'd store the wood once they found it.

"That's almost as long as I've been with the department," Angie told Cam. "Forty-three years. You know, you work for the college for *ten*, you get a mug. Twenty, you get a nice pen. I'm comin up on an Edenville *rocking* chair, myself."

"Angie, you're turning left up here," Syd called from the back.

"Yep," confirmed Angie. She swung the van so fast Cam was shocked a hubcap didn't fly loose.

"Can we slow down?" Madeline asked. She looked green. She gripped McCall's sleeve, but he shoved her off.

"Almost there!" Angie announced. "See, most people," talking to Cam again now, "say the Renfield blood does somethin *bad* to ya. Never been my experience. Fact, I think drinking the water here made me smarter. I have a head for *all* department matters like you wouldn't believe. Numbers, addresses, dates . . . Got every class schedule and every address of every faculty member ever passed through Slitter, right up here." Tapping her temple as she whipped around another corner, somehow managing to hold on to the steering wheel with one hand. "For instance, that professor who ran off with the redheaded co-ed, got the ski trips canceled? Lived at 77 Applecore Lane. Right next to the Mithers, actually."

"Angela," McCall snapped. "Really would be nice if you focused on the road."

"Road, ha!" Angie slammed the van into a driveway. A metallic clunk-grind as some part of the undercarriage smashed against the curb and was lost into the gutter.

"We're here," said Angie with a smile.

The house was a squat brown thing in a neighborhood of homogeneous squat brown things. The day was overcast and somewhere out there, a small dog barked endlessly.

The group climbed out of the van a little groggy and worse for wear. The ride had been maybe fifteen minutes door to door, but Cam had to take a moment to breathe through his mouth, gulping the early September air with relish. Madeline looked even worse than he did. She rested a hand against the van and stared at the ground. Angie, on the other hand, was already marching up the short stub of a driveway to the door.

"Come," said McCall, placing a hand on Cam's shoulder. He led him to the house. Angie already had the shitty dented screen door open, and was waiting, smiling, for McCall to knock.

Cam didn't like this vibe. Nor did he like that they'd called it a raid. People die in raids.

He'd waited for Quinn to come home last night so he could talk to her about all this. But when he'd finally relented and texted her to ask if she was still at her mom's, she'd just written, *YEP*. So he'd left it alone. Focusing for too long on his phone screen made his eyes ache anyway.

McCall knocked on the door. Cam took a moment to look around. Wes and Syd stood a ways behind him. Madeline was now hobbling up the driveway. Someone could have told Cam the entire neighborhood was abandoned and he would have believed it.

Until, that is, the door creaked open, and Chett Neeves emerged from the shadows.

He glanced around at everyone. "Must be my birthday."

"Morning, Chett," McCall smiled.

"Ben," Chett nodded. "Wes."

"Sneeze," Wes greeted him.

Chett crossed his arms. "So what's . . . ?"

"Well, brass tacks." McCall smoothed his tie over his stomach. "Our new channelman here gave me a rather intriguing report yesterday."

Chett gave Cam such a withering look that Cam had to look away. He watched a V of geese honk by overhead.

"I thought you decided *channelman* was an outdated term," said Chett. "Considering some of them are women or—"

"Right, right," said McCall. "Certainly. But that's beside the point. Cameron informed me—us—that you have a piece of the pie right here in your very home."

Chett smirked. "I, ah . . . I sold it."

McCall's demeanor flickered. He ran his tongue around his mouth. "Come again."

"I sold it," Chett repeated. "At a flea market, last summer." He wheeze-laughed. "How much did *Professor* Marion see?"

"I . . . know your family pretty well," said Cam, blinking.

"Right, so my Auntie Ethel," said Chett. "You know she was a collector, too. She had a cribbage board, stained right down the middle. She had this wooden doll, a—"

"Why don't we come in?" said McCall. "Just wanna see."

Chett stepped aside and McCall shoved his way into the house. Angie followed cheerfully after. Wes and Syd nudged their way past Cam after that. He glanced at Madeline. She shook her head, standing on the lawn.

"I'm not going in," she murmured. "I don't like the raids."

"You . . . want me to stay out here with you?"

She shook her head and forced a smile. "Too much despair at these things. I don't even know why I came."

Cam watched her wince for a moment, then went in, letting the screen door clap shut behind him.

Chett's house was impersonal and dusty. He owned a beanbag chair and a tube television. Cam had the urge to turn it on just to hear the old blink and hum of the early aughts. He followed the line of faculty limply as they shuffled through the house.

"I'm telling you," said Chett, "I sold my aunt's entire collection. Last thing she had was a set of knives. Sold that, too. Wooden handles, all—"

"Chett, I'm sorry," said Syd. "But if you're lying, you know you can save your breath." She began to unbuckle her small hand.

Chett scoffed. He stood in the corner of his barren, dim living room as the sub-department pawed through his things. Wes lifted a corner of the bent window blinds, peering outside at a weedy backyard. A garden gnome stared glumly back at him, cracked and sun-bleached.

"You remember who bought it?" he asked. "The trunk. We've got the cribbage board, I remember that one."

"We have the knives, too," said Syd. She draped her straps on the back of a chair that was puking up its stuffing from several duct-taped wounds. She bared her small hand, unfurled its fingers. Cam could hear the knuckles crack. She grunted, knelt, and placed her hand in the center of the floor. She closed her eyes.

"You think I'm a fool," said Chett from the doorway. His face twitched indignantly. "But I'm not lying. I was glad to be rid of it. All of it. Anytime you cut a vegetable with those knives, you could be nowhere *near* your finger, and you'd *still* cut yourself. Every time. And the trunk? The trunk *moved* at night. I heard it sliding around on the floor. I've seen it slide into my room. It slides *backward*. Then it turns around. And when it looks at you, you . . . lose time."

"Oh, the trunk looks at you?" McCall sneered.

Chett nodded solemnly. "And when it opens . . . The noise . . . The *voices* . . . It's not just a trunk anymore. It's a magnifying glass. It—"

"It's not here," said Syd. She rose, leaning on Wes to do so. She opened her eyes. "He's not lying. It's somewhere else."

"Where?" McCall snarled.

Syd lifted her shoulders, wrapping her hand back up. "Don't know."

McCall was breathing hard through his nose now. "Can't you try again?"

"Ben." Syd glared at him. "I saw what I saw. There's no trying it again."

McCall ran his tongue around his teeth. Something bulged in his throat. Something unnatural.

He strode across the room to Chett and placed a hand on the man's shoulder, looked down at him. He pursed his lips, shook his head.

"Sorry," said Chett. "It was before you came here. Before you told that *ridiculous* story at the alumni house. I'm surprised anyone believed you at all." He glared around at the others. "Surprised at *all* of you." He wheeze-laughed. "And now you're probably going to kill me over a stupid—"

He was cut short by McCall's hand. The fingers tightened. They dug into the sinews and cords of Chett's shoulder. His knees buckled a little.

"Okay," he said, his laugh faltering. "Ow."

"Ow?" said McCall. He tilted his head, brought his face closer to Chett's. His throat continued to bulge. To swell. "What ow? This?" McCall clenched his hand harder. Chett cried out. "This ow? Is *this* ow? Oh, you *poor* man. If this is too much, we can bring the fucking Giving Tree in here," jerking his head at Madeline outside, staring helplessly through the screen door. "She'll feel it up right *for* you." And he dug his fingers in harder.

Chett's face screwed tight with pain. His forehead was beginning to sweat. McCall went on: "Did you know that's her talent? Hm? That she's mortally empathetic? That poor Madeline Narrows could be whittling away *right* now because she's trying to make *you* suffer less?"

"Okay," Chett gasped. "I get it."

"All that pain just . . . eats away at you. Not that *you'd* know with your perfectly fine, non-rotting body."

"Ben," said Syd. "It's fine. We'll keep looking."

McCall's eyes widened and he swiveled his head like an owl to glare at her. "Keep . . . looking? Do you even understand . . ." He gagged, the thing inside his throat expanding. He addressed the group. "Who here will be dead within the month? Hm? Wesley, how long before you drown in yourself?" He called out louder, "Madeline, how long will it be before you're just bones and pain? Didn't Syd wriggle her little fingers against your ribs and tell you it'd be *weeks*? And Cam . . ." He locked his eyes on Cam's. "I'd say you're about a week away from feeling your eyes pop. We should have thrown you on the bleeder when we found you. Sucked the answers out of you and been *done* with it."

Cam pressed his back to the wall. His hand floated up and began to pick nervously at his beard. His ears rang. "Bleeder?" he whispered.

"I shouldn't have listened to you!" McCall yelled at Madeline. Then he turned his gaze back on Chett and smiled, lifted his shoulders, and he sounded more than a little insane as he said, "But you sold it. Ha! *We're* out of time and you *sold* the one thing we needed. Damn you, Sneeze. Damn you."

His face rippled and twitched. For a moment, Cam thought he was about to scream at Chett. Really let loose.

But he didn't.

Benny McCall tilted his head back like a snake. His eyes rolled up and his jaw grew wide. A low droning growl rolled out his throat. And out came the thick, dripping tendril of his tongue. It rose straight up, ripping out between his teeth in one long winding drool. It was not one tongue, Cam saw, but several. Dozens. All overlapped and woven together, but twitching and writhing of their own accord, like living scales, glistening in the dim gray light. The tongue grew to be a foot, two feet, three feet, in length. Cam could see the massive swell in McCall's throat where this tentacle was unspooling from deep within his chest. He imagined it curled there like a sleeping beast.

Chett screamed. The stupidest thing he could have done. McCall whipped his tongue into Chett's open mouth and shoved it all the way in.

Chett's throat expanded as the tongue wormed its way down, down. His arms flailed. He beat at McCall, who now held him by both shoulders. McCall turned his head back and forth, eyes ecstatic, tongue digging, exploring. Chett made horrible noises. Horrible. Blood dripped down his chin. His legs gave but McCall held him upright. Then McCall took a great, roaring breath. Chett's eyes twitched and his entire body convulsed as McCall ripped out his tongue by its roots.

Blood spattered fast onto the floor as the wriggling roots of Chett's tongue quivered and danced in the air. How it was still moving after being wrenched from its home, Cam didn't know. He watched, head light and stomach roiling, as McCall lifted it up between two fingers. He placed Chett's tongue gently on the very tip of his own, and all the other tongues around it squealed in delight, wrapped around the new one, pressing it down, pressing it into the nest, welcoming it, all bloody and hot. The broken spurting roots wove themselves home, and McCall slurped his tongue back inside himself, down into his chest. Chett's own tongue squirmed as it slid behind McCall's teeth, leaving a film of blood across his lips. He wiped the film from his mouth with the back of a hand, smearing it across one cheek. Chett collapsed, bleeding fast. His lips had split. Something in his nose had cracked. His face was skewed and spurting. His jaw was limp and done.

McCall put his hands on his knees and bent down low over Chett. Mocking, in Chett's own voice, "I *sooold* it. Fuck you." McCall spat on him.

Nobody moved. Cam wasn't even breathing. He yanked beard-hairs from his chin with shaking fingers.

"Take him to the bleeder," said McCall in his own voice, wiping more blood off his face. He sucked it off his fingers. "See if he won't tell us where the damn thing is."

"He has the wrong initials," said Wes. "He won't know. Besides, we don't have room."

"Take him anyway. Recycle someone else! And take *that* asshole." Jerking his head at Cam. "Show him where we'll stick him if he doesn't continue to cooperate."

Grim-faced, Wes scooped his hands under Chett's shoulders. He nodded at Cam. "Feet."

Next thing he knew, Cam was helping toss Chett into the back of the van. Madeline sat in the back with him, holding Chett's head in her lap, stroking his hair with fingers that were shrinking visibly, the knuckles growing stranger and more warped every time they touched his skin.

"I'm so sorry, Chett," she whispered. "It'll be worth it, though. You'll see. We're going somewhere *better* . . ."

Cam wandered into his office. He stared at Chett's desk. Then, to his surprise, he heard Chett's voice coming down the hall. He looked out toward McCall's office and saw the man talking on a cell phone in Chett's nasally drone.

"Uncle Chetty would *love* to come to your bat mitzvah," said McCall, eyeing Cam down the hall. "But I'm a little busy with grading this weekend . . ." He winked at Cam, and pressed his office door shut.

"It's how he keeps attention off us," said Wes, appearing at Cam's side. "He has an entire drawer of phones. Calls it his dead-voice drawer."

"And no one ever suspects?"

"You'd be surprised."

"So that's his . . . blood talent?" Cam guessed.

"Yeah, if you want to call it that." Wes coughed. "Here." He slapped a pair of work gloves against Cam's chest. "Let's go grab Sneeze from the van. And I'll show you the bleeder."

CHAPTER SEVENTEEN

A PERFECT ECOSYSTEM

For that first whole night she was underground, Quinn had really hoped Cam might come for her. But the second night? After Slitter had her thrown back in the cell so she could "prepare her mind" for tomorrow's ceremony? That second night, she doubted it.

She spent hours pawing at cracks in the walls, trying to see if she could widen them. She couldn't. She wriggled her fingers around the seams between the walls and floor. Nothin. She yanked at the window bars with her probably-infected hands. They wouldn't budge.

Someone shoved apples and oranges through the bars and told her it was "breakfast time, sweetie." She smashed the apples (hard little red guys) against the edge of the sink. They spattered white chunks onto her face, and cracked open to reveal a number of razor blades, glass shards, and pins. The oranges were even worse. The shit inside the oranges made her gag. Another bit of hazing, maybe. Another "rite of passage."

After a while, the ladies came and forced her into a wooden chair, tying her down so she wouldn't "be rude and run away in the middle of your own party," as Winnie put it, cinching Quinn's wrists tight with extraordinarily strong fingers. When she was secure, they carried her into the main chamber of the undercampus.

Along the wall, beneath the massive sweep of tapestry, the women had set up a long table of polished white birch-bark, more beautiful than any table Quinn had ever seen. Larger than any table she'd ever seen, too. They sat her at its head, Greta at her side. Slitter sat across from them, far away at the table's other end. They had dishes piled high with steaming meat, brass goblets filled with ever-flowing wine. They smoked, too. Joints and glass pipes and bowls of chocolate edibles passed from hand to hand. Quinn leaned limply toward one as it passed under her nose. Greta laughed.

"*We* can't eat before the ceremony," she said. "It's best to go in on an empty stomach." She had a wreath of sunflowers woven about her head. Someone placed a similar one on Quinn.

"I didn't take you ladies for potheads," said Quinn.

"Well, I can only stomach about two glasses of wine," said Marcia, blowing out smoke. "Not like when I was *your* age."

"But we like to keep the celebration going," said Cindy. She lifted a glass pipe molded in the shape of a spider, the little bowl of bud cradled between its eight hands. "To Greta and Quinn."

"To Greta," everyone called. "To Quinn!"

"And to Matthew, our Philosopher High," added Winnie.

"To Matthew!"

"Thank you, girls," said Slitter from down the table. He gnashed something between his teeth. Quinn could see his plate was covered in something other than the meat everyone else was eating. It looked plasticky, thin and gross. He smacked his lips. "Now. Ms. Quinn Rose Carver-Dobson. I think it only fair that I give you a brief explanation of what you're looking at."

"I would *love* that," said Quinn.

"Well." Slitter wiped his mouth with the back of a hand and adjusted the legs of his mobile chair so he sat a little higher. "For years, the Mind of God shoved my consciousness up and down His manyworld Spine, sharing Himself *end*lessly with me. Until I finally, simply . . . burst. A year into my retirement."

"Big bummer," said Quinn.

"But one day, I had a dream of many women feeding from the open veins along my wrists. I was instructed to tell my wife, Belinda," nodding at the withered old woman next to him, dead-eyed, drinking from a goblet with shaking hands, "to ask me any question she wanted. Anything at all. The Mind assured me she would receive the answer she sought. Now, Belinda had a cousin who supposedly drowned in Bartrick Lake. She asked what truly happened to him. And the Mind instructed me to feed her from my eyes." As if on cue, he grunted, and the contraption strapped to his skull hissed steam. Fluid slurped away into the tanks.

Just like Cam, Quinn thought.

"The Mind showed Belinda the truth. *I* was a mere filter for this truth, the Aether flowing through my eyes containing whatever answers its drinker craved. A rare talent indeed. But the Mind exacted a toll through my body. Belinda was . . . translated. The Mind assured me it would be alright; she would cocoon and rehumanize overnight, only to transform again at her will. It told me that whenever she shed her skin, I should eat of it. She would drink of me, and I would eat of her. A transaction that would offer us both strength and longevity." He gestured to the stuff on his plate. "I have eaten of her . . . *many* times."

"So you think it's worth it?" Quinn asked the table.

Greta said coldly, "I'd rather die than not know what happened to my Clare bear."

"Well, I don't share the same sentiments about my boyfriend," said Quinn. "I don't need to know *shit*. And I don't know where the wood is, so."

"But what about your friend?" Slitter purred. "The one who drags the deer."

Quinn froze. Blood whooshed in her ears.

"She . . . She's not *here*, is she?" she asked.

"No," said Slitter. "But you could locate her . . . very easily."

Quinn said nothing.

"You see," said Greta, smiling and adjusting her flower crown. "We're a *community*. We all have reasons to be here. People and things we've lost. Matthew helps you *see*. Sure, there's a price, but when has lunch ever been free?"

"It's too steep," Quinn murmured. "I don't . . . need to know that bad."

Greta gave her a pitying look. "I've heard other women say that, too. *I* said it. And I shied away, at the very last second. But . . ." She swallowed. "But I was wrong. It's destroyed my marriage, Quinn. Not that it was stellar to begin with. But all the same. I came back to Renfield to finish what I started. To find the answer I need. I know you understand the feeling I'm talking about. I know that *you* know that once Renfield has hooked you, it never leaves you alone."

Quinn said nothing.

Winnie added, "That's why we all have such a hard time leaving the county. It just . . . doesn't leave *you*. The nightmares, the depression, the *itch*. You always find your way back. Am I wrong?"

The women around the table nodded.

"So even if you don't care for your boyfriend, which," Greta rolled her eyes, "I get—I know there's something more that you *do* care about. Something that's haunted you. Changed who you are on a DNA level. So what's a little more mess? Why not fuddle around with your DNA just a *little* more, if it means smoothing out that wrinkle?"

"None of us regret it," said Winnie. "We all feel more balanced. Happier. Don't you want that? Don't you want to feel happy? You always wonder what's *wrong* with you, but . . . you don't have to."

Cindy chimed in. "It's nice and cool in the caves. Hot flashes? Forget em. Bad knees? Thing of the past."

"Besides," said Marcia, "some of us *do* live aboveground. I prefer the undercampus, but you *can* live in a house."

"Are you fine not knowing?" Greta asked. "Or would you rather be transformed?"

Quinn, like most of us, had often entertained the question of what she'd do if someone offered to make her a vampire, or a werewolf. Would she do it? Which one would she rather be? She'd always felt she'd rather be a werewolf. Seemed easier to manage. But she had never considered becoming a molting, insectile . . . thing. Would it be worth it, to know what had happened to Celeste? Would it be worth giving up her life in Brooklyn to live here, in Edenville? To weave a cozy little home for herself among these women?

Pfft, said her brain. *What life in Brooklyn?*

"You don't eat people, do you?" she asked.

"God, no," said Winnie. "And only Matthew eats the husks."

Slitter chomped on something stringy. "This one's Deborah's."

Deborah lifted her goblet like this was a compliment.

"And you'll let me go?" Quinn asked. "My hands need attention or they'll get infected."

"Oh, the ceremony will help with that," said Cindy. "It really *does* strengthen the body. Did you know I'm actually ninety-four this year? Matthew is a hundred and eight, thanks to our husks."

"And of *course* we'll let you go," said Marcia. "We'll even help you find a spot in the community. A role. *Just* for you. The Edenville Players could use a new creative directooor," she singsonged.

"It is a perfect ecosystem, Quinn Rose Carver Doboon," said Slitter. "The husks sustain me." Suddenly he gagged, loud and wet, on a hunk of Deborah. "And what my body recycles back to you all," he tapped an eyetube with a broken fingernail, "grants you knowledge beyond your wildest imaginings. That is the beauty of Renfield's rot. It may not seem to have an order. But there *is* a method to its madness. It isn't a horror. It's nature, only different."

His face darkened. "But there are other worlds where the rot is . . . worse. And I would be very interested in trading knowledge with *you* regarding access to these other . . . poisoned realms. It is high time I cure them my*self*, now that it seems my so-called *savior*," his lip twitched in anger, "has abandoned me. They were meant to arrive on this plane last spring, but they have . . . evaded me. I have waited nearly thirty years for them in this skin. On other planes, it has been . . . significantly longer. And I am tired of waiting for my cure.

"But my impatience is a heart-thing, and of course, the Mind cares not for hearts. The Mind has *refused* to tell me the location of the rot-root, the *cure,* or where lies the tapestry-door. My hope is to enter that door, gather my other selves from their respective planes, and amass my own search party of copies of myself. *I* will find the root myselves, without any *help* from my supposed savior. But the Mind did say *you* would come and assist me, willingly or no. That your Campbell Peter Marion would know the location of the door to the Spine. So I apologize for the way my girls have treated you thus far, but the Mind *did* indicate it would be . . . necessary. To gather the information I need. And I hope, now, that I have persuaded you to *willingly* trade the whereabouts of your current partner for the whereabouts of your . . . old friend." He grinned cruelly.

"So that's what I'd be to you?" Quinn asked. "Information and . . . and *food*? So you could keep letting these women suck your dick another hundred years?"

"We'd be food for each *other*. No need to paint it in such a crass light. Besides, I am quite fond of the collection this self has acquired." He stroked a finger down Belinda's face. She continued chewing blankly, unflinching. He gazed around the table lovingly. "No need to belittle them. I have *freed* them of the burden of relying upon their own minds. I consider that . . . quite the accomplishment."

"Right." Quinn frowned at the table.

"Well." Slitter sucked husk off his teeth with a wet smack, then fiddled with his joystick to steer his chair away from the table. It clunked and steamed on its slipshod steampunk legs. "You have some time to consider how *willing* you will be in this transaction. Perhaps when you see exactly what I have to offer, you will alter your tune. Perhaps you will *decide* to lead us to your beloved Campbell Peter Marion. *He* will provide me with the information I require, or he will suffer a very lengthy demise.

"My cane! I am too full to sit forward."

One of the women scurried up to him, handed him his eagle-headed cane in both hands, like a ceremonial sword. He leaned back in his seat with a sigh, and used the point of the cane to shove his joystick forward, laughing as he teetered away from the table, leaving the women gathered there laughing at the ceiling on command. Leaving Quinn chewing at her lip, wondering what she was going to do.

CHAPTER EIGHTEEN

SHE'S A LADY

When Cam was thirteen, he grew a boil beneath his balls. He could barely sit still in class, it ached so bad. He'd been so embarrassed about it that he hadn't told a single adult. No, Cam just took a lighter and a needle into the bathroom and *very* carefully lanced this third ball himself. It was his greatest accomplishment. He hadn't even known his body could do this. There are *so* many fluids a body can make, and the bloody gray ooze he was able to squeeze out of that thing gave him such a high that he felt hollow for weeks. None of the zits he popped, scrabs he clawed off, anything at all—none of it quite scratched the itch of that third ball.

His class had a scary story contest around Halloweentime, so Cam whipped up a little ditty called, "The Extra Balls," about a boy going through puberty whose balls had dropped, and then another set dropped, too. And another. Aaand another. By the time this kid had dropped a fifth pair into the same sack, he could no longer sit down.

Cam shared the piece with his parents. As an only child, he had no one else to show off to. They'd been *very* concerned. His teacher, too. She'd even written him a note: "I don't think we can share this with the rest of the class, but your understanding of craft displays a mastery for your age group that is enviable. It's also worth noting that your piece gave me nightmares. You must be the youngest Cronenberg fan there is."

Cam didn't know what a Cronenberg *was*.

Not yet, anyway.

"The Extra Balls" sparked a lifelong fascination with horror. And Cam wondered now, as Chett Neeves gurgled blood onto his gloved hands—if it hadn't been for that boil, would he even be here at all?

He felt the sunflowers watching with intense fascination as they carried Chett into Slitter Hall. Felt their eyes through the walls as he and Wes hauled Chett down the stairs.

Cam wondered if he'd ever had another person's blood on him like this. He'd never been in a fight. Never driven anyone to the hospital. He'd lived a charmed life.

He didn't feel very charmed anymore.

At the door to the sub-basement, Wes grunted and unceremoniously dropped Chett's feet. Chett gakked up more blood, dark and chunky, from his mouth and nose. He mewled, sending bubbles up from deep within his ruin of a jaw.

"Is he gonna live?" Cam asked.

Wes was fussing with a large thing of keys. He glanced at Chett over his shoulder. "Oh yeah, he'll be fine. They always look like that."

"They?" Cam echoed stupidly. "Always?"

Wes gave him a sardonic smile. "Look like *that*, yeah." He found the right key and swung open the door. It was hot inside the hall. Wes shoved the keys back in his pocket and picked up his half of Neeves again.

Only now, as they carried Chett into that Hell-hot underdark, did it occur to Cam to ask what they were going to do with him.

"You heard Benny," said Wes, grunting with effort as he waddled backward. "Take him to the bleeder."

"I don't know what that is," said Cam. "You *must* know I don't know what that is."

"And I *said* I'd show ya," said Wes, grunting. "Patience."

They came to the large metal vault door. Machinery churned and pumped inside. Cam glanced at the door to the tunnel, imagined the golf cart waiting lonely on the other side. Wes dropped Chett's feet again and dug into his pocket for the keys a second time. "Goddamn . . . fuckin . . . things . . ." He located a thick, dark key, and jammed it into the lock. Turned it. Bolts inside the door began to whine. Gears ground.

Wes smiled proudly. "Built this myself. My bachelor's is actually in Engineering. Used to get high with my roommate and design some *weird* shit. Some of it was just coked-out nonsense, but *some* of it? Some of it ain't bad. The thing *inside* here, though, was designed by our buddy Benny. Said he saw it in another world."

"So he's actually been to other parts of the Spine."

"So he says." The door clicked and Wes gripped the wheel-handle.

"But you believe him," said Cam.

Wes sighed. He cleared his throat. "Not always. Personally, I suspect that no matter how *better* it may seem, no matter how much therapy you attend? There's always nowhere left to go but further down."

"Then what the fuck, why help?"

"Because what else am I supposed to do before I hack up both lungs and die in my own gin-spit?" He pulled the door open with both hands, like he was opening an ancient tomb. Cam stepped inside. The air tightened his skin.

"We've been pumping the AC down here strong over the summer," said Wes. "If there's one fault with this stupid machine, it's that it overheats like a motherfucker. Here." He grunted, hefted Chett's ankles up again. Jerked his head at a metal slab in the center of the room. It looked like a rusted autopsy table. "Bring him here."

They dropped Chett on the slab and Wes clapped Cam on the shoulder. "I'll get some music goin." He went to a Bluetooth speaker standing on the metal sink bolted to the wall. "Hope you like Tom Jones."

While Wes fiddled with the speaker, Cam had his first real opportunity to take in the room. The bleeder.

The bodies.

The room was huge, its ceiling taller than made sense. Cam couldn't see how it didn't cut into the floor above. The room was concrete and metal, all rusted-over. If cool air weren't humming through the vent overhead, Cam could tell the room would be volcanically hot. Pipes wound in every direction, clanging and thrumming. But the main eye-catcher was the pair of gigantic cylinders along the back wall. Giant rotating turbines with horizontal shelves. The shelves rotated the way cars on a Ferris wheel do, staying balanced and upright as they turned around and around in slow, eternal circles. Every shelf was a slab of rusting metal. On every slab was a single body and a short pole, vines of IV tubes snaking down into arms and mouths. Each wheel must have been lined with a dozen or more people. Spinning endless, like hot dogs at a gas station.

Against his better judgment, stomach clenching, glasses fogging, Cam stepped closer.

The bodies were naked except for the metal straps holding them tight to their shelves, and the large diapers wrapped around their laps. The bodies that appeared to be female had bras on as well. They *all* had IV tubes leading into their arms, and larger tubes down their throats, clamped in place with bright white medical tape. There was a clank, a grind, and Cam watched as thick brown sludge pumped its way down the mouth-tubes.

"Lunch time!" said Wes. He laughed.

Some of the bodies moaned around their tubes. Let out stifled gags.

But this was not the worst of it. The worst was the massive metal helmet strapped to each body. Big jags of metal latched to the front of their skulls, bolted in place along the sides. Spires of metal prodded down into the eye sockets, and big hypodermic needles pumped endlessly into tubes, whirring fast like the gears of sewing machines. The tubes ran up to the back of the machine. Cam peered around it and saw twin glass canisters filled with fluid. They were large. Many gallons sloshed inside.

"That's . . ." But his throat was too dry to finish.

"Interplanal Aether," said Wes. "If you're feelin fancy. More colloquially, it's—"

"Spinal fluid." Cam winced. The heat was making his eyes burn. His throat dry. "I'm familiar."

"So that's basically the gist," said Wes, still fussing with his phone and the speaker. "Anyone who isn't as cooperative as you, we just plug em in and pump out what we want to know. McCall drinks that stuff, and the visions transmute to him." Wes grimaced, shook his head. "Tasted it once. Not for me."

"Did you see anything?" Cam was still taking in the scope of the machines, the room, the bodies bleeding constant visions from their eyes.

"Sort of," said Wes. "I saw this . . . valley where the trees bleed? Cut open an oak and it spurts dark red. Fuckin nuts. But not really of any use. *Here* we fuckin go!"

"She's a Lady" began to boom against the walls. Some of the bodies groaned in recognition, fear. They flinched, but Cam couldn't imagine you'd want to move very much, not with two giant metal spikes pumping into your head.

"Alright," said Wes over the music. He clapped his hands, dancing to the machine. "*Now* I feel like I can focus. Let's recycle . . . you." He slapped a button on the engine and the turbines ground to a halt, presenting one slab in particular. A young man, with graying hair. Wes unhooked the chains holding his slab and dug out the tubes. The man retched horribly as the feeding hose whipped up out of his throat. Cam had to swallow the sour taste of bile, look down at his Chett-stained shoes. Wes stopped the twin whirring needles in the man's helmet, and wrenched it free. The face below, withered and caked in blood, spatters of brown lunch mush, opened its tongueless mouth like a dying fish. Wes unfolded wheels from the bottom of the slab and pushed it to the far wall. The wheels screamed against the concrete. He opened a metal grate in the wall Cam hadn't noticed before, and dumped the body down a dark chute within. He punched a button on the wall. Flames burst to life within the chute, and Wes slammed the grate shut before Hell could lick out into the room.

Wes danced back to the table where Chett lay and Cam stood awkwardly, wobbling a little on his feet, feeling light-headed. Wes shook his head. "He hasn't produced any fresh Aether in *months*. Not a very good student, either." He coughed, and the smell of juniper seemed to singe Cam's nostrils. "Alright. Help me out with Sneeze here. I can *never* find a vein."

Wes sang along with Tom Jones as he took the still-dripping recycled helmet and brought it to Chett's slab. The twin eye-pikes glittered in the yellow work lights. "Whoa, whoa, whoa, she's a lady. Talkin about that little lady . . ."

"Don't you want to clean the blood off first?" Cam asked. Chett was still covered in it, vomiting down in chunky red strands over his chin and his shirt.

"Oh sure," said Wes. "Hold this." Shoving the helmet into Cam's hands. Cam held it, did not move a muscle. Wes retrieved a pair of scissors and cut Chett's shirt from his body. He yanked off the man's jeans and underwear, and Cam looked up to spare Chett this final indignity.

"Damn, Sneeze," Wes whistled. "Never woulda guessed." He strapped Chett down. His wrists, ankles, and a thick leather strap across his neck. He cinched them tighter than seemed necessary. Then he took the helmet from Cam and positioned it over Chett's skull. There was a side panel on the helmet that looked like it belonged in the last century, all metal knobs and brass switches, glass gauges. Wes fiddled with it and the thing began to whir. Cam watched as the pikes turned, then burrowed their way down into Chett's skull. The helmet steamed, the pikes lifted, cranked back down. Chett woke up screaming, jerking against his restraints.

"We've got," Wes shouted over the noise, shaking a can of some unmarked spray, "this Renfield shit. Keep him from getting infected." He sprayed Chett's entire writhing body with a silver mist. "You know about the Edenville Butcher? Old biology teacher? They *say* this was one of her experiments. Practically magic. Bottles and bottles of it in the basement of the college center. Feels fuckin fan*tast*ic on your balls. Here, keep it." He chucked the can at Cam. "Now help me find that vein."

Cam stuck the can in his back pocket and tried to help, but he'd never done this before. Wes would poke the needle in, swear, then swim the needle around inside Chett's arm, searching for a vein. Swear again, slide the needle back out. By his third attempt, Cam almost passed out. Later, he wouldn't even remember the rest of the procedure. He remembered greasing up the food tube, helping shove it down Chett's throat. He remembered standing before the turbine as Wes took two great lengths of chain and added Chett Neeves to the wheel. But the tissue between these moments, Cam would never recall. Over it all, Tom Jones sang on and on and on.

As Cam watched the wheel of the bleeder slowly turn, he noticed that every shelf had a strip of masking tape along its edge. He read the names as they went around:

Chelsea Mendez.

Cooper Marks.

Calais Mueller.

Cassandra Maywell.

Conner Matthews.

Then came a slender body with short red hair. By the time her name rolled around, Cam wasn't surprised at all.

Clarity Mither had been here all along.

"Vermont certainly looks different this time of year," he murmured.

"Hah?"

Louder, "You told me Clarity was in Vermont."

"Oh." Wes hawked phlegm onto the floor. "Yeah, well, you knew that was bullshit."

"They all have the same initials." *My initials.*

"Yeah, except for our boy Sneeze here. He'll be an outlier."

"Why do we all have the same initials?" *We,* he realized he'd said *Why do* we. His eyes darted to the grate in the wall, flames still flickering within.

"Dunno," said Wes. "Benny claims that on some other plane, seers like yourself are called channelmen. Like shamans, ya know? He thinks it's an inside joke from the Mind. C.M. Channel Men? I don't know. Adios!" Chett's body churned away over the top of the machine and was gone from sight.

"And that's that." Wes grinned. "Let's wash up and see what Angie's got for lunch."

When Wes had his back to him, washing his hands at the sink, Clarity Mither came around again. Cam watched her arrive.

He couldn't explain why he did what he did. Maybe it was because Quinn was right after all. Maybe it was the "same initials" thing. Maybe it was a Grinch-esque change of heart.

But whatever the reason, when Clarity came around the bleeder, Cam dug a finger under one of her straps. Just a single flick of the wrist, so that one of her hands could wriggle free. She twitched as he did this. Then she was gone, up and away around the machine.

When Wes asked Cam to shut the door behind him, already far down at the end of the sub-basement hall, humming to himself—Cam left it open just a crack.

"Now," said McCall with a sigh, "we wait."

Tom Jones's "Green Green Grass of Home" was purring out of Wes's speaker now as they sat around Slitter Lounge, eating delivery from

Pancake Planet. It was a pretty glum scene. Madeline wasn't eating. She sat hunched, arms wrapped around herself, staring at the floor.

McCall shoved a waffle into his mouth. Cam watched him chew. Wondering when that mouth would be coming for *him*.

"Think he'll give us anything good?" Syd asked.

"One can only hope," said McCall.

"It's just the two, right?" said Madeline. "Just two pieces left?"

"Indeed," said McCall, eyes far away as he scrrraped a bite off his fork.

"Do you know what they are?" asked Cam.

"Now, yeah," said Wes, chewing a pancake egg salad sandwich. "We've had an idea about the other one for a while, but Neeves's trunk we weren't sure about."

"We're only missing part of one of the eyes," said Syd. "And a length of the left leg."

Wes snorted. "That eye-piece has been missing for thirty years."

"It is a . . . special case," said McCall, gazing up at Slitter's portrait. Slitter's cane. "Cameron, you're not eating."

"I'm not hungry." And he didn't think he would be for quite a while.

McCall began to say something else, then gagged suddenly, reached into his mouth, and removed a molar. He dropped it on his plate. It clattered loud. He looked around at everyone. "Well. It's official, if it wasn't already. *My* body is giving up on me as well."

He glared across the table at Cam. They *all* looked at him, and Cam's skin tightened under the weight of their eyes.

McCall licked syrup and blood off his lips. "Your time is just about up . . . Cameron."

CHAPTER NINETEEN

GRETAMORPHOSIS

No more than an hour after their dinner around the large birch table, the grand chamber under Edenville had transformed into a chaotic bacchanal. Little old ladies were everywhere, drinking wine straight from the bottle, laughing madly. Two of them knelt over a third and held her hair back as she puked on a pile of rocks. Pairs making out, tongues worming into each other's wrinkled mouths, hands fumbling at each other's crimson robes. Inhuman shadows cackled over the ceiling, danced along the walls, moving to the bass-shaking, earth-core beat, booming from hidden speakers. It was so throbbing-loud Quinn was surprised there hadn't been a cave-in yet.

Luckily, the ladies ignored her. She was worried they might force-feed her something, or mess with her already-brutalized hands, pulsing hot and useless against their restraints. They'd cleared the table away, but had left Quinn tied to her chair on the dais.

Greta appeared before her. "How ya doin?"

Quinn glared. "Stupendous. They do this for everybody?"

"I know, isn't it awesome? Always good to have an excuse to celebrate. And they're celebrating *our* freedom."

"Freedom from what?"

"From the bonds of ignorance!" Greta shouted. "Tonight, we know the things we've *yearned* to know. Tonight, we receive blessings from our Philosopher High—and the Mind." She threw her hands up. "Praise to the Mind!"

Every woman within earshot took up the cry. "Praise to the Mind!"

Quinn had to admit, the communal aspect of this place had a certain pizzazz to it. It appealed to the theater major in her who wanted to snort coke off bathroom sinks. She wanted to get high and fuck someone onstage, in the dim of the ghostlight after-hours. She wanted to . . .

She wanted to breathe.

Slitter's chair whined and hissed as its four metal legs sproinged onto the dais. He worked the joystick with the end of his cane (a feat of hand-eye coordination that *was* impressive), moving his legs in a mockery of dance. His other hand held a large shining mug. Quinn recognized the E.C. sunflower logo. Slitter drank red wine from it in great gulps, head tilted far back. Wine splashed over his chin, the tubes in his eyes. He grinned and his teeth were stained deep purple. He flung his cane into the air, and called out, "Release her!"

Hands frantically untied Quinn from behind. After hours sitting there in the middle of an old-lady spider-rave, she could barely move her arms, they were so numb. Her hands did not look well. She turned to see who was untying her. It was Greta, still in her sunflower crown. She smiled at Quinn, helped her stand, and said, "Here we go."

Slitter lifted his hands again. The entire system of tunnels went silent at once. The music cut out, and all the women leered into the center of the chamber, at Quinn and Greta and Slitter.

"Greta Marie Mither," he rasped. "Quinn Rose Carver-Dobson. What a *treat* it is to have you here tonight." He pushed his joystick forward. The throne took two hobbling steps, then stopped. He knelt his chair in front of Greta and Quinn, front legs bending inward until he was eye level with them. He stank of dogshit and rotting garlic. He spread a hand in the direction of the giant tapestry on the wall. "We are but cells, existing in a vast organism far beyond our comprehension. But *tonight*, we celebrate the fact that our Mind offers us even *scraps* of what It has created, as It dances lonely among the stars." He gazed wistfully at the tapestry through his tubes. His blackened lips trembled. The wrinkled purple scalp gleamed. After a moment, he grinned and turned to address his entire congregation. "Tonight! We celebrate the ascension of two sisters. Their metamorphosis will grant them the answers they desire. Greta. Step forward."

Greta stepped forward. She seemed very nervous but very excited.

"I," said Slitter, "do not know the answers nor the questions. The Mind once spoke unto me, 'Matthew! Be a vessel for my voice! Give these women the peace they seek!' Who am I to question that dream? *I* am but a single mind spread over many selves, and *this* self is but a filter. Greta Marie Mither. Do *you* have a question in your heart?"

"I do," she said in a small voice.

"I know," said Slitter. "*It* is smarter than us all. And if It demands a fee in exchange for knowledge, who am I to question Its will? Greta Marie Mither. Do you accept this price?"

"I accept, High Lord."

Slitter smiled, reached up a thin hand, and undid the brass nozzle latched around his right eye. He cranked it clockwise. Steam hissed out around the seam. He peeled the tube away. Yellowish strands squelched between the tube and the puckered red skin around his socket. Fluid oozed from the charred black inside. It dribbled down in cream-of-mushroom globs against his cheek. A small yellow light burned deep within his skull.

Slitter held out his hands, palms up. "Then drink of me, and be satisfied."

Greta lifted her trembling fingers to his face. He was just out of reach enough that he had to twist the knob of his chair, grind the joints in his legs even farther down, bending unevenly. He bowed to her, and she cradled his head in her hands. She licked her lips. Then she slid out her tongue and put her mouth to his eye. She closed her eyes. Her jaw worked as she moved her tongue around and lapped at the inside of his hole. Slitter reached up a hand and held the back of her head, holding her mouth to his skull as she drank, gagged, and swallowed. Quinn could hear her murmuring happy noises as she sucked at his brain, as she opened her mouth and ran her tongue around the rim of Slitter's socket. She moaned.

"Yess," Slitter cooed. "Goood. Get every last drop, dear girl."

Quinn fought hard not to vomit. She wavered on her feet. She felt someone dig into her arm, steadying her. She turned her head, and Cindy was there at her side. She'd amassed even more pairs of glasses since they'd last met. Quinn had a sudden image of the glasses like Mardi

Gras beads. She couldn't imagine what Cindy had done to earn all those during the celebration.

At last, Greta stepped back. She licked her lips again, and suddenly, she gasped. She threw her head forward, face twisting with intense pleasure. She fell to her hands and knees. She retched. Moaned. She cried, and she laughed at herself for crying. She pawed at the stone floor.

"Clarity," she sobbed. "My baby. I'm sorry. I'm so sorry. I see you. I shouldn't have let you go. I'm sorry. I shouldn't have let you gooo," she wailed. She beat her hands against the dais.

The women wailed with her. It was deafening. But no one touched her. None of the women went to her or comforted her. It must be part of the whole bit. You gathered your answer alone while everyone else just screamed at you.

Slitter turned to Quinn. "Quinn Rose Carver-Dobson. Your turn has come. Step forward."

The cavern went silent again, except for Greta's sobs.

Quinn stepped forward.

"Do you have a question in your heart?" Slitter asked.

Greta gagged again. Quinn looked down. Something green was throbbing under the woman's skin, spreading from her mouth through her cheeks.

"I do," said Quinn.

"I know," said Slitter. He reached up and undid the clasp of the tube around his other eye. Steam poured out. More chowdery globs chunked out of his socket. "Do you accept the price that answers will impose upon your body?"

Greta retched. She writhed on the floor, began to seize. Green froth bubbled out of her mouth.

"Look not at her," said Slitter. "At *me*. Do you accept?"

"Will it hurt?" Quinn asked.

"Only a moment," said Slitter.

Greta was on her back now. Gasping and bucking her hips. Bones were shifting and popping all over her body. Her neck was twisting un-naturally.

"Seems like it'll be a few moments," said Quinn.

"Do you *accept*?" said Slitter, more coldly.

"I do," she said, lifting her chin. "I accept . . . High Lord."

He grinned. Bent his head to her. "Then drink of me, and be satisfied."

Quinn reached for him. Reached for the oozing socket, the little yellow eye burning deep within, smoke curling out.

She reached up, up . . .

And wrapped her hands around the cane in his lap. She pulled. He caught it, but it wrenched free easily from his old grip, sent her toppling back onto the ground. Her head cracked against the rock and when Slitter roared, she wasn't sure if she was actually hearing him or if her brain was on fire.

"Heresy!" Slitter bellowed. He yanked the joystick back. His chair lifted off the ground, front legs rearing and kicking at the air. He swung his chair down and Quinn rolled out of the way just in time. Steel slammed into the rock where she'd been just a second before. She scrambled between the metal legs, around the back of Slitter's chair. There were too many wires and tubes. *Fuck it,* she started pulling at them indiscriminately, smacking them with the cane. *Just break whatever, it won't help him.* Machinery hissed and whined; goo spurted into her face, her eyes, blinding her for a moment. She tried to wipe it away but flashes of the woods exploded through her mind. Flashes of Celeste in a hospital. Celeste kneeling by a brook on the edge of town, hands twisting the neck of some small, squealing animal. And it struck her, then: if she'd accepted Slitter's offer, she would, in fact, know what had happened to Celeste.

That hurt.

Slitter roared again and whirled around, swiping at her with one long, bony hand. She ducked, blinking rapidly, trying to clear the gunk from her eyes.

Now the women were falling on her, scratching at her, pulling her hair. She swung the cane at them, and they fell back. One of them stumbled backward into Slitter's chair. The gears inside began to whine as the chair tilted up and fell on its side with an iron *crunch*. A great howl went up among the women, all of them crying at the ceiling in a massive echo of Slitter's hoarse, gargling screams.

"Get her!" he shrieked.

Quinn stuck the cane against the ground, used it to prop herself onto her feet. As soon as she stood, someone was grabbing at her ankle. She looked down, saw Greta clutching at her. Skin green and scaly, eyes bubbling.

"Fool!" Greta spat. "Ungrateful little—"

Quinn rammed the end of the cane against Greta's face. The bone cracked open and a chunk flew away. Black eyes blinked and rolled underneath. She hissed. Her jaw cracked in half, teeth rotating, chin splitting into a razorous mandible. Legs burst from her chest, her stomach, the sides of her ribs. They kicked at the air as Greta's body shook and popped like a corn kernel, skin sloughing away in favor of a hard green shell, brackish rivulets of blood running away onto the floor. She clicked her new jaw at Quinn, and Quinn fucking bolted.

They were clutching at her, grabbing at her clothes, the flesh of her arms, with those scrabbly lacquered nails and dry skin. Quinn elbowed them out of the way left and right, kicking at them, shoving them back with her forearms like they were a swarm of bats. She swung the cane over her head, felt it crack against someone's side. She kept having to wrench her arms and legs away from the women as she fought her way off the dais.

"Fuck *off*!" she yelled at one woman as she rammed her elbow into the woman's nose. The woman's face turned inside out, flipped around, and became a rattling black set of mandibles that bit at Quinn's shoulder.

She heard a wet bursting noise behind her. She turned, stumbling, and saw that the women were *all* popping and transforming. Exploding out of their skins. She saw Cindy and Marcia and Deborah in the crowd, snarling at her with sharp teeth. Their skin swelled, turned the same sick shade of green that had infected Greta. They split at the seams, ripping out of their skin so their entire faces slicked away, eyeballs rolling back and popping onto the ground. Eight large, bloody sharp studs wrenched out of their stomachs and ribs, and they fell forward so they could chase her in their glistening, hard emerald skin and legs made of bone. More of them swarmed over the ceiling, covering the entire cavern like ants.

Quinn screamed, squeezed her eyes shut, and *ran*. She made it up out of the cavern into a tunnel, slammed her hand onto the wall and ran her fingers along its side, groping at the stones and dirt as she sprinted blind up through the rock. Up, up, she went. She felt her ears pop. Her skull roared.

She found herself in a tunnel that was getting smaller, smaller. Tighter, tighter. She shoved her way into it, wriggling her arms first, throwing the cane up in front of her. Women clawed and bit at her ankles, tore into her calves. But the tunnel was too tight for them to follow. Their hard green bodies wouldn't fit, their spidery legs wouldn't bend the right way. She shoved them off as she dug at the dirt and rock, broke her fingernails against the cave, scrambling up, up, so tight she couldn't breathe.

And then she collapsed onto hard-packed dirt. The air seemed to open around her with a *whoosh* and she scrambled onto her hands and knees, whirled about. She could see the hole in the wall she'd squeezed through. The bricks were broken in and jagged around its mouth and . . .

Wait, bricks? Wall?

Quinn blinked, panting. She dug into her hoodie pocket, found Dad's lighter. It took her a few tries ("Come *on*, Marilyn"), but she finally flicked it on and looked around. She was in some kind of maintenance tunnel. Not like the tunnels farther down, which seemed naturally-made. This was a sewer or something. Pipes and wires leading off in either direction. Slivers of light from her left.

She wobbled to her feet and leaned against the cane. She caught her breath, keeping her eyes locked on the hole in the wall. Nothing came through.

"Okay," she murmured. "Go Crows."

The tunnel was low enough that she had to hunch as she walked along, cane in one hand, lighter in the other. Finally, the main pipe she'd been following along the ceiling curved up, and light spilled out from a slim hole above. She could see a tiled ceiling up there. She snapped the lighter shut.

"No spiders, no spiders, no spiders," she muttered as she hefted herself through the hole. She had to squeeze her way around the pipe but when she came out, she found herself in the middle of a concrete floor, in some nondescript maintenance room. There was a door. She creaked it open, and looked out onto some kind of common room. A group of what she assumed were students sat around a table with dice and papers and a large map.

She crept up behind them, heart still hammering. When they noticed her, they almost jumped out of their chairs.

"Where is this?" Quinn asked.

"It's . . . Kleave Hall?" one of the students said. He swallowed a nervous lump. "You're in Kleave Hall. On the quad. East Camp. W-we're just playing D&D." Like, *Don't hurt us.*

"Okay, thanks," said Quinn. She started to limp away.

"Hey, wait, do you need help?" he called after her. "What happened? Are you okay?"

Quinn shouldered her way out of the dorm double-doors onto the quad. It was night, and there were very few students out. They all glanced at her, giving her wary looks. She offered them tight smiles as she limped past. "Hi. How are ya. How ya doin." Gripping the cane more tightly with each step. The wood dug into her wounds.

By the time she hit the main drive, all she could do was wheeze and say, between breaths, "Ichabod." As if Cam could feel her out here, giving this word mass.

The sunflowers of West Camp cocked their heads at her as she hobbled by. She nodded at them, "How are ya." And a breeze rattled through their leaves in answer.

"Okaayy," said Quinn, shivering. "Yep. It's Ichabod. Ichabod . . ."

She said it all the way out the North Gate and across Rackell, up the hill to the Nethers. "Ichabod," she wheezed, jangling down the middle of the street in the night, battered and bloodied, but still human. Saying "Ichabod" between teeth that were getting rapidly more gritted and grinding and hateful. "Ichabod. Ichabod. *Ichabod.*" As she limped on Slitter's cane toward Cam.

CHAPTER TWENTY

ICHABOD

Cam was throwing shit into a bag when someone burst through the front door. His stomach clenched. His time had come. They'd tired of him. They were gonna throw him on the bleeder and pump him dry.

Footsteps clomped up the stairs. He looked around wildly for a weapon. He ended up grabbing an umbrella, held it in both hands, and just managed to spin around, wielding its tip at the door—when he saw Quinn standing there. Breathing hard. Bleeding from dozens of cuts and gouges. One of her feet stood crooked. She glared at him.

Cam lowered the umbrella. "Jesus. The hell happened to—"

"Ichabod," she said, between breaths.

"Where *were* you, I thought—"

"Wha . . . ?" She laughed. Head back, open-throated at the ceiling, "HA! Where *was* I?" She stuck her chin out at him, tried to stake the word through his brain. *Why aren't you getting this?* "Cam. Ichabod. We're fucking *done* here."

"I thought you were with your mom."

Her eyes widened. She gestured around the room. "Without *any* of my shit? What the fuck, Cam?"

"Well, I thought you were pissed."

"You thought . . . Cam." She limped toward him, clung to his arms.

"Ow," he said. "What are you—"

"Cam, I was *underground.* Look, I'm not explaining this to you right now. Ichabod. We're going."

"Hold on, what is—"

She gripped him more tightly, digging her broken fingernails into him so hard her entire arms ached. "Cam, there's no holding on. Let's. *Go.*"

"What are you . . . holding?"

"Cam, *where* are the keys?"

He didn't answer.

"Campbell!"

He was staring at the cane.

She shoved him away. "You fuck. What is wrong with you? You're not *listening*. Ichabod!"

Slowly, he lifted a hand and pointed. "Is that . . . Slitter's cane?"

She blinked, then turned defensively, putting herself between him and the cane. "What about it?"

"Where . . . did you get it?"

"Underground! I was underground! Cam, this is . . . Where are the goddamn keys?"

The cane. He could give them the cane. Maybe they would let him live. Maybe they wouldn't shelve him after all. Maybe he could still be special and maybe they'd even take him with them as they walked through the giant.

Quinn whacked his arm with the cane. "Are you hearing me?"

"Ow, yes! I just . . . Why don't you . . ." He licked his lips. "Just . . . give me the cane and I'll give you the keys."

She gaped at him. Then whacked him again. "You're trying to *bargain* with me?" She whacked his other arm, drove him back against the wall, the end of the cane against his sternum. "I said my goddamn *veto* word. We should be in the car *right*. Now." She jammed the cane into his stomach. Air whooshed out of him and he fell to his knees.

"I'm not making a fuckin deal with you, asshole," she said. She caned his back, between the shoulders. He fell forward onto the floor. She hit him again. "Where are the car keys?" And again. "Where are the keys?" And again. "I'm so *sick* of your bullshit, you traitor! Where are the keys?!" And again.

And again.

*　*　*

Finally, her arms began to tremble. She looked down at the cane in her hands. Her blood was smeared across the eagle head. And as she looked more closely at it, she saw the sliver of dark stain curling from the carved feathers, around the shaft and down.

"Oh shit," she said. She dropped the cane like it was on fire. *That was Renfield wood. That wasn't me, that was . . . That was the wood.*

Cam groaned on the floor. "Jesus, Quinn . . . Fuck . . ."

Without thinking, she dug into his pockets, eyes wild with panic.

"Quinnnn," he groaned. "My back . . ."

She said nothing. Just kept frantically pawing at him for the keys. When she finally found them, she got up and limped out of the room, his voice trailing after her. "Quinn, wait . . ."

She paused briefly in the kitchen to fill a glass of water from the sink. It occurred to her that if she'd just beaten her boyfriend with Renfield wood, drinking Renfield water wasn't exactly a smart move. But she was so thirsty, she filled a second glass and slugged that down, too, then limped back out into the night.

The few yards from the door to the car were long. The Nethers felt dark and abandoned. Quinn realized they had never met anyone else who lived here. Perhaps they'd always been alone.

She had trouble opening the car door. The wind had picked up. It tried to press her back. She glanced up at the door to 1896, half expecting to see Cam there, stumbling after her. But he wasn't. Yet.

Leave him. He left you first.

Finally, she was behind the wheel. She whipped the car out of their parking spot so fast it gave her the spins for a second. She cranked the wheel around and suddenly, Cam was outside, shouting over the wind, swinging the cane over his head, "Wait!" But Quinn was already facing the road. She slammed her foot on the accelerator.

The road curved around the trees, the leaves beginning to churn madly, and as she came around the bend down the hill—she saw a woman standing in the middle of the road. She wore nothing but sagging white underwear and a sweat-stained bra. Covered in blood and snot and bile, she gaped at Quinn. She had swirling black holes where her eyes should be. And when she opened her mouth, Quinn could see far down her throat, for she had no tongue.

But worst of all—she looked like Celeste.

Quinn rammed the wheel to the side. The girl's face screamed by her window. The car slammed into the trunk of a tree so hard, the airbag exploded, firing a reeking pink gas into the car. Quinn gagged on it, stomach roiling, hands floating around in dizzy circles. She burped acid, then Cam was at the window, ripping open the door. "Fucking *fuck*, Quinn."

Quinn shoved him away. Suddenly, the girl was grabbing at him. She clung to Cam, moaning. Quinn scrambled away from her, into the passenger seat.

"What are you?!" she screamed.

But Cam held the girl back, almost like he was protecting her. He held her at arm's length, inspecting her face.

"Who the shit is that?!" Quinn cried. "What the fuck is going on?!"

"Quinn, stop it! You don't recognize her?"

Recognize who? Celeste? Why did Celeste have sharp red hair? Why wasn't she blond? Why was she *here*? Quinn didn't feel like her brain was working right. She felt like the wood had already poisoned her through her wounded hands.

"Shit, Quinn," said Cam, holding the girl upright. "It's Clarity Mither."

Bent, April 2018

Little Catie Mason is the strongest body I've ever had. Her skin lasts for ages. It grows with me, even becomes fertile for new life for a time. She *wanted* me to inhabit her, pulsing in her organs and her blood. And because of this, her skin was a gracious host for decades.

Until I began to spit out teeth. The roots simply rotting away, snapping clean off. The first I lost were molars, their absences easy to hide in the back of my mouth. But this latest is a canine. My smile will have a hole now. People will notice.

I'm spitting this canine into the sink when Madeline Narrows comes into the bathroom. We haven't met yet, but I recognize her. That thin frame, the sundress. Always, those sundresses. Her closet is *full* of them. I know this because every time I've been in this day before, I've leapt into Madeline at this precise moment. When I awoke this morning, in fact, I had planned to do the same. Madeline's empathy makes her a reliable skin, and makes her well-loved among colleagues and students alike. Every other time I've been on Earth, her skin has served me well.

But I've promised myself this loop will be different. Besides, the fuss over where Catie Mason has gone is always a bit frustrating to navigate. *Every* time, I seem unable to avoid people noticing that Catie has entered a bathroom with no windows and no other exit, and has vanished from that room entirely. It would be foolish of me to suffer through that inconvenience yet again.

So today, instead of carefully shredding Catie's hollow sack of skin into the toilet and walking back out of the bathroom as Ms. Madeline Narrows, I decide to try something new. Perhaps this will be the kickstart my cycle needs in order to end differently. Perhaps *this* decision will have a positive impact on events that will not yet occur for thousands of years.

It's an idea, at least. A worm can always dream.

She offers me a polite "Hello" and heads for one of the stalls. Then turns, hand on the stall door, and says, "Are you alright?"

I have my canine pinched between two fingers, just over the trash bin set in the bathroom wall. I swivel my head around, give Madeline a tight-lipped smile, and pointedly drop the tooth into the trash. "I'd say I'm fine, but you'll see right through that, won't you?"

She leans against the stall door, smiling uneasily. "Do I know you?"

"We've never met," I say, washing my hands. "But I have a memory for things that haven't happened yet." One of Catie's fingernails slides off as I press it. No pain, no blood. Just gone.

"Where are you from?" Madeline asks.

"Lillian."

She nods. "So that's your blood talent."

I roll my eyes. "You're one of those people who call the *curse* a talent."

"But it is." She steps forward. "Don't you think remembering the future is a talent?"

"No," I say, ripping a paper towel from the dispenser, losing another nail as I dry my hands.

"I know most people believe Renfield corrupts, but I don't think that's true," she says. "I think of my 'affliction,'" she air quotes, "as a gift. Feeling others' pain for them? That *helps* people."

"It'll kill you."

She smiles like she doesn't believe me. "I'm a little more optimistic than that, Ms. Mason. Sorry, I just . . . recognized you."

I wince, but I should have expected this. If I didn't want to be known, I should not have run for mayor.

There is such a long period of *waiting* I have to endure as Catie, and I have not yet tired of the possibilities I can fill that time with. I've had families, raised children. I've become a librarian, read as many Earth-books as I could stand. I've taken up astronomy, discovered new beings at the bottom of the ocean, become a high school teacher, opened a ceramics studio . . . This time around, I've joined the local government in Bent. It's turned out to be the perfect cover for my . . . ulterior interests.

As always, Catie has held on for nearly forty-five years. I can't imagine any other host lasting that long, but no other host I've had is as *enthused* as

Catie Mason. In the backseat all the while, stirring around the rear of my brain. Watching everything. She had not a moment of regret for offering herself to me.

But nothing lasts forever, of course. And as I look at my wrinkled, sagging face in the bathroom mirror, I know the time has come. I'll need *some*one soon, even if it isn't Madeline.

"It's nice to meet you," she says. "I work at the college. One of the writers." She gestures vaguely at the bathroom door, to the event hall outside, filled to the brim with writers.

"Poetry, if I'm not mistaken," I say.

"Yes!" Pleased. Then shaking her head. "You probably haven't heard of any of my ”

"I haven't. But I'll be reading some of it soon." I offer my hand, let her shake it. Let her feel things about me through my skin. "It's a pleasure to meet you officially. You're a *lovely* body."

I leave her there looking dumbfounded.

I emerge from the women's bathroom into a large, sun-flooded space. It's a perfect spring evening. The rolls of green hills outside the tall windows are picturesque. They are awarding some Big Award for nonfiction to Benjamin McCall—the first Black man to ever win—and tonight is a Big Deal Banquet to honor him.

I remember not caring for this event. I remember not *ever* caring for it, in all the times I've been here. It's a distasteful show of wealth and breeding, thinly disguised as a literary highlight of the cultural calendar year. Everyone standing around, congratulating themselves on what a fine job they've done, nominating a person of color this year instead of another milk-skinned idiot. They all say, *It's so great he's won*, like they're not the ones who were keeping him from winning in the first place.

At least there's an open bar in the corner.

I lean against it, order an old-fashioned. When Catie's body came of age, she ordered her first legal drink. *I* ordered her first legal drink. By that time in my skin's life, I'm so caught up in girlhood that I forget myself for a moment. I'm so stricken by the magic of *finally* being legal to drink that I'm stunned, open-mouthed, surrounded by my "girlfriends," trying to decide what drink I'll order. The bartender staring at me. And all I can think in that blush-blinking moment is that someday I will meet Sydney Kim, and *her* favorite drink will be old-fashioneds, and this can be something we bond over, so I order the damn thing and . . . here I am.

It was strange, forgetting who I was. Actually *believing* for a moment that I was some young girl, instead of ageless old Yennigen. Like the night after prom, when I let Allen Jacobs feel me up in the back of his dad's convertible. Even letting Jacobs *take* me to prom in the first place. I'd actually wanted to *go* to prom. I'd *wanted* him to kiss my neck, and I felt my body press itself closer to his as he did. *You're forgetting yourself, Yennigen*, I thought. Then, *So what?* as Jacobs slid his hand up between my thighs. *This part of the cycle is only waiting, anyway. I deserve some fun . . .*

But by the time I reach this literary event, the waiting has long been over. Wheels are deep in motion. I have killed people. Have seen myself reflected in their eyes, a wrinkled hard woman with piercing eyes and short white hair. I have stood over graves and said, "We only wanted the wood. *Now* look at you. Your teeth are in your fucking throat." I have watched people choke on their own parts, and I have turned, disgusted, to my cronies (I've had *cronies*—young stud-boys who'd fuck me in exchange for the manual labor my slow-rotting arms cannot always perform), and I've said, "Smother him." I've walked away without a backward glance, listening to the muffled screams of the dying as they are buried alive.

Slow and steady, I have gathered pieces of the tapestry. It has taken me years, but I have finally completed nearly half of the giant. I keep it in a storage unit on the edge of town. I live alone in this life, so this process has been relatively easy. In other lives, when I've had families, I have had to be more creative. But there is a certain leisure to living alone. And soon, the giant will be complete. My lost tooth is a harbinger of the end of my time in Catie Mason, and the end of my time on Earth.

Is this what the philosophers intended for me when they shoved me down that well? To recreate this doorway at *any* cost? Or would they be horrified by what I've become? I think not. Considering the swiftness with which Marran slit Eddick's throat, I can't imagine they'd be anything other than supportive of the actions I've taken to secure the pieces of this doorway. No, I think the steamy-eyed High Bastard would appreciate the life I've made for myself here. I have made *quite* the life.

Sometimes, part of me whispers, *Then keep it. There's no need to go further down. You have a life here, in Bent . . .*

But then I remember the splendors of that other world. The one that caged me for eons. Those vast forests, the sprawling towers of its cities. The gleam of the sun along the brass hulls of its airships. I remember how goddamn *glorious* it would be to rule that place. And I swear to myself, again, that I will make it back down there. I will find a way to *break* this cycle once and for all. To secure for myself the kingdom I have always dreamt of ruling: Yennigenia.

It's a working title.

"Excuse me. Mayor Mason?"

The bartender has just slid my drink across to me when I hear Madeline's voice. I turn, and there he is. Standing very tall in front of me. Holding a glass of champagne in one hand, his crystal award tucked under his arm. Madeline wrapped around his side. He sticks out a hand to greet me. "I'm sorry, I didn't mean to startle you. I'm Ben McCall. Madeline said she just met you, and I wanted to introduce myself. You were one of the ones who recommended my book to the committee."

"I did," I say, only just now remembering I've done this. I shake his hand. It practically swallows mine. "Yes, fascinating work. Congrats on your award. Well-deserved. You could kill someone with that." Pointing at the thing's sharp edges.

"Oh." He laughs nervously. He says something that makes Madeline laugh, too, and they share a cute little banter. I can't remember how long they've been dating, but it seems serious from the looks on their faces. From the way he slides his arm around her shoulders and she tucks into him. I sip my drink, smile like I'm listening. I'm not. I can't even hear them over the din and the fucking fancy-pants quartet by the big window. My eardrums have begun to deteriorate.

"Well, I'm glad to hear that," I say. I can tell I've interrupted the middle of a sentence. To cover, I quickly add, "You gave a fine acceptance speech. Most winners brag more."

"Oh, my mom always said to be humble, so . . ." He smiles again. Then a frown jerks over his face. He runs his tongue around his teeth. *Ah yes,* I remember. *The tongue.* I remember that it pains him. I wonder if Madeline considers it a talent or a curse. Or both.

"I don't mean to impose," he says, "but . . . Madeline mentioned you have a . . . particular interest in local history?"

I sip my drink, smack my lips. It hurts a little. My lower lip has begun to slough off in the last six months or so. I've covered up the loose flesh with lipstick, but still.

Perhaps that's another reason I allowed myself to be such a girl. It was *fun* while it lasted. Wearing lipstick and dresses. Too fun, actually. When Catie's body overdosed on cocaine on its twenty-third birthday, I finally decided enough fun. I began rebuilding the tapestry the very next day.

"I do," I say. "A *big* interest."

"Well," he clears his throat. "I've been working on this . . . new book about some of the local lumber companies and their use of slave labor in the late 1700s. I was wondering if I could talk to you sometime about some of Bent's archives, or—"

"Oh, absolutely," I say, cutting to the chase. "Here." I hand him my drink, then dig around my purse for a business card. I manage to locate a very crumpled one, and hand it to him.

"Give me a call tomorrow, and we'll set something up," I say. "Always happy to . . . support local artists."

McCall looks at the card in awe, as if he can't believe how easily this great opportunity has presented itself. He glances at Madeline. She gives his arm a supportive squeeze.

"Perfect," he says, pumping my hand again. "I will. Thank you so much."

"My pleasure," I say. "Congrats again on the award."

I slug the rest of my drink and walk away as he and Madeline share a kiss. His cheeks bulge as he extends that tongue deep inside her mouth. Her knees give and she clings to him for support.

I remember when Catie's body drew attention like that. I don't miss it. Aging has permitted me to work in peace, without distraction from the heart.

As I walk away, Madeline and McCall are approached by an older woman I recognize as one Winnifred Hetch. I pause, and watch from a distance. I can't hear them, but I know Winnifred is asking Madeline if she's ready to fulfill her destiny as savior of the Spine. Has she found the rot-root yet? Is she ready to meet with the Philosopher High?

Madeline, of course, has no idea what she's talking about. These questions are meant for me. They've *always* been meant for me.

Winnie finds me at farmer's markets, at school, at home. When I am freshly Madeline, in the spring of 2018, there always comes a day when Winnie approaches me and tells me it is time to fulfill my duty. She has a surprisingly large, pearl-handled pistol in her purse, and sometimes she sticks it to the small of my back, demanding I "embrace the prophecy of the Mind." Which always makes me laugh. Sometimes I refuse to come along and she actually pulls the trigger, rupturing my kidney so that I am forced to take *her* skin. But another of those spiders always tracks me down. The High *always* gets what he wants. Always captures me, crucifies some poor bastard to the tapestry, and *shoves* me through its cold, dark maw.

Until today.

Today, McCall ushers Madeline away, leaving Winnie in the middle of the hall, looking lost and confused.

I slip out a back door, laughing to myself.

Yes. This time, things are already different. The smug High bastard will probably spend the rest of his Slitter days wringing his hands, just *hoping* for another vision of the savior his god promised. The "savior" that arrived and then vanished just as quickly, without healing anything at all.

Good. Fuck him.

"You have a *lovely* home," I tell McCall as he hands me an iced tea. He sits next to me on the couch in his living room. There's a picture window across from us, facing his front yard. It's a sunny day, all grassy-green and robinsong. The sprawling neighborhoods of the Mill do have their suburban appeal, I'll admit. Cozier than my drafty penthouse in Bent.

He clinks his glass against mine. "I hope you don't mind I don't have any booze in the house."

"Not at all," I lie, swallowing the bitter taste of tea. "So. Benjamin. What *exactly* can I help you with?"

"Well . . ." He frowns, runs his tongue around his teeth. "Can I be honest with you, Ms. Mason?"

"I don't know. Should you be?"

"I'm worried I might not be able to. But . . . Madeline *says* you have a talent to know what people ask before they ask it? And she . . . I hope you don't mind, but she *felt* that you could help. When you shook hands."

"Did she? Hm. Well." I place a hand upon his arm. "Then you can tell me *anything*, Benjamin. I promise I won't report you." This could be anything. This day is so new, so excitingly *fresh*.

"That's great, because I don't know where else to turn, and . . ." A smile flickers over his mouth, but doesn't catch. "For starters, then . . . There's no book. I'm not researching enslaved lumber workers or . . . anything like that."

"I figured."

He spreads his hands. Pauses. Then: "When I was a kid, my mom used to work in the Falls. She had the night shift at a convenience store there. Used to bring home these . . . liqueur chocolates that I *loved*. But . . . they were *made* in the Falls as well."

"Tinker's candy has been known to cause cancer," I say.

"Exactly. And worse."

"It . . . mutated your mouth," I guess. "Gave you a *blood* talent." As if anything in this sinkhole valley could be beneficial.

"Yes." He nods. "That's *exactly* what happened. I, I must have eaten *hundreds* of those things. And they . . . changed me." He takes a long, shaking sip of his tea. "I didn't know until I was fourteen. Her name was Jasmine. We were in the back of my older brother's car, just . . . sitting in the driveway. I'd stolen a bottle of my father's whisky. We kissed—my first ever—and my tongue . . . *embraced* hers." He can't look at me. Tells his story to the floor. "The next thing I knew, it was . . . pulling on her, *pulling* . . . My brother helped me bury her, deep in the Shembels. He doesn't . . . speak to me anymore.

"It happened again when I was eighteen. I was drunk at a party—I used to play football—and . . . one of the cheerleaders . . . kissed me. I forgot myself. Her name *was Jules*." His voice slips into a feminine register, high and young.

He rubs his lips, closes his eyes. Seems to be thinking of the right way to continue.

He must figure it out, because he rises off the couch and says, "Wait here."

He leaves the room, and returns with a large cardboard box. Things sliding and thunking around inside. He drops it on the coffee table. Before he opens it, he says, "When I went to college, I . . . drank. Heavily. I couldn't stop. It became a game I played against myself. How well could I hide the body? How well could I maintain my schoolwork—my football scholarship—while I *hunted*, and *lied*? The answer . . . shocked me. I remember attending morning classes with rum in my coffee, eyeing all my classmates, my tongue . . . growing with every sip, every . . . taste.

"I drank well into my thirties. Well into my career as a writer. Until I met Gloria. She helped me. For a long time, I was able to keep myself from hurting her, or anyone else. I attended meetings, I . . . had myself under control. But I should have known. There *are* no roads out of Renfield, or so they say.

"We'd decided to have a child. We were . . . We were *trying* to have a child. I suppose I'd had a long day of teaching. I'd had a manuscript rejected *again*. It just happens so *fast*. All of a sudden that bottle you keep hidden in the cupboard is in your hand, and I crawled into our bed and I . . . took her. I don't *know* how it happens. But it . . . When it was done, I cut her tongue from mine. I couldn't have it inside of me. But it *regrew* itself." He swallows, voice cracking. "Madeline is the first person I've trusted myself to be with since then."

I stand, deeply interested. "And the box?"

"It's phones," says McCall. He removes the lid and stands back, like its contents might spring out at us. I peer inside. It is, indeed, phones. Many, many cellphones, ranging in size and variety from the sleekest, most current iPhone to the oldest, brickiest Ericsson.

He digs into the box, extracts an old gray Samsung. "This belonged to an Amanda *Davis*." He enunciates the name like I should recognize it. I don't. He sticks his arm deeper into the box, digs out a pink Razr flip phone. "Rene Nelson." When he sees this name doesn't ring a bell either, he digs deeper, unearths a big block of a Nokia. "Toni *Ridge*way." He tosses her back into the box. Scoops out great handfuls of phones. "Paige, Michelle, Teá . . . I don't even *know* who some of these belong to anymore. I don't know if anyone is still looking for them, or . . . This is *decades* of addiction, Ms. Mason. But I—I haven't touched alcohol in three years and seven months. Madeline calms the urge. She *takes* it. I feel bad, but it's true. I don't want to drink when I'm with her. At all. But I can't . . . I can't keep *this* from her any longer. She *thinks* it's just the drinking. She doesn't know about the . . . dead-voice box. I call it."

"She doesn't know about *any* of this?" I laugh. "That's . . . quite the feat." I'm impressed he's hidden this from me-as-Madeline several times now. I had no idea.

"I can keep it all in my head," he says. "Mostly. Which tongue belongs to which phone. I'm terrified to take notes in case Madeline finds them. But sometimes, I can't keep it all straight. I lose track, and I have to power a phone down for *good*. When I stop using a voice—telling Amanda's mother I'm fine, I'm just traveling; or Rene's horrible uncle I'm still not interested; or Paige's poor ex-husband I *still* need space—I'm *killing* that person. Killing them more dead than when I buried them in *bags* in the Shembels." His voice trembles.

I nod slowly, taking this all in. I'm trying not to laugh, because he seems so distraught about this. So remorseful. But it's all so funny and fascinating and *new*.

"Poor Madeline," he says, shaking his head sorrowfully. "Every time we kiss, I *feel* that other me prodding at her. That Renfield me that emerges when I drink." He runs his tongue around his teeth. "I feel her absorbing it, but one day, her talent won't be enough. And I'll . . . I *love* her. But I worry every second of every day that I will be her end. One day, without thinking, I'll . . . I'll have a beer! And I'll take her voice, Ms. Mason. The drink . . . will *consume* it."

"Well." I sip my tea. "That is quite the tale."

"I'm sorry if this too much," he says quickly. "You can arrest me, you can—"

"Do you think I have some kind of cure?"

He gives me a desperate look. "If you know Renfield history, you can *help* me find that candy. Help me figure out how this all began. I've asked other people. Discretely, hypothetically. Pharmacists in the Falls. But you know what they *all* said? 'Them's the breaks. That's Renfield for ya.'"

"Oh, Benjamin." I shake my head at the box. "So sad to be alone with a secret like this."

"But, but *you* have resources. You're the mayor! Have you . . . heard of anything like this?"

"I haven't," I say. "But! I do believe I can help unburden you from this curse."

His eyes widen gratefully. "You can?"

"Of course. Be happy to."

He begins to cry, he's so relieved. "Thank you. Oh god, *thank* you . . ."

"But first: Why don't we have a quick snack? I'm famished, aren't you?"

He sniffs. Glances between me and the phones. "How can you even *think* about eating?"

"Problem-solving makes me hungry. I'd brainstorm much more fluidly if I weren't doing so on an empty stomach."

"O . . . okay." He shakes his head. "I . . . have some sandwich stuff, I could . . ."

"Oh, that won't be necessary." I fucking hate sandwiches. "Tell me, Benjamin. This is a very specific question, but . . . Do you have any *berries* on hand?"

HEARTS VS. MIND

I was alone in my room when the body crashed the party. I'm the youngest sibling of three, the invisible one, and I lived in the loft far from everyone else. Sometimes I think it was my father's joke to call me Clarity. Sometimes I wonder if I did it to myself.

When the screaming began, I came downstairs to the second-floor balcony of our old home on Applecore Lane. I looked down at everyone, a ghost in the ceiling. My parents had a big Fourth of July party every year. The living room was filled with people. And there, in the center of the floor, was a mangled thing. Purple and gnarled. Everyone was screaming at it.

It'd rained all week, and the corpse had washed up from the woods beyond the backyard, smashed through the glass doors to the patio. Flooding was happening all over the county. It was a bad week—some people thought a flood in Renfield meant the end. The blood in the ground was finally rising up, and coming for us all.

Of course, the world went on. But my parents saw this dead, waterlogged creature as an omen. A warning. After a century and a half, the Shembelwoods finally wanted the Mithers *gone*.

Later, people started throwing rocks through our windows at night. We don't know who they were. But we knew that if the forest was tired of us, other Renfielders would be, too. They wouldn't oppose what they saw as the will of the woods. It wasn't long before my parents moved us to Furrowkill, where we would be safe from superstition and, more important, "safe from the eyes of the giant."

But truth be told? I feel like the giant is the only one who ever really saw me. I loved the constant sense of being watched in this county.

That's why I returned to Renfield. Why I only applied to Edenville College.

If I couldn't be seen *here*, I figured I'd throw myself through the window at the *next* Fourth of July, and then everyone would see Clarity for sure.

Clarity Mither, "My Bedroom Is Rotting"

CHAPTER TWENTY-ONE

THE OLD BIOLOGY BUILDING

The car definitely wouldn't start. He'd tried it five times now, while Quinn ranted on about the tunnels.

"Hundreds of them," she said. "And they all have these, these red robes and they're these half-spider *things*, and . . ."

Finally, Cam took the key out of the ignition and leaned back, sighed. "We're dead in the water, folks. Shit." He rubbed his shoulder, squeezed his eyes shut. "You really got me with this fuckin cane." He had it tucked between his legs.

Quinn eyed the stained eagle head. Why was he still holding it? She tore her eyes from it, wriggled uncomfortably in her seat, then frowned. "The hell am I sitting on?" She reached under herself and extracted a metal spray can.

"Oh shit," said Cam, snatching it from her. He'd forgotten he left it there after driving home from campus. "Here, hold out your hands."

She almost didn't. But she figured she couldn't end up in *worse* shape, so. She held up her wrecked palms and he sprayed them. It was cold, and tingled like good ChapStick on bad lips. Pins and needles snaked up her wrists, as if her hands had been asleep. She flexed her fingers. Better. *Much* better.

"Thank you," she said. "What is that?"

"Renfield's not all bad," he said, with significantly less *I told you so* malice than he might have on any other day. He turned to the backseat. "Clarity? Lean forward."

The eyeless, tongueless, mostly-naked girl leaned into the front seat, making Quinn flinch. She hadn't been a big fan when Cam had ushered the girl into the car with them. Still twitchy from the crash.

But watching him extend this kindness to Clarity changed things. As she watched him spray Clarity's crusted sockets (and as Clarity opened her mouth for him, moaning with relief as the spray hit her hollow lower jaw), Quinn realized something had happened to *him*, too. Just as she'd squeezed herself through a narrow tunnel to survive, Cam had been squeezed as well.

As he sprayed Clarity down, he told Quinn briefly about the tapestry, the Spine. The bleeder. The tongues.

"Clarity was there in the basement," he explained. "I let her go."

Clarity jerked out a blind hand, fumbled for his wrist, and squeezed. She made noises they couldn't understand. Sad but grateful. She fell back drunkenly into the backseat.

"Your ankles," said Cam, handing the can back to Quinn.

"Thanks." She sprayed herself, glancing at him warily. He fiddled with Slitter's cane, turning it this way and that.

"You wanna look under the hood?" Quinn asked.

Cam blinked like he'd forgotten what they were talking about. He glanced out the windshield, then snorted, rolled his head on the seat to give her an *Are you kidding*. "Quinn, I don't know shit about cars. Plus we only *have* half a hood." He nodded through the cracked windshield at the crumpled stretch of metal that used to be a hood.

"Well, do you have service?"

Cam pulled out his phone. "No. You?"

Quinn held up her hands. "I don't even have a phone."

"What do you mean?" He showed Quinn his screen. "You texted me."

She squinted at his phone, reading, then punched his arm. "*Fuck* you."

"Ow! What did I—"

"You really think that sounds like me?" She ripped the phone from him, scrolled through the messages. "When have I ever used the word *pusillanimous*? I can't even *spell* that. *God*. You pusillanimous *prick*." She chucked the phone at him, looked out the window.

"Alright," said Cam. He leaned down, scraped his phone off the floor.

"We can't stay here. We have to do something about her." Nodding at Clarity. "Get her to a hospital or . . . something."

"We can't *walk* to a hospital. I don't even know where there *is* a hospital. It could be miles."

"Maybe we'll get service somewhere if we—"

"And the tunnels are all over!" Quinn waved a hand at the dark. "Literally, like, everywhere. I went in through the library and came out on the quad."

Cam shivered at his own memory of the undercampus. "Then let's just take her back in the house. We have internet there, we can—"

"What if they tracked me? What if they come up through the floor?!"

Cam sighed. "Well, we have to at least get her some water or something." He looked around. House lights tinkled through the leaves. "Maybe one of these—"

"No." Quinn shook her head hard. "They could be more old ladies."

"Okay, then what do *you* fucking suggest?"

Quinn twisted Dad's lighter between her fingers. Looked around. "We're pretty shaded here. Not many cars come down this way. Maybe we could just wait here until dawn."

"Because they won't be looking for you at dawn."

"They'll have to go back to work." She raised an eyebrow. "You're not concerned about the faculty looking for *you*?" Flicking her eyes at Clarity, breathing heavily in the backseat.

Cam picked at his beard, looking down at the cane. He was waffling, he realized. As soon as he'd laid eyes on the cane, he'd forgotten himself. He'd already chosen to free Clarity. He didn't think McCall would show *that* much gratitude for the cane if Cam had already proven himself a liability like that.

Weeeaak, the eagle head seemed to snarl at him. The same voice he'd heard thrumming from the tapestry. *Coulda been a special special boy, Caleb. Chose instead to be scared . . . and weeeaak . . .*

He took both hands off the cane like it was burning. He shoved his glasses (now bent from being caned) up his nose. He took a breath. "Right. No, right. I mean . . . I hope they're not."

"We should burn that," said Quinn, staring at the cane.

Cam shook his head. "I don't know if we'll be able to. We just have to keep it from them. Until—"

Laughter. Out there in the windy night.

They both turned in their seats. Clarity's hollow face gaped at them balefully from the backseat. But beyond that, out the back window, they could see a parade of women marching into 1896, just visible around the bend in the road. They were laughing and bumping against each other, leering and calling Quinn's name. Cam's name. All wearing their scarlet robes.

Quinn slid down in her seat, swearing under her breath. Cam followed suit.

They didn't move for several minutes. Finally, Quinn peered over the back of her seat. The women were retreating. But they were waving to one woman standing in the doorway of the town house. A woman who shut the door when the others left, sealing herself inside. *Just in case someone comes back.* She could imagine Slitter's voice giving the order.

"They left a guard," she said.

"Just one?" Cam sat up. "We can take her."

"Cam, I'm telling you, she's a spider."

"Oh, come on."

"You . . ." She blinked at him. "You don't believe me? What about the shit *you've* seen?"

McCall's tongue wormed into his mind.

"Point taken," said Cam. "Okay, maybe there's somewhere on campus we can hide. Spend the night. In the morning, I can . . . I'll ask Angie for the key to the van. Say we smashed our car and I just need to borrow it for a bit. Then we drive the *fuck* out of here."

"But what if Angie is . . . one of them?"

"Then we *steal* the van, I don't know. Clarity, can you last the night?"

Clarity nodded. She even perked up and, with effort, managed to mouth a word that sounded like *house.*

Cam and Quinn looked at each other.

"What house?" Quinn asked.

Clarity held out a hand. Tried another word. "Pha."

"I didn't get that one either," said Cam. He looked at Quinn. She shook her head.

Clarity wriggled her fingers. She tried again, enunciating so hard the cords in her neck tightened. "Pha. Ng."

"Phone!" Quinn cried. "Give her your phone."

Cam obliged. Clarity held it for a moment, then handed it back to him. She moved her head back and forth. "Nngg. Oh. Shh." She worked her mouth around. Put her teeth together, hissed through them.

"Note!" Quinn cried again. "Cam, she wants to type. Pull up your notes thing."

Cam did, handed the phone back to her.

Clarity stared emptily at the windshield, furrowed her brow, then typed. Her thumbs moved confidently over the keys, and when she handed the phone back, the message was surprisingly coherent: There's a sviyseiff campus. Wear camp. In field. Once haunted, but isn't any more I think. Should be safe

"Sieve yes campus?" Cam tried.

"Howwss," Clarity said. "Off."

"House off campus," Quinn translated. "Oh." She snapped her fingers. "I am *nailing* this. Where? West Camp?"

Clarity nodded vigorously. Her short red hair flopped across her face.

"I know what she's talking about," said Cam. "You mean the old biology building?"

Another vigorous nod.

"That's only a fifteen-minute walk from here," said Cam. "We can make that. Hunker down, protect the cane."

"And it's safe?" Quinn asked. "No one goes there?"

Clarity held out her hand for the phone again. She typed even more confidently this time, handed the phone back within seconds.

Wypp9w3e ri be qg7nt3e vy5 3v3rywh3re ge43 is so

"Great," said Quinn.

Clarity leaned against Quinn as they walked, limping along on the cane (which they wrapped in a towel so no one had to touch it). Quinn had pulled a blanket out of the back of the car, too, and wrapped it around Clarity's shoulders. Clarity's legs hadn't been used for the better part of a year, and they wobbled dangerously beneath her. But she limped along on Slitter's cane fine enough. With Quinn's support, they were making good time.

Crossing Rackell Street was the main stressor. Luckily, no cars passed. They had to sneak through North Gate to avoid the guard in the shack by the main gate, then stuck to unlit paths as well as they could. When they turned toward West Camp, the flowers lifted themselves a little, and followed the trio along the sidewalk. At one point, a campus security car cruised by, and the three of them ducked. The sunflowers swept over them, giving them shade.

"Are the flowers on our side?" Quinn whispered.

"I wouldn't bet my life on it," said Cam.

They cocked their heads at him.

The large wooden fence at the edge of Slitter's parking lot loomed tall and dark.

They squeezed through its gate one by one, stuffing Clarity through first and following close behind. The field beyond was a sea of sharp gray leaves, waist-high. They charged through them and saw, up ahead, the old house. Sagging, rotten, and flaky. A two-story colonial job that leaned too far forward for its own good.

They stumbled up onto the porch and eased the front door open. The tattered remains of a living room seemed to blink at them, surprised to have visitors. Before they stepped into the building, Quinn swung an arm out, blocking Cam. "Wait. Vibe check." She stared into the room for a moment. Then nodded. "Okay, I think we're good."

"Thanks, detective," Cam muttered.

It seemed that the Edenville Butcher had moved on from her old haunt. That, or she never existed in the first place. Cam found himself wanting to ask Chett about it, and felt a fresh pang of guilt.

Quinn flicked her lighter on so they could see, and Cam shoved a broken old armoire against the door. Moonlight cut through the shades on the two windows of the far wall. They propped Clarity up in the corner and sat on either side of her. Quinn took the cane and held her lighter to it. It took a few tries to get a spark to catch. "Come on, Dad . . ." But finally, a small flame wavered to life. She let it lick the head of the cane. It lingered for a moment, then blew out. She dropped the cane, clapped her lighter shut, and slumped to the floor.

"You should've left it," she said. "Whatever they're doing isn't our concern anymore. We can just leave."

"I know. I . . ." He blinked at her with his bright red eyes. He pursed his lips, like a *sorry* or a *You were right* was trying to get out but he was stopping it.

They looked at each other in the moonlight for a long time, breathing softly together.

Clarity coughed, moaned.

"You wanna tell us what happened to you?" Cam asked. He offered his phone again. "You can try typing it. I think we both want to know how you ended up in that basement."

Clarity took the phone in both hands.

They waited patiently, silently, as she typed. She typed for a long time. When she was finally done, the edges of the horizon over the field were just beginning to brighten. Quinn's eyes were fluttering shut.

Clarity handed the phone back to Cam. He read a little. Most of it was legible, some of it was gibberish. But he got the basic gist. He handed it to Quinn and dug at his eyes while she read. His entire body and brain hurt.

"What do you think?" he asked.

"What do you mean?"

"What do you think we should *do*?"

"Well, I don't know who that is." She pointed to a name on Clarity's note.

Cam nodded. Solemnly, he said, "I do. I've been writing about them."

"Who are they?"

"I'm not sure," said Cam, rising and looking out the window at the dawn. "But from what I can tell, they're a . . . collective of worms with a singular consciousness. Parasites or something. They jump from host body to host body and they've been doing it for . . . ever." He tasted the name. "Jopp Yennigen." He looked at Quinn. "If Yennigen is here, in Edenville? It's my personal opinion that they need to be stopped. They're cruel and cold. And they're not going to stop until they get the Shattered Man back online."

Quinn sighed. She wanted so badly to say again, *It's not our problem.*
They should just leave it all alone. But then Clarity rested her head on
Quinn's shoulder, and she softened. If there was something in Edenville
that was taking and torturing girls, Celeste would want her to do something about it.

"Okay," she said. "So we find a way to destroy the tapestry. Maybe it'll
be easier when it's all together? Add the last pieces and just . . . chuck a
Molotov at it, be done. Then drive the fuck back to Brooklyn."

"You have a Molotov on you?"

Quinn shrugged. "How hard can they possibly be to make? You have
your wallet?"

"Yeah, but—"

"Great." She ticked off their errands on her fingers. "Then we go to the
liquor store, the old Mither house, *back* to Slitter Hall, and then home."

"And you don't want to just . . . Ichabod?"

"Fuck yes I do. But . . ." She placed a hand on Clarity's head. "But first
I think we should burn Edenville to the goddamn ground."

Cam picked at his beard. Then nodded.

"Okay," he said. "Clarity, how does that sound to you?"

Clarity gave a weak thumb's up, then spun a middle finger in a big
circle. *Fuck you, Edenville.*

Cam glanced at his phone. "We have another two hours before Angie's
at her desk. So we might as well get some sleep."

"I'm so there," said Quinn, already closing her eyes.

As Quinn and Clarity slept, Cam sat there, staring at the cane on the floor.

If what Clarity had written was true, they were up against something
horrible. Something monstrous. Something not even remotely human.

He took the phone and read through her story again. He read until his
phone turned itself off. Then he nodded himself into a nightmare about
his tongue splitting into worms, and wriggling down his throat.

CHAPTER TWENTY-TWO

"MY BEDROOM IS ROTTING," BY BENNY MCCALL (CLARITY'S STORY)

She'd been awake when the needles plunged into her eyes. She felt them suck at her brain, pumping for seven long months of rusted, boiling darkness as she rotated on her metal spit. The pain was sublime and endless, and worst of all, she knew her dormmates wouldn't come for her. Her parents, sleazy Terrence and simpering Greta, wouldn't come.

No one would even notice she was gone.

Clarity sat on the porch of the old biology building. It was just an old house. Maybe it looked more scholarly inside, but she had never been inside. The house sagged and paint-peeled over her head. The field of tall gray grass surrounding it was frozen in the cold. Frost sparkled under the moon. She hugged her knees tight to her chest, took a long drag off her Noxboro, blew gritty smoke at the stars. She breathed in the cool February air, and felt the eyes of the Renfield giant blinking at her through the trees, from the clouds, from the grass.

Even though she hated the way Noxboros coated her tongue with that weird dirty film, they did have a strange blueberry tint, hiding just beneath the nicotine, that soothed her. Clarity grew up smoking these. Bumming them off older kids at parties, smoking them behind Lillian Academy's gym at sunset with Parker Bailey, who kept trying to kiss her.

Clarity had never kissed anybody. The dating pool at her hippie-dip private school hadn't been big enough for her to be interested in anyone (there were only fifty kids in each grade). The dating pool at Furrowkill High was much bigger, but Clarity had been too pissed by the move to care. Screw her parents for making her switch schools just before senior year, even *if* they had their reasons.

The first thing she did when she came back to Renfield was buy a pack of Noxboros. They tasted like home. And she was proud that she'd allowed herself to live long enough to earn buying a pack of her own, with*out* Parker Bailey's fake ID. The second thing she'd done was dye her hair in the dorm sink. She didn't want people pointing at her signature old-money blond on the quad, whispering, *That's that Mither girl.* So she'd hackjobbed her way into a homemade bob, all uneven and short, but new and therefore acceptable. She dyed it a bright red, left the communal sink looking like a crime scene. None of the other girls on her hall said anything, though. Clarity suspected they *all* had their own private embarrassments.

She blew out smoke, ground her cigarette butt onto the porch. Hugged her knees tight again, pressing her back against the wall. She shivered, wishing she'd worn something more substantial than her purple leggings. She checked her phone. Time to be moseying anyway. It was almost time for her meeting.

The meeting.

The thought of it made her heart lurch.

She stuffed the pack of Noxboros in her backpack, grabbed her phone, and stepped off the porch onto the grass. She turned and waved at the old house. "Thank you." She was grateful it'd allowed her a quiet beat off campus. A half-hour to clear her head, away from Haywood Tower's stifling fifth floor, where all her floor-mates were hunkering down for a movie night. Microwaved popcorn, Swiss Miss, the whole song and dance. Jordan even bought rum with her fake ID.

No, Clarity didn't have the time or the heart for a movie night. Not tonight.

Tonight, she had a meeting with Professor McCall.

*   *   *

Clarity had spent winter break in Furrowkill, watching *Breaking Bad* in bed. She'd been so burningly happy to be home after finals (her first finals ever), and she'd greeted her parents with such Christmasy aplomb, that she'd actually convinced herself she was excited to be home for the holidays. That was a mistake, of course. Charlie, now a junior at Syracuse, brought his girlfriend home. She made everyone cupcakes.

It was horrible.

They were delicious.

That, and Jess was going through her third breakup with the same girl (a senior at Cornell who clearly didn't give two shits about Jess, if you asked Clarity). So between the two of them, there wasn't much energy in the house left for Clarity. But . . . when had there ever been?

After the third season of *Breaking Bad*, she'd found herself looking forward to returning to Renfield, despite a dull and long first semester at E.C. Even though she hadn't suddenly morphed into the cool young thing the Disney Channel had promised her she'd transmogrify into when she turned eighteen. Instead, she'd sat in her dorm room for so long, staring at the ceiling and listening to Agnes Obel and Florence + the Machine, that the room seemed to be rotting around her. As if it was alive, muscles and organs pulsing on the other side of the wall. She imagined cracking away the plaster to reveal veiny meat. This was the same stupid, sedentary shit she'd done throughout high school, at Lillian Academy and then Furrowkill High. The same stupid shit she'd be doing for the rest of her life.

Why do I want to go anywhere, she asked her journal, *when all I do there is sit and wish for more?*

She tromped through the frozengrass field and squeezed back through the tall wooden fence. She crunched her way across the lot toward Slitter Hall. Sunflowers lay dead across the gravel, stretching across the pavement in long, frozen tendrils. They crackled beneath her boots in the dark. She stared at the ground, crunching along through the bitter, silent night.

The boots had been a Christmas gift from Dad. Whenever he saw her in them, he'd point at them like he was admiring something *he* owned. "They look good on you," he'd say, the same way a sane person might say, "That painting looks *good* on that wall over there." Like she was a thing, to be decorated and spun slowly in a corner. Like the elaborate gold-draped Christmas tree on its little rotor, revolving forever in the corner of the Mither living room. Dad had clearly always wanted a girl who attended a small liberal-arts factory and wore boots like *these*. Whatever, it was a fine gift. It just made her feel bought.

It was one of those death-still winter nights when the campus felt like a forgotten warzone. All the slopes and hills completely frozen, the grass studded with ice. Patches of snow had solidified here and there along the greenish mud. The only light came from the moon and the streetlamps, black-painted old metal, burning white orbs along the paths.

A beautiful, apocalyptic night. It made Clarity feel alive, but only barely, like a stranger in a barren atomic waste, wandering from camp to camp, looking for survivors. No one else was outside. The windows across campus were all lit warm and orange. She imagined herself an orphan, looking in from outside, freezing in the Dickensian cold. She kept her head bent, her breath tucked against her chest to keep her chin warm, as she went up the steps and into Slitter Hall.

It'd snowed significantly over the last month, and in the frozen pits of late January, that snow had stomped and slushed into a gritty, salty mush. The students had been back from winter break for three weeks, and already the carpet in this vestibule was irreparably stained and salted and wet.

She swiped her student E-card on the reader, pushed the inner door open. The hall was silent. Smelled of books and cold stone. She gazed down at McCall's office door.

It took her a moment to begin walking toward it.

She first met Professor McCall at the annual Richard P. Hardscratt (Class of 1978) Alumni/ae House Dinner. Only five Creative Writing students were invited every year, mostly juniors and seniors, and the occasional underclassmen whose parents were celebrities or legacies or both. Clarity *was* a legacy (her parents actually met at Edenville), but she had a hunch that wasn't why they'd invited her. Professor Flannery had shared the story she'd been writing in her fiction workshop with Professor Kim (not that Clarity *said* he could do that), and Professor Kim claimed it was top-notch work. She and Flannery had been encouraging her to read at the coffeehouses (fuck that).

Clarity didn't get the fuss. She'd had the idea for the piece in a dream, and she never put much stock in dreams. It was a weird sci-fi story about a wriggling of worms. An alien parasite stuck in an endless cycle of pain and waiting. Clarity could relate, even though the worms were psychotic and murderous. Even though writing this story made her eyes burn for some reason.

But it was just some silly thing based on a weird-ass dream. Not nearly as interesting or personal as the thing she was writing about her room. About how you can spend so much time sinking in a room that it begins to rot.

"You're sitting on the floor," she wrote, "with your back against the wall, typing out your little fantasy stories to keep yourself company, just like you've done since you were nine, and suddenly the room clenches around you. Like it's feeding on you. Like when you came up the throat of the Haywood Tower elevator, Room 507 was just *waiting* to digest you. And when *you* rot, the room rots with you. And this happens in every bedroom you ever know, until you hate the very *idea* of bedrooms."

So Clarity found herself invited to this dinner with all these hoity-toity people. She'd even walked into town to buy a nice dress. One of the ladies at the clothing store helped her, leering at her hungrily in the mirror as she admired herself. She was surprised how good she looked. Her short red hair, perfectly sharp above this sleek black dress. She wished she had cleavage to show off, or a butt, or anything really. She even took a picture of herself and sent it to Jess—an extremely rare display of sisterly affection. "lol," she wrote, "flat as a board." Jess, in another unprecedented display of sisterly affection, sent her a picture back, in front of *her* mirror, in her dorm at Cornell. She, too, was uncurved. "The Mither curse," she wrote.

So how did this man, this Benny McCall, take notice of Clarity? This short, flat, transparent girl? Why did he deign to kiss *her*, to probe his tongue inside her mouth, tasting her in a way she'd begun to assume she did not deserve to be tasted?

Clarity wasn't sure.

But there he was. Man of the hour at the Alumni House Dinner, at which Clarity knew zero other people. She just kept stuffing cheese and crackers in her mouth in the corner. And for whatever reason, his eyes had landed on her.

There were plenty of other adults around, all of Clarity's professors. But all of them were acting . . . off. The entire department. They'd seemed fine earlier in the day, during class, but then McCall had gathered them all in some side room during the cocktail hour before the dinner, and they'd emerged . . . different. Whatever McCall had said to them, it'd spooked them good.

Clarity would later deduce that this was when McCall gathered the entire department together and told them his tale about the Spine. He and Wes began building the bleeder the very next day.

McCall came up to her after the department dispersed (all of them drinking with shaking hands, whispering furtively in corners). Her mouth was full of cheese when he introduced himself. She'd been shocked. He was so handsome up close. She didn't know what to say. They'd all been assigned his book of essays over break (the one that won the Bent Literary Citizen Award last spring), but she hadn't bothered to read it. Homework over the holidays? Gimme a fuckin break. Literally.

But now that he stood before her, she regretted she didn't have anything to say to him.

Luckily, *he* did have things to say. He told her he'd already begun reading some of the pieces from students he'd be working with this semester, and he'd found her piece about worms very intriguing.

"Remind me what the main character's name is?" he said.

Clarity pronounced it very clearly. "Jopp Yennigen."

McCall repeated the name, moving his tongue around his teeth. "Yes . . . I can't wait to discuss it with you. By the way, I *love* your hair." Running a finger along its very edge.

Professor Narrows appeared at his side, wrapping an arm around his, looking concerned. Clarity fled, feeling suddenly embarrassed that she had even *dared* tread on an adult woman's territory.

But then he'd been all flirty in class the next day, complimenting Clarity's piece pro*fuse*ly to Professor Flannery, making Clarity blush in front of everyone. And suddenly, she found herself thinking of McCall all the time. She thought of his large, rough hands moving over her. Thought of his eyes locked on hers. Thought of him *seeing* her, holding her.

Before their first meeting, Clarity had doused herself in perfume. She shaved her whole body, thinking, *Yeah right*, the entire time. She'd only done that once before, just for herself, just to see what it was like. It was awful. But college was alien territory. This was only the first week of her second semester. Ya never know.

Alone together in his office, McCall had been very complimentary. He liked Jopp Yennigen a lot. But he didn't love her other story (because they'd been allowed to submit two for their workshops with him). Didn't have any interest at all in "My Bedroom Is Rotting."

"I don't think it's *bad*," he'd assured her. "I simply like *this* one more." Sliding the slim sheaf of papers across the desk at her. A paper copy of "Yennigen's Travels," by Clarity Mither. He'd circled things in red, slashing blood across each page.

"But I feel more passionate about the bedroom one," she said.

"Ah. I see."

And then he'd gotten close to her. Come around the desk and sat on its edge, his strong legs to either side of her. He'd played with her new hair. She hadn't been able to breathe.

McCall told her he'd *pay* her to continue writing the Yennigen piece. He'd do *any*thing for her. He said this very close, directly into her ear. She thought she was going to melt into the floor.

Blinking rapidly, she said as assertively as she could, "I'm sorry. I want to write what I want to write. The bedroom piece feels important to me. The Yennigen one . . . is for fun."

"But it's important to *me*," said McCall. "I'm *very* much looking forward to seeing how it ends." He waved the pages at her. "*Does* Jopp return to that world and establish Yennigenia once and for all? Do they *find* all those pieces of wood? You mention part of a trunk or . . . something . . ." He flipped through the pages, frowning.

Clarity had, indeed, added an element from her own life to "Yennigen's Travels." Her parents had gotten her the steamer trunk as a gift for her seventeenth birthday, back when they'd lived in the old house at Applecore Lane. Her mom bought it at a flea market in the Mill, finding it very fancy and quaint. But when it started sliding around the loft at night, Clarity realized it was made of bad wood. She'd locked it in the closet, listened to it bang against the door a few times before it settled down. She never opened that closet again. When they moved, she left the trunk behind.

Something about the way McCall spoke about this trunk settled it for Clarity. She wouldn't be telling him a goddamn thing about it. He could know *anything* else about her—but not that. She didn't know why, but something was going on around this man. Professor Narrows had seemed light and bubbly last semester. But now that she and her boyfriend worked together, she seemed thinner, twitchier. Everyone in the department did. McCall was adding a strange energy to campus. Clarity didn't know why, but she could feel it.

So even though he'd ended that first meeting by asking her to consider writing more Yennigen, then telling her how pretty she was, and *kissing* her, long and deep, lips softly sliding hers apart so he could taste her— Clarity just *knew* that telling him about the trunk would be bad news.

The next day, she'd gone to the first coffeehouse reading of the spring semester. She'd tromped all the way out to Slitter Auditorium, determined to read part of her bedroom piece, in spite of her lifelong fear of public speaking.

McCall was reading right before her. And when he got to the podium, he said, "This is from a new piece I'm working on. It's called 'My Bedroom Is Rotting,' by Benny McCall." He'd flashed a look up at Clarity in the audience, and she'd begun shaking in her seat.

When Professor Narrows called her name to read, she shook her head wildly and slunk down farther in her chair. She didn't know what else to do. She shook her head until Professor Narrows awkwardly moved on.

She stormed down to McCall after the reading. He was wading through a sea of other co-eds toward the door, laughing them off with that laugh that sounded like a cloth bag filled with smashed rocks. Clarity pushed her way up to him just as he was heading out the auditorium door and she said, breathless, "You stole my story."

He glanced over his shoulder at her. His eyes gleamed. He said, "Yes, I did." And the door closed on him, leaving Clarity speechless.

So here she was, one miserable week later. Stamping snow and ice off her boots in Slitter Hall. Here she was, walking *down* that hall, heart punching at her ribs. And here she was, sitting in McCall's office for a second time.

He smoothed his tie across his stomach, ran his tongue around his mouth. He gazed at her across the desk.

"Here's the thing," he said. "You're a bright girl. Pretty, too. So I'll make you a deal. I'd like you to continue writing about Jopp Yennigen. Or I'll continue stealing the work you're *really* fond of."

Clarity chewed the inside of her cheek. She realized that despite his power over *her*, she had a power over him, too. What would happen if she told Professor Kim that he'd kissed her? He'd be 300 percent fucked, that's what.

She tossed her new hair a little. "What's it worth to you?"

"What's it worth?" He frowned. Then stood, and came around the desk to her. He tucked her hair behind her ear, ran his tongue around his mouth. Standing behind her, he ran his hands down from her shoulders over her chest. "It's worth everything to me." Without thinking, she reached up and felt his arms. Strong, thick arms. Then he lifted her, turned her around. She didn't know what to do. She ran her hands over his chest. She kissed his neck. That's what they did in movies, right? He tasted like carpet.

"I've never," she said, without quite knowing what she'd never.

"It would mean so *much* to me," he purred. "I *need* your words, Clarity."

She sucked his earlobe. Between breaths, she murmured, "Why do you care . . . so much . . . about Jopp Yennigen."

He breathed into her hair. Took a fistful of it and pulled her head back, so that he could whisper in *her* ear now.

"Because," he murmured as he kissed her neck. "I *am* Jopp Yennigen."

"The fuck." She tried to shove him off, but his hand held her fast by her hair. "Let go."

"Want me to prove it?" he asked.

"I want you to let *go* of me."

He threw her into the chair, knocking the wind out of her. Then went calmly to a section of the wall that he popped open, and began to pour himself a drink.

"There are . . . parts I can't remember," he said. "Pieces I can never recall."

"Okay, so you memorized my fucking story, so what?" She swallowed a hard knot of fear.

He smiled at her, sat on the edge of his desk with his drink. Then proceeded to tell her parts of her own story she didn't even know. He told her about the deadman's well. Told her about the rot-root, hidden somewhere at the bottom of the Spine. He told her about Catherine Mason and the tapestry and how the real McCall had once come to Yennigen for help—so Yennigen had eaten him. Had taken that tongue for themselves, and shredded Mayor Mason's broken shell in McCall's garbage disposal.

"And here I am," said McCall. Said Yennigen in McCall's skin. "So if you know how my story ends this time around . . . I'd really like to know."

"Bullshit," she said, without believing it was bullshit.

McCall frowned into his drink. He tsked. Set his glass down on the desk. And then his throat began to bulge.

Clarity only made it halfway to the door before he shoved himself down her throat. He left her bleeding on the carpet while he called her mom. From far away, she listened to him tell Greta Marie Mither that everything was fine. She heard the odd tilt in her mother's voice that said Greta did not believe him.

* * *

For seven horrible months, she held on. For an entire purgatory of time, she kept the trunk buried. Held in the back of her mind where those metal spikes couldn't reach. Even as she bled out vision after vision of Yennigen and the manyworld—she refused to reveal the trunk.

She would rather die than help Jopp Yennigen.

CHAPTER TWENTY-THREE

EMERGENCY FACULTY MEETING

"I saw the door was open," Angie said as she led McCall downstairs. Madeline followed closely behind them. McCall was taking the steps two, three at a time with his long legs, and Angie had to pause between words to keep up. "As soon as I . . . looked inside, I . . . called Wesley, but he said . . . to tell *you* straight away."

McCall charged down the hall of the sub-basement. He didn't say a word. *Hadn't* said a word since Angie came into the lounge where he and Madeline were grading papers, and announced that the bleeder room had been left unlocked.

When they burst into the boiling concrete room, Wes was already there, kneeling by one of the turbines. He held the spent shell of Clarity's helmet in both hands. A trail of droplets ran from his feet out the door. Blood and ectoplasm mixed, as well as a greasy patch of dried vomit, where Clarity had apparently paused and puked before continuing her escape. The large metal fan turned overhead, tired and grinding. It sent a slow spinning shadow over the dried fluid on the floor. Sweeping over like a death-bird, and away. Over, and away. *Whoosh . . . whoosh . . .*

Wes put the helmet down and stood, slapped dirt off his hands.

"She pulled herself out of it," he said. He coughed. "That's supposed to be impossible. She'd have to unscrew the things herself. From her own skull."

"She's tenacious," said McCall. "I assumed her constitution would be weaker, but I suppose I was mistaken . . . Dammit!" He kicked the helmet across the room. It broke against the wall in a clanging mess. Some of the bodies on the machine winced.

McCall went around the back of the bleeder to the Aether-tanks. He held his hand under a spigot, poured a small puddle into his palm, and slurped it into his mouth. He smacked his lips, shook his head. Then slammed his fist against the machine.

"Hey," said Wes.

"Still nonsense," McCall snarled. "Nothing useful at all. Fuck!"

Syd appeared in the doorway. "Heard there was a commotion."

"Mither escaped," said Wes.

Madeline ran her eyes along the bloodied trail, the vomit. "That poor girl. Clarity was such a good student." She put a hand to her heart. "Her story about the bedroom—"

"Oh, fuck the bedroom," said McCall. "Who was the last person down here?"

A beat of silence.

"Am I on goddamn *mute*?" said McCall. "*Who* was—"

"It's my fault," said Wes. "When we brought Sneeze down here, I told Marion to close the door behind me and I . . . guess he grew a conscience."

"Luckily not a very big one," said Syd. "He could've sprung everyone."

"She *knew* something," said McCall. He waved a hand at Syd. "You felt it." He pointed at Madeline. "*You* felt it in her work. I even *tasted* a glimpse of it, but . . ." He breathed a long, exasperated sigh. "It's gone. Fucking gone!"

"It's okay," Madeline cooed, draping her arms across his shoulders from behind. "We can find her."

Wes spat bloody blue onto the concrete. "Yeah, if we have time."

"We don't," said McCall. He put his hands on his hips, completely ignoring the Madeline wreath he now wore tight about his shoulders. He ran his tongue around his mouth. Around and around. Thinking hard with a bitter, tight expression.

"Maybe someone else will see," said Madeline. She nodded at the rotating shelves. "Maybe the Mind will *tell* us where—"

"No, no, *no*." McCall shook his head. "They're useless. I *want* Marion. I want the fucker who *should* have been here in the *first* place." He whirled on Madeline. "*You* were the one who had the bright fuckin idea of letting him run loose. Are you proud of that now? Hm? Look at what he's done."

"Alright," said Syd. "No need to lose our heads."

Madeline's hands retreated against her chest. She looked wounded, exhausted. "Ben . . . I was just trying to help. I can tell you're upset." She shivered, skin quivering. "But—"

"Stop," he hissed. "Stop eating my feelings. I can *feel* you digging. This is *my* fuckin anger, *I* wanna feel it. Dammit!" He massaged his forehead and groaned. "I can feel him rotting. I can *feel* McCall giving up. We have a day, maybe, before I *need* someone new."

Madeline looked like a kicked dog. She wanted to go to him again. She wavered there, in the middle of the room.

"For Christ's sake, Madeline," said Wes. He coughed, deep in his throat. "It isn't Ben. It *hasn't* been for a year and a half. It *told* us that. Sat us all down and told us McCall is gone. It's *just* worms. Stop trying to reason with it."

Madeline flicked desperate eyes around the group. "I was trying to *help*. Clarity's mom was drawing too much attention. I . . . I *thought* if we didn't just kill Marion—"

McCall ignored her. "Where is Marion now? Does anyone know?"

"It's possible he's . . . absconded," said Angie.

McCall turned to her. "Since when?"

"Well, a few of my girlfriends were looking for his partner last night and they said the house looked . . . Well, like they'd left in a hurry. But their car is there. Smashed."

"Smashed?" McCall echoed.

"Wrapped around a tree." Angie shrugged. "Maybe Renfield sent them another surprise and they panicked, tried to leave on foot."

"They can't have *walked*," said McCall. "The nearest town is . . . what? Bent? That's a twenty-minute drive. I can't imagine they'd have walked it."

"Maybe Syd can track them," Madeline suggested. She brightened, stepped forward. "If she touches the car or something, would that work?"

"Objects only have about an hour's residue," said Syd. "*People* I can read for quite a ways back, but anything inanimate, it . . . I mean, if they haven't touched the car in the last hour, we're out of luck."

Madeline chewed on this for a second. "Okay, is there a way for you to—"

"There isn't a *way,* Madeline," McCall growled. "She said it wouldn't. Work."

"Well, hell." Wes cleared his throat. "Don't you *remember* where they went? Since you've been here before, Captain Worms?"

"I can't even remember books I read last *year,*" said McCall. "Let alone something that may or may not have happened to me *thousands* of years ago, my time. Besides, I've never *been* Benny before. This is all new territory."

"Can we track his cell phone?" said Madeline.

Syd laughed. "Do you know how?"

"I don't know, they always do that in movies. Can't we—"

"Oh my god, Madeline." McCall sighed.

"Well, look," she said. "I'm sorry. I'm just trying to brainstorm here. Don't talk to me like I'm a child, Ben."

"You *are* a goddamn child," said McCall. "I *told* you I'm not Ben and *still* you insist on cooking me *dinner* and telling me about your fucking *day.*"

"Aw come on man," said Wes. "Don't be a dick about it."

"Baby," said Madeline. She went up to him, put a hand on his arm. He glared. "We'll *find* him. You're just upset. You're not yourself, you're all stressed. Ever since you won that award, you've been *so* stressed, and—"

Suddenly, he had her by the throat. It happened so fast the others barely even saw him move. Madeline blinked at him. His fingers were so large they stretched all the way around her neck. His throat bulged.

"I'm not *well*?" he said. "I'm fucking *worms,* Madeline." He snarled in her face. "Worms. Why do you *insist* on not understanding that?"

"Because you're my Benny," she rasped. Her hands moved over his wrist. He tightened his grip.

"Alright." Wes moved behind McCall, put a hand on his shoulder. "Come on, let her go."

McCall shot out his fist, slammed his knuckles into Wes's windpipe. He crumpled, wheezed and hacked long spatters of blue filth onto the floor.

Syd and Angie inched closer together, closer to the door. McCall eyed them with a malice so hot and angry they were suddenly rooted to the spot.

"You wanna help her?" McCall asked. "Hm? Come on." Wes kept coughing and retching on the floor. "Come on. Stop me. Go ahead."

No one moved.

Madeline pawed helplessly at his arm. "Benny . . . Please . . ."

He turned back to her. The tongue slithered inside his jaw.

"I should have taken you when I had the chance," he said. "But I could take you now." His fingers ground into her. "I could jump right into you and you'd *let* me. You'd *open* yourself to me, you . . . worthless . . . fucking . . . meat."

Madeline's eyes widened. She gasped. Blood squirted out between McCall's knuckles.

"That's enough," said Syd.

"Then *make* it enough," he spat.

Wes turned onto his belly, tried to get up. McCall carried Madeline, dripping, to him and placed a shining shoe on the back of his head. He ground Wes's face into the floor, until Wes's arms gave out and he flattened against the concrete.

"Someone stop me!" McCall called out. Madeline whimpered and beat at his arm as he *squeeeezed*, harder and harder. Blood ran between his fingers. She tried to pry his hand from her throat. It wouldn't budge. It only tightened.

"Come on!" McCall cried around the room. "Someone *do* something!"

No one did.

"That's what I figured," he said.

And he closed his fist.

Tendons snapped inside Madeline's neck. Her mouth flew open. Blood coughed out. The air *popped* as McCall crunched the bones and ground them together. Things squished and spurted as McCall wrenched his hand back and forth, cracking her spine apart. Madeline's head lolled to the side, and toppled off her body, exposing jagged ends of bone, tube, muscle. For a moment, McCall held on to the ragged top of her exposed spine. Her hands clawed at him for another few seconds, then twitched down to her sides. Her entire body convulsed. McCall dropped it and let it writhe on the floor as it leaked blood and urine.

He picked up the head, one of her eyelids still twitching. He dug his fingers between her teeth and cracked her open like a nut. He horked several times, like a dog about to vomit. Then with an explosive roar, the tongue ripped out of his mouth. It dug into Madeline's bleeding, wrecked jaw and wrapped itself about her tongue. He had to wrench her mouth open wider to get it out, snapping cords, wrestling the jawbone back and forth.

Angie and Syd would think of this image every day until they died. But they couldn't look away. McCall snapping Madeline's tongue out by the roots, his other tongues squealing in welcome as he slid hers onto his appendage.

He wiped the blood from his lips, and was about to speak when he clutched at his stomach and groaned. He bent in half, retching. Wes was still trapped under his foot, and when McCall vomited, it splattered across Wes's back. Thick, dark chunks of gut spewed onto his shirt. Wes managed to shove himself out from under McCall's shoe. He scrambled back against the wall.

McCall took several deep, hitching breaths. He blinked up at the ceiling fan. "Ohh my. Benny didn't like *that*. Did you, Benny? Noo . . ." He grimaced, grabbed his stomach again, lurched forward. His eyes swept around the room. Syd and Angie huddled together by the door, Wes with his back against the wall, wheezing. Madeline, hollow and dead in pieces on the floor.

"Ohh, he's *mad* at me," McCall laughed. "Shoving me out of his skin. Pulling all . . . the switches. Shutting down." He grit his teeth in pain. "I'll have to use someone else soon. *Any*one else." He glared at Wes. "Even Falls trash like *you*."

He limped toward the door. Over his shoulder as he went, "Let's work on finding Marion. He can't . . . be far . . ."

In his wake, there was a moment of silence as Madeline spread across the floor. The fan overhead . . . *whooshed* . . .

When the slick dark puddle of Madeline Narrows reached the tips of Wes's shoes, he pulled them back, hugged his knees to his chest. The puddle grew larger, and this time he didn't move at all. He let the blood soak over him. He felt like he deserved it.

"At this rate, there won't even *be* a Creative Writing department," said Syd. "Who's going to cover her classes? Or Chett's?"

Wes coughed, said nothing.

They listened to the fan and the grinding turbines of the bleeder.

"I'll get a mop," said Angie.

She and Syd left Wes on the floor, blood soaking into his lap.

Suddenly, he laughed. He put a hand into the puddle, brought it to his face, and ran the blood over his cheeks. He laughed again, and sobbed.

Splashing her blood across his face with both hands, he cackled and hollered and screamed. All the pain, all the years of feeling that Madeline had soaked into her blood, now soaked into his.

CHAPTER TWENTY-FOUR

THE MITHER RUINS

At the end of *The Shattered Man*, the Committee betrays Caleb Wentley and nails him to the doorway. The doorway Caleb has just spent a hundred pages of blood, sweat, and tears helping rebuild. But Caleb doesn't die. Not exactly. He awakens in the realm of the Man. Nothing but stone and shadow and flame. The broken bodies of the Committee lay strewn around him. The Shattered Man has rejected them all, the very moment they stepped through His door. *Try-hards,* He calls them. *Bootlicking sycophants.* But He offers Caleb new life. A life of servitude, but life all the same.

Caleb refuses. Instead, he seals the doorway using the . . . power of love or something (Cam can't remember what bullshit MacGuffin he used). The Shattered Man, furious, retaliates by separating Caleb into three doughy, misshapen gummermen. He sends them up through the doorway just before it folds in upon itself, and tells them to find a new pawn, a candidate for the creation of a new door. One perhaps even more efficient than Crazy Frank LaMorte.

The book ends in a metafictional loop, in which the narrator is revealed to be Cam himself. The gummerfolk, he knows, are now hunting *him*.

But in real life, things are already going differently. Cam has snapped out of the spell the sub-department has woven for him. Caleb was a follower up until the end, but Cam is smarter. He's not going to be turned into gummerfolk. Not today.

They ended up sleeping until the late afternoon. When everyone was awake, jumpy and sore, they went over the plan again. Then Cam slipped out of the house toward Slitter Hall.

He twitched wildly as he made his way across the parking lot. He felt like he should be limping. This was the desperate scene near the end of the film when the protagonist limps back into his office, hoping to grab the MacGuffin from his desk (the file, the USB drive, the hat, whatever). He nods at everyone as he enters the elevator, pretending everything is normal.

Cam found himself sliding into this role, limping a little even though he wasn't injured. His back and ribs ached from the beating Quinn had given him, but his legs were working fine. He made his way up the short stone steps of Slitter Hall, passing a couple students he recognized but couldn't name.

"Afternoon, Mr. Marion," they greeted him.

He gave them all curt nods.

Tense strings played in his head. He imagined the way the camera would sweep over his shoulder and pull in tight on Angie as she looked up from her computer, clearly shocked to see him here, at her desk.

"Oh," she said. "Good afternoon."

He read her surprise as a very bad sign.

"Hi, Angie." He leaned over her desk and smiled warmly but probably unbelievably. "How was the rest of your day yesterday? After the raid."

"Boring," she said. Her eyes flicked over his shoulder. Now he could tell: his smile *wasn't* believable. But neither was hers. They'd definitely noticed Clarity was missing.

"Hey, is anyone using the van today?" he asked quickly.

"I . . . don't believe so. Why?"

"Our car broke down yesterday," said Cam. "Someone recommended a shop over in . . . the Mill?" He swallowed awkwardly. "So I wondered if I could use the van to . . . drive over there."

If everything were normal, Angie might simply *offer* him a ride. But instead, she rose unsteadily from her chair. "You know, I . . . I think I left the van keys with Wes after the raid. Why don't I go . . . I'll go ask him if he still has them. You . . . You wait *right* here."

"Sure thing," he said, offering another plastic smile. He watched her as she went out to the hall.

For a moment, there was still some hope that everything was fine.

Wes's office was to the left, in the same cluster as Cam's. McCall's was to the right. If Angie turned left, she might be telling the truth. In that case, Cam could—

Aaand she turned right. Shit.

Cam lurched over her desk, shoved some papers around, knocked a few of Angie's bobblehead penguins to the floor. Nothing, no keys. Angie's big purple purse sat on the far edge of the desk. He grabbed at it, and it fell, spilling its contents onto the carpet behind her desk with a loud clatter. Keys jangled onto the floor. Not the van keys, but still.

He went around the desk and crouched down, grabbed the keys, and was shoving Angie's shit back in her purse when McCall's voice cracked into the room: "He's not here."

Cam froze. McCall sounded breathless, like he'd just run from his office. He probably had. Cam pressed himself to the floor, dug his cheek into the carpet, praying he was fully hidden.

"He was *just* here," said Angie.

But McCall was already off down the hall, his voice farther away. "Where are the others? Where's Syd?"

Cam waited a moment, then peered over the desk. All clear.

He threw Angie's purse back on the desk and crept out into the hall, around the corner to the stairs, less than a second before McCall and Syd came around from the other end. Cam shot a look over his shoulder just before he hit the door to the parking lot—and ran smack into Wes.

His face was clean and red, like he'd just taken a long but necessary shower.

Cam didn't move.

"Did you know garden gnomes are supposed to be good luck," said Wes. He sounded hypnotized.

"Sure," said Cam, eyes wide.

"Poor Chett. He had a nice gnome in his yard, and we *still* got him."

They stared at each other for a full beat.

Then Wes cleared his throat and stepped aside, holding the door wide open.

"Just promise," he said softly, "if shit really goes sideways? You do the same for me."

Cam held up three fingers. "Scout's honor."

Wes nodded. And Cam darted past him.

He ran up and down the rows of cars, clicking Angie's fob until a dented green VW Bug booped itself unlocked. He wrenched open the door and tried to dive inside, but the seat was too far forward. He jammed the button on the side of the seat and was stuck waiting as it slowly ground itself backward. "Come on, come on . . ."

McCall burst out of the hall. "Cameron!" He started to run toward Cam, tie flapping back over a shoulder.

"Good enough," Cam told the seat. He ducked fast into the car, closed the door—and just managed to lock it as McCall got his fingers around the handle.

"You fuck!" McCall screamed at him. He beat at the window with his palms, then straight-up punched it. The window spiderwebbed. "Cameron!"

"It's Campbell!" Cam yelled back. The engine roared to life and so did the radio, blasting Tom Jones's "It's Not Unusual" at full volume. Cam swore (*Does* everyone *in the department have a freaking Jones fetish?*), and threw the car into reverse. He slammed his foot on the accelerator, felt the tires crunch over McCall's shoe. McCall howled in pain. Cam thrust the car into drive. He skidded around the lot, blaring the horn three sharp times. Quinn and Clarity slid out of the gate as he pulled up to it. Quinn stuffed Clarity into the backseat, and as she was climbing in after her, McCall grabbed her. Quinn whipped around, shoved him with the cane.

"The cane!" he roared. "Give me the cane!"

"Eat it!" she yelled, cracking it across his nose. McCall fell back and she pulled the cane inside the car, slammed the door shut. Cam sped away, leaving McCall in the middle of the parking lot, one leg at an odd angle, jaw working in tight circles, tongue squirming in its lair as he howled.

"How could you have let him out of your fucking *sight?*" McCall snarled at Angie. His throat roiled.

"Oh, what?" she said, reorganizing her bobbleheads. "You gonna take *my* tongue, too? You're killing this entire department."

McCall put his hands on the desk and leaned into her face. "You think you're untouchable. But if that's true, then *why*," his voice shifted into Madeline's, "didn't you save me?" It shifted again, into Clarity's. "Or me?" Again, into Chett's. "Or *me*?"

Angie held her chin up. "Your hunger will break you one day."

"I doubt it," said McCall, leaning back and straightening his tie. He turned to Syd. "What here did he touch?"

"That," she said, nodding at Angie's purse, already undoing the straps of her small hand.

"Can we cool it with the Tom Jones?" Quinn shouted. She'd found a large pair of Angie's sunglasses in the console and was sliding them onto Clarity's face. "I don't know what a sexbomb is, but I'm really not here for it."

Cam punched the radio knob. He shook his head, blinking rapidly. Tom Jones had brought back memories of the bleeder, made his eyes itch. "This is insane."

"It's only gonna get worse."

"How do you know?"

"Because this is clearly a goddamn movie, Cam," she snapped. "You *wanted* to be in a movie and now we freakin are. And clearly, we still have the climax to look forward to, so." She put a hand on Clarity's leg. "Is there any way you can tell us where we're going?"

Clarity made a series of gargling noises.

"Did you get any of that?" Cam asked.

"Not at all," said Quinn. "Sorry."

Cam drove on, following Rackell Street as it turned north into County Road 7. If only his phone hadn't died, or Angie had some GPS, or— But then he remembered.

"Angie!" he said. "She mentioned someone used to live by the Mithers. On . . . Apple Something Street?"

"Appuh Guh!" Clarity cried. "Appuh Guh!"

"Applecore, yes! Applecore Lane. If we can just get up to Lillian and ask someone for directions, we'll be great."

"Okay, go Crows," said Quinn. "So just . . . follow signs for Lillian."

"Yeah, what signs?" The county road was covered entirely in trees. Thick-leafed oaks that blotted out any view of the pavement more than thirty feet ahead.

"I'm sure we'll see signs," said Quinn.

They drove for a minute in silence.

Cam shook his head. "This is stupid. So stupid. We *should* just leave."

"We can't let that *thing* keep stealing people's voices," said Quinn. "And you're right, we can't let them have access to any other world. Or . . . vice versa. Remember the gummerfolk at the end of—"

"Yeah, I remember my own *book*, thanks." Cam wiped sweat off his forehead. His scalp itched. His body ached. The road was blurry, and he'd *really* bent his glasses. When he slid them up his nose with a pinkie, they just bent more.

They drove through nearly half an hour of winding roads, dotted with individual houses squatting amongst the trees, before they reached a sign that read LILLIAN, 3 MI.

"We got a sign," Cam announced.

Soon, they arrived at a cutesy town square that reminded Quinn of *Gilmore Girls*. A picturesque gazebo in the center of a big green lawn, a little New Englandy church, a high school, a deli, a general store—all of it clustered tight together.

"It's like *Back to the Future*," said Cam. He waved awkwardly at an old man in a Bent Whalers T-shirt as he crossed the street. He felt like a fugitive. All these people minding their own business in this little town. Which of them were normal and which of them had "talents"? What had Renfield done to them that he couldn't see now, in the bright of day?

Quinn rolled her window down. "Hi, excuse me?"

The old man turned. "Yes. What can I do ya for?"

"We're trying to find Applecore Lane."

"Ahh, Applecore, eh?" The man leaned into the car and gave a series of halting, only slightly confused directions. Cam kept his eyes straight ahead, eyeing the street directly in front of them in case they needed to speed away. In case this "man" suddenly tried to eat them.

"Thank you *so* much," Quinn finally said.

The man patted the car, frowned briefly at Clarity, moon-faced behind Angie's purple sunglasses, then continued ambling toward the deli on the corner.

"Ugh," said Quinn, rolling up her window. "His breath smelled like pee. Turn left."

She managed to navigate them to the northwestern outskirts of Lillian, to a road that ran alongside Bartrick Lake. The water was pretty and glistening, and Quinn shuddered at the thought of what might be hiding beneath its surface.

They came to a strip of large houses, set far back from the road and separated from the rest of the world by tall fences.

"What number?" asked Cam.

Clarity held up fingers, flashing them to indicate 7-9.

And there it was. A large Tudor-looking, three-story motherfucker atop a hill, at the very peak of a winding driveway, leading up from a spiked black metal fence topped with falcons. There was a large brass plate set into the fence that had lost one or two screws, and now hung at an angle. A faded realty sign from Motherwell & Clarke leaned in the grass. Clearly, no one was buying. But Quinn could still read the metal plate:

Mither
79 Applecore Lane

As Cam brought them up the driveway, they could see just how much disrepair the house had fallen into, in the one year it'd been abandoned. Windows boarded up with plywood. Weeds sprouting over the cracks in the little path from the side of the house to the front door. Shingles had fallen, the siding had warped. It seemed not like the house was rotting, but that the earth was twisting it somehow, shaping it into an art piece, and a warning. Renfield was reclaiming its own.

They parked at the end of the drive, alongside the garage. They were right at the edge of the woods. The trees lining the backyard were still and watchful under the sun.

Clarity gave a small moan. She didn't like being back here.

"How do we get in?" Cam asked.

Clarity gestured, incredibly vaguely, around the side of the house, to the back door. They helped her along, letting her use the towel-wrapped cane for support.

The slabs of plyboard covering the sliding glass doors of the patio had fallen inward. They groaned as the trio stepped over them, into the house. Inside, the place was close and damp, dusty and hot, yet somehow sticky-cold all at the same time. The vibe was not good at all.

"Alright, where we lookin?" Quinn asked. "Your room?"

Clarity nodded. She grunted, and pointed up.

"Okay." Quinn took her arm. "We're gonna go up together, okay? Cam, you wanna stay down here, keep a lookout?"

"They don't know we're here," he argued.

"I'm sorry, what I meant was: Cam, stay the fuck here and make sure no one sneaks up on us."

"Fine, dick."

"Amazing. Be back in a jiff." Quinn led Clarity up the stairs.

Cam listened to them clomp across the second-floor hall. They tromped farther away, up some other set of stairs. Then silence.

He looked around the kitchen. Empty and picked-over. He kicked at a smooth gray stone. He idled around in circles, kicking at dead leaves, broken glass. It was strange, being in this lightless, lifeless house. It was so . . .

A sound down the hall.

Cam froze, peered out from the kitchen. Shadows gazed back. Another sound. Something sliding across the hardwood.

"Hello?" he said, because that's what people say. It's what *he'd* write someone saying, if he was writing this.

The sound came again. A low, heavy *ssslide* across the floor.

"Hello," said Cam.

And as if it were saying hello back, the trunk slid into view. Auntie Ethel's eternity trunk.

He laughed. "Oh. Of course."

The trunk slid closer. It was tattered and dark-stained, fraying at the edges. He could see why Clarity had left it behind. Then again, his senior year of college, they'd had a big trunk just like this for their coffee table, him and the three other dudes he lived with. It was a nice piece of furniture, all things considered.

The trunk slid closer. Its black brass handles clattered. The stain across its lid was dark and jagged.

"Hello," said Cam, a third time.

The trunk opened. Swung its lid all the way back in a creaking *thunk*. It was dark inside. Darker than it should be. Cam leaned forward to see why it was so dark in there and he saw stars. Constellations, galaxies, black holes. The stars became eyes, and the eyes blinked at him, and he fell to his knees. Tears began to burn in his eyes, and his mind was suddenly blank except for the numbing sensation of how small he was. How tired. How he should just crawl into the trunk and let it digest him. Let the world forget him.

"Hello," he said limply.

Hello, the trunk echoed back.

Clarity's loft was a long, narrow room. At one end were two closets and a bathroom, and at the other was the short staircase leading down to the second-floor hall. It smelled of sawdust and time.

Being back in her old haunt was doing something to Clarity's stomach. It kept twisting and turning. She wished horribly that she could see. She wanted to cry, but her body was too dry. She kept giving these mewling gasps, letting them vibrate out into the endless dark of life without eyes. Quinn's hand groped out from the fog and held hers.

"I gotcha," she said in a soft voice. "Where would the trunk be?"

Clarity grunted.

"The closet?" she guessed.

Clarity nodded, shifting her weight on the cane.

Quinn went to the closet and peered inside. "Nothing."

Clarity grunted.

"The other closet?"

Clarity nodded.

Quinn went to the other closet, but there wasn't anything in there, either.

She threw up her hands. "I don't know, man. Where else would it . . ."

Her eyes landed on the wall behind Clarity. She went pale, and cold.

Clarity grunted inquisitively.

There, just over the stairs, so they hadn't seen it when they'd entered the loft, was a giant green-black cocoon.

"Clarity," Quinn whispered. She didn't move. "Come to me. Come to me *right* now. Follow my voice. Just . . ."

Another voice stirred within the cocoon, gurgling in its thick, wet net. "Clarity?"

Greta's face pressed through the edge of the husk. Quinn could see the bulges of her eyes swiveling around and around until they landed on her daughter. She grinned. She pressed forward through the cocoon, snapping its threads between her fingers.

"Clarity Anne," she cooed. "Ahh. I've been waiting for you . . ."

The trunk had spent a year all by its lonesome. Bumping down the stairs, wandering into rooms and back out again. Like a dog wondering when its owners will return. It had not shown anyone eternity for a long time. It was *thrilled* to show Cam . . . everything.

He felt abysmally drunk. He could feel his body kneeling on the floor of the old Mither home. Could feel hot trails of salt worming down his cheeks. But his mind was elsewhere. His mind was falling up, up, into the stars. It was the worst spins he'd ever had. Sliding endlessly forward without moving at all. The trunk sent him rocketing over the surface of a massive, black glimmering lake. No—no lake at all, but the back of some great winged beast. Its giant leathery arms beat at the stars, contained stars, were under and around stars. It *was* space, and outside of space. Lobster-esque limbs dangled uselessly from its carapace, twitching at the velvety darkvast. Cam could see the knobbly ridges of vertebrae knuckling up from its hide, from its short stub of tail, up to the throbbing, glowing mass of its brain, its skin the translucent hue of an ocean-bottom alien, mind and organs completely visible. And that *mind*. A swirling chaos of weeping and light. It thrummed. A deep beat that said, over and over, *You're worthless. You're worthless.* And as Cam flew over the glossy hide of its back, the Leviathan turned—and looked at him.

Cam whimpered. Someone put a hand on his shoulder. From a colossal distance away, he heard Syd's voice: "He's traveling."

Wes: "Where?"

And McCall, cold and bitter: "Doesn't matter. We got what we need."

Space slammed shut. Cam blinked, but could not make sense of all the shapes and colors around him. Couldn't see that McCall now stood over the trunk, one shoe atop the lid. A tire tread was smeared across the shoe's shining black surface. He'd stood on the trunk like a hunter with his prey.

"Worthless," said Cam, his mouth hanging open. "Worthless." Long spiderweb strands of saliva and tears dribbled off his chin. "Worthless . . ."

"We should let him live," said Wes.

McCall leaned down, and sneered into Cam's face. "Where's the cane, asshole?"

"Worthless," said Cam. "I'm . . . worthless . . ."

McCall stuck his fingers under Cam's chin and tilted Cam's face to his. "Where. Is. The cane?"

"Please don't take my voice," Cam managed to drool.

McCall laughed. "We'll see."

There was a shout from upstairs. McCall glanced at the ceiling. He nodded at Syd and Wes, somewhere behind Cam. "Stay with him. He won't go anywhere."

"And if he tries?" Syd asked.

"He won't."

"How do you know?"

"Because he'll be unconscious." McCall backhanded Cam across the side of his skull.

Greta popped a long fingernail through the film of the cocoon. A jet of brackish fluid spurted out. She slid her finger up, slicing, sending gunk slopping onto the floor. She wrestled herself free, face cracking apart as she molted and fell naked from the wall, skin shining red and new. There was film across her eyes. All eight of them. She swiped them clean, and they blinked sideways. Clearly, she hadn't finished rehumanizing.

Quinn shoved Clarity behind her. "What do you want with her?"

"*Want* with her?" Greta gave an odd, desperate laugh. "I don't *want* anything with her. She's my daughter."

"I won't let you turn her."

"You don't understand," said Greta, inching closer to them, like a monster out of some old film. Halting, dragging steps across the floor. "When they're born, children take pieces of your heart. I . . ." Something in her throat clicked. "I dreamt of seeing you again, Clare bear."

Clarity shrunk behind Quinn, holding to the back of her hoodie, leaning hard against Slitter's cane.

Greta paused. "Don't be afraid of me. I'm sorry I couldn't come sooner. Your father wanted nothing to do with Renfield, especially after you disappeared. But I *knew* I needed to come back. I knew you weren't in *Vermont*." She crept forward again. "Matthew showed me where you were. The *pain* you've endured. Oh, Clarity, I'm so sorry . . ."

"It's not your mother," Quinn said over her shoulder. "Take or leave what I have to say, I know we don't know each other, but . . . that's not your mom anymore. Not fully, at least."

"She's a bitter woman and a heretic!" Greta snapped. "A blasphemer! Denier of gifts! Her words are *poison*."

"Look, the gift I denied? Would have turned me into a monster-person. Would *you* have taken that gift?"

Clarity shook her head.

"Exactly."

"But it was for *you*!" cried Greta. She stretched out her hands, reaching for Clarity. "I did it to find *you*."

"Then why were you waiting here?" Quinn asked.

Greta beamed. The warm, zealous smile reserved only for those who have been baptized in blood. Her many eyes blinked separately. "Because this is where the Mind said she would be. It *told* me you would bring her here. Praise to the Mind."

"You're really not sounding any *less* culty," said Quinn. Again to Clarity, "Look, I know it's your mom and all, so I'll leave it to you. Do you *want* to go with this woman? Just say the word. Understand that she just fell out of a fucking cocoon. Not to bias you or anything."

Clarity hesitated. Then shook her head slowly.

Greta's face flickered. Its bones twitched and popped. Quinn pushed Clarity farther behind her.

"The Mind warned me you might try to keep her from me," said Greta. Something dark was beginning to pump through her veins, her skin shading itself a muddy green. "That's why I asked the patrol to stop by. To make sure my vision played out as planned. To make sure I had *help*." She laughed. Her arms shook and cracked backward. She was shuddering and shifting as she crept closer and closer. Quinn kept backing away, farther and farther into the corner. Farther and farther from the stairs. "If I'm not mistaken, they should be here any moment."

"Who?" Quinn asked, though she had a sinking feeling she already knew.

And she was right. Greta smiled and said, "The Philosopher High, of course. I'll have my daughter, *he'll* take back his cane. And you, Quinn? *You* we'll just bury." Her jaw burst and she fell onto the legs cutting through her ribcage. She thrust herself forward, running toward them, hissing and spitting.

Quinn spun out of the way as Greta charged. Greta cracked her skull on the wall, leaving a wide trench in the plaster, sending a crack up to the ceiling. She turned and hissed again, clicking the sharp points of her mandibles, undeterred. She leapt forward, legs skittering across the floor as Quinn and Clarity ran back across the room.

Quinn jumped down the steps, pulling Clarity after her. "Come on, come on!"

Clarity stumbled and fell and suddenly, one of Greta's legs was pinching her shoulder, pulling her back. Clarity let out a guttural, rasping scream. She swung the cane blindly as she was yanked backward, back into the loft.

Quinn grabbed Clarity's ankle and held on tighter than she'd ever held on to something in her life. For a moment, it felt like they might rip the girl in half.

Finally, Greta's grip loosened. She toppled forward. Quinn kicked her in the stomach, launching her into the air, all the way down the loft steps. She thudded against the floor below with a sickening crunch. Her legs wobbled under her as she tried to stand.

"Eat . . . you," she hissed. She rose unsteadily to all four feet. "Kill you . . ."

Quinn and Clarity held each other. Clarity had a ragged, slow-seeping wound across her shoulder. They didn't move. Greta stood between them and the rest of the house.

They were trapped on the steps to the loft.

Syd was kicking the trunk to shards. Cam's eyes fluttered open. Through gray static, he could see the wide expanse of the floor, Syd's shoe crashing down onto the trunk. McCall's shoes were gone.

Finally, Syd reached down and wrenched the lid off. Panting, she pressed her small hand to the wood, and nodded. "We got it."

"Good," said Wes. "Now, I say *we* take it back to the tapestry. Leave Captain Worms behind."

"What about the cane?" Syd asked.

"Fuck the cane. Don't we have *enough*? Let's tack this to the tapestry, slit Marion's throat onto it, and walk through. It *should* work."

"Quinn," Cam grumbled against the floor, too groggy to move. "Quinn . . ."

"Fine," said Syd. "Let's . . . Oh shit, who did you invite?"

"What do you mean?" Wes asked.

Cam swiveled his eyes up. Syd was looking at the open mouth of the living room, where the sliding glass doors once stood. Outside was the green swath of lawn, the woods. And crawling out of the dirt at the edge of the trees were several leering old women. He could hear them bickering as they dug their way out of the earth. "We should have taken the ninth tunnel . . . Shirley, it's faster if we go through the sixth . . . It's *not* shorter, Susan, you're *awful* at directions . . ."

"Shhhit," said Wes. "What do you wanna do?"

"Grab Marion and let's hoof it," said Syd.

Cam felt hands under his arms. Felt Wes's breath hot and minty in his face. Whispering, "Sorry, buddy. Don't worry. I got a plan."

Wes was dragging him out of the house.

"Quinn," he moaned. "Quinn . . ."

Women were pouring out of the ground like ants. Now that Cam was upright, was moving outside into the daylight, he could see that some of them were pulling thick ropes. They pulled and pulled. Steam rose from the hole.

And out came Matthew Slitter in all his glory, throne-chair glittering in the sun. He laughed as they undid the ropes tied about his mechanized legs.

"Quickly now, girls," he said. "I can smell my cane."

Cam still couldn't move. He felt drugged. Felt like his skull wasn't on right. He couldn't tell if it was from the trunk or McCall or both. But he was coherent enough to feel it when Wes pulled him up short. Coherent enough to see the wall of women standing between them and the cars.

"Ahh," said Slitter as he pounded his chair across the lawn toward them. It clunked and whirred unevenly. "Campbell Peter Marion. At last. You reek of wood."

Greta's jaw clicked itself wide open, revealing her throat.

"Clarity Anne," she hissed. "You come with me right now. Or—"

Someone grabbed her from behind. She spun around, hissing, and there stood McCall. He held one of her rear legs in one large hand. He yanked, and Greta toppled forward, mandibles smacking against the floor. Clarity and Quinn remained frozen.

McCall reeled Greta in, pulling on her leg, hand over hand.

"I always hated our phone calls," he growled in Clarity's voice. "You're a terrible mother. And worse, you're between me . . . and the cane."

Greta spun onto her back, thrust her legs at him. He fell over backward and they dug into each other, tearing, roaring. McCall's tongue ripped through the air, wrapped itself about Greta's throat. She bit at it, and he whipped it back, blood and saliva flying.

"Come on," Quinn whispered. She shoved Clarity past the brawl as they tore into each other, sending spatters of blood, red and green, across the walls. She shoved Clarity down the stairs to the first floor just as McCall and Greta crashed onto the steps. Shards of broken banister rained down on Quinn as she shoved Clarity forward. "Go, go!"

"Thief of tongues!" Greta spat. "Killer! Cutter!" She drove the sharp point of a leg into McCall's chest. He howled, elbowed the leg, and it cracked, split. He grabbed it, wrenched it in half. Greta screamed, collapsed, spurting green onto the floor.

"Breaker!" she hissed at him as she tried to crawl away, bloody stump twitching. "Taker of daughters!"

"Shut . . . *up*." McCall took her head in both hands and tore it from her body.

Quinn and Clarity burst out onto the yard, skidding to a halt just before they ran into Wes and Syd, and Cam slung between them.

"Ahh," said Slitter. "Quinn Rose Carver-Dobson. De*light*ful."

At the sight of him, Quinn's blood ran cold. She could only imagine what Clarity must be feeling right now. Jerked around with no sense of what was happening.

"I was . . . just leaving," Quinn panted.

"On the contrary," said Slitter. "We were just about to bargain."

"You and me?" She spat on the ground between them. "Forget it."

"He means me and him." McCall emerged from the house behind them. He tossed Greta's head onto the ground. It rolled and came to a stop against Slitter's throne-leg. He glanced down at it, then frowned up at McCall.

"And who are you?" he asked.

"Jopp Yennigen," said McCall, straightening his crooked and bloodied tie. "Your savior."

Slitter's face went slack. For a moment, he looked in awe at McCall. Then he barked laughter, and wrung his hands gleefully. "Well, well." He stomped his chair-legs in the grass. One jerked woundedly where Quinn had caned it. He grinned. "So you're here after all. Ha! Perhaps my impatience was premature. Perhaps *this* is where we were always meant to be."

McCall said nothing.

"You look well," said Slitter. "Such a handsome hide."

"Wish I could say the same," said McCall.

"Okay, this is a nice stand-off and all," said Quinn. "But I don't think we're really a part of it, so." She made a move toward Angie's car. The women hissed at her. Cindy and Marcia, Winnie and Deborah, and a dozen others. She froze.

McCall nodded at the mechanical throne. "So you can't walk in *any* vertebra, is that it?"

"The chair is traditional," said Slitter, voice rising a little, like this was an appalling thing for McCall to say. "It represents the High's sacrifice of the body in service to the Mind. We *all* have our versions of them, my many selves. This particular machine we built from a design off a trader in the Dreamcoast. A fascinating vertebra, the Dreamcoast."

"So, what?" said McCall. "You finally realize I wasn't gonna save you? You gonna collar me and find the rot-root yourself?"

"Not necessarily," said Slitter. "I *realize* that you care not for the depression of the Mind. Have no . . . vested interest in making the Spine a more habitable place. I was foolish to think you would be sympathetic to my cause. The Mind *did* warn me, after all."

"And you couldn't have realized this *before* shoving me down that well?"

Slitter wagged his head. "Perhaps. Regardless, here is what I have on offer. Take me to the tapestry, and I will let you free. I'll find the root myself, and you may travel the Spine at will. Build Yennigenia, if you can. But you must also allow me to have Ms. Quinn Rose Carver-Dobson. She has insulted us, and must be punished."

"Fuckin deal," said McCall. "I don't know who she is, anyway. What about the others?" He nodded at Wes, Syd, and Cam.

"You know, I thought I'd *need* Campbell Peter Marion," said Slitter, "to locate the tapestry in your absence. But *your* being here is serendipity. Perhaps the Mind wasn't lying after all. That is a relief." His voice was wet with gratitude. "Even if you *are* seventeen months tardier than expected. But now that you're here, we may dispose of the rest of them." He turned. "Winnifred?"

Winnie appeared beside him. She was dirty and red-robed, but other-wise just as perfectly coiffed and well-crafted as when Quinn had met her. Her nails were perfect. And she was holding a gun. She leveled it at Syd.

"Praise to the Mind," she said.

Wes leapt forward. He shoved Winnie's arm up just as the gun went off. Syd flew back, blood flying from her neck. Cam collapsed to the ground. The women swarmed over Wes and Winnie as they struggled over the gun. More shots went off. This hadn't exactly been Wes's plan, but it would do.

He yelled, "Go! Get in the car!"

"Fool!" Slitter roared.

McCall's tongue whipped into the air. He snarled at Clarity, dove for the cane. Quinn yanked it from Clarity's hand and swung it at him. He caught it in his tongue. The thick tendril wrapped around its length and for a moment she held on as they wrestled back and forth, before he ripped it from her grasp, sending her sprawling onto the dirt by Cam's side. Clarity screamed. Quinn turned over in time to see McCall lifting her over his shoulder.

She grabbed Cam, dug for Angie's keys in his pocket. Next thing she knew, she was shoving Cam into Angie's car, closing the door just as Winnie threw herself at the window. She snarled through the glass, jaws breaking apart. "Ungrateful little cur!" Then the window exploded. Winnie's face blew apart. She shuddered and slid down to the ground, spilling blood and glass into the car, into Quinn's lap. Behind her, Wes held the smoking gun in the air for a moment longer, before the women tore him into pieces.

Quinn didn't think, she just drove. Speeding backward down the driveway. Leaving Clarity behind. Leaving the last of the bloodywood in the hands of the spiders, Slitter—and Jopp Yennigen.

CHAPTER TWENTY-FIVE

BURN IT TO THE GODFORSAKEN GROUND

"Alright," said Cam. He ran a hand over his face, sniffed. Blinked. He had to shout over the wind roaring through the broken windows as they drove. "That's twice now we've barely escaped in this same stupid car. I don't think we get a third, I mean . . . I think next time one of us isn't coming with. Statistically speaking. This late in the game."

"Then let's just go," said Quinn. "Fuck it. We tried, we failed. Let's Ichabod."

He sighed, blinking hard. He probed at a spot in his skull. Winced. His fingers came away red. He shook his head. "You don't really think that."

She drove.

"Quinn, they *have* Clarity. And more important, they've opened the doorway. Or they will. Shit's going to come *through*. The gummerfolk."

"Shit already *has*," she said. "Here." She drifted onto the shoulder of the road, turned off the engine, and they sat there, catching their breath.

"I *want* to help Clarity," said Quinn. "I do. But they're literal monsters, Cam. What are we supposed to do?"

"I was wrong," he said. "*This* is our chance to do something great."

"Yeah, but *I'm* also my first priority. And I don't know how to help her now. Or anyone. Jesus, are you okay?"

He looked green. Suddenly, he threw open the door and puked.

"Goddamn," he muttered. He spat bile onto the grass. Leaned back, closed his eyes. Softly, "We should've just taken her to a hospital. Gotten out of here."

"They'd come looking for us. We would've still had the cane."

"We could have tried harder to destroy it," he said, like an apology.

Her face softened. "How?"

Cam sat with his eyes closed.

"Cam?"

"I'm just . . . tired," he said. "Just beat. My brain . . ."

Quinn watched him breathe. Then she pursed her lips, put the car in drive, and drove them back south, toward Edenville, shaking her head and thinking, *This is so fuckin dumb*, the entire way.

She found a liquor store on the north side of town. She left Cam in the car and went in. Then marched back out because she'd forgotten the Society ladies had taken her wallet. She lifted Cam up, dug *his* out of his back pocket, and marched back in.

"You *look* like you could use a drink," said the gruff man behind the register.

Quinn, who had a huge crate of Millett's Everclear before her on the counter, gave him a withering look. She pointed at the wall behind him. "Throw in a packa Noxboros, too."

When she shoved the crate through the broken car window and climbed back into the driver's seat, Cam licked his lips and said, "I'm sorry."

She paused. Sighed. "I know."

"You don't have to forgive me."

"I don't."

Another pause.

"I think," she said, "when we're done here . . . we're done."

Cam absorbed this without moving. After a beat, he nodded. "Okay."

"Okay."

"But what do you want to do first?"

"The fuck you mean?" Quinn stuck a cigarette between her lips, lit it, and jerked a thumb at the box in the backseat. "We're gonna burn this place to the godforsaken ground."

"Well, then it's a good thing Wes slipped the golf cart key in my pocket," said Cam, holding up a ring of keys.

Quinn frowned. "What golf cart?"

* * *

Clarity fought like hell as McCall carried her down the burnt tunnel to the tapestry room. He dumped her in the corner, ignoring her fists beating against him. He made her listen as he took the cane and bolted it to the wall with the biggest fuckin nails Clarity had ever heard. They boomed through the ancient classroom. The image of those nails blasting through *her* was enough to keep her from trying to escape. Had she been able to see, Clarity would have observed that this nail gun had been modified, and was in fact larger and uglier than any nail gun she'd ever known. The size of its ammunition was biblical.

Slitter watched in silent, hand-wringing anticipation as McCall took the lid that once was Auntie Ethel's and fastened it to the giant. Slitter was flanked by a small coterie: Marcia and Cindy, and Deborah. The giant glared down upon them all. Clarity could feel Him hum. Could feel that He had unique plans for everyone. He had special plans for *her*.

McCall nailed the wood in place. *Boom.* He stepped back, scratched the side of his head with the nail gun. "That look right to you?"

Slitter approached the tapestry. He inspected it. Nodded. "Impeccable."

"Good." McCall sighed. "Whew. Long fuckin day."

"Well, don't dally," Slitter snapped, turning to face McCall. "Staple her to it and be done with it. Open Him, for Mind's sake!"

"Oh, I have *better* plans for her," said McCall. Clarity felt him put a hand on her head. She shoved him off. He chuckled. "There's a vertebra, much further down, where they tie their channelmen to trees. Use them to predict the weather, the changing tides of government, and more."

"Oh yess," said Slitter. "I have *many* such pets."

"I've never had my own before. And such a *pretty* one. Right, Mither?"

Clarity spat at him. She must have missed horribly, because both men laughed, cruel and loud.

"Then what death will you use to unlock His door?" Slitter asked.

"Guess." McCall aimed the nail gun and pulled the trigger. Slitter's head jerked back. He'd sprouted a nail diagonally from his left cheek. The point of it drove the tube from his right socket, sending cracks along the glass. Purplish blood squirted out.

He looked surprised. Then laughed, and snarled. "You wormy alien bast—"

McCall fired a quick succession of nails through Slitter's face, shattering his teeth, shredding his bushy eyebrows. The nails whipped right through him, pinning shreds of flesh and hair to the jagged terrain of the tapestry. Slitter's withered hands flailed, his chair reared back, and as he toppled onto the moldy carpet, more nails ripped straight through his skull, thunking into the uneven wood behind him. Aether dripped off the nail-ends onto the floor. The women screamed in a Greek chorus, beating their chests, tearing at their hair. They lunged for McCall, but when he leveled the gun at them, they froze.

"That's right," said McCall. "And don't follow me through. I'm tired of you philosophers and your—"

A low *boom* rippled through the room.

If Clarity still had eyes, she would have seen the Renfield giant beginning to burn. The lines of Him darkened along all those tabletops, picture frames, nightstands, and Slitter's cane. The wild hair began to bleed out black, inky tendrils across the boards. The shoulders began to crack and heave. The nails with Slitter-scraps still stuck to them—they popped free and clattered to the floor, the gore on them sucked into the bloodlines of the wood, which were no longer lines of stain but gouges, revealing a deep, deep shadow behind the wall.

And the eyes. The eyes began to slice over the room. Moving back and forth. Clarity could hear them sawing across the wood.

McCall's breath in her ear. In her own voice, he laughed at her. "Feel that? His door . . . is open."

CHAPTER TWENTY-SIX

FINGERS FROM THE OTHER SIDE

Cam drove the golf cart down the tunnel. His eyes burned and his entire body ached, but he kept going. The box of booze sloshed in Quinn's lap at his side.

As he'd unlocked the door to the tunnel, he'd thought about all those people still on the bleeder, strapped down in unending darkness. He thought of the pumps in their eyes. *Sorry, Chett.* But there was no time for that now.

Quinn stuffed the bottles with rags as they drove—strips of blanket they'd ripped apart from some E.C. quilt Angie had in her car. Cam wondered what work anniversary that'd been from. Thirty years working for the college? Well, it was rags now.

Time is nothing but rags in the making.

They knelt outside the tapestry room. The door was open. Quinn put the box on the ground. She and Cam looked at each other.

"Ready?" he asked.

Quinn nodded, and was about to say something when she heard Slitter scream. The women wailed. Then a *boom.* So low and resonating Quinn couldn't even call it a sonic boom. It was like the dark itself became brighter, more . . . full. Like the shadows around them were beginning to boil into a stew-like thickness, a glowing morass of solidified whispers, the teeth-itch feeling of steel scraping on bone, the crack of branches in the dead of night, your closet door easing itself open. The tunnel became a synesthesia of horror. With every beat of her heart, Quinn felt screams pump through her veins. She saw agony roiling on the walls. She tasted salt, rot, sulfur, heartbreak. Like Willy Wonka had handed her a gum-ball and said, *Chew this. It's a nightmare.*

"Ohh yes," said McCall inside the room. They heard him take a big snoutful. "That's the good shit."

"We gotta chuck these," said Cam. "Now."

Quinn flicked her lighter against one of the rags. It wouldn't go.

"Dammit," she said. "Come on, Dad, I need you now."

"Is someone there?" McCall's voice rolled through the open door. "Marion, is that *you*?"

"Quinn," Cam hissed.

"I'm trying!" she hissed back. "Dad, come on, man, don't be a dick." And the spark caught. She held the flame to the rag of the first Molotov. She had, obviously, never lit one before. She thought it might even explode in her hand. But the flame clung to the rag perfectly.

"Shit," she said, holding it away from her. "Okay. Go Crows!" And she tossed it into the room. It exploded in the middle of the spider-lady throng. They screamed and spat and ripped themselves apart, becoming burning, smoking sausage-things. They charged at Quinn through the doorway, and she smashed another bottle into Cindy's face. The women behind crashed into her, toppling through the door into the tunnel, swallowed by flames.

It was a satisfying sight. Quinn watched them burn with relish.

Until they began to weep.

"We tried to help you," cried Marcia.

"Why would you do this," cried Cindy.

"We *loved* you," they cried as one, as they wilted and blackened and died. Flames licked up the tunnel walls, to the flower-roots overhead.

Clarity cowered deeper into the corner, desperately turning her head, trying to hear what was happening.

McCall paid attention to none of this. He stood transfixed before the tapestry. He got close to it, and watched as small gray fingers with tiny black nails began to wriggle between the cracks of the wood. Eyes blinked out from the shadows of the giant's seams. They swiveled around inhumanly. Fingers clawed at the wood, digging their way through. Digging their way *up* from further down the Spine.

"Fascinating," said McCall. "I've never known what you are. But I'm coming for—"

"The fuck you are," said Cam. McCall turned just in time for Cam to smash a bottle across his face. McCall collapsed without a sound. Cam looked down at the jagged mouth of the bottle in his hand, wondering if he had it in him to stab McCall, rip out that tongue.

Something grabbed him by the throat. Something oozing out from the cracks in the tapestry. Its face woobled out from the darkness and the oak, gums gnashing, skin sloshing around.

The gummerfolk were coming through.

He gasped and clawed at the hand. Suddenly, Quinn was at his side, prying those slippery, inhuman fingers loose. Finally, she managed to wrench Cam's throat free. He sputtered and held out his hand, rasping, "Molotov."

But before Quinn could respond—the wood exploded outward. Shards of it flew across her face. She put up her hands to shield her eyes, and splinters burrowed themselves into her skin. She dove behind one of the pyres of scattered desks around the room, as Cam flew back hard against the wall. Shards grazed her forearms and her shoulders, and they *burned*, like the darkness on the other side of the door was boiling. But when the room grew suddenly colder, so cold Quinn could see her breath, she knew that wasn't true. Whatever was out there wasn't hot. It was bitter, bottomless cold.

She looked up to see dozens and dozens of gummerfolk pour through. They slipped and slid and tripped and glid across the floor, stumbling over McCall without stopping. Cam and Quinn were both hidden out of sight, Clarity pressing herself small into the corner. More gummerfolk poured through, and stranger things as well. Things flew out of the tapestry, beating at the air with wings of bone. Things crawled and scampered and slimed. An entire stampede. Cam and Quinn kept their heads down, hands over their heads, as these things shoved their way onto Earth.

Suddenly, Cindy was screaming. Quinn couldn't believe she was still alive. She kept her head down, and listened to the horrible slobbering gags of the gummerfolk as they worked their mouths onto Cindy's charred limbs. One slid its jaw over her head, and the screams were muffled. There was a great *pop*, and Cindy was silent.

Someone needed to reach the Molotovs. Someone needed to end this.

The stampede abated, and darkness swelled from the open door. Shadows flooded the room in thick ribbons of ink, growing like ivy across the walls, wriggling up through the tiles of the ceiling, jostling the work lights, so the pale green light of the room began to flicker. Fingers wrapped themselves in dense sheets around the edges of the tapestry. Something within began to moan. Some ocean-bottom beast pulling itself up from the depths. The fingers around the edges all clenched and whitened their knuckles as they hoisted this thing from the void of the Spine.

McCall began to twitch. He groaned and put his hands to the floor, began to lift himself. His arms shook. He opened his mouth, his tongue splashed onto the floor. His breath steamed in huge clouds. The entire tentacle of his tongue steamed, its many little appendages all hot and wriggling. He growled, deep and inhuman. *"Marrrriooonnn."*

Quinn whipped her head around, trying to locate the box of Everclear. It was still sitting by the door. Clarity was crawling toward it.

"Clarity!" she hissed. Quinn prayed to anyone who was listening, then tossed her lighter across the floor. It hit the side of Clarity's hand, and she flinched. Then she realized what it was. How close she was to the box. She gave Quinn a thumb's up.

McCall was almost on his feet now. He rolled his shoulders back, dripping liquor, almost losing his balance. He lifted his tongue to the flickering ceiling and let out a foghorn bellow that made Quinn clap her hands to her ears. He was silhouetted perfectly by the doorway, so that fingers framed him all around. It was oddly beautiful, and the image would sneak up on Quinn in strange moments for the rest of her life. She'd find herself, for instance, having a cider at sunset in August, watching the fireflies dance around the trees. And there would be McCall, framed by darkness and fingers. Calling her name through the years with that monster of a mouth. His voice not just one anymore, but legions. All crying out at once, *"I'll take your tongues, and tell your families and your friends . . . horrrrible things."*

He swung his head. Threw a desk against the wall, where it exploded into bits. His eyes practically glowed in the flickering dim as he swept his gaze over the room, searching. Quinn ducked behind a different desk, stayed there until she was sure he hadn't seen her. McCall growled again, taunting them, egging them to come out. *"I'll tell them you never loved them. Tell them they've faaailed youu. I'll make them listen as I fire a gun into the phone. Make them think it's their fault you're gooone."*

Heat rippled by the side of Quinn's head. She looked over, and saw that Clarity had managed to light one of the cocktails. She cocked her hand back, and chucked it as hard as she could at McCall.

But she wasn't strong enough. The bottle exploded by McCall's feet. Close enough that tongues of flame licked at the roots growing deep around the giant. Far overhead and miles away, Quinn could hear the sunflowers scream in agony.

But McCall stepped back from the fire and laughed. He spoke in Clarity's own voice. "Nice try, Mither!"

And Quinn realized the wooden edges of the doorway weren't burning. Flames rolled off them like oil off feathers.

"Smoke!" Cam hissed. Quinn looked across at him, frowning. "Cigarettes!" He gestured wildly, trying to explain as concisely as possible what Wes had said about his father. "Noxboros filter the curse! It won't burn unless you—"

McCall charged and kicked him against the wall. Kicked him again until he was silent.

Clarity was struggling to light another Molotov. Quinn scrambled over and lit it for her.

"You've done enough," she whispered. As if she'd been waiting for this, Clarity collapsed onto the floor. Quinn took her fresh pack of cigarettes from her pocket, dug into it. She tilted her mouth to the flame on the Molotov rag.

"Bon voyage, humans!" McCall cried in many voices. He looked even more grotesquely picturesque now, the fire at his feet lighting him from below, the finger-thing bellowing from beyond. McCall threw back his head and laughed. "I won't miss this world a bit."

"Fuck you!" Cam screamed, running at him with the shard of broken bottle.

McCall turned to him, and *burst*. Worms exploded out of his skin and shot through the air. Hundreds of them. Pale, bone-colored maggoty little things. McCall's body deflated like a used balloon. The tongue splattered onto the floor and cracked apart into thousands of squirming pieces.

"Oh," said Cam. And the worms dug into his skin. They shot into his mouth, past his tongue, down his throat. They burrowed into his eyes, wriggled into his pores, down his ears, into his pants. He writhed and jerked. Then he was still. He looked down at McCall's limp skin. He looked up at Quinn and Clarity, huddled together in the doorway. He grinned.

"I am not skin," said Cam, cold and alien. "I am that which writhes within."

Quinn lurched to her feet. She had four Noxboros stuffed in her mouth. She held the burning bottle in one hand and she screamed at McCall, at Yennigen, at the doorway, at the woman who took Celeste, at Slitter and Spider and Glasses, and even at Cam—at *all* of it—she screamed, "Go fucking Crows!"

The thing in the blackness behind Cam roared. Roared so loud it blew Quinn's hair back, turned some of it white. She saw fangs begin to emerge from the wall. Like a lanternfish, rising from the bottom of the sea.

She threw the Molotov. Whatever had guided her hand when she tossed the lighter guided her again, and she swore fealty to whatever it was for the rest of her days.

Fire crashed into the opening of the tapestry. The thing bellowed again, and the teeth, the fingers, retreated. The wood began to char, the sunflowers screamed louder. But even better, fire exploded down Cam's body. On the floor, the tongue caught fire, too. It squealed its own many-throated pain. Bits began to melt along the floor. They wriggled and squeed, curling in on themselves, flopping back and forth.

Cam's eyes were bright and hateful, and as he burned, he leapt into the tapestry, just as it collapsed on top of him and he fell in a screaming whoosh of smoke and embers.

Quinn and Clarity took turns choking down Noxboros, chucking more Molotovs at the giant, until there was nothing left. Until fire was spreading up the tendrils of the roots, and the aboveground screams of Slitter's flowers were deafening.

They sat there together, until the tapestry was no more than a heap of glowing ash.

A tongue was inchworming its way across the floor. Quinn picked it up between two fingers, held it out to Clarity.

"This yours?" she asked.

Clarity opened her mouth. Quinn placed the tongue inside. Its roots dug their way into Clarity's jaw and she grimaced as it attached itself to her. She worked her jaw around. She swallowed. And said in a deep, gravelly voice, "I don't think so."

"Well," said Quinn. "You wanna try another? We could find a—"

"I want to eat and drink as much as humanly possible," said Clarity.

"If you like pizza, there's this place in Leaden Hollow that—"

"Yes," said Clarity. "Literally anything." She choked up a little. "Thank you." She threw her arms around Quinn.

"Alright." Quinn nodded. "Okay." She patted Clarity's head. "You're okay. You're . . ." Her voice caught, and she began to cry. She cried hard, for a long time.

She cried until she realized they'd switched positions, and Clarity was now holding *her*, stroking her hair. And still she cried, until Clarity murmured in her ear, "We should go. The tunnel is burning."

"Okay." Quinn sniffed. "Okay. Here. I'll help you stand."

"Thanks," Clarity growled as they rose.

"Don't mention it," said Quinn, flakes of burning root falling into her hair. "Now let's find ourselves a road outta Renfield."

CODA

A ROAD OUTTA RENFIELD

In the morning, Sydney Kim will awake in Bartrick Regional Hospital with a hole in her neck. Winnie's bullet punched straight through, and the wound is already healing without complication.

But Syd won't know that when she wakes up. Disoriented, she'll rip the IV from her hand. She'll thrash and claw at the nurses holding her to the bed. She'll clutch one of them by the front of his scrubs and pull him close. She'll hiss, eyes wide, voice rasping even worse than before, "Get. Me. A *phone*."

The walls of the bleeder room are remarkably thick, and even when Slitter Hall begins to crumble and smolder around it, the people there will remain safe on their rotating shelves. Safe, that is, until the Edenville Fire Department cracks apart Wes's high-security door and lets Angie into the room. She clutches the one penguin bobblehead she's managed to rescue from the rubble of her desk. His beak melts halfway down his face as she holds him to her chest and surveys the dozens of moaning bodies.

Then she'll nod at the grate in the wall, and say, "Dump em in the hole. Junk the machines. Make sure my department lives on."

The E.F.D. will oblige. They've covered up worse scandals for the college.

One by one, they'll slide the bodies down the chute. Chett Neeves will manage to gargle a mostly-intelligible *wait*, just before he is swallowed by the flames.

But all of that will happen in the morning.

* * *

As night swept over the campus, Quinn helped Clarity into the passenger's seat of Angie's car. She climbed in behind the wheel and they sat for a moment, breathing together, in the parking lot of Slitter Hall.

"Do you think Yennigen made it through?" Clarity asked.

"Oh boy," Quinn sighed. "Ya know, at this point? I *barely* understand what's going on. So I . . . have no idea. I sorta don't give a shit."

"Same."

It was dark, with no moon. Smoke was streaming from Slitter's windows, and billowing about the clock tower of the college center. Through the open holes of the broken car windows, they listened to the flowers die. They almost felt bad.

"Sorry about your mom," said Quinn.

"It's okay," said Clarity. "I don't know why she was looking for me so hard. Never seemed to care before."

"She seemed nice, though. Before she was a . . . whatever."

"She wasn't."

"I was trying to be nice."

"I'd rather you be honest."

Quinn put a hand on hers. Clarity wrapped her fingers around Quinn's. "I hear ya," said Quinn. "Well, I don't know about you, but these last few days really put me through the wringer."

Clarity gave her a bleak look with her empty sockets. "Yeah," she said, in a voice that wasn't hers. "It's been a real doozy."

"Let's change the vibe." Quinn turned the radio on, cranked the dial to the first station she could find. "Sooner or Later," by the Grass Roots. One of Dad's favorites.

"Awesome," she said. "Go Crows." If God did indeed live inside the shuffle button, God was certainly saying something now. Maybe not today, or tomorrow. But sooner or later, love was gonna find her.

She pointed the car toward North Gate, away from the fire and the scream-flowers. She sped off campus as the flowers shook their fists at her. She didn't even bother stopping for her stuff at good ole 1896. Just drove right down Rackell Street, and back up the hill down which she and Cam had driven so long ago. When they reached the overlook of the Billows Road, she did not look back. Did not give Edenville a second glance. It didn't deserve one. And when they passed the hump in the road that had killed Celeste, Quinn didn't stop for that either. Not even when that woman with the deer dragged herself back across the road ahead and glared at Quinn through the windshield.

No, Quinn just tightened her grip on the wheel, jammed her foot on the gas, and felt that old ghoul thump dead beneath her wheels.

ACKNOWLEDGMENTS

Oh gosh, where even to start. Ya know, in January of 2018, I had Cam's nightmare—the one that opens this book. Mine was slightly different. There was a dog in it. But the main elements are all the same: the attic, the gooey interdimensional creatures, the poem. I awoke at, like, three a.m. and made a note on my phone called "Pencil Man," because that was the Man's name in *my* nightmare. I drew the original sketch of the giant that morning, and have not stopped doodling Him since.

In its original conception, this novel was about a married couple, Cam and Quinn, and their son, Caleb, who kept drawing these creatures he called the poorly made (aka the gummerfolk). They whispered to him through his bedroom wall. I'm sad that some elements of that original concept have fallen by the wayside over the years. Like the men in suits who approach Cam in the park and tell him he can see the future. Or the implant the faculty dig into his brain, with those long wires reaching down through his spine. Or that time Clarity went to a school dance and got to kiss the boy she liked. The funeral butterflies, that guy on the subway, the long-lost ruins of Presz'dre Mar… It's bittersweet looking back on these ideas and knowing they'll remain in the murky nothing of unexistence. But I'm happy that other elements *have* remained, and evolved, even. There *is* a Caleb in the book. Quinn *does* have a bad encounter with soap. And although their original host-character, Check Miller, is no more, Jopp Yennigen still kicks ass.

Which is all to say, I guess the old cliché is true: *so* much goes into a novel, from conception to completion. So many people influence even the tiniest details along the way. To thank everyone responsible for this *thing* you now hold in your hands, this amalgamation of four years' worth of *stuff*, would be impossible.

But let's kick shit off with a *massive* thank-you to the incredible Claire Harris at P.S. Literary Agency. Claire, thank you for pulling Renfield County out of the slush. I am so so grateful for you every single day. Go Crows! And speaking of grateful, oh *man* am I grateful for Vedika Khanna at William Morrow. Vedika, I gave you the sweatiest pitch over Zoom, but you trusted that there was a novel in there somewhere. I can't thank you enough for taking a chance on this world. You and Claire knew I could write a novel long before *I* knew that. And thank you to Ariana Sinclair, editor extraordinaire! Ariana, thank you for taking over for Vedika with such enthusiasm. You helped smooth out so many wrinkles and tighten so many bolts that I didn't even know were loose! This ship wouldn't be able to fly if not for your kind and thoughtful hand.

Thank you, Kashinda Carter, for giving this an insightful, sensitive read and for giving such wonderful feedback. I was overjoyed to hear how much you liked the book.

Thank you, Andrea Molitor, for your hard work on copyedits. Your note about how "sprent" is a great word truly made my year!

Thank you to the entire William Morrow team: Rachel Kahan, Kaitlin Harri, Kelly Cronin, Amanda Hong, Leah Carlson-Stanisic, Suzanne Mitchell, Yeon Kim, and Emily Bierman.

Y'all are *awesome*, and I am wildly lucky to be working with you.

Speaking of amazing teams, thank you to the entire crew at P.S. Literary Agency. What an incredibly kind, giving group of humans. To everyone at PSLA, as well as Taryn Fagerness and Alec Frankel & Debbie Deuble Hill at APA—thank you all for helping bring *Edenville* to the world.

Thank you to all the people who read early drafts of this: Tarver Nova, Maureen O'Leary, Ashley Pecorelli, Hannah Peterson (who suggested the McCall/Clarity kiss), and the legend himself, Jamie Sheffield. Jamie, thank you for being a constant source of inspiration, affirmation, and homemade booze. I couldn't ask for a better writing companion. Our craft talks around the fire keep me goin!

Big shout-out to: Dad, Springfield Apartments, the Groves Branch Library, the Red Hook Library, the Boardman Road Library, the Lubbock Alamo Drafthouse, the Ground Hog (RIP), Brandon Lee, Chris Brown,

Ben Hennesy, Jesse Rogala, Jennifer Skura Boutell, Jeanne Asma, The Tuesdayers!, Matthew Vassar, Cindy & Terri, and of course Mozzie & Tex. Thank you for all the late-night talks. Go Bucks.

Thank you to my wonderful OG cast: Michael Rinere, Kristin Battersby, and the unbelievably talented Vin Craig. It felt so magical being in the room with you all as we read through this beast for the first time together. Once a week, for a month and a half, we sat around my table and read. What an *incredible* gift. Kristin and Mike, y'all breathed such life into Cam and Quinn. I didn't know how human they were until our reading. Which is funny, because I spent four years with them in my head. And Vin, thank you for listening to all my rants about spider-ladies and tongue-monsters. Go Turkeys.

Speaking of good listeners—thank you most of all, Mom. Thank you for *always* being there. I'd be lost without you.

ABOUT THE AUTHOR

Sam Rebelein holds a BA in English and Education from Vassar College, and an MFA in Creative Writing from Goddard College, with a focus on horror and memoir. His work has appeared in a number of speculative fiction publications, including *Bourbon Penn, Planet Scumm, The Deadlands, Press Pause Press, Coffin Bell Journal, The Dread Machine,* Ellen Datlow's *Best Horror of the Year*, and elsewhere. He currently lives in Poughkeepsie, New York. For more about Sam (and pictures of his dogs), follow him on Twitter @HillaryScruff and Instagram @rebelsam94.